ASHLEY
Carter

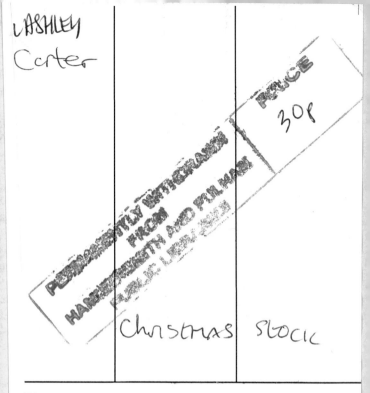

PRICE
30p

Christmas Stock

Please return/renew this item by the last date above. You can renew on-line at

www.lbhf.gov.uk/libraries

or by phone
0303 123 0035

Hammersmith & Fulham Libraries

A PRINCESS BY CHRISTMAS

BY
JENNIFER FAYE

Published in Great Britain 2014
by Mills & Boon, an imprint of Harlequin (UK) Limited,
Eton House, 18-24 Paradise Road, Richmond, Surrey, TW9 1SR

© 2014 Jennifer F. Stroka

ISBN: 978-0-263-91323-1

23-1014

Harlequin (UK) Limited's policy is to use papers that are natural, renewable and recyclable products and made from wood grown in sustainable forests. The logging and manufacturing processes conform to the legal environmental regulations of the country of origin.

Printed and bound in Spain
by Blackprint CPI, Barcelona

In another life **Jennifer Faye** was a statistician. She still has a love for numbers, formulas and spreadsheets, but when she was presented with the opportunity to follow her lifelong passion and spend her days writing and pursuing her dream of becoming a Mills & Boon® author, she couldn't pass it up. These days, when she's not writing, Jennifer enjoys reading, fine needlework, quilting, tweeting and cheering on the Pittsburgh Penguins. She lives in Pennsylvania with her amazingly patient husband, two remarkably talented daughters and their two very spoiled fur babies, otherwise known as cats—but *shh*…don't tell them they're not human!

Jennifer loves to hear from readers—you can contact her via her website: www.jenniferfaye.com.

CHAPTER ONE

AT LAST HE'D lost them.

Prince Alexandro Castanavo of the Mirraccino Islands stared out the back window of the cab as it snaked in and out of traffic. He'd never driven in New York City but his concern deepened when they swerved to the berm of the road. While all of the other traffic was at a standstill, they kept rolling along.

When the cab suddenly jerked to the left, Alex's shoulder thumped into the door. He reached for the armrest and his fingertips dug into the hard plastic. What had he done to deserve the cabbie who thought he was a grand prix driver?

Alex jerked forward as the car screeched to a halt in front of a traffic light. At least the guy obeyed some traffic rules. Another glance out the rear window revealed a bread delivery truck behind them. He breathed a sigh of relief. No one was following them. But then again, how could they? He doubted many people drove as erratically as this cabbie.

"You can let me out here?"

"No. I get you there quick."

Alex reached for his wallet, but before he could grab it, the car lurched forward. He fell back against the seat. What was up with this guy? Didn't he know that he'd make more money by taking his time?

"You don't have to hurry."

The man grinned at him in the rearview mirror. "Hurry? Sure. I hurry."

Alex inwardly groaned. He was about to correct the man when he realized that every time the man spoke, he took his eyes off the roadway. It was best not to distract him if Alex wanted to reach his destination in one piece.

He silently sat in the backseat while the cabbie jockeyed through the streets of Manhattan. Alex stared out the side window as a fine snow began to fall. Cars and people abounded in every direction, seemingly undisturbed by the deteriorating weather. Garlands and festive wreaths adorned the fronts of buildings while pine trees and shiny ornaments decorated the shop windows. Christmas was definitely in the air, even though it was still a few weeks away.

City life would definitely take a bit to get used to. Not that he planned to live it up while in town. Unlike his usual need for high visibility on behalf of the kingdom, this trip required stealth maneuvers, especially since he'd gone against protocol and stolen away without his security detail. Although in his defense, it was a necessity. Trying to elude the paparazzi was tricky enough, but doing it with an entourage would be impossible.

Soon the stores faded away, traffic thinned out and rows of houses dotted each side of the street. One last glance out the rear window assured him they hadn't been followed. At last, the tension in his neck eased.

When a loud clicking sound filled the car, he noticed they'd turned onto a cobblestone roadway. It was a narrow residential road with no parking on either side.

Alex sat up a little straighter, taking in the sweeping willow trees on either side of the street. This must be the exclusive neighborhood of Willow Heights, aptly named.

The homes in this area sat back off the road. They were older mansions that were well kept and still stunningly beautiful. Being here was like stepping back in time. A wrought-iron signpost came into view. It stood in front of a stone wall and read: The Willows.

Alex glanced up at the stately home with its old-world charm. He wasn't sure what he was expecting. When the problem at the palace had come to light, there had been no time for detailed planning. He'd moved directly into action. His mission was to draw out this game of cat and mouse with the press—not knowing how much time would be needed to resolve his brother's latest fiasco.

The driver turned in to the gated driveway. "That is some swanky place. You some rich muckety-muck?"

He wasn't sure what a muckety-muck was, but it didn't sound good. "No."

"You stay long?"

He wished he knew. "I'm not sure."

"When you need a ride. You call. Freddy take you."

English might be Alex's second language, but this man made him feel as if it was his first—the broken English combined with a very heavy accent left Alex struggling to understand what the cabbie was trying to say. But one thing he knew was that he wouldn't be summoning Freddy for another ride—anywhere.

The paved driveway led them to a spacious three-story flagstone mansion. By the looks of it, this place dated back a century or two. The owner certainly had done a fine job keeping up the outside. Ivy grew up one wall and its vines were dusted with snow. It didn't even come close to the enormity of his family's palace, but the large, sweeping porch draped with garlands gave the place a warm, homey feel.

The car pulled to a stop and the driver cast him a big, toothy grin. Alex reached for his credit card to pay the fare but paused. On second thought, he grabbed some cash from his wallet. It was best to keep his true identity under wraps for now.

Once he and his luggage were settled on the sidewalk, the cab raced off down the driveway. Alex's shoulders slumped as the adrenaline wore off and fatigue weighed him down. He stifled the urge to yawn. He'd never been so happy to have his feet on solid, unmoving ground; now he just had to find his room and get some shut-eye before he dropped from exhaustion.

"Welcome," chimed a sweet voice.

He turned, finding a young woman coming up along the side of the house, lugging a big cardboard box. Her reddish-brown ponytail swayed as she made her way toward him. Her beauty captivated him, from her pink-stained cheeks to her full rosy lips.

Her breath came out in small white puffs in the frigid air. Her forehead creased with lines of exertion from carrying a box that was far too big for her.

Alex sprang into action. "Let me take that for you."

She looked hesitant but then relented. "It goes on the front porch."

"Your wish is my command."

They strolled side-by-side along the walkway. She cast a curious glance his way. "Are you all right? You looked a little shook up when you got out of the cab."

"You wouldn't believe the cab ride I had here." He stopped at the bottom of the steps. "I think the cabbie drove off the road more than he drove on it."

"I take it you didn't enjoy your adventure?"

"Not at all. I am very grateful to be here in one piece. Remind me to think twice before I call that cab company again."

The young lady smiled and he found himself smiling

back. This was not good. He knew better than to encourage the attention of women. It only complicated things when they wanted more than he could offer.

He forced his lips into a flat line as he moved onto the porch. The box landed with a thunk. He turned around to find the young woman standing just behind him.

As he dusted off his hands, he took in her white winter jacket with the logo for The Willows stitched in blue thread on the chest. His gaze skimmed downward, catching her snug jeans and the wheat-colored work boots that completed her ensemble. He drew his gaze up from her peekaboo curves. At last his gaze made it to her eyes—her big brown eyes. He wondered if she knew how beautiful she was. The guys must go crazy over her.

"Thank you for the help." Her gaze strayed to his luggage and back to him. "Can I help you? Are you part of the wedding party?"

"No, I'm not." His voice came out deeper than normal. "I want to check in."

"Rooms are by reservation only."

This young woman must be mistaken. "I have a reservation. Now, if you could point me in the direction of the person in charge."

The young lady pulled off a glove and held out her hand. "You're speaking to her. I'm Reese Harding. And you would be?"

He stepped closer and wrapped his cold fingers around her warm ones. Her skin was smooth and supple. He resisted the urge to stroke the back of her hand with his thumb. When his gaze caught hers, he noticed the gold flakes in her eyes.

"Allow me to introduce myself. I am P—" He caught himself just in time before blurting out his formal title. It took him a moment to recall the alias he'd used on the registration. He'd borrowed his mother's family name. "Alex DeLuca."

Then, realizing he'd held on to her hand longer than necessary, he released his hold on her. He never let a woman affect him to this extent. Being awake more than twenty-four hours was definitely impacting him. If only he could sleep on planes, it'd help.

"You own this place?" he asked, just to make sure he understood her correctly.

"Yes, I do."

His brows gathered as he studied her. She certainly seemed awfully young to be running her own business. "If you don't mind me asking, how old are you?"

"I can assure you I'm older than I look."

Well, now she had him curious. "And that would be—"

"Twenty-five." Her dimpled chin lifted. "Don't tell me you're going to card me too?"

"Um…no." He glanced away. He was letting himself get off track. It must be jet lag, because he wasn't here to pick up women—even one as captivating as the woman standing before him. "About the room—"

"The place is full up until Monday."

"Monday?" That was impossible. The muscles in his neck and shoulders tightened. "I made the reservation for today."

"If you'd like to make another reservation, I can check our calendar." She turned and stepped inside.

He strode after her, closing the door behind him. "I assure you I have a reservation, if you'd just check."

With an audible huff, she stopped in the foyer and turned. "Listen. I don't have your reservation. In fact, I've never spoken to you in my life. I would have remembered the accent."

He would have remembered her honeyed voice, too.

She was as attractive as she was frustrating. "Someone else must have taken my reservation. Surely you're not the only person who works here." Then again, this place was smaller than he'd been expecting. "Are you?"

Her forehead crinkled. "No, I'm not. But anyone you'd have spoken to would have checked the online system and known we were booked."

Not about to give up, he thought back to the phone call when he'd made the reservation. "It was a woman I spoke to about getting a room. She sounded a bit older than you. She took my information."

She frowned. "Maybe you do have a reservation. It's possible it didn't get entered in our system." She lowered her head and shook it. "But it doesn't change the fact that I don't have anywhere for you to stay. We are hosting a wedding this weekend."

He'd boarded three different flights today just to be sure he'd lost the paparazzi. And he'd suffered through a long layover in the Atlanta airport, cramped in a chair. All he wanted to do now was enjoy a warm meal and a soft bed. He held back a yawn. Rather make that a soft bed and then the warm meal. Anything else was unacceptable.

He straightened to his full six-foot-three-inch height and pressed his hands to his waist. He swallowed his frustration and strove for a professional tone. "What about my deposit?"

Her lush lips gaped and her face paled. "You made a deposit?"

"Yes. Check your computer."

Her eyes widened. "Mr. DeLuca, I'll definitely check into getting you a full refund. I'm truly sorry for the inconvenience."

He glanced around at the historic mansion. His gaze scaled up the rounded staircase, taking in the stained-glass window on the landing. There had to be room some-where—even if it took a bit of juggling.

"Since you've already accepted my money and this place looks spacious enough, I am sure you can set up accommodations for me until this wedding is over." He flashed her one of his camera-ready smiles. "After all, I traveled a long way to get here. Now I expect you to hold up your end of the arrangement."

Her lush lips pressed into a firm line as though she were considering her options before speaking. "Why don't you follow me into the lobby while I clear up this snafu?"

Without another word the spitfire strode away. Her well-rounded hips sashayed from side to side like the metro-nome from the days when he'd been forced to take piano lessons. Only the swing of her backside mesmerized him in a way the silly rhythm keeper from his childhood never did. He stared at her until she disappeared back down the hallway.

Alex gave himself a mental jerk. He couldn't let himself get distracted—no matter how beautiful the distraction. He had a job to do. A mission to complete. His sole duty was to protect the crown of the Mirraccino Islands from a messy scandal—one that would most certainly rock not only the palace walls but also the entire nation.

CHAPTER TWO

REESE HARDING STRODE to the back of the mansion, trying not to let the tall, dark stranger get under her skin. All the while, she ignored the prickling sensation at the back of her neck. Let him stare. She wasn't going to go all soft because he was drop-dead gorgeous and his mere touch made her fingers tingle.

Her gut told her that he was used to getting what he wanted—when he wanted—but it wasn't going to happen today. There honestly was no room. And by the way he could make her heart race with just a look, it was for the best.

Reese marched into the office just off the kitchen. She suspected that her mother had accepted his reservation. If that were the case, Reese might very well have a legitimate problem. And she'd have no one to blame but herself. When her mother had finally come out of the dark place she had disappeared to after Reese's father unexpectedly died, she had been so excited to see her mother's desire to help with the inn that perhaps she'd let her mother have too much freedom.

"Hey, honey." Her mother peered in from the kitchen. "What are you doing? You just tracked a trail of snow over my clean floors."

"Sorry." Reese continued rummaging through the

stacks of bills and correspondence on top of the big oak desk. "I need to find something."

"Can I help?" Her mother's face lit up. "I'm feeling like my old self now and would really like to be more helpful around here. I could organize the office for you."

"Mom, we talked about this. I like it the way it is. I can usually find what I'm looking for." And she would this time, too, if Mr. DeLuca didn't have her all flustered. "Besides, we don't want to rush things. You're doing so well and all, I just don't want—"

"I know, honey." Her mother patted her back. "It's just nice to be needed. So what are you looking for?"

"There's some guy waiting in the foyer claiming to have a reservation for tonight. Do you recall taking a phone call from an Alex something or other?"

Her mother's graying head tilted to the side. "I'm not sure. A lot has been happening around here lately."

Reese stopped shuffling through the papers in the organizer and looked directly at her mother. "This is important. Think real hard. Did you take a reservation from a man with a foreign accent?"

Her mother's forehead crinkled. "When would he have called?"

"Last week." Reese grabbed another stack of papers, looking for anything that would confirm that man's words.

"Seems to me I might recall speaking to someone with a foreign accent. I remember because the connection wasn't very good."

"Really? You remember him?"

"If I took his reservation, the money will be in the computer."

Her mother was right. She was wasting her time searching through all of those papers. She could pop on the computer and confirm Alex's deposit had been made. She pushed a button to start the computer.

"I'll leave you alone to figure things out." Her mother made a beeline for the door.

Reese logged into the resort's financial account. There was indeed a deposit—a huge deposit. Surely she'd misread the amount. Even after she blinked and refocused, the same enormous dollar figure remained. Her heart picked up its pace as excitement coursed through her veins. There was more than enough cash here to rent out the entire mansion for a month.

She then checked the inn's online reservation system. There was no mention of Mr. DeLuca. How was that possible?

After some quick sleuthing, she determined that her mother had bypassed the online reservation system and taken his information over the phone manually. Oh, what a mess! She'd have to sit her mother down and have a firm talk about procedures so they could avoid these issues in the future.

Still, this influx of cash was just what they needed to pay the upcoming tax bill, not to mention the bank loan. *Calm down. You're getting ahead of yourself.*

It wasn't like she could accept his money. She didn't have one single room to offer him. All she could do was offer Mr. Sexy Accent a full refund and hope he'd go away quietly.

But nothing about the man said he'd easily back off from what he wanted. Everything from the man's every-strand-in-its-place dark hair to his tailored white shirt that covered an obviously buff chest and down to his polished dress shoes said he was used to getting what he wanted when he wanted and the way he wanted it.

Nonetheless, she didn't have the ability to accommodate

him, much less the obviously large party that he planned to host. With a weary sigh, she grabbed the checkbook to write out the refund. The pen hovered over the check and her grip tightened as she thought of turning away all of that money.

She wrote out his name and the amount. Life wasn't fair. In the past year or so, with the economic downturn, she'd had a hard time attracting people to The Willows and now she was having to turn away this obviously affluent guest because of a clerical error.

She really did feel bad for him. Then a thought occurred to her. The least she should do was help this man locate some other reasonable accommodations.

Armed with the check and her address book, she returned to the foyer. Upon finding her mother and Mr. DeLuca conversing in lowered voices, she paused by the staircase. Neither of them seemed to notice her presence. What in the world was her mother saying that was so engrossing? The man rocked back on his heels and laughed. The sound was deep and rich.

When she stepped off the carpeted runner and onto the dark, polished wood floor, her boots made a sound. Both her mother and Mr. DeLuca turned her way. Reese's hold on the sizable check tightened. It was best to get this over with quickly.

The man caught her gaze with his deep blue eyes. She was struck by their vibrant color, but beyond that they told her nothing of the man's thoughts. Talk about a poker face. What sort of things did this international hunk keep hidden from the rest of the world? And what twist of fate had brought him to her doorstep?

The rise of his brows had her averting her gaze, but not before her pulse spiked, causing her heart to flutter. Why was she so intrigued by this stranger? So what if he came from another land and had the sexiest way of rolling his *R*s? He was still just a guy and she wouldn't let herself want something that she knew could never be. Her attention needed to remain on the mansion and keeping it afloat.

"Ah, there's my daughter." Her mother leaned toward Mr. DeLuca as though they were old friends. "I'm sure she'll have cleared everything up for you. It was nice to meet you. I hope we can talk again." Her mother's eyes twinkled as a mischievous grin played across her lips.

Once they were alone, Reese pulled her shoulders back. "Mr. DeLuca, I've verified your reservation and I must apologize for the inconvenience this has caused you. My mother made a mistake when she gave you the reservation. She didn't realize that we already had a prior commitment."

The man remained silent, not appearing the least bit interested in helping her out of this awkward situation. She held out the hefty check, but he didn't make any attempt to accept it.

"This is the full amount you paid. I double-checked." When he still didn't move, she added, "The check will cover your full deposit."

"I don't want it."

"What? Of course you do. That's a lot of money."

Tired of playing word games, she stepped up to him and stuffed the check in his hand. For the second time in less than an hour, his touch caused a jolt of awareness to shock her nerve endings.

Her gaze lifted and she noticed his eyes were bloodshot, as though he'd been up all night. Then she noticed the lines bracketing his eyes and the dark shadow of beard trailing down his squared jaw. She was tempted to reach up and run her fingertips over the stubble.

She clamped her hands together. "If you'd like, I have

the phone numbers of other facilities around the city that might be able to accommodate your party—"

"That won't be necessary," he said firmly. "I am staying here as arranged."

"But—"

"There are no more buts. I am staying." He pressed the check back into her hand. "And don't tell me again that there is no room. Your mother informed me otherwise."

"She did what?"

He sent her a knowing smile. "She told me there's a bedroom available. It's in some private apartment until one of the guest rooms opens up."

What in the world had gotten into her mother? Sure, she used to be impulsive back before the disaster with Reese's father, but since then she'd been so reserved, so quiet. Now she was getting active in the inn, which was great, but why in the world was she handing out her daughter's bedroom to this total stranger?

Reese shook her head, trying to dispel the image of this tall, dark, smooth-talking stranger in her bed. "She shouldn't have done that, not without talking to me."

His voice softened. "She seemed certain you wouldn't mind. After all, it's only until the other guests check out."

"But that's days away. They aren't leaving until Monday." And the apartment was so small that they'd be bumping into each other, day and...night. She swallowed hard.

At that moment, approaching footsteps sounded on the stairs. Relieved at the interruption, Reese turned away. Sandy, in her blue-and-white maid's uniform, descended the steps with her dark brown ponytail swinging back and forth. The young woman's eyes lit up when they landed on their latest guest. It would appear that being left in the lurch by the father of her child wasn't enough to make Sandy immune to Mr. DeLuca's charming smile.

"Do you need something, Sandy?" Reese asked, hoping the girl would quit openly ogling the man.

Sandy came to a stop next to them. "I…uh…finished cleaning all of the rooms." She tore her gaze from Mr. DeLuca and turned to Reese. "Do you need anything else today? I don't mind staying longer."

"Thanks. But we're good. Enjoy your evening off."

"Um…sure. Thank you." Sandy almost tripped over her own feet as she kept glancing over her shoulder at Mr. DeLuca.

Reese turned back to him, refusing to let his tanned features, mesmerizing blue gaze and engaging smile turn her into a starstruck teenager. "Where were we?"

"We had just resolved my accommodations until the wedding party checks out. Now, if you'll show me to my room."

She pressed her lips firmly together, holding back her response until she gave it some thought. The truth was most women would probably stumble over themselves to have this hunk of a man sleep in their bed. But she wasn't most women. Men couldn't be trusted—no matter how well you thought you knew them.

But this arrangement was all about business—nothing more. What was a few nights on their old, lumpy couch? As it was, she didn't sleep all that much anymore. The concerns about meeting this month's payroll on top of the loan payment kept her tossing and turning most nights.

"I must warn you that the room is nothing special. In fact, it's rather plain."

"Is it clean?"

She nodded. The linens had just been changed that morning. "But I'm certain it won't be up to the standards you're used to or even the normal standards of The Willows. And…and—"

"And what?"

She shook her head. "Nothing important."

She couldn't bring herself to let on that it bothered her to share her tiny apartment with him. And no matter how much she reminded herself that it was business, it still felt personal having him slide between her sheets and lay his head on her pillow. Her pulse picked up its pace. Her gaze strayed to his bare ring finger before she realized her actions and refocused on a nondescript spot just over his left shoulder.

Maybe if he wasn't drop-dead gorgeous she wouldn't be overreacting. But for the first time since she'd started the inn, her hormones were standing up and taking a definite interest in a man. Not that he'd be interested in a college dropout like herself—even if quitting school hadn't been a choice but rather a necessity.

He looked pointedly at her. "If you have something else on your mind, you might as well get it out in the open now."

Heat crept up her neck as her fingers tightened around the check. No way was she confessing to her nonprofessional thoughts. "I was just concerned about where the rest of your party would be staying."

"There's no one else coming. I am the only guest."

"Just you?" Her gaze moved to the check that was now a bit wrinkled. "But this deposit covers all six rooms."

"I am a man who values his privacy."

That or he was so filthy rich that he didn't have the common sense God gave a flea. But hey, who was she to argue with some sheikh or eccentric recluse?

But the money in her hand came with some sticky strings. She'd have to open her home up to him for five days and four nights. She suddenly regretted not doing more with the upkeep of the apartment. But her limited funds had to go toward the debts her father had left as her inheritance. Soon the creditors would be calling and she wasn't sure what she would tell them.

She glanced up at the staircase and balcony with the large stained-glass window. Her mother's family had owned the mansion for generations. She didn't want to think about the tailspin her mother would go into if they had to turn this place over to the bank—not now that her mother had almost recovered from her father's deception. So if it took bunking with this man to secure the necessary funds, she didn't see where she had much choice in the matter.

"Well, Mr. DeLuca, it looks like you've rented yourself a mansion."

What would it be like having a sexy roommate? Did he sleep in boxers? Or perhaps in the buff? And more importantly, did he walk in his sleep? Heat swirled in her chest and rushed up her neck. After all, a glimpse wouldn't hurt anyone.

The lines on the man's tanned face eased and a hint of a smile played at the corners of his full lips. "Now that we're housemates, you may call me Alex."

She wasn't so sure getting personal with him would help her roving thoughts, but she wasn't about to turn away his kindness. "And you can call me Reese."

CHAPTER THREE

THIS WAS WHERE he was to stay?

Alex followed Reese into the tiny apartment. He wondered who lived here or if it was just kept as a spare unit. Although seeing the older furniture and the coziness of the place, it didn't resemble any of the inn's photos he'd observed online. This place definitely wasn't meant for guests.

Reese swung open the door to a small bedroom. "This is where you can sleep."

He stepped up behind her in the doorway and peered over her shoulder. The decorations consisted of miniature teddy bears of all colors and designs. He'd never seen so many stuffed animals in one room. It was definitely interesting decor.

The most important feature was that it had a place for him to sleep. In the middle of the room stood a double bed sporting a royal-blue duvet with white throw pillows. Definitely nothing fancy, but at this point it didn't matter. He didn't think he could take one more step.

And to be honest, staying in these private quarters, as primitive as they were, would only make him that much harder to find. It'd been way too easy to tease the press with a juicy morsel of information about how he'd lost his heart to an American. But what no one knew was that he wanted no part of the *L* word. He'd witnessed firsthand how devastating it could be when you've lost the one person you loved with all of your heart. He refused to let himself become that vulnerable.

"Dinner is at six." Reese backed out of the doorway. "Do you need anything else?"

He stepped past her and hefted his suitcase onto the bed. "Your mother mentioned the room has a private bath."

Reese's brows rose sharply. "She was mistaken."

"I don't think so. She sounded quite certain."

Reese crossed her arms and tilted her head until their gazes met. "Well, she was mistaken, because she was talking about her room and she's not about to give it up to you or anyone."

"You seem very protective of your mother."

"She's all I've got in this world." And without another word, Reese turned and left.

Alex stood there staring at the now empty doorway, mentally comparing the image of the smiling older woman with the very serious young woman who seemed less than happy to have him here. There was a definite resemblance between the two as far as looks went, but the similarities stopped there. He rubbed the back of his neck before stretching. He was probably making too much of the first meeting. He'd see things clearer in the morning.

At last, he gave in to the urge for a great big yawn. The unpacking could wait. After being in transit for much longer than he cared to remember, it'd feel so good to lie down and rest. Just for a moment. After all, it was almost dinnertime.

He leaned his head back against the pillow. Maybe this trip wasn't going to be as bad as he'd imagined. For the time being, he could be a normal person without people looking at him with preconceived notions of what a royal should say or do. For just a bit, he'd be plain old Alex. A regular citizen. A mere tourist. Something he'd never been in his whole life.

The next morning, Alex awoke with his street clothes still on. He'd only meant to lie down for a moment. His stomach rumbled. He hadn't even made it to dinner. Then the events of the prior evening started to play in his mind.

He groaned as he recalled how in his exhausted state he'd been less than gentlemanly, demanding to have his way. He scratched at his two—or was it now a three?—day-old beard. He definitely owed Reese an apology.

After a hot shower and a much-needed shave, he started to unpack. He moved to the dresser and pulled out a drawer. He froze when he spotted a light pink lacy bra. What in the world?

His gaze moved to the right, finding a matching pair of undies. They weren't much more than a scrap of lace with a couple of pink strings. Immediately the image of Reese came to mind. This must be her bedroom. And these were her things. He slammed the drawer shut, but it was too late. His imagination had kicked into overdrive.

Not only had he been unfriendly last evening, but he'd even stolen her bed right out from under her. He groaned. He wasn't so sure an apology was going to be enough to earn his way into her good graces.

He removed a pair of jeans and a sweater from his suitcase—the clothes he'd borrowed from his brother. They were more casual than his normal wardrobe, but this trip called for a very casual appearance. He and his fraternal twin, the Crown Prince Demetrius Castanavo, still wore the same size. Not that his brother would even notice the missing clothes, much less care about them. He had more important things on his mind at the moment.

Alex's next task was styling his temporarily darkened hair. He didn't want anyone to recognize him too soon. Let the paparazzi continue with their hunt. After all, the fun was in the chase. And it'd take them awhile to find him in this out-of-the-way inn.

As he worked the styling gel into his hair, he mulled over his brother's situation. He sympathized with Demetrius. The thought of being responsible not only for the royal family but also for an entire nation was, to say the least, a bit overwhelming. He just hoped Demetrius would come to terms with his inherited position as crown prince and not cause any further incidents—such as the potential scandal everyone was working so hard to cover up.

Next Alex added some saline drops to his eyes to refresh the colored contacts similar to the ones he'd used while he'd been on vacation a few months back. He blinked a couple of times, then inspected his image in the mirror. A smile pulled at his lips. For today, he was no longer Prince Alexandro. He was just plain, ordinary Alex. But first he had some royal business to attend to.

He stepped into the living room and heard a knock at the door. A man handed him a tray of food and Alex's mouth watered. It'd been a long time since he'd been this hungry. He thanked the man and barely got seated on the couch before he took his first big bite.

After finishing every last drop of the herb soup and devouring the turkey sandwich, he logged on to his computer. He scanned one news site and then another and another. His plan wasn't working. The paparazzi weren't following his jaunt to the U.S. the way he'd hoped they would. In fact, he'd fallen out of the headlines. This was not good. Not good at all.

He'd definitely have to up the stakes if he wanted to gain the press's fleeting attention. Uncomfortable with the idea of throwing out a juicy bit of information, he nonetheless started typing a note from a fictitious palace employee to a popular internet gossip site about his recent "activities." This was the only way to keep them from sniffing out the truth—the scandal that was his brother's life. He just wondered what lengths he'd have to go to in order to keep up this charade.

He was able to keep working into the afternoon and catch up on some important emails related to Mirraccino's shipping commerce. Once he'd pressed the send button on the last email, he made his way downstairs. He'd just found his way to the kitchen when Reese came rushing out of it carrying a stepstool. All bundled up in her coat and fuzzy pink earmuffs, she came to a halt when she noticed him blocking the hallway.

"Good afternoon." Her voice was cool and there was no hint of a smile on her face.

This would be so much easier if he hadn't stumbled upon her skimpy undies. Even now he wondered if she had on a matching blue set. Or perhaps she preferred deep purple. Or maybe they were polka-dotted.

"Could you move aside? I was on my way out the door."

He gave himself a mental jerk. He wasn't ready for her to go—not yet. "I smell something delicious. The aroma wafted the whole way upstairs. What is it?"

She lowered the collapsible stool to the floor and leaned it against her leg. "It's homemade marinara sauce. But it's not ready yet. If you want to make yourself comfortable in the living room just off the foyer, I'll make sure someone lets you know when dinner is served."

"Do you want to join me?"

"I can't. I'm headed outside to do some work." She hefted the silver stool.

"But I wanted to speak with you."

"Can it wait? I have a couple of things I need to do before dinner."

"Of course." He kept what he hoped was an impartial expression on his face. "It's not urgent. May I help you?"

She shook her head. "I've got it."

As she headed for the front door, an uneasy feeling came over him. The ladder looked as though it'd seen far better days. Combine that with the ice and snow and it'd undoubtedly add up to trouble. Perhaps this was a way he could earn himself some points with her. But more than that, something told him Reese could use a helping hand—even if she was too stubborn to admit it.

As it was, he'd never been any good at just sitting around doing nothing. If he'd been at the palace, he'd be busy dealing with one situation or another. His country was quite involved with the exportation of its fine wines and fruit as well as being a shipping mecca. But he had to keep in mind that while he was in New York, he was plain Alex on holiday. Still, that didn't mean he had to sit around doing nothing.

He rushed off to grab his coat from the apartment. On the way back down the stairs, he happened upon a young man rushing up the steps, taking them two at a time. The guy had stress marring his face as a distinct frown pulled at his mouth. The guy grunted a hello as he rushed past. Alex couldn't help but wonder if that was the groom.

Why in the world did people put themselves through such stressful situations? He had no intention of saying *I do* any time soon—if ever. He'd seen firsthand how powerful love could be. And when it was over, it left people utterly devastated.

If he took the plunge it would be for something other than love—something worthwhile. After all, a meaningful union was what was expected of a prince. It was his duty.

Lost in his thoughts, Alex yanked open the front door. His hand grasped the brass handle on the glass storm door and pushed. At that moment, he saw Reese off to the side. The door bumped into the stool with her on it. The contraption teetered to the side. Reese jumped off just in time.

"Are you okay?" Alex rushed to her side.

"I'm fine." But she didn't look happy to see him—not that he could blame her.

"I didn't expect to find someone standing in front of the door."

"It's my fault, I should have moved over to the side a little more, but I was having problems stringing the lights right above the door."

He glanced at them. "They look all right to me."

"Look at them from down here." She led the way into the yard, oblivious of the deepening layer of snow.

Alex followed her. When he turned back, he found she'd transformed the porch into a beautiful winter scene. There was garland lining the front of the porch. Small artificial pine trees strung with white lights stood guard on either side of the front door. And then there were strands of white twinkle lights the whole way around the porch, giving it a soft glow.

As Reese stood there puzzling over how to finish stringing the lights, her full lips pursed together. If he were impulsive—like his twin—he might consider stealing a kiss just to see if her lips were as sweet as they looked.

Alex turned to look out over the quiet street. The thought of kissing her still pulled at his thoughts. Besides probably earning him a slap for his effort, he knew kissing her was the sort of spontaneity that had gotten his brother in a world of trouble. Alex still didn't understand how the crown prince could elope with a woman he had only known for a handful of weeks. Frustration churned in Alex's gut. No one would want an impulsive ruler, including Alex himself. That's why the elopement had to be dealt with immediately and quietly without the encroachment of the press.

Alex glanced in Reese's direction to find her big brown eyes studying him. Her gaze was intense and put him off center because it was as if she could see through him—see that he was a fake. Or maybe it was his guilt from not introducing himself properly as the prince of the Mirraccino Islands that had him uneasy.

But it had to be this way. Keeping his identity hush-hush was of the utmost importance. He didn't know this woman any better than a person on the street. There was no reason to take her into his confidence and expect her to keep it. To her he was nothing more than a paying customer—end of story.

Her brow crinkled. "Is something wrong?"

"Not that I can think of."

"Okay. I just thought with you standing out here in the cold instead of inside in the warmth that you must need something important."

This was his opening. He didn't have a lot of practice at apologies and for some reason he really wanted to get this right.

"There's something I have to say." When he had her full attention, he continued. "I am sorry about our first meeting. I was way out of line."

There was a flicker of something in her eyes, but in a blink, it was gone. "Apology accepted. But it wasn't all your fault. You were expecting a room to be waiting for you. No one could blame you for being upset."

"But then to kick you out of your own bed—"

"Don't worry. I don't sleep much anyway."

Before he could inquire about her last statement, she

headed back to the porch to adjust the strand of lights on the banister.

"What do you think?" Reese returned to his side.

He didn't really notice a difference. "Looks much better."

"I don't know." She crossed her arms and studied the lights strung from one end of the porch to the other. "It's not perfect, but I guess it'll have to do."

"Do you always decorate so elaborately?"

She shrugged. "I wouldn't bother, but each home along Cobblestone Way is expected to light up their homes for the holidays."

Reese climbed on the unstable stepstool. When she swayed slightly, Alex rushed to her side.

"Let me do that for you." He held out his hands for the string of lights.

"Thanks, but I've got it. I know exactly how they go."

Instinctively he placed a hand on her hip to steady her while with his other hand he gripped the stool. The heat of her body seeped through her jeans and into his hand, sending a strange sensation pulsating up his arm.

She glanced down at him and their gazes caught for a second more than was necessary. Then she turned away and attempted to string the lights on three little hooks above the door.

"There. That should do." With his hand aiding her, she climbed down the few steps. "Would you mind plugging them in?" She pointed to the outlet on the other side of the porch.

He was glad to help, even if it was just something small. And the fact that this independent woman let him do anything at all must mean that he was making a little bit of progress with her. He liked that thought—not that he was going to let this budding friendship go too far. But it would be nice to have someone around with whom he could strike up a friendly conversation. He quickly found the end of the extension cord and plugged in the additional string of lights.

He turned around to find that she'd returned to the front lawn to inspect her own handiwork. Deciding that she had the right idea, he did the same. He glanced up at the house, finding it looked just as good as before. "You did a great job."

"It's no big deal. But it's nice to know that someone enjoys my efforts."

"Do you need help with anything else?"

"Actually, I do."

Her answer surprised him. "Tell me what you need."

"After dinner, I need to go get a Christmas tree."

She was going to chop down a tree? She might have the determination, but he wasn't so sure that she had the physical strength. He wondered whom she would turn to if he wasn't here. The thought of her leaning on another man didn't sit well with him.

Ignoring the bothersome thought, he followed her back to the porch and helped collect her supplies. "I must admit this will be a first for me."

"Where exactly are you from?"

He didn't want to lie to her, but he knew that he couldn't be totally honest. With his accent there was no way he could pass for an American. There had to be a way around this tricky topic.

He decided to turn things around. "Where do you think I'm from?"

"I don't know." She tilted her head to the side and eyed him. "Let me think about it."

Spending time with Reese could be trickier than he'd imagined. He didn't want to lie to her, but telling her about his homeland was not an option. Maybe he should have stayed in the apartment and avoided her altogether. He inwardly groaned. As if that would be possible with them being roommates.

Besides, he already had a date with her. Correction. He had plans with her.

Oh, boy, was he in deep trouble, and it was only his second day in New York.

CHAPTER FOUR

THIS WASN'T A good idea after all.

Reese closed the side door to the garage and inhaled a steadying breath. She'd been far too aware of Alex at dinner. The deep rumble of his contagious laughter. The way his eyes crinkled at the corners when he smiled, making him even more handsome—if that was possible. And the way he listened to her as though each word she uttered truly mattered.

This was not good.

What had she been thinking inviting this man to go pick out a Christmas-tree with her? It wasn't as if she needed any help. Since her father's death, she'd been managing everything on her own. Why should that change now?

But she reasoned that Alex was an important guest. His enormous fee would help her meet this month's bills… she hoped. It was definitely a good incentive to make his stay here as pleasant as possible. And perhaps he'd recommend his friends stay at The Willows the next time they visited the city.

And if they were all as easy on the eyes, she wouldn't complain. After all, looking didn't hurt anything. It was getting involved with men that set you up for a world of pain. Just ask her mother. And even Reese had been involved with someone after her father died who'd promptly dumped her when he found out she wasn't a rich debutante. The memory still stung. How could she have been so foolish as to fall for her ex's promises?

In the end, she'd learned an important life lesson—don't trust men with your heart. Eventually they'll hurt you when you least expect it.

As for Alex DeLuca, she was so far out of that man's league that it was laughable. So what was she worrying about? She could relax and enjoy having some company for once.

She pressed the automatic garage door opener and started the truck. It coughed and sputtered and the breath caught in her throat. *Please don't let this be another thing I need money to fix.* As though in response to her silent prayer, when she turned the key again the engine caught. She exhaled a pent-up breath and put the vehicle in drive.

In no time at all, Alex was seated next to her. "Reese, thank you for allowing me to ride along."

The *R*s rolled off his tongue in such a divine way. She stopped herself just short of swooning. He could definitely say her name as often as he wanted. Realizing that she was letting her thoughts wander, she reminded herself that he was her guest—nothing else.

"Um…sure. No problem." In an effort to keep her thoughts from straying, she turned on the radio and switched stations until holiday music filled the air. As an afterthought, she said, "I hope you don't mind some music."

"Not at all. Back home my mother used to always have music filling the…house."

She noticed his use of the past tense and then the awkward pause. She wondered if he too was a member of the lost-a-parent-prematurely club. It was not something she'd wish on anyone—no matter the circumstances. But then again, maybe she was reading too much into his choice of words, as English was obviously his second language.

In an effort to change the topic of conversation to something more casual, she said, "That's right, I was supposed to guess where you're from. I'm not great with placing accents, but I'm thinking somewhere in the Mediterranean. Maybe Italy?"

"Very good guess. Maybe you are better at figuring out accents than you think."

English definitely had a different ring to it when Alex was speaking. It had a sort of soothing melody. She could listen to him talk for hours.

"If you don't mind me asking, what brought you to New York?"

"Business. Or should I say, I am between business negotiations. With people being out of the office for the holidays, I decided to stay in New York and experience a white Christmas."

"You hope."

"What?"

She could feel his gaze on her. "I meant you hope to see a white Christmas. Snow around these parts is hit or miss. The snow we're getting now might be all we get until after the New Year."

Was it possible he had no family to go home to? Why else would he rent out an inn for the holiday? Pity welled up in her. She couldn't blame him for not wanting to spend Christmas alone. She'd had a taste of that when her mother was having problems. It was lonely and sad, filled with nothing but memories.

Which led her to her next question: How did such a handsome, obviously successful man end up alone? Surely he wouldn't have a hard time finding a date or two. Oh, who was she kidding? He could probably have a different date for breakfast, lunch and dinner, seven days a week, and still have plenty leftover. Perhaps if her life were different she might have given him a chance.

Alex cleared his throat. "Are you sure we're going in the right direction? We're heading into the city."

She had been distracted by their conversation, but she couldn't imagine she'd turned the wrong way. Just to be sure, she glanced around at the landmarks. "This is the right way."

"But I thought you said we were going to cut down a Christmas tree."

"I said I was going to get one, but I never said anything about cutting it down." She glanced over at him as he slouched down in the seat and adjusted his ball cap. "I'm sorry to disappoint you. But this is really much faster and easier for me."

"Is it much further?"

"Not far at all. In fact, we're here."

She stared out the window at the familiar city lot that was cordoned off with fencing. Pine trees ranging in size from small chubby little guys to tall slender ones littered the lot. People from old to young meandered around, pointing at this tree and that tree. Smiles covered their faces and the years rolled away as each seemed to step back in time and remember the childhood fascination of choosing their very own tree for Santa to leave presents under. If only that feeling of wonderment stayed with everyone. Instead some learned the hard way that things weren't always as they appeared. Sometimes life was nothing more than an empty illusion.

Reese's jaw tightened at the grim thought. Anxious to get this over, she said, "I'll just go check out what's available that will fit in the foyer. Feel free to look around."

"What about a tree for yourself?" When she cast him a puzzled look, he added, "You know, for the apartment?"

"I don't want one. After what happened…oh, never mind. I just don't have the time to bother."

She threw open the truck door and hopped out. She'd already circled around to the sidewalk when Alex's door opened. She noticed that he had the collar on his jacket pulled up and his hat shielded a good portion of his face. He must be cold. If he was here long enough, he'd get used to the cold weather.

He stepped up to her. "Let me know if you need any help."

"I will. Thank you."

His gaze moved up and down the walk. If she knew him better, she'd say he looked stressed. But that couldn't be the case. Who got stressed going to the Christmas tree lot? Maybe a single mom of six active little kids. Now that could be stressful. But not a single grown man.

So what was the true story? Why was Alex all alone for the holidays?

What had he been thinking to agree to come to this very public place?

Alex glanced around to see if anyone had noticed him. It was far too early in his plan to have his true identity made known. Or worse, for someone to snap a picture of him and publish it on the internet. He pulled his ball cap a little lower. Sure, he had his disguise in place, but he knew that it would not hold up under the close scrutiny of the press's cameras.

He slouched a bit more and avoided making eye contact with anyone. Fortunately no one seemed to pay him the least bit of attention. The people meandering about seemed more interested in finding the perfect Christmas tree than the couple of dozen other shoppers.

Thousands of holiday lights were strung overhead. This town certainly had a thing for lights, from the little twinkle ones to big flashing signs. He gazed at the trees, wondering what it'd be like to be here with his own family choosing the perfect tree—not that he had any immediate plans for a family. He knew a proper marriage was expected of him, but the thought didn't appeal to him. His duty was to look after his father, the king.

After all, if it wasn't for him, his mother, the queen, wouldn't have been shot by a subversive. The poignant memory of his mother taking a bullet in the chest brought Alex up short. Because of one thoughtless act, he'd devastated lives, leaving his father brokenhearted and alone to shoulder the weight of Mirraccino's problems.

That long-ago day was still fresh in Alex's mind. He'd grown up overnight and learned the importance of rules and duty. He didn't have the luxury to wonder what his life might be like if he were an ordinary citizen. He was a prince and with that came duties that could not be shirked—the consequences were too much to bear.

Still, that didn't mean he should forgo his manners. And thanking Reese for her hospitality would be the proper thing to do. He stopped in front of a chubby little tree that would look perfect in the apartment. It'd certainly cheer the place up.

A young man with a Santa hat and red apron approached him. "Can I help you?"

"I'd like to buy the little tree in the corner."

The guy eyed him up as though wondering why he'd want something so tiny. The man rattled off a price and Alex handed over the money.

With the little tree stowed in the back of the pickup, Alex sought out his beautiful hostess, who was pointing out a tall, slender tree to an older man with a white beard.

His cheeks were chubby and when he laughed his round belly shook. Alex wondered how many times children had mistaken him for Santa. Even the man's eyes twinkled when he smiled.

The man glanced at Alex before turning back to Reese. "This must be your other half. You two make a fine-looking couple. Is this your first Christmas together?"

"We're not together." Reese's cheeks filled with color. "I mean, we're not a couple. We're…um—"

"Friends," Alex supplied.

Although on second thought, the man's observation did have some merit. In fact, the more he thought of it, the more he wondered if the man was on to something. Reese would make any man the perfect girlfriend.

She was certainly beautiful enough. When she smiled, she beamed. And in the short time he'd known her, he'd gotten a glimpse of her strength and determination.

She'd make the ideal fake girlfriend.

After all, he was supposed to be in the States because of a love interest. And with the speed with which he'd had to put this plan in motion, he hadn't had a chance to find someone to fill the role. But if the need arose, would Reese be willing to play along?

Something told him that with some gentle persuasion, she could be brought round to his way of thinking. Okay, maybe it was more a hope than a feeling. But for now none of that mattered. Hopefully his brother's rushed marriage would be resolved quickly and quietly so that involving Reese wouldn't be necessary. But it never hurt to be prepared. His father's motto was Hope for the Best, But Be Prepared for the Worst.

Perhaps Alex should do a little research and see what challenges he would be up against with Reese. He'd probe the subject with her when they were alone in the truck.

Alex leaned over to Reese. "You found a tree?"

"Yes, I did. I think it'll be perfect." She pointed to the tree the man inserted into a noisy machine. Alex watched as the tree's limbs were compressed and bound with rope.

"It'll make a great Christmas tree. You have good taste."

Reese turned to him and smiled. Such a simple gesture, and yet his breath hitched and he couldn't glance away. Big, fluffy snowflakes fluttered and fell all around them. And the twinkle lights reflected in her eyes, making them glitter like gemstones.

"As soon as they bundle it up we can go home." She moved as if to retrieve the tree, breaking the spell she'd cast over him.

Alex, at last gathering his wits, stepped forward. "I'll get it."

She frowned as though she were about to argue, but then she surprised him by saying, "Okay."

With the tree secured in the bed of the truck, Alex climbed in the heated cab. He rubbed his hands together. "I remembered everything for this outing except my gloves."

Reese's face creased with worry lines. "You should have said something. Here, let me crank up the heat."

"Not necessary. The sting from the pine needles is worse than the cold."

"Let me know if you need anything when we get back to the house. Antiseptic cream, maybe?"

"I will." This was his chance to broach the subject in the forefront of his mind. "What did you think of Santa back there mistaking us for a happy couple?"

"That he needs a new pair of glasses."

"Surely being my girlfriend wouldn't be so bad, would it?"

Once stopped at a red light, Reese gave him a long look.

He started to feel a bit paranoid, as though he had a piece of lettuce in his teeth or something. "What?"

"I'm just looking for some sign that you hit your head when you were swinging that tree around."

"Very funny." When she smiled, a funny sensation filled his chest. "You still haven't answered my question. Would I make good boyfriend material?"

She jerked her gaze forward just as the light changed. "You can't be serious. We—we don't even know each other. And I'm not looking for a relationship. Not with you. Not with anybody."

"Understood." He was at last breaking through her calm reserve. He couldn't push her too hard too fast. "I was just hoping your rejection of the idea of us being a couple wasn't a personal one. After all, I showered and shaved today. My clothes are clean," he teased. "And I carried that great big tree for you."

"That's the best you can come up with?" She smiled and his breathing did that funny little tickle thing at the back of his throat again.

"Pretty much. So if circumstances were different, would I stand a chance with you?"

"I'll give you this much, you are persistent."

"Or maybe I'm a glutton for punishment." He sent her a pleading look.

"And I'm sure those puppy eyes work on all of the ladies, don't they?"

He sat up a little straighter. "Is it working now?"

The chime of laughter filled the truck. "If you aren't a salesman, you certainly missed your calling."

Did that mean he'd sold her on the idea that he was worthy of a second or third look? He didn't know why her answer had suddenly become so important to him. It wasn't as though this part of his plan had to be implemented—yet.

Still, he found himself enjoying the smile on her face. It lit up the night. She should definitely do it more often.

Reese tramped the brakes a bit hard for a red light, jerking him against the seat belt. "I'm sure you'll make some lucky lady the perfect boyfriend."

It was his turn to smile. "Thanks for the ringing endorsement. What would it take to tempt you to play the part?"

"Of what? Your girlfriend?"

In for a penny, in for a pound. "Yes."

She laughed. "Fine. If you must know, if by chance I was looking—which I'm not, but if I were—you might have a chance. But I seriously don't have the time…if I was interested."

"Ouch."

"Is it your hands?"

"No. It was my ego. It just took a direct hit."

She shook her head and smiled. "I'm sure you'll survive."

He leaned back in the seat as she skillfully guided them homeward. With Reese behind the wheel, Alex relaxed enough to let his thoughts wander.

How was it that someone so beautiful and entertaining could be single? Surely she wouldn't be alone for long. The image of Reese in someone else's arms took shape in his mind and with a mental jerk, he dismissed the unsettling idea. Her future relationships were none of his business. Period.

CHAPTER FIVE

PEACE AND QUIET at last.

Reese smiled to herself. The wedding party was off for the rehearsal and dinner. They wouldn't be home until late. She'd even let the staff go early. After all, it was the holiday season and there was nothing here that she couldn't manage on her own. And her mother was upstairs watching her favorite crime drama.

"Reese?" Alex's deep voice echoed down the hallway.

"In here." She was kneeling on the floor, sorting strands of twinkle lights.

He stepped into the room. "What are you doing?"

"Trying to get these lights to work. I need to replace the lightbulbs—one by one. Someday I'll have to buy new strings, but not this year." They would light up—even if she had to sit here all night exchanging the little bulbs. "What do you need?"

"I finished with my work and wondered if I could lend you a hand."

"You spend a lot of time on your computer, don't you?"

"It's a portable office. It allows me to work from anywhere."

She pulled out another bulb and replaced it with one she was certain worked. Still the strand remained dark. "So this isn't a holiday for you?"

"I would rather keep busy. I am not good at sitting around doing nothing." He knelt down beside her. "Let me have a try."

She glanced at him, surprised anyone would voluntarily offer to fix Christmas lights. Before he had a chance to change his mind, she held out the strand to him. "Good luck."

He moved closer. His warm fingers brushed over hers. His touch lingered, sending an electrical current up her arm. The reaction frazzled her common sense. She stared into his eyes as her heart pounded in her ears. He was the first to turn away. A sense of disappointment plagued her.

Regaining her senses, she jumped to her feet. She took a step back, hoping to keep her wits about her. She'd been avoiding him since that awkward moment with Santa—er, that man at the tree lot. Why the man had assumed they were a couple was beyond her. It wasn't as if she looked at Alex with dreamy eyes. Okay, so maybe she just had. But it was just for a moment. And it wasn't as if she was truly interested in him.

But then Alex had continued the conversation in the truck. What was that all about? She still wasn't certain if he had just been joking around or if he'd been hitting on her. At least she'd set him straight—a relationship wasn't in her plans. She refused to be lied to by another man.

Alex pushed a small lightbulb into the socket. Nothing lit up. "I don't smell any food cooking. That's a first. This place always has the most delicious aromas."

In that moment, she realized in her exuberance to let everyone have the evening off that she hadn't thought about dinner. And she didn't have a good history with the stove. Anything she put near it burned—to a crisp.

"I'm afraid that I let the staff have the evening off. With the wedding party gone for the evening and the holidays approaching, I thought they would enjoy some time off. So I'm not sure what to do for dinner, as I'm an utter disaster in the kitchen."

"It doesn't have to be anything fancy. In fact, simple sounds good."

Against her better judgment, she was starting to like this guy. "How simple were you thinking? I can work the microwave, but that's about it."

His brow arched as amusement danced in his eyes.

"Hey, don't look at me like that. A person can't be good at everything. So how about a frozen dinner?"

His tanned nose curled up. "Or we could order a pizza?" He loosened a bulb from the strand. "They do deliver here, don't they?"

She nodded. "I'll check to see if my mother will join us. I'll be right back with the menus."

She rushed out of the room and up the stairs to the little apartment that she'd been sharing with her mother since her father's death two years ago, when her life had changed from that of a carefree college student with the whole world ahead of her to a college dropout, striving to keep a roof over her brokenhearted mother's head.

Not that she would have ever made any other choice. Her mother had always been there for her—she'd made her smile and wiped her tears. Now it was Reese's turn to pitch in and help. That's what families did—took care of each other.

"Hey, Mom," Reese called out, bursting through the door of their apartment. "How do you feel about—"

The words died in her throat as she noticed her mother sitting before a tiny Christmas tree on the coffee table. It was lit up and had a few ornaments on it. What in the world? Where had it come from?

Her mother was staring at it as if she were lost in her

thoughts. Was she thinking about the past? Was her mother remembering how Reese used to beg her father for her very own Christmas tree?

The memories Reese had been suppressing for so long came rushing back. The image of her father's joyful smile as he held a tiny pine tree in his hand had her chest tightening. Back then he'd call her his little princess, and she'd thought the sun rose and set around him. How very wrong she'd been.

"Mom?" Her voice croaked. She swallowed hard and stepped closer to her mother. "Are you okay?"

Her mother blinked and glanced up at her. "I'm fine. But I'm glad you're here. I just had a phone call and your aunt isn't doing well."

Relieved to find that her mother wasn't sinking back into that miserable black hole where she seemed virtually unreachable, Reese asked, "What's wrong with Aunt Min?"

"She's having a hard time adjusting since Uncle Roger passed on. That was her neighbor and she agreed to come pick me up. I know with the holiday approaching and the wedding this weekend that this is the wrong time to be leaving you alone, but no one knows your aunt as well as me."

Reese wasn't so sure about her mother leaving to comfort someone who was grieving. She knew for a fact it was not an easy position to be in. But her mother appeared to be determined, and she supposed there was nothing she could say to change her mind.

"What can I do for you?" Reese asked, ready to pitch in.

"Absolutely nothing. You already have your hands full here." Her mother gave her a hug. "I've got to pack before my ride gets here."

Her mother was headed for the bedroom when Reese called out, "Mom, where did the tree come from?"

"Alex. He thought you might like it."

Her mother disappeared into her bedroom and Reese turned. The long-forgotten handmade ornaments on the little tree caught her eye.

Well, if he was so interested in having a Christmas tree, he could have it in his room—er, her room. She unplugged the lights, carried the tree to the bedroom and pushed aside her collection of miniature teddy bears—some that were as old as she was and some that were antiques collected from her grandmother and yard sales.

She'd always planned to update the room, but once she'd formally withdrawn from college, she'd packed up her apartment and put everything in storage. There wasn't time to worry about knickknacks when there was an entire inn to run. And now she was just too tired after working and smiling at the guests all day to be worried about redecorating a room where she barely spent any time.

She glanced at the bed with its comforter haphazardly pulled up. She imagined Alex sleeping in it. There was something so intimate about knowing that the Mediterranean hunk was sprawled out in her bed. Just as quickly as the thought came to her, she vanquished it.

He was a man—not to be trusted. And he'd only gone and confirmed her thoughts when he went against her wishes with the little Christmas tree—even if it had been an effort to be considerate. Conflicting emotions churned in her stomach. Why couldn't he leave well enough alone?

Not needing or wanting the aggravation, she pulled the door closed on the room. And that's exactly what she needed to do with Alex—close the door on this thing that was bubbling just beneath the surface.

He'd put this off long enough.

Alex retrieved his phone from his pocket. It was time

to let the king know that he was safe. In return, hopefully he would have good news as well. Perhaps this mess with his brother, the crown prince, had been quietly resolved. Then Alex could pack his bags and catch the first flight home—away from his beautiful hostess, who muddled his thoughts and had him losing focus on his priorities.

He dialed the king's private line. The phone was answered on the first ring, as though his papa had been sitting there waiting for him to call.

"Papa, it's me, Alexandro."

"At last, you remember to call."

"I had to move quickly and quietly in order to elude the paparazzi."

"Tell me where you are so I can dispatch your security detail."

"No." Alex's body tensed as he envisioned the dark expression settling over his papa's distinct features. It wasn't often that someone said no to the king. In fact, this was the first time Alex had done it since he was an unruly child. "I have to do this. It's the only way to protect the family. If your enemies learn of Demetrius's rash actions, they'll make it a public scandal by painting him as unfit to rule. They'll gain more support for their planned takeover."

"That's not for you to worry about. The royal cabinet has that under control."

He wanted to believe his papa's comforting words, but Alex had his own sources and they all told him that these subversives meant business. He knew that no matter how old he got, his papa would still try to shield him from the harsh realities of life. But now wasn't the time for being protective. There'd already been one uprising that year. They couldn't risk another.

"I understand, Papa. But trust me when I say I have to do this. It's for the best. As long as the press is curious of my activities, they'll focus on me instead of sniffing around the palace for a piece of juicy gossip."

The king let out a long, weary sigh. "I'll admit that it has been helpful. So far only the necessary staff know of this debacle. The councillor seems to think we should be able to clear this up soon...if only your brother would come to his senses."

"You're still opposed to this marriage?"

"In these uncertain times, we need a strong liaison with one of our allies." There was a strained pause. "If only this girl had some important connections."

His papa sounded much older than he'd ever heard him before. Alex's gut knotted with frustration. When was his older twin ever going to learn that he had responsibilities to the crown, the kingdom and to their papa, who would never step down from the throne until he was secure in the fact that his successor was up to the challenge of safeguarding the kingdom. His father had never rebounded fully after the queen's death. And now his health was waning.

Alex recalled how he'd made it to her side as she drew in her last breaths. Pain arrowed through his chest. She'd told him to take care of his papa. He'd promised to do it. And that's what he'd been striving to do ever since. Not that anything he did could make up for his part in his mother's death.

"Don't worry, Papa. I know what I'm doing."

Alex's thoughts strayed back to their visit to the Christmas tree lot.

You two make a fine-looking couple.

The more he thought of Santa's words, the more he was certain he was right—Reese had the right beauty and poise to pull off the plan he had in mind. Perhaps it was time he started figuring out ways to fit Reese into his agenda.

"Papa, everything will work out. When the time is right, I'll call for my security detail."

There was another pause. He wondered if the king was debating whether or not to command he change his plans and return home immediately.

"Alex?" The sound of Reese's voice trailed down the hallway.

"Papa, I must go. I'll call again soon." And with that he disconnected the call and switched off his phone. "I'm coming." He reached for the cabinet next to the sink, searching for a glass.

"Oh, here you are. I thought maybe you changed your mind about dinner and decided to cook instead."

"I don't cook, either. I just got thirsty." And he truly was thirsty after tap-dancing around, trying to pacify his papa.

After he downed a glassful of water and set it aside, he turned to her. "What did you need?"

"I ran upstairs to get these." She held up an array of menus.

She'd been in the apartment and that meant she must have noticed the little Christmas tree that he'd decorated to cheer up the place. Her mother had supplied some old ornaments. So why hadn't Reese mentioned it?

"Here." She stepped closer with her hand outstretched. "Pick your favorite."

He waved her away. "You pick. Whatever you choose will be fine."

Her gaze didn't meet his. "Are you sure?"

He nodded. He'd made enough decisions for tonight. He didn't feel like making any more, even if it was something as simple as pizza. In some ways, he used to envy his brother for being the crown prince, with the way people looked up to him. But as Alex got older, he was relieved to have been delivered second. It was very stressful and tiring making decisions day in and day out that impacted so many people.

Sure, to the world being royalty was all glamour and five-star dinners and balls. But behind palace walls in the executive suite there were heated debates, and the newspapers were quite critical of the decisions made by the monarchy. There was no way to please everyone all of the time.

But in this one instance, Alex was needed to keep the Mirraccino Islands together and peaceful. He would do whatever it took to keep the paparazzi from finding out the truth. Because he knew all too well what happened when a royal forgot his allegiance to the kingdom—the price was much too dear.

He cleared the lump in his throat. "While you call in the order, I can set up the tree in the living room."

"Did you get the lights to work?"

"Yes, I did. It was one bulb that was burned out. I replaced it and at last, there was light."

"Thank you." Her tone held no warmth. "Um, about the tree…I usually set it up over there next to the staircase. But I can do that myself—"

"Consider it done."

"I thought maybe you'd be tired of decorating."

So she had noticed the little tree. And it didn't seem as though she was pleased. Sure, she'd told him not to bother, but he'd thought she was too busy to do it herself and would enjoy the surprise. Her cool demeanor told him that her reason for not wanting a tree went much deeper than that.

"Christmas is one of my favorite holidays." He wondered if maybe she'd open up a little.

"That's nice." Her frosty tone chilled him. "I put the boxes of decorations next to it."

"You'll need to show me. I don't know how you want it decorated."

"Oh, that's easy. I always start with the white twinkle lights. Then I add gold ribbon and red glass ornaments."

"Do you trim the tree by yourself?"

"Yes. I find it is easier. I know how it should look, so why bother explaining how I want it when I can just as easily do it myself? In fact, you don't need to bother with it. I'll just place this call and be right back."

Reese strode out of the room like a woman on a mission. He thought it was sad that she insisted on doing so much around this place by herself. It sounded very lonely. Well, this Christmas would be different. He walked over to the tree and moved it to a spot next to the steps.

This Christmas he'd help her find the joy of the holiday.

CHAPTER SIX

WHY DIDN'T HE listen to her?

Reese frowned when she returned to the foyer. Alex was busy stringing the lights. And he didn't have the tree in the right spot. She usually moved it a little closer to the stairs to keep it out of the way. She knew she was being picky. She'd known for a long time that it was one of her faults. But things must be in their proper place or it drove her to distraction.

Alex turned to her. "I went ahead and started."

She nodded, trying to not let it bother her that the tree was out of place. Or that the lights needed to be redone if they were going to make it the whole way to the top.

"You don't like it?"

She knew that he'd tried his best and she really did appreciate it. She shifted her weight from one foot to the other and continued holding her tongue. Why did it have to bother her so much? She was being silly.

"What is it?" His eyes beseeched her.

She let out a pent-up breath. "The tree needs to be moved back out of the way."

"I know. But it is easier to decorate it here."

"And the lights, they need to be spread out a little more or you'll run out before you get to the top."

He arched an eyebrow. "You can try to get me to quit, but I won't. I'm going to help you decorate this tree."

"You're stubborn."

"And you're picky."

"Something tells me we have that in common." She could give as good as she got.

He smiled. "Maybe I am. But I know what I like."

His gaze was directly on her as he stepped closer. Her heart shot into her throat, cutting off her breath. His gaze dipped to her mouth before returning to meet her curious stare.

"You're very beautiful." The backs of his fingers brushed her cheek.

She should move, but her feet wouldn't cooperate. Shivers of excitement raced down her neck and arms, leaving goose bumps in their wake. She stared into his mesmerizing blue eyes, drowning in their depths. It'd been so long since a man had been interested in her. And she hadn't realized until now how lonely she'd become. After Josh—

The memory of her ex jarred her to her senses. She stepped back. This couldn't happen. She'd promised herself that she'd keep men at a safe distance.

Alex's hand lowered to his side. If she didn't know better, she'd say there was a flicker of remorse in his eyes. What should she say to him? After all, he wasn't Josh. Her ex had been needy and demanding. Alex was thoughtful and understanding. They were opposites in almost everything. So why was she backing away? After all, he'd soon be moving on and returning to his home—far away.

Maybe she shouldn't have backed away. Maybe she should have satisfied her curiosity to see if his kisses were as passionate as she imagined them in her dreams.

But the moment had passed. There was no recapturing

it. She moved to the tree and knelt down to start adjusting the string of lights.

"Could you help me on the other side of the tree?" She tried to act as though the moment hadn't shaken her.

"Just tell me what you need me to do."

To Alex's credit, he let the awkward moment pass without question. By the time they moved the decorated tree into the correct position, Reese had to admit that she'd enjoyed her evening. Alex was actually quite entertaining with his various bits of trivia. Who would have guessed it?

It wasn't until after the wedding guests streamed through the front door that she was able to lock up the house. She climbed the steps to the tiny apartment, anxious to call it a night. She was just about to close the door when she heard footsteps bounding up the stairs. She didn't need two guesses to know that the heavy footsteps didn't belong to the anxious bride across the hall or one of her smiling attendants. No, it was the one man who got under her skin. She thought of rushing off to her mother's bedroom, but she felt the need to thank him for making a chore that normally came with some harsh, painful memories into a pleasant experience.

She turned to him. Her gaze settled on his lips. The memory of their almost kiss sent her stomach spiraling. "I—I'm heading to bed. I just wanted to thank you for the help tonight. If it wasn't for you, I would still be working at it."

"You're welcome. And it turned out well, even if it isn't exactly how you normally do it." His brows drew together as his gaze swept around the room. "What happened to the little Christmas tree?"

"I moved it to your room. I thought you could appreciate it better in there."

"But I did it for you."

"And I told you that I didn't want a tree."

"But the tree downstairs—"

"Is the price of doing business. Guests expect an inn to be decked out for the holidays, and it's my job to fulfill those expectations. But that doesn't mean I have to decorate my personal space."

"I was only trying to help."

"That's not the type of help I need." The words were out before she could stop them. Exhaustion and worry had combined, causing her thoughts to slip past her lips. "I'm sorry. I didn't mean to snap at you."

He shook his head. "You're right. I thought—ah, it doesn't matter what I thought."

The hurt look in his eyes had her scrambling for an explanation. "It's just that Christmas brings back bad memories for me and my mother. And I'm afraid that it'll upset her. I'll do anything to keep her from going back to that lonely dark place where she went after my father died."

He eyed her up as though he were privy to her most private thoughts. "Your mother seems like a strong lady. Perhaps she's stronger than you think."

Reese shook her head, recalling how her mother had crumbled after learning that her father had been on his way to his mistress when he'd died in a car accident on Christmas Eve. Loss and betrayal combined to create the perfect storm to level her mother—a woman she'd always admired for her strength. It had brought her mother to her knees and Reese never wanted to witness anything so traumatic again.

Reese pressed her hands to her hips. "You don't know her like I do."

"That's true. But sometimes an outsider can see things someone too close to the situation will miss."

She lifted her chin. "And what exactly have I missed?"

"Did you know it was your mother who got out the Christmas decorations for me to use on the little tree?"

"You must have pressured her. She wouldn't have voluntarily gotten those out. Those were…were our family ornaments, collected over the years."

"Actually, it was her idea. She insisted I decorate it for you. She thought it would make you happy."

No, that wasn't possible. Was it? Reese took a step back. When the back of her knee bumped into the couch, she sat down. What did this mean? Had she been so busy that she'd missed seeing that her mother truly was back to being herself?

"I had no idea it would upset you so much."

"It's just that…that my father always made Christmas such a big affair. It's hard to think of it and not think of him." But she failed to add the most painful part. She couldn't bring herself to admit that her father had left them on Christmas Eve for another woman. And he'd spent their money on that woman…buying her a house and leaving them in debt.

Alex stepped forward and took a seat beside her. "I didn't know."

"My mother didn't mention it?"

"She said that it has been awhile since you two celebrated Christmas, and she thought it was time you both had a good one."

Reese's heart filled with an unexpected joy. "She really said that?"

He nodded. "Otherwise I wouldn't have gone through with decorating the tree without your approval."

If this was okay with her mother, who was she to disapprove? Maybe it hadn't just been her mother who'd been deeply affected by her father's actions. In the past couple of years, Reese had been so busy worrying about keeping a roof over their heads that she hadn't realized how much her father's actions had hurt her. Or how she'd let her father steal the magic of the holiday from her.

Reese turned to Alex. "I'm sorry I was so grinchy about it."

"Grinchy?"

"Yeah, you know the story, *How the Grinch Stole Christmas?*"

"I'm not familiar with it."

"I didn't think there was anyone who didn't know that story. You must have lived a sheltered life."

"I had books, but they were educational."

"Like I said, you lived a sheltered life. Don't worry. I'm sure we can find you a copy somewhere and broaden your horizons."

"My horizons are plenty broad," he protested. "Would you mind if I brought the tree back out here?"

"Suit yourself." She most certainly wasn't the only one used to having her way.

As he strode away, she wondered why it had taken a total stranger from another land to open her eyes and help her see her life more clearly. It was as if she'd been living with tunnel vision these past couple of years, focusing on protecting her mother from further pain and keeping their home.

And though Alex was certainly a nice distraction, she couldn't let herself lose focus now. The Willows was far from being out of debt. In fact, even with Alex's generous fee she still might have to let go of Sandy, the maid and a single mom. The thought pinched at her heart.

With it being Christmas, surely there would be a miracle or something. It wasn't as though she was really a grinch, but if she had to eliminate Sandy's position at Christmastime, the comparison with that fictional character would hit far too close to home—heartless.

"Here we go." Alex strode back into the room.

She noticed how when he entered a room, his presence commanded attention. She wasn't sure what it was about him that gave her that impression. It could be his good looks or his six-foot-plus height. But no. It went beyond that. It was something much more significant, but she just couldn't put her finger on it. Maybe it was the way he carried himself, with a straight spine and level shoulders. Or the way he had that knowing look in his blue eyes. She sighed in frustration, unable to nail down exactly what was so different about him.

Alex paused. "Did you change your mind?"

"Oh, no. I guess I'm more tired than I'd originally thought."

"After I plug in this cord, would you mind turning out the lights? There's nothing like the glow of a Christmas tree."

She got to her feet and moved to the switch.

When the colored bulbs lit up the chubby little tree that to Reese resembled nothing more than a branch, she doused the overhead light. But it wasn't the tree that caught and held her attention. It was the look on Alex's face. For a second, it was the marvel of a little boy staring at a Christmas tree for the first time.

"Isn't your Christmas tree like this?" She was genuinely curious.

He shook his head. "It's quite tall and it's more formal, similar to the one you have downstairs."

"You mean it doesn't have candy canes and little bell and penguin ornaments?"

Again he shook his head. "No. Everything has to be picture-perfect. The way my mother would have wanted it."

A little voice in the back of her mind said to let the comment pass, but she couldn't. She wanted to know more about him. Maybe if she demystified him, he'd have less of a hold on her thoughts.

"Your mother…did you lose her?"

The words hung heavy in the air.

At last, Alex nodded. "She died when I was a teenager. Christmas was her favorite holiday. In fact, Papa still has the—the house decorated like she used to do. On Christmas Eve, for just a moment, it's like she's still there and going to step into the living room at any moment."

"It's good that you have such happy memories to hold on to."

"Enough about me. I'm sure you have special memories of the holidays."

She waved away his comment. "They aren't worth getting into."

She wished she could concentrate on the good times, but her father's betrayal had smeared and practically obliterated them. In her mind, that man was not worth remembering. Not after what he'd done to them. She stuffed the memories to the back of her mind.

This was why she no longer enjoyed the holidays— they dredged up unwanted memories. She wished she had nothing but good memories, like Alex. She envied him.

"I'm going to sleep." Not that she'd close her eyes any time soon. "Would you mind turning out the lights before you go to bed?"

"Not a problem." He smiled at her and her stomach fluttered. "But before you go, there's one other thing."

With nothing but the gentle glow of the little tree filling the room, it was far too romantic. Her gaze returned to his lips. They looked smooth and soft. She wondered what it'd be like to meet up with him under the mistletoe. Realizing she'd hung some downstairs for the bride and groom to indulge in, she wished she'd saved some for up here.

Alex cleared his throat. As her gaze rose to meet his, amusement danced in his eyes. Surely he didn't have a clue what she'd been thinking. Did he?

"What were you saying?" She struggled to do her best to sound normal and not let on that her heart was racing faster than the hooves of the horses who pulled the carriages around Central Park.

"I don't want to embarrass you, but did you know you have a leak in your roof?"

She nodded. "I had it fixed last week. I just haven't gotten around to getting the interior repaired."

"I could take a look at it. If you want."

She shook her head. "You're a paying guest. Not hired help."

"But I am volunteering."

Why did he always have to push? Well, this time he wasn't getting his way. "I don't need your help."

He stared at her long and hard as though trying to get her to change her mind. "Understood. I'll see you tomorrow."

At last she'd gotten through to him. "Good night."

She turned and headed back down the hall. She could sense his gaze following her, but she refused to glance back. He created a mixed-up ball of emotions in her that constantly kept her off kilter.

And what unsettled her the most was the fact that she liked him. No matter how much he pushed and prodded her, beneath it all he was genuinely a nice guy. Although he was awfully tight-lipped about his past and his family. She noticed how every time he started to mention a piece of his life, he clammed up. What was that all about?

Time passed quickly. In no time at all, Alex moved across the hall to the executive suite. He was amazed by how hard

Reese worked every single day, from the time she got up before the sun until she dropped into bed late at night. He soon found himself bored of the internet, even though his leaked letter to the paparazzi had worked as he'd hoped. Now the gossip sites were filled with all sorts of outlandish stories, but the most important part was that they were looking for him. He just had to keep his disguise in place a little longer.

He thought of Reese and how she'd react upon learning he was a prince. Somehow he couldn't imagine she'd treat him any different if she knew the truth. Or was it that he didn't want her to treat him different? He liked their budding friendship—in fact, he liked it very much.

Guilt plagued him for not being more open with her. She'd been kind and generous with him—he wanted to treat her with the same sort of respect. He considered telling her everything, but in the next thought he recalled how deviating from the plan had cost his mother her life.

Alex paced back and forth in his suite. It was best for everyone to keep up the pretense of being a businessman—which he truly was back in Mirraccino. What he needed now was something to keep him busy.

It was still early in the morning when he strode across the hall to Reese's apartment and rapped his knuckles firmly on the dark wood door. No answer. After having lived with her for the past few days, he didn't think anything of trying the doorknob. When it opened, he stepped inside.

"Reese, are you here?"

Again, no answer.

He glanced around, pleased to find that the little tree was still centered on the coffee table and a cottony white cloth with little sparkles had been placed around the base. Maybe at last Reese was starting to find her holiday spirit.

Though the place was clean, it was showing its age. It was very striking how different this apartment was from his polished, well-kept suite. He turned in a circle, taking in the details. The yellowing walls could use a fresh coat of paint. And the ceiling was missing plaster where the roof had leaked.

A thought started to take shape. He might be of royal blood, but that didn't mean he hadn't gotten his hands dirty. Thanks to a very patient maintenance worker who used to be put in charge of him whenever he got in trouble as a youth, he'd learned a lot. Probably a lot more than most people of his status. And it wasn't until now that he realized what a gift it was to have a practical skill set.

He set off to the downstairs in search of Reese. When he couldn't locate her anywhere, he ended up in the kitchen. The chef was there. He was a unique guy, tall and wiry and about Alex's age, maybe a little younger. But his worn face said that there was so much more to his life's story than cooking for pampered guests. Above all that, the guy seemed like an all-around fine fellow.

"Good morning, Bob. Have you seen Reese this morning?"

"Morning. What would you like for breakfast? I can whip you up something in no time. If you want to wait in the dining room, I'll bring it in to you."

"That won't be necessary. I can eat in here." Alex set about getting himself a cup of coffee before Bob could make the offer. "About Reese, have you seen her?"

"She passed through here awhile ago, mumbling something about business to take care of. She wasn't in a talkative mood. Come to think of it, I haven't seen her since. In fact, I'm not used to this place being so utterly quiet."

Bob's last comment stuck with Alex. He never really thought about Reese keeping her staff on duty just for him.

That certainly wasn't necessary. He could fend for himself. After all, he was supposed to be just an ordinary citizen— not royalty. He'd have a word with her later.

"Do you like working here?" Alex took his cup of black coffee and sat down at the marble counter.

"I'm lucky to have this job. Reese helped me out at a really bad time in my life." Bob turned back to the stove. "If it wasn't for Reese, who knows where I would have ended up."

"I take it she's a good boss?"

"The best." Bob turned from the omelet he was preparing and pointed his spatula at Alex. "And I won't stand by and let someone hurt her."

Alex held up his palms innocently. "You don't have to worry about me. I'll be moving on soon."

"Good."

"Now that we have that clear, I was wondering if you might help me with a special project."

Bob wiped his hands off on a towel. "Depends on what you have in mind."

"I have some extra time on my hands and I'd like to put it to good use."

"Well, if you're looking for things to do, you can sight-see or hit the clubs. They don't call it the city that never sleeps for no reason."

Alex shook his head. "I had something else in mind. But I'll need your help."

Bob sat an empty bowl in the sink. After a quick glance at the omelet, he stepped up to the counter. "What exactly do you have in mind?"

CHAPTER SEVEN

"WHAT ARE YOU DOING?"

Reese glared up at Alex, who was standing on a ladder in the corner of the living room. With a chisel in one hand and a hammer in the other, he turned. Was that guilt reflected in his blue eyes?

"I got bored." He lowered the hand tools to the top of the ladder.

She crossed her arms. "So you decided to make a mess of my apartment?"

Her gaze swept across the room, taking in the drop cloths covering everything. Cans and tools sat off to the side. And then her gaze settled back on the culprit. Alex was flashing her a guilty grin like some little boy caught with his hand in the cookie jar. But she refused to let his good looks and dopey grin get to her.

"Alex, explain this. What in the world are you doing?"

"Fixing the ceiling."

She frowned at him. What was this man thinking? Obviously he hadn't been when he made the hole in her ceiling. It would cost a small fortune to repair it—money she didn't have. She'd already made the rounds to the banks. No one was willing to help her refinance The Willows. She was officially tapped out.

In fact, she'd returned home determined to figure out a

way to meet next month's payroll. She really didn't want to let Sandy go before Christmas. Reese would do anything to keep that from happening, but sometimes the best of intentions just weren't enough.

"Alex, do you know what a mess you've created? There's no way that I'll be able to get someone in here to fix it."

"You don't need to hire anyone. I have this under control."

Her neck was getting sore staring up at him. "Would you get down off that ladder so I can talk to you without straining my neck?"

He did as she asked and approached her. He was so tall. So muscular. And as her gaze rose up over his broad chest and shoulders, she realized having him step off the ladder was a big miscalculation on her part.

His navy T-shirt was stretched across his firm chest. Her mouth grew dry. Did he have to look so good? Specks of crumbled plaster covered him, from his short dark hair to the jeans that hung low on his lean waist. She resisted the urge to brush him off—to see if his muscles were as firm as they appeared.

"If you'd give me a chance, I think you'll be impressed with what I can do."

She didn't doubt that she'd be very impressed, but her mind was no longer on the repairs. Her thoughts had tumbled into a far more dangerous territory.

Her gaze settled on his mouth. Was he an experienced kisser? With his sexy looks, he was definitely experienced in a lot more than kissing. The temperature in the room started to climb. When she realized that he was staring back at her, waiting for a response, she struggled to tamp down her raging hormones.

"You need to stop what you're doing. This—this is a

bad idea." She didn't know if the words were meant more for him or for herself.

"Really, I can do this. I used to help—" He glanced down at the carpet. "The guy who fixed up our house when I was a kid. I learned a lot."

She groaned. "When you were a kid? Are you serious?"

"Trust me."

She resisted the urge to roll her eyes and instead glanced back up at the looming hole in her ceiling. A cold draft brushed across her skin. A band of tension tightened across her forehead. She couldn't leave the ceiling in this condition; she'd go broke trying to keep the place warm.

"Seeing as you started this project without my permission, you can't possibly expect me to pay you to do the repairs."

His blue eyes lit up. "I agree. And truthfully, I did try to ask you before starting this, but when you were gone for the day, I thought I'd surprise you."

"Humph…you certainly achieved your goal." She eyed him. "You know I really should toss you to the curb. No one would blame me. Tell me, do you always go around vandalizing people's homes?"

His dark brows drew together. "That's not what I'm doing. And I've never done this for anyone else."

"What makes me so special?" She stared at him, looking for a sign of pity in his eyes. And if she found it, she didn't care what it cost her. She would show him to the door. She didn't do handouts.

His gaze was steady. "The truth is you'd be helping me."

"Helping you?" That wasn't the answer she'd been expecting. Before she could say more, the phone rang. "Don't move. I'll be right back."

She walked away, still trying to wrap her mind around what had gotten into him. She'd bet ten to one odds he didn't know what he was doing. She really ought to bounce him out on his very cute backside...but she needed the money he'd paid to stay here. Being hard up for money really did limit one's options—she hated learning things the hard way.

Of course when she answered the phone and found an impatient creditor at the other end, it did nothing to improve her mood. The man wanted to know why they hadn't received a payment for the past month. After she tap-danced her way into an extension, she walked back into the apartment. Alex was back up on the ladder, making the hole in her ceiling even bigger. She inwardly groaned.

"Do you ever listen to instructions?" She didn't even bother to mask the frustration in her voice.

He glanced down at her and shot her a sheepish grin. "I want to get as much done today as I can."

"And what if I tell you that I want you to stop?"

His gaze searched hers. "Is that what you really want?"

"It doesn't matter what I want. I don't have the money to hire a contractor. I've got creditors calling and wanting to know why they haven't been paid." She pressed her lips tightly together, realizing she'd spoken those words out loud.

"Are things really that bad?"

She shrugged, not meeting his gaze. "I'll turn things around. One way or the other."

"I'm sure you will." He glanced back at the work waiting for him. "In the meantime, I better get back to work, because I don't want to miss dinner."

She cast a hesitant look back at the hole in the ceiling before turning back to him. "You promise you know what you're doing?"

He smiled and crossed his heart. "I promise."

With effort, she resisted the urge to return the smile.

She wanted him to know that she was serious. Was it his sexy accent that made his promise so much easier to swallow? Or was it something more?

"Okay. I have a few things to do before dinner."

She reached the doorway when he said, "You know you don't have to keep Bob around on my account. I can fend for myself."

"This is his job and he's counting on a paycheck. The stubborn man doesn't accept anything that might be construed as charity."

Alex sent her a knowing smile. "Sounds like the pot calling the pot black."

"It's kettle. The pot calling the kettle black."

"So it is. And you, my dear, are the pot."

With a frustrated sigh, she turned her back on Alex and the crater-size hole in the ceiling. She had bigger problems to solve. Like finding a way out of this horrendous financial mess that she'd inherited. The thought of her father and how much trouble he'd brought to her and her mother renewed Reese's determination not to fall for Alex's charm. She needed to keep things simple where men were concerned—especially where Alex was concerned.

Not yet.

Alex groaned and hit the snooze setting on his phone, silencing the loud foghorn sound. He'd been having the most delightful dream and Reese was in it. He'd been holding her close with her generous curves pressing to him. A moan rose in his throat as he desperately tried to recreate the dream.

She'd been gazing up at him with those eyes that could bend him to her will with just a glance. He'd been about to kiss her when the blasted alarm interrupted.

Try as he might, there was no returning to Reese's arms.

He rolled over and stretched. Days had turned into two weeks and his body had adjusted to the time change. He wondered how much longer he'd be here.

For the first time, the thought of packing his bags and catching the first flight back to Mirraccino didn't sound appealing. This chance to be a regular citizen instead of a royal prince was far more appealing than he'd imagined— Reese's face and those luscious lips filled his mind.

The images from his dream followed him to the shower—a cold shower. After all, it was only a dream, a really hot dream, but a dream just the same.

He pulled a pair of jeans from the wicker laundry basket. Reese had generously offered to show him how to do his own laundry. He had much to learn, but he didn't mind. However, when he pulled a T-shirt out of the dryer to fold, he frowned. It was pink. Pink?

He balled it up and tossed it aside. His thoughts turned back to his beautiful hostess. Maybe if he were to tell her the truth about himself he could—what? Ask her to hook up with him? No. Reese wasn't the love 'em and leave 'em type.

He pushed the tormenting thoughts to the back of his mind as he finished up his laundry and sat down at his computer. He typed his name in the search engine. In no time at all, there were thousands of results. Good. He had their attention now. His gaze skimmed down over the top headlines: *With Rising Tensions in Mirraccino, Where Is Prince Alexandro? Is Prince Alexandro on a Secret Mission? The Mirraccino Palace Is Mum about Prince Alexandro's Absence.*

The headlines struck a chord with him. He should be at home, helping his papa. Instead he was here, repairing a hole in the ceiling for a woman whose image taunted him at night while her lush lips teased him by day. Still, he was doing an important function. As long as the press was sniffing out stories about him, his family could function under the radar.

A couple of older photos of him popped up on social networks with new tags. They were of him posing with beautiful women. All of them were strangers to him. He honestly couldn't even recall their names. Once the photos were taken, they'd gone their separate ways. *Then he saw one headline, proclaiming:*

Did the Prince Ditch Duty for Love?

His clenched hand struck the desktop, jarring his computer. No, he didn't. But no one outside of the family would ever know that he was doing his duty—no matter how much it cost him. No matter how much he hated keeping the truth from Reese.

His gaze roamed over the headlines again and he frowned. No one was going to win his heart. He didn't have time for foolish notions of Cupid and hearts. When it came time for him to marry, it would be because it was what was expected of him.

He wouldn't set himself up for the horrendous pain he'd seen his father live through after his mother's death. Or the years of loneliness. It had almost been too much to observe.

Yet Alex couldn't let the headlines get to him. They created the attention he wanted—even if they poked at some soft spots. He supposed under the circumstances he couldn't be choosy about how the swirl of curiosity happened as long as it worked.

Perhaps it was time to feed the press a few more bread crumbs. He wrote an anonymous email that because of his security precautions would be impossible for the paparazzi to trace.

To whom it concerns:
I have inside information about Prince Alexandro Castanavo's whereabouts. For a little extra money I have photos. But this information will not come cheap. It'll be worth the hefty price tag. Let's just say the prince is not off doing diplomatic work. Time is ticking. This offer has gone out to numerous outlets. First come, first served.

He smiled as he pressed send. That should spark some interest.

Not about to waste any more time, he set aside his laptop and headed straight to Reese's apartment to check on the primer he'd applied to the walls and ceiling. All the while, his thoughts centered on Reese. He desperately wanted to be up front with her about everything.

But he knew people weren't always what they seemed and that sometimes they were put in positions where they were forced to make choices they might otherwise not make. This financial crisis Reese was facing was one such instance where she might do something desperate to bring in money to keep this place afloat.

And what would be easier than selling the story of a prince undercover while the crown prince eloped with a woman he barely knew? But another voice, a much louder voice inside him, said he was being overly cautious. Reese was trustworthy. And the time had come to be honest with her…about everything.

CHAPTER EIGHT

THIS WAS THE answer to her problems.

It had to be.

Reese stood in the inn's office, staring at the paintings she'd completed back before she'd dropped out of school. They'd been viewed by notable figures in the art world and generous offers had been made. Of course, in her infinite wisdom, she'd wanted to hold out, so she'd turned down the offers. She'd dreamed of one day having her own gallery showing. Of people requesting her work by name. But all of that had come to a crashing end one snowy night.

Now her only hope to hang on to the only life she'd ever known came down to selling these paintings. And if she didn't sell them, she'd have to let Sandy go just days before Christmas. The thought made her stomach roll.

Who ever said being the boss was a great thing?

Sometimes it just downright rotten.

And this was most definitely one of those times.

"What's put that frown on your face?"

She glanced up to find Alex leaning casually against the doorjamb. A black T-shirt stretched across his broad chest. The short sleeves strained around his bulging biceps as he crossed his arms. No one had a right to look that good.

When her gaze lifted to his mouth, he smiled. Her stomach did a somersault. What was it about him that had her thinking she should have taken more time with her makeup or at least flat ironed her hair into submission instead of throwing it haphazardly into a ponytail?

She swallowed hard and hoped her voice sounded nonchalant. "I was thinking."

"Must be something serious."

"I—I just figured out a solution to a problem." She moved away from the canvases, hoping Alex wouldn't be too curious.

"That's great—"

"Did you need something?" She shuffled some papers around on her desk to keep from looking at him. "Please don't tell me there's a problem with the apartment."

"Not like you're imagining. I'm almost finished."

"Really?" This good news was music to her ears.

"Yes. But I wanted to talk to you about something."

"Can it wait?" She sent him a pleading look. "I was on my way out the door."

He didn't say anything at first. "Of course it can wait until later."

"Good." She didn't need any more problems right now. "Do you need anything while I'm out?"

"Actually, I do." He stepped up to her desk. "And your offer keeps me from having to call a cab."

She laughed. "Come on. What was that cabbie's name? Freddy?" Alex nodded and she continued to tease him. "I'm sure Freddy would love to give you a ride."

Alex shook his head vehemently. "That is never going to happen. I think he had delusions of being a grand prix driver."

She patted Alex's arm, noticing the steely strength beneath her fingertips. As the zing of awareness arrowed into her chest, the breath caught in her throat. She raised her head and their gazes caught and held. Was he going to kiss her? They'd been doing this dance for so long now that it had become pure torture. The wondering. The imagining.

Her gaze connected with his. Definite interest reflected in them. Would it be so bad giving in this once and seeing if he could kiss as well as she imagined when she was alone in the dark of the night, tossing and turning?

Alex cleared his throat. "Do you have pen and paper?"

"What?" She blinked.

"I need to write you a list."

"Oh. Right."

Then, realizing she was still touching him, she pulled her hand away, immediately noticing how her fingers cooled off. He was definitely hot and in more than one way. And she'd just made a fool of herself. She'd only imagined he was interested in her. Her cheeks warmed as she handed over a pen and notepad.

His gaze was unwavering as he looked at her. "I appreciate you doing me this favor."

He wrote out the short list before reaching into his back pocket and pulling out some cash. He handed both over to her.

"I don't need money. After all, it's my ceiling that you're repairing. The least I can do is pay for the supplies."

"And you wouldn't be paying for those supplies right now if it weren't for my idea to surprise you and start the job without your permission."

She had a feeling that the money was being offered because he felt sorry for her. But he made a valid point. With that thought in mind, she folded the money and slipped it in her pocket.

"I should get going. I have to get the truck loaded up." It wasn't until the words were out of her mouth that she realized she'd said too much.

Alex glanced back at the canvases. "Are those what you need put in the truck?"

"Yes. But I've got it."

He strode over to her paintings. "What are you doing with these?"

How much should she tell him? She found herself eager to get his take on her plan. After all, it wasn't as though she could talk to any of the staff. She didn't want to worry them. And her mother, well, even if she was still at the house, she wouldn't understand. She'd beg Reese to keep the paintings—that they were too precious to part with.

But other lives were counting on her now.

Alex stepped over to the cases that held what she thought were her three best pieces of work. "Do you mind if I take a look?"

She did mind, but she found herself saying, "Go ahead. Just be careful. I can't let anything happen to those."

She had to admit that she really was curious about his reaction to her work. Would he like the pieces? Her stomach shivered in anticipation.

Alex took his time looking over each piece. He made some very observant comments that truly impressed her. If she didn't know better, she'd think that he too was an art student.

"Those are very impressive."

"Do you mean it?"

"Of course." He made direct eye contact with her. "You're quite talented."

Sure, she'd been told her work was good by experts, but there was just something about Alex seeing her work that made her feel exposed. Maybe it was that a stranger's opinions could be swept aside, but Alex's impression of her art would stay with her. For a moment, she wondered when his opinion had begun to mean so much to her.

"Do you still paint?"

She shook her head. "I don't have time for things like that these days."

"This place must keep you busy." He glanced back at the paintings. "Are you planning to sell these?"

"I'm going to speak with some gallery owners about showing them. I'm hoping that they'll fetch a good price. A couple of years ago, I had people interested in them. But back then I had bigger plans. I wanted to keep them and have a showing. But life took a sharp turn before any of that could happen...if it ever would have."

"I am sure it would have."

"Are you an artist?"

He shook his head. "I don't have an artistic bone in my body. I can only appreciate others' work. And you're very good."

"Thank you. At one point in my life I thought I'd have a future in art. I'd been dreaming about it since I was a little girl. But things change."

"You shouldn't give up on your dreams. No one should."

She shook her head, wanting to chase away the *what if*s and the *maybe*s. "That part of my life is over."

"You're young. You have lots of choices ahead of you."

"My mother needs me. I won't just abandon her like... erm...it doesn't matter. I don't even know why we're talking about it. I need to get these in the truck and soon I'll have the money to keep the doors to this place open."

What was taking her so long?

Alex paced the length of the living room. She'd been gone all day. How long did it take to talk to a couple of people? Surely they'd worked all of the details of the sale out by now. After all, he hadn't just been boosting her ego—she really was talented.

Now that he'd made up his mind to be honest with her about himself, he was anxious to get it over with. He doubted she would take the news well at first. She might not even believe him. But hopefully he'd be able to smooth things over. He couldn't imagine what it'd be like to have Reese turn her back on him—not speak to him again. His chest tightened. That couldn't happen.

He retrieved his laptop and settled down on an armchair, hoping to find a distraction. He logged on to his computer, anxious to see what the latest gossip consisted of. As long as it was about him and his fictitious romance and not his brother's real-life romantic disaster, he'd be satisfied.

The sound of a door closing caught his attention. He quickly closed his laptop and got to his feet. "Reese, is that you?"

She stepped into the living room. "Yes."

Her tone was flat and her gaze didn't quite reach his. He couldn't help himself—he had to know. "How did your day go?"

Her eyes were bloodshot and her face was pale. "It doesn't matter. I have some paperwork to do. Is there anything I can get for you?"

"Yes, there is." All thoughts of his need to tell her of his background vanished. Comforting her was his only priority. He attempted to reach out to her, to pull her close, but her cold gaze met his—freezing him out. His arms lowered. "You can talk to me. Tell me what happened."

Her eyes blazed with irritation. "Why do you always have to push? Why can't you leave things alone? First it's the Christmas tree. Then it's my apartment. You can't fix everything."

He took a step back, not expecting that outburst. "I am concerned. I'd like to help if I can."

"Well, you can't. This is my problem. I'll deal with it on my own."

No matter how much she wanted him to walk away, he couldn't. The raw pain in her brown eyes ate at him. Reese was the pillar of strength that everyone in this mansion leaned on. It was time that she had someone she could turn to for support.

"You don't have to do this alone."

"Why do you want to get involved?"

"I'd like to think that we're friends and that you can turn to me with your problems."

"You are my guest and I am the manager of this inn. That's all we are to each other." A coldness threaded through her words.

His voice lowered. "You don't believe that."

"I can't do this now." She turned away.

Acting against his better judgment, he reached out, wrapping his fingers around her forearm. "Don't push me away. Talk to me. Maybe there's something I can do to help."

She turned back, her gaze moving to his fingers. He immediately released her.

She sighed and lifted her chin to him. "I know you're trying to be nice, but don't you understand? You can't help. No one can."

"Something can always be done." He signaled for her to follow him to the couch. "Sit down and tell me what happened. If nothing else, you might feel better after you get it out in the open instead of keeping it bottled up inside."

She glanced around as though looking to see if anyone was close enough to overhear.

"Don't worry, Bob is at the market. And Sandy had to leave early because her little girl got sick and needed to be picked up from day care."

"Oh, no. Is it anything serious?"

"Not from what I could tell. Sandy said the girl hadn't felt well that morning, but she had hoped that whatever it was would pass. Apparently it didn't."

"So we're alone?"

He nodded. "Except for the groundskeeper. But I rarely ever see him inside the mansion. The only time I ever did see him inside was when I first arrived here and he'd dropped by to give your mother a pine cone wreath."

"Yes, Mr. Winston is very good to Mom."

It was good to know that there was someone around watching out for Reese and her mother. But that didn't mean Alex couldn't do his part, too.

"Sounds like Mr. Winston has more than one reason for keeping the grounds looking so nice."

Reese's fine brows drew together, forming a formidable line. And her eyes darkened. What in the world had he said wrong now?

CHAPTER NINE

"That's impossible."

Reese sat back, stunned by the thought of her mother liking Howard Winston. Her mother was still recovering from the mess after her father's death. Her mother would never let another man into her life, not after the way they'd been betrayed. It wasn't possible. Men weren't to be trusted.

"Are you so sure?" Alex persisted. "I mean, I only saw them together a couple of times, but there was definitely something going on there."

"They're just friends." Reese rushed on, unwilling to give his observation any credence. "Mom would never get involved with another man. Not after…after my father."

She'd almost let it slip that her father was a horrible, lying, conniving man, but she caught herself in time. Airing her family's dirty laundry to a stranger—well, Alex wasn't a stranger any longer. And the truth was she didn't know what he was to her.

Still, she didn't like to talk about her father—with anyone. The man wasn't worth the breath to speak his name. After all, he hadn't even loved them. His own family. He'd scraped off their savings and spent the money on his new woman—the woman he had left her mother for on Christmas Eve. And he'd been such a coward that he'd only left a note. He couldn't face them and admit what he'd done.

The backs of her eyes stung. Why did she still let the memory get her worked up? Two years had passed since her father's betrayal had come to light and her mother had crumbled.

Alex got to his feet. "I didn't mean to upset you. I thought you might be happy about your mother having someone in her life."

"I—I hadn't noticed." She choked the words out around the lump in her throat. "I've had a lot of other things on my mind. This place can take a lot of time and attention."

"Then maybe what you need to do is get out of here."

Her eyes widened. "You mean leave?"

He smiled, hoping to ease the horrified look on her face. "I am not talking about forever. I was thinking more along the lines of an early dinner."

"Oh." Heat flashed in her cheeks. She didn't know why she'd jumped to the wrong conclusion. Then again, maybe she did.

On the ride home, she'd been daydreaming about packing her bags and heading somewhere, anywhere but here. Not that she would ever do it. But sometimes the pressures got to be too much. Just like tomorrow, when she had to tell Sandy that she would have to lay her off. But she would hire Sandy back just as soon as possible—if there was still an inn to employ her.

Alex shifted his weight from one foot to the other. "If you want, we can leave a note for Bob letting him know he can have the evening off."

She shook her head. "I can't afford to splurge."

"Maybe you misunderstood. This is my treat. I think it's time for me to get out of here and check out a bit of

New York City. And who better to show me some of the finest cuisine?"

She arched a brow. "Are you serious?"

He nodded.

He was probably right about her getting out of the house. A little time away and a chance to unwind would have her thinking more clearly. Oh, who was she kidding? There was no way she'd unwind when she knew that she had the horrible task of laying off one of her valued employees, who was more a friend than a worker.

After her father's betrayal, she'd closed herself off, only letting those closest to her in. And the three people who worked for her had gained her trust and friendship. They were a family. They'd filled in when her mother wasn't capable of doing more than caring for herself. They'd been there to support her, to cheer her on, and she couldn't love them more.

Alex shot her a pleading stare. "Surely sharing dinner with me can't be that bad of an idea."

Reese worried her lower lip. She really had no desire to go out, but he was, after all, the paying guest—a guest who'd spent a lot of his time fixing up her private apartment. Giving him a brief tour of Rockefeller Center and dinner was the least she could do.

"I did hear Bob mention that he still needed to run out and buy his girlfriend a Christmas present. I'm sure he wouldn't mind leaving early. I'll give him a call."

"And I'll change out of these work clothes into something presentable."

When he turned away, she noticed how his dark jeans rode low on his trim waist and clung to him in all of the right places. The man was certainly built. She swallowed hard. Any woman would have to be out of her tree to turn his offer down.

She struggled to sound normal. "Um, sure. I'll meet you back here in ten minutes."

He nodded and headed for the steps.

If he was going to dress up, she supposed she should do the same thing. She mentally rummaged through her closet. She didn't own anything special. The best she could do was her little black dress. It was something she kept on hand for hosting weddings.

Some funny feeling inside her told her this dinner was going to be a game changer. They wouldn't be quite the same again. But in the next breath, she assured herself she was making too much of the dinner. After all, what could possibly happen?

What would it take to make her smile?

Alex sneaked a glance at Reese's drawn white face. The lights of the tall Christmas tree reflected in her eyes, but the excitement that had been there when they'd decorated the tree back at the inn was gone. He had to do something to make things better. But what?

She still hadn't opened up to him. Sure, he'd surmised that her plans to sell her paintings today hadn't worked out, but it went deeper than disappointment. He'd been hoping that when he took her out on the town, she'd loosen up and temporarily forget her problems. So far it wasn't working.

"Maybe stopping here was a bad idea." Alex raked his fingers through his short hair.

"No, it wasn't." She reached out and squeezed his hand. She smiled up at him, but the gesture didn't quite reach her eyes. "It's just that I used to come to Rockefeller Center every Christmas with my father. Back then the tree looked ginormous to me."

"I am sorry that it now makes you sad."

She shook her head. "It's not that. It's just that back then things weren't so messed up. At least, I don't think they were. I'd like to think that part of my life was genuine and not riddled with lies."

"What lies?" Had he missed something she said? Impossible. He was captivated by her every word.

She shook her head and turned back to the tree. "It's nothing. Just me rambling on about things that aren't important."

He stepped in front of her. "It sure sounded important to me. And I'd like to understand if you'll tell me."

"Why do you care? I am just your host."

"And my friend," he added quickly. Then he stopped himself before he could say more—things that he, the prince of a far-off land, had no right saying to anyone. His feelings were irrelevant. His duty was to the crown of Mirraccino. That was what he'd been telling himself for years.

She smiled up at him. "You're very sweet. It's surprising that you're not taken yet."

He pressed a hand to his chest. "Who would want to kidnap me?"

She laughed. "Your English is very good, but I'm quickly learning that you aren't as familiar with some of our sayings. What I meant was I'm surprised that you're not in a committed relationship."

His thoughts briefly went to the king and his insistence that Alex formalize the plans to announce his engagement to Catherine, an heiress to a shipping empire. The entire reason for the match was political positioning. Combining her family's ships with the ports of Mirraccino would truly make for a powerful resource and secure Mirraccino's economic future. It didn't matter that he and Catherine didn't have feelings for each other. An advantageous marriage was what was expected of him—his wants and desires did not count.

As dedicated as Alex was to the crown, he'd never been able to visualize a future with Catherine. In fact, they planned to get together after Christmas and discuss their options. His gut told him to end things—to let her get on with her life. He didn't like the thought of her waiting around for him to develop feelings for her that obviously weren't going to appear. And marrying her out of pure duty seemed so cold. But it was what his family wanted—what they expected.

Catherine was beautiful and he did enjoy her company, but there just wasn't an attraction. That spark. Nothing close to what he felt around Reese. Now where had that come from? It wasn't as though he was planning to start anything with Reese. The last thing his family needed was another complication.

He didn't want to think about himself. It was Reese who concerned him. "Who put that sadness in your eyes?"

She swiped at her eyes. "It's no one. I—I mean it's the problems with the inn. I just need a quick influx of cash."

"What can I do to make it better?" He would do anything within his power—aside from risking his nation.

A watery smile lit up her face as she shook her head. "You've already done enough."

"But how?" He was once again confused. "You mean my reservation?"

"No, by being a caring friend."

Before he had a chance to digest her words, she was on tiptoes and leaning forward. Her warm lips pressed to his. The breath caught in his lungs. Sure, he'd fantasized about this—heck, he'd dreamed of this—but he never imagined it could be this amazing.

She was about to pull back when he snaked his arms around her waist and pulled her closer. Her hands became pinned against his chest. The problems of the Mirraccino nation and the crown's expectations of him slipped away as the kiss deepened. When she met him lip to lip and tongue to tongue, no other thoughts registered except one—he was the luckiest man alive. Nothing had ever felt this right.

She worked her hands up over his shoulders. Her fingers raked through his hair, causing the low rumble of a moan to form in the back of his throat. Her body snuggled closer but with their bulky winter garb he was barred from enjoying her voluptuous curves pressed to his.

He nibbled on her full bottom lip, reveling in the swift intake of her breath. She wanted him as much as he wanted her. The only problem was they were standing in the middle of Rockefeller Center—and in front of the Christmas tree, no less. Not exactly the place to get carried away.

Still, he couldn't let her go…not quite yet. He'd been with his share of women, but they'd never touched a part of him deep inside. It was more than physical—not that the physical wasn't great. But there was something more about Reese, and in that moment his brain turned to mush and he couldn't put his finger on exactly why she was different.

A bright flash startled him out of the moment. His eyes sprang open and with great regret he pulled away from her. Immediately the cold air settled in, but his blood was too hot for him to be bothered by the crisp air.

"What's the matter?" Reese asked.

"I—I thought I saw something. I am certain it's nothing."

His gaze scanned the area, searching for the person with the camera. Had the paparazzi tracked him down? Had they snapped a picture of him holding Reese close?

He studied the other couples and families with small children. It could have been any of them. He was making too much of the situation. If it was the paparazzi, he couldn't imagine they'd worry about hiding. He was just being paranoid without his security detail.

When he turned his attention back to Reese, she glanced up at him. Her cheeks had bright pink splotches. He couldn't decide if it was the dipping temperatures or embarrassment. And now that the cold air was filling with white fluffy flakes, his brain was starting to make connections again. He owed her an apology.

Years of being a prince had taught him that there was a time and a place for everything. This was not the time to ravish her luscious lips—he needed to keep things low-key between them. He still had yet to reveal his true identity to her. But he would fix that this evening—no more secrets.

He gave her hand a squeeze. "My apologies. I shouldn't have taken advantage of the moment."

"You didn't." Her gaze lowered. "I'm the one who should be apologizing. I started it."

She had, but he was the one who'd taken it to the next level. When she started walking, he fell in step next to her. Hand in hand, they moved as though they'd been together for years.

She glanced over at him. "Are you still up for going to dinner like we planned?"

"Do you still want to go?"

She nodded.

He was hungry, there was no doubt about that. But food wasn't what he craved. He swallowed hard, trying to keep his thoughts focused on his mission tonight—being honest with Reese without chasing her away.

Big snowflakes drifted lazily to the ground. They quickly covered her hair, reminding him of a snow angel. He'd never seen anyone so beautiful. It was going to be hard to stay focused on his priorities when all he wanted to do was get closer to Reese. If only his life were different....

In that moment, he heard the king's clear, distinct voice in his head. *Your life is one of honor—of duty. You must always think of the kingdom first.*

And that's what he was doing, but each day it was getting harder and harder to live by those rules. He glanced at Reese. Definitely much harder than he'd ever imagined.

CHAPTER TEN

REESE WAS SURPRISED by how much she was enjoying the evening. The trendy restaurant had been mentioned by a few of her guests and she now understood why. It was cozy with soft lighting and a few holiday decorations scattered about. And the tapas menu was simply divine. She loved trying a bit of this and a bit of that.

And thanks to the deteriorating weather, the restaurant was quiet enough to make conversation. Everything was going fine until Alex turned the conversation back to her. After the waiter delivered the coffee and a slice of triple-chocolate cake, Alex studied her over the rim of his cup.

He took a sip of the steamy brew before returning it to the saucer. "Tell me about him?"

Reese's heart clenched. "Who?"

Please don't let him be asking about her father. She never spoke of him...with anyone, including her mother. And she certainly wasn't about to sit here in public and reveal how that man had lied to their faces before betraying her and her mother in the worst way.

Alex leaned forward, propping his elbows on the edge of the table. "I want to know about your ex-boyfriend. The man who broke your heart."

She let out a pent-up breath. Josh was someone she could talk about. It'd taken her time to sort through the pain he'd caused, but in the end, she'd realized his lies were what had hurt her the most—not his absence from her life.

"Josh was someone I met in college. He was a smart dresser with expensive tastes. I was surprised when he offered me a ride home from a party one night. When he dropped me off, he was impressed by my family's mansion—if only I'd known then what I know now. Anyway, he insisted I give him my phone number."

Sympathy reflected in Alex's blue gaze. "He was after your money?"

"Yes. But I was too naive to know it then. I let myself get so caught up in the thought of being in love that I let it slide when things always had to be his way. And when he'd criticize my outfits, I thought it was my fault for being so naive about fashion."

"What a jerk." Alex's jaw flexed.

"When my father died, things changed. Josh transformed into the perfect gentleman. He said all of the right things and even talked of us getting married. He made me feel secure."

The memories washed over her, bringing with them the forgotten embarrassment and pain. She blinked repeatedly. She'd been wrong—recalling her past with Josh hurt more than she'd been willing to admit.

Alex reached across the table and squeezed her hand. In his touch she found reassurance and a strength within herself that she hadn't known was there.

She swallowed down the jagged lump in her throat. "Everything was fine until he learned I wasn't an heiress. In fact, I was in debt. Poorer than a church mouse. I don't know if I'll ever get out of debt before I'm a little old lady."

"You're so much better off without him. He isn't worth your tears."

She ran her fingertips over her cheeks, only then realizing that they were damp. "Once Josh knew I couldn't support him, he stopped coming around and didn't return my calls. But by that point, I was so busy looking after my mother and keeping the bank from taking the house that Josh's absence got pushed to the back of my mind."

"I'm so sorry he hurt you like that—"

"Don't be. It's done and over with. I don't want to talk about him anymore." And she couldn't bear to think of that time in her life—it was truly her darkest hour.

"They say talking about things helps you heal."

"I tend to think that chocolate heals all." She took the last bite of chocolate cake and moaned at its rich taste. "Now it's your turn. Tell me more about yourself."

"Me?" His eyes widened. "I'm boring. Surely you want to talk about something more interesting."

She shook her head. "Fair is fair. I told you about my no-good ex. Now it's your turn to tell me something that I don't already know about you."

He leaned back in his chair as though contemplating what to tell her. Then he glanced around. She followed his gaze, finding the nearby tables empty. Her anticipation grew. He was obviously about to take her into his confidence—what could be so private?

"What if I told you I'm a prince?"

Disappointment popped her excitement. "I'd say you have delusions of grandeur. I thought you were going to be serious."

He leaned forward as though he were going to say more, but her phone chimed. She held up a finger for him to give her a moment as she fished the device out of her purse. "It's my mother. I have to get it."

She got to her feet, grabbed her coat and rushed to the exit, where she'd be able to hear better without the background music. She stepped out into the cold evening air when the chime stopped. Drat. It could be important. She better call back.

The snow was still falling, enveloping everything in a white blanket. Not many people were out in the wintry weather. Those who were had their hoods up and kept their heads low as they moved along the partially cleared sidewalk. Only one man was taking his time and gazing in the various restaurant and store windows. It seemed awfully cold to be strolling around. But to each his own.

The wind kicked up. She turned her back to the biting cold and pulled up the collar on her coat. She'd just retrieved her aunt's number when she heard a man's voice call out. She turned around.

"Hey!" The man who'd been window gazing was now staring at her. "Yeah, you."

Beneath the harsh glare of the street lamps decorated with tinsel, Reese spotted a camera in the man's hands. He lifted the camera and in the next instance a bright flash momentarily blinded her. She blinked repeatedly.

He stepped closer. "What's your name?"

She stepped back. "Excuse me."

Who was this guy? And why had he taken her photo? People on the sidewalk paused and stared at her as though trying to figure out if they should know her. Like a deer in headlights, she froze.

"Come on," the man coaxed. "Give me a pretty smile."

Reese put her hands up to block the man's shot. "I don't know who you are, but leave me alone!"

"How old are you, honey? Twenty? Twenty-two?"

She went to turn back toward the restaurant when she stepped on a patch of ice. Her arms flailed through the snowy air. Her feet slid. Clutching her phone in a death grip as though it could help her, she plunged face-first toward the pavement.

* * *

Alex smiled as he traced Reese's steps to the exit.

The evening had gone better than he'd ever imagined. The tip of his tongue traced over his lower lip as he recalled the sweetness of Reese's touch. She sure could turn a kiss into a full-fledged experience. He just hoped that once he convinced her he was telling her the truth she'd understand, because he wasn't ready to let her go—not yet.

He pushed open the glass door when he saw Reese sway and fall to the ground. The sound of her name caught in his throat. He moved into action as a flash lit up the night—the paparazzi. Right now, his only concern was making sure Reese was okay.

Alex knelt beside her sprawled body. His chest tightened as he waited for her to speak. "Reese, are you okay?"

"I…I don't know. The fall knocked the breath out of me." She turned over on her backside. "My arm hurts, and my knees."

"I'm so sorry." When she started to get up, he pressed a hand to her shoulder. "Sit still for a second and take a couple of breaths."

Alex glanced around, spotting a man with a camera farther down the sidewalk. His gut instinct was to go after the man, but he wouldn't leave Reese. She needed him.

The photographer took a moment to snap another picture before he escaped into the night. Alex was certain that it would end up in the gossip rags that night, but his only concern was Reese.

And this incident was all his fault. He'd gotten caught up in the moment—only thinking of his need to comfort Reese—to be with her. He'd failed to follow any of the safety protocols drilled into him as a kid. He'd gotten so comfortable in his anonymous role that he'd forgotten just how easily things could unravel. Now once again, his rash decision had hurt someone he cared about.

That thought struck him.

He cared about Reese. It was true. But he didn't have time right now to figure out exactly what that meant. Right now he had to determine if she was all right to move. He needed to get them both off this city street. Luckily, with the inclement weather, not that many people were out and about.

"This is my fault." Alex held his hands out to her. "The least I can do is help you up."

"I've got it."

"You need help. You're sitting on a patch of ice." He continued to reach out to her. "Take my hands."

When she went to reach out to him, she gasped.

"What is it?"

"My right arm. I had my phone in my hand and came down on my elbow."

"How about your left arm? Is it all right?"

"I think so."

He gripped her good arm while she held the injured arm to her chest. An urge came over him to scoop her up into his arms and hold her tight, promising that everything would be better, but he knew that could never happen. He'd waited too long. Too much had happened. Things had gotten too out of control.

And now when Reese found out the truth—the whole truth—she'd look at him with an accusing stare. She was hurt because of him. And he couldn't blame her. None of this would have happened if only he had stayed back at the inn. He'd had a plan. A good plan. And he'd abandoned it.

He noticed the grim line of her lips as she cradled the injured arm and he felt lower than a sea urchin. "I am taking you to a hospital."

"I don't need to go. It's just a sprain."

He sent her a disapproving stare. "I insist the doctors have a look at you."

Deciding that her black heels were definitely not to be trusted on the slick sidewalk, he wrapped his arm around her waist. Even though most of the walkway had been cleared, there were still patches of snow and ice. His arm fit nicely around her curves. The heat of her body permeated her clothes and warmed his hand.

At the truck, he paused by the passenger door and opened it for her.

She cast him a hesitant look. "You're going to drive?"

He nodded. "You can't drive with your arm injured. How far to the hospital?"

"It's just a few blocks from here."

"Good." He helped her into the truck and then set out to get her some help.

"I don't understand what that man wanted."

"What did he say to you?"

"He wanted my name and I think my age. If this is some sort of human interest story for the local paper, they have a strange way of conducting themselves."

"Did he mention which paper he works for?"

"I don't even know if he works for a paper. That's just my best guess. When I first spotted him, he was staring in windows. I didn't know what he was up to."

Mentally Alex kicked himself for letting this happen. He was certain that photographer had known who he was and had most likely tracked him from Rockefeller Center to where they'd had dinner. Well, it wouldn't happen again. When he got back to the inn, he would be placing a call to Mirraccino to update the king on the recent turn of events and would request that his security detail be dispatched immediately.

Worry and guilt settled heavily on his shoulders. There was no excuse for his poor behavior. How would he keep Reese from hating him?

In one evening, he'd broken his promise to himself to follow the rules and keep those closest to him safe. He glanced at Reese, who was still holding her arm. He'd failed her in more than one way.

He should have trusted her with the truth about himself before now. But at first he'd worried that she'd sell the information. And then he'd enjoyed his role as plain Alex and selfishly didn't want her treating him differently. Now he'd waited too long.

CHAPTER ELEVEN

WHY WAS HE acting so strangely?

Reese sat on the edge of the emergency-room exam table and studied the drawn lines on Alex's handsome face. She recalled him apologizing and blaming himself for her injury. What was up with that? He hadn't even been outside when she'd slipped.

Why did she have this feeling she was missing something? She was about to ask him when the doctor entered the room.

The gray-haired man in a white coat had a serious expression on his face as he introduced himself and shook her good hand. "The films show you didn't break any bones. However, you have some minor cuts and abrasions. The worst injury is a contusion to your elbow."

Alex's hands clenched as he stood next to her. "How bad is it?"

His worry and anxiety were palpable. Had he never seen anyone get hurt before? If this was how he reacted to scrapes and bruises, she was really glad there was no blood.

The doctor's brow arched as he took in Alex's presence.

Reese spoke up. "It's okay. He's my friend."

"All in all, she's lucky. We'll clean her up and give her some anti-inflammatories to help with the swelling. She'll be sore for a day or two, but she'll feel better soon."

Reese detected the whoosh of breath from Alex. She'd swear he was more relieved than she was over the diagnosis. Although the thought of a cast was not one she would have relished when she had to take over the maid duties. How exactly would she have changed linens one-handed? Or managed any of the other tasks?

It seemed to take an eternity until she was released from the hospital. She tried to talk to Alex, but his moodiness wasn't of any comfort. When he did speak, it was only in one-syllable answers. You'd think he was the one who'd been hurt, not her.

It was all his fault.

Reese had been put in harm's way. She'd been hurt. And it was all because he hadn't taken the proper precautions. It wouldn't happen again.

With her snug in bed, Alex moved into action. He had some explaining to do. His papa would not be pleased— not that he could make Alex feel any guiltier than he already did.

While he spoke with the king, Alex scanned the internet trying to locate the photo from this evening, but no matter what he typed in the search engine, nothing popped up. He was certain the man with the camera had been part of the media and not just some fan. So where was the picture?

Alex braced himself for some fictitious story to accompany the photo. He just hoped that it wasn't too scandalous. His family had been through enough with his brother's overnight marriage to a practical stranger.

"You should have listened to me!" The king's voice vibrated the phone. "How badly is the girl injured?"

"She's going to be sore for a while, but there's nothing serious."

"You know that you must make this right. Her injuries

are the result of your poor judgment. You shouldn't have been out in public without your security detail."

"I'll do my best to make it up to her."

"Make sure you do. We don't need her turning to the media with a sob story or worse. We're already dealing with enough here."

He would take care of it. But first he had to be honest with her. He just hoped that with her being so loyal to her mother and her need to hang on to this mansion that had been in her family for generations that she'd be able to understand his loyalty to his family and the crown.

"How are things with Demetrius? Have the issues been resolved?"

"Almost. We need another day or two. Can you make that happen considering everything that just occurred?"

"Yes." That was his duty, no matter what.

Alex raked his fingers through his hair and blew out a long slow breath. "I'll make sure our plan does not unravel because of tonight's incident. I already have a backup plan in motion. I will step things up and take care of Reese at the same time."

"I don't like the sound of this. The last time you had an idea, you snuck out of the palace and took too many risks with your safety. This time I insist you tell me about this backup plan."

Alex rolled out his plan for his papa. He also took into consideration the king's suggestions and made a few adjustments until they were both satisfied.

"What about Catherine?"

The muscles in Alex's neck tightened. "I'll speak with her when I get home."

The logical thing would be to go to Catherine and formalize the marriage that their families were so eager to see take place. But how was he supposed to make a commitment to a woman he didn't love?

His priority now was speaking with Reese. He'd do that first thing in the morning. Somehow he had to make her understand his choices were for the best—for all concerned.

She was, after all, understanding and generous with her employees. These were just two of the qualities that he admired about her. He just hoped she'd extend him the same courtesy.

CHAPTER TWELVE

BEEEEP! BEEEEP!

Who in the world had their finger stuck on the front-door buzzer?

Reese groaned. She rolled over and opened one eye. It was still dark out. What in the world? Her hazy gaze settled on the green numbers on the clock. It wasn't even 6 a.m. She still had another half hour to sleep. Maybe they'd go away.

Beep. Beep. Beep.

Another groan formed deep in her dry throat. She wasn't expecting anyone. Maybe one of the employees had forgotten their pass card. Wait. No one came in this early.

Well, she wouldn't know what was going on until she answered the door.

She clambered out of bed and grabbed her old blue robe. Her elbow throbbed. There was no way the wrap on her arm would fit easily through the sleeve. Instead she draped the robe over her shoulder while holding her arm to her chest.

Her bare feet padded quietly across the floor. The door to Alex's suite was just down the hall from hers. There were no sounds or light coming from his rooms. Lucky him. He was probably still enjoying a peaceful night's sleep. Whatever had her out of bed at this hour had better be important.

She glanced through the window that ran down each

side of the front door, finding Mr. Winston standing there. What in the world?

"Please come inside." She held the door open for him. "What are you doing here at this hour?"

"I was up early, reading the paper while drinking my coffee, when I stumbled across something you need to see."

"Couldn't this have waited a few more hours?"

"No. In fact, I got here just in time."

"In time for what?" She was thoroughly confused. She really needed a piping-hot cup of coffee to wash away the cobwebs in her mind.

"Read the headline." He held the morning paper out to her. "It'll explain everything."

She accepted the paper and unfolded it. Her eyes immediately met a black-and-white photo of Alex. Her gaze skimmed the headline: Royal Prince Finds Love.

The breath caught in her throat as she read the words once more. Below the headline was a picture of her on the sidewalk with Alex next to her. Her mouth gaped. The photo had been taken last night.

She struggled to make sense of her rambling thoughts. This is why the man on the sidewalk had been questioning her? Alex was a prince?

How could that be true? Alex was royalty? Impossible.

Then their conversation at the restaurant came rushing back to her. She read the headline again. He had been telling her the truth. Alex was an honest-to-goodness prince.

"It's true," she said in astonishment.

"You know about this?" Mr. Winston's gaze searched her face.

She hadn't meant to say the words aloud. "He mentioned something about this last night."

"Do you understand the trouble we're going to have here?" The groundskeeper wrung his hands together. "I already had to escort two reporters off the property and close the gate. Thank goodness your mother isn't here."

It wasn't just her mother who would not approve of the three-ring circus going on in front of the property. Ever since Reese's father had died, the snooty neighbors had stuck their collective noses up in the air. They didn't approve of the inn. They'd even gone out of their way with the local government and business associations to try to block her from opening The Willows. They didn't want their exclusive neighborhood blemished with a bunch of riffraff.

This latest scandal of sorts would only add fuel to a fire that had finally died down to small smoldering embers. And it was all Alex's fault—correction, it was all Prince Alexandro Castanavo's fault.

She glanced toward the window. "Do we need to call the police?"

Mr. Winston rubbed his gloved hands together. "I don't think it'll be necessary at this point. But if that fella you've got staying here decides to stay on, you might have a real problem on your hands. Do you want me toss him out?"

"Um…no. I'll take care of him." She worried her bottom lip as she figured out what to do next. "Until he leaves, can you keep the press off the property?"

"I can try. But they could sneak around back without me knowing."

She tapped the folded newspaper against her thigh. "I'll call Bob and ask if he can come help you. Surely they'll get bored and go away soon."

"I wouldn't count on that. They seem to be rapidly growing in numbers."

"Please do your best. And thank you for helping."

Mr. Winston's face softened. "No need to thank me. I'm just glad I was up early and saw the paper."

She marched up the steps, coming to a stop in front

of Alex's room. She lifted her hand to knock on his door when her robe slipped from her shoulder. The cool early-morning air sent goose bumps rushing down her skin.

What should she say? Why had he kept his identity a secret? What was he doing here at The Willows? The un-ending questions whirled round in her mind.

Maybe it'd be best if she got dressed before confronting him. It'd also give her a moment to figure out exactly what she was going to say to him. Most importantly, she wondered if he was truly going to come clean about last night.

Reese called Bob and then rushed through the shower. The more she thought about how Alex had duped her, the angrier she got. And to think she'd started to trust him—to open up to him.

Minutes later, she returned to his door. With her good hand, she knocked.

There was no answer.

She added more force to her rapid knock. "Alex, I know you're in there. Wake up!"

There was a crash. A curse.

The door swung open. Alex stood there in a pair of box-ers. His short hair was scattered in all directions. "What's wrong? Is it your arm?"

"No." She drew her gaze from his bare chest to meet his confused look.

"Reese, what is it?"

"This. This is what's wrong." She pressed the paper to his bare chest. When the backs of her fingers made con-tact with his heated skin, a tingling sensation shot up her arm and settled in her chest. She immediately pulled away. Now wasn't the time for her hormones to take control. She had to think clearly.

He grabbed the paper and without even unfolding it to read the headline said, "I can explain this."

"So you know what's in it?"

He nodded. "I planned to explain everything in the morning. Speaking of morning, what are you doing up so early? The sun isn't even up yet."

"The sun may not be up, but that didn't stop the reporters from blocking the sidewalk and spilling out into the road. My neighbors are going to have a royal hissy fit over this one."

It wasn't until the words were out of her mouth that she realized her poor choice of words. She looked at him as he moved to the window facing the road and peered out. He was a royal prince. It was taking a bit for her to wrap her mind around that image. To her he was still Alex, who'd stood on the ladder plastering her ceiling. The same Alex who'd kicked back in her living room enjoying a pizza. And the Alex who'd kissed her last night.

She stared at him. His muscled shoulders were pulled back. His tanned back was straight and his head was held tall. And when he turned to her, his faraway gaze said he was deep in thought. His nose was straight and his jawline squared. He definitely looked like a very sexy Prince Charming.

In that moment, it struck her that she was speaking to an honest-to-goodness prince. Royalty. The accusations and heated words knotted up in her throat.

As though he remembered she was still in the room, his gaze met hers. "Do you mind if I throw on some clothes before we get into this?"

Realizing that she was staring at his very bare, very tempting chest, she nodded and turned away. "I'll meet you downstairs."

She headed for the door without waiting for his answer. She needed to talk to him, but not like this. Once he was dressed, she'd be able to have a serious conversation with him.

When she reached the ground floor, she glanced out the front window, finding Mr. Winston strolling along the perimeter of the property. He was such a good guy. She couldn't imagine letting him and the others go. How could she let them down?

She gave herself a mental shake. She would deal with that problem later. Right now she needed to deal with her guest—the man she'd begun to think of as a friend—the man she'd shared a kiss with the night before. She paced the length of the living room. How long did it take to throw on some clothes?

She walked to the foyer and glanced up the staircase. There was no sign of him. With each passing moment, her irritation rose. Why hadn't he been honest with her? Why all of the dodging and evasiveness?

When he finally stepped into the room, she stopped and met his unwavering gaze. His hair was still damp and a bit unruly. He'd put on a blue sweater and jeans. His feet were still bare. She drew her gaze upward, refusing to be swayed by his good looks and his royal breeding. There was something different about him.

"Your hair, it's lighter."

"I started washing out the temporary hair dye."

She openly stared at him. "There's something else."

"I didn't put in the colored contacts."

Instead of a vibrant blue, his eyes were a blue-gray.

"Is there more?" He'd really thought through his charade. Her gaze skimmed over him, looking for any other changes.

"That's all."

She tilted her chin up. "You owe me an explanation. And it better be good. Real good."

"I meant to tell you—"

"When? After you got me under your spell? After we—" She pressed her fingers to her lips.

She hadn't meant to go down that path. In fact, she hadn't meant to mention the kiss, but she just couldn't forget it. Nor could she dismiss the way his touch filled her stomach with a sense of fluttering butterflies.

"It's not what you're thinking. I'm staying at The Willows because I needed someplace quiet to stay."

"Someplace where you could hide from the press?"

He nodded. "This place is private enough while still being close to the city."

"And this explains why you could afford to rent out the whole place. But why weren't you up front with me?"

"I didn't have a choice—"

"Everyone has a choice. When we started getting closer, I started opening up to you about my past, but you still remained quiet."

"You don't know how many times I wanted to open up to you." He stepped up to her, but she backed away. His gaze pleaded with her. "I really do have a legitimate reason for not telling you the truth. Will you sit down and hear me out?"

She moved to the armchair while he took a seat on the end of the couch. "I'm listening."

Frustration creased Alex's face. "You must believe me when I say the kiss last night was real. And if you deny it, you'll only be lying to yourself."

The memory of his breath tickling her cheek. The gentle scent of his spicy cologne teasing her nose. And then his warm lips had been there, pressing against hers. Alex was right. The kiss had been out of this world.

"You mentioned something about a duty. A duty to do what?" she prompted, trying to keep not only him but also her own thoughts on target.

"To protect my country at all costs."

Reese rubbed the shoulder of her injured arm, trying to ease the dull ache. "Go on."

"I'm sorry about last night with that reporter. You were injured because I didn't follow protocol—again."

"Again?"

He paused as though searching for where to begin. "I was rebellious when I was younger. I hated all of the rules and protocols. I didn't understand their importance. When I was fifteen, I got in an argument with the king before a public outing."

"I'm guessing that was a no-no."

Alex nodded. "I ignored the mandated protocol of staying with the bodyguards at the event and took off into the crowd. With the guards chasing after me, the king and queen were not fully protected. A gunshot by a subversive meant for the king struck—struck my mother."

Reese sat back, stunned by the traumatic event in Alex's childhood. She reached out and squeezed his hand. Sympathy welled up in her for the guilt a fifteen-year-old should never have to experience.

"Before my mother died, she had me make a promise— to take care of Papa. I've kept that promise ever since. It's the very least I could do after what I did."

"Your mother must have loved your father dearly."

"Not always. Theirs was an arranged marriage."

Reese had heard of them existing in some cultures, but she found it startling that people would marry for something other than love. "How did they meet?"

"My grandfather wanted Mirraccino's wine industry to flourish beyond our nation's boundaries. He'd determined the best way to do that was to join forces with one of Italy's major wine producers and distributors. And during one of those meetings, my grandfather was introduced to my mother. It was then and there that my grandfathers came to agreement to merge the families through marriage."

"I can't imagine having to marry someone that you don't love."

"As a royal, one must always do their duty. It's an expectation that starts at birth." Alex shrugged.

"Lucky for your parents it all worked out—"

"Not quite. If only I'd have followed the rules, she... she might still be here."

"You can't blame yourself. You were young and kids don't think before they act."

"I grew up fast that day. I swore I would toe the line and protect my family at all costs—even at the risk of my own safety. I couldn't bear the thought of losing them both."

"And that's why you kept your identity from me—you were protecting your family?"

"I'm here on a most important mission for my country."

"A mission?" Alarm bells rang in her mind. What sort of situation had he gotten her mixed up in?

"If I tell you, do you promise that it'll go no further than you and me?"

She worried her bottom lip. She wanted to know. She needed to know. But what if it was something bad? She eyed up the man she knew as Alex. Her gut told her that he was a good guy, even if he had misled her.

"It'll stay between us."

The lines in his face eased. "My country is a small group of islands in the Mediterranean. It has a strong hold in the shipping industry and wines."

She listened as Alex revealed some of the history of his islands. She was amazed that his small country could have an uprising. When she thought of a sunny island, she thought of peaceful beaches and lazy afternoons. It just showed that she spent too much time wrapped up in her own little part of the world.

After he explained about his brother's impulsive marriage, Alex looked her directly in the eyes. "So you see how my brother's impulsive behavior would be disastrous for our nation."

She wasn't so sure she saw the situation the same as him. "So what you're saying is that you don't believe in love at first sight?"

He shook his head. "No, I don't. I believe in lust and need. But love...well, it grows over time. Like my parents' marriage."

Reese got his message loud and clear. The kiss last night meant nothing. A pain pinged in her chest. She sucked down the feelings of rejection. After all, it was only a kiss. Right now, she needed to hear the rest of Alex's explanation.

"So you think your brother married this girl just so he could have his way with her?" Reese didn't even know his brother, but she wasn't buying that story.

"I didn't say that."

"Sure you did. But something tells me if he looks anything like you that he could have almost any woman he wanted. So why would he offer marriage if he didn't love her?"

Alex paused and stared off into the distance as though he were truly considering her argument. "Maybe you do have a point. Perhaps he was genuinely infatuated with her."

She laughed in frustration and shook her head. "You just won't give in to the fact that your brother might truly love this woman and that your family is trying to tear them apart."

She was about to ask him what he would do if his family tried to come between them, but she stopped herself in time. After all, there wasn't anything for his family to disrupt.

Alex frowned. "It doesn't matter if he loves her or not. He's the crown prince. A wife will be chosen for him. Just as was done for my father and his father."

She wasn't going to argue his brother's case. It was none of her affair. But the pack of reporters outside was a different matter. "Now that you have the press off of your brother's trail, what are you going to do? The press can't camp out on my sidewalk. The neighbors are probably on the phone with the police right now."

"I have a plan, but I need your help."

The little hairs on the back of her neck lifted. "What do you want me to do?"

He held up the paper. "I need you to play the part of my girlfriend."

CHAPTER THIRTEEN

"I COULDN'T BE more serious."

Alex sent her a pleading look that had a way of melting through her resistance. He wanted her to be his pretend girlfriend? Her, Reese Harding, the girlfriend of an honest-to-goodness prince?

The phone started to ring. This was the perfect excuse for her to escape his intense stare. His eyes on her made her heart race and short-circuited her thoughts.

"You've got the wrong woman." She started for the hallway.

"Reese, please wait. Hear me out." There was a weary tone in his voice that stirred her sympathy.

She stopped but didn't turn around. She knew that if she did she'd cave. And she just wasn't ready to give in to him just yet. "I need to get the phone."

"Let the answering machine pick it up. This is important." He cleared his throat. "I know I made a mess of this. I'm truly sorry."

She nodded, letting him know that she'd heard him.

"Will you at least look at me?"

Reese drew in a deep breath. Part of her wanted to keep going out the door and let him know that what he'd done couldn't be forgiven with two little words of apology. But another part of her understood where he was coming from.

He'd been doing what he thought was right and necessary to protect his family. How could she fault him for that?

"I wouldn't ask you to do this if it were not a matter of national security."

Her gaze narrowed in on him, trying to decide if this was the truth or not. "National security? Shouldn't you be talking to some government agency?"

"Not the United States." He got to his feet and moved to stand in front of her. "My country is in trouble."

That's right. He was a prince. Not Alex the repair guy. Not Alex who helped her decorate the Christmas tree. And certainly not Alex the laid-back guy who enjoyed an extra-cheese pizza.

"I don't think I can help you. I run an inn. I'm not an actress. I could never pretend to be a rich debutante or some ritzy character."

"But you have something better than money and a well-known name."

"And what's that?"

"You are a woman of mystery. A woman who has the press waiting to eat out of your hand."

She was really getting confused. "What exactly is it you want me to do? Pose for the cameras?"

"In a way, yes."

She shook her head. "I'm not a model. The black dress that I wore last night and ripped on the pavement was my best dress. You'll have to find someone else."

"That isn't possible."

"Sure you can. This is New York City. The place is crawling with single women. And I'm sure a lot would clamor to be seen on your arm."

"But they're not you—the mystery woman in the photo." He glanced away as though he hadn't meant to blurt that part out. "We could make this a full-fledged business deal."

"A business deal?" She pressed her good hand to her hip. "It's really that important?"

He nodded. "If you were to continue our charade, I would pay off the debt on The Willows."

She stared at him. "You can't be serious. Nothing could be that important."

"Trust me. It's of the utmost importance." He leaned back in the ladder-back chair. "When this situation is behind us, you will own The Willows outright. Maybe then you can go back to art school and follow your dreams."

Reese placed a hand on the archway leading to the foyer to steady herself. Had she truly heard him correctly? Impossible. No one could toss around that much money…except maybe a prince. But what struck her even more was the desperation reflected in his eyes. How could she turn him down with so much at stake?

But did he know what he was asking of her? Did he know that her heart was still bruised by the way he took her feelings so lightly? Did he know that kiss was the most amazing thing to happen to her in a very long time?

Pretending to be his girlfriend would only stir up more unwanted emotions. She shouldn't even consider the idea. It spelled trouble with a capital *T*.

"If I agree, how long will this charade go on for?"

"Not long. Once my brother and the king have the situation settled, the press will find another story to interest them. The paparazzi's attention span is quite short."

"So we're talking a few days?"

"Perhaps longer."

"A week? Or two?"

"Maybe longer." When her mouth gaped open, he added, "No more than a month. At most."

Her gut told her to back out of this agreement as fast as possible—to save herself. But another part of her fancied the idea of dating a prince—even if it was all a show. Above all, she wasn't ready to say goodbye to Alex.

Before she could change her mind, she uttered, "Fine. You have yourself a fake girlfriend."

"There's one more thing you should know."

Her stomach tightened into a knot. "There's more?"

"We need to return to Mirraccino first thing in the morning."

"What?" He couldn't possibly be serious. This was just too much. "But I can't leave. It's Christmastime. I—I don't even have any presents bought for anyone."

He sent her a weary smile, as though relieved. "You can buy your gifts in Mirraccino and I'll make sure they're shipped in time for Christmas."

She frowned at him. "You seem to have an answer for everything."

"This is a once-in-a-lifetime proposition. How can you pass it up?" When she didn't say anything, he added, "If I didn't truly need your help, I wouldn't have asked."

"But what about The Willows? I can't just turn my back on it. And thanks to you, the place will most likely be booked solid through the New Year."

He smiled. "See, I told you things would turn around."

"Don't smile. This isn't good. I don't know how to do everything."

"How about your mother? She could run the inn while you're away."

"My mother? I don't think so."

"Why not? She seems fully capable to me. In fact, she seems to feel a bit left out. She almost glowed when your aunt needed her. Sometimes people need to be needed."

"And you think that she could run this place on her own?" Reese shook her head. "If you'd seen her after my dad died. She was a mess. No, it'd be too much for her."

"I don't think you give her enough credit. Maybe you've been caring for her for so long that you don't even see that she's recovered and ready to take on life if you would just let her."

"And what if something goes wrong and I'm out of the country?"

"Mr. Winston can help her."

Reese's mind replayed how Mr. Winston had always been there, trying to cheer up her mother. And over the past year, he'd made it his mission to bring her a bouquet each day from the flower gardens. She realized that her mother had seemed to spring back to life during that period. Was it possible it had something to do with Mr. Winston?

Her hands balled at her sides as she considered that maybe her mother didn't need her hovering anymore. Maybe it was time her mother stood on her own again.

She tilted her chin up and met Alex's steady gaze. "Tell me what you expect from me in exchange for this all-expenses-paid vacation to some Mediterranean island."

He reached into his pants pocket and pulled out a small black velvet box. "You'll need to wear this."

Reese's heart thumped. She'd always dreamed of the day a man would present her with a diamond ring and ask her to be his wife. What girl didn't at some point in her life? But not like this. She didn't want a fake engagement.

"I can't pretend to be your fiancée."

He gestured to the box in her hand. "Open it before deciding."

She had to admit she was curious to see the contents. The lid creaked open. Inside sat a ring with a large pink teardrop sapphire in the center with diamonds encircling it. The breath caught in Reese's throat. She'd never seen anything so beautiful. Ever.

"Is it real?"

"Most definitely."

"Where did you get it?"

"I had it shipped from Mirraccino. I hope you like it."

At a loss for words, she nodded and continued to stare at the stunning piece of jewelry. She was tempted to slip it on her finger...just to see how it'd look. After all, she'd probably never, ever hold something so precious in her hands again. Talk about your once-in-a-lifetime experiences.

Her gaze lifted to find Alex studying her reaction. She closed the lid and held it out to him. "I can't take this. It's too much. What if I lose it or something?"

"It's perfect for you. And you won't lose it. You're very responsible."

"But people will think that you and I...that we're something we're not."

"That's the point. I need people to talk about us instead of about my family."

As tempted as she was to place the magnificent ring on her finger, she returned the ring box to his hand and wrapped his fingers around it. "We'll be living a lie."

"Why does it have to be a lie? I am giving you this ring. That's a fact. You and I are friends. That's another fact. What stories people make up beyond that is out of our control."

"Still, it'll be a lie of omission."

"And sometimes a little white lie is more important than the truth. If your friend were to ask you if she looks like she put on weight and she has, would you tell her that she's fat?"

"Of course not." It wasn't until the words were out of her mouth that she realized she'd fallen into his trap.

"I just need a little diversion to keep my family safe and the country at peace. Please help me."

How could she turn away? And it wasn't just about

him. It was about the innocent people of his nation, who hadn't signed up for a scandal. Maybe she could help him. Maybe…

"I—I can't give you an answer now." No way was she jumping into this proposition without thinking it through—without the pressure of his pleading stare. "I'll have to think it over and talk to my mother. I'll let you know."

"By tonight."

"What?" He had to be kidding. This was a huge decision for her, to step into the spotlight with a prince and pull off some sort of charade. "I need more time than that. There are things to consider. Arrangements to be made."

"I'm sorry, but this has to happen before someone lets the bat out of the bag—"

"It's cat." When he sent her a puzzled look, she added, "Lets the cat out of the bag."

He sighed. "Someday I'll get all of your sayings straight."

Reese's mind had moved past Alex's loose grasp of idioms. She envisioned escaping the cold and snow to visit a far-off island. And what was even more tempting was being on the arm of the sexiest prince alive.

Some people would think she was crazy to even hesitate. But they hadn't lived the past two years of her life. If they had, they'd be cautious, too.

Still, the thought of jetting off to paradise with Alex made her heart flutter. It'd definitely be the experience of a lifetime. Could she honestly pass up a chance to spend more time with him?

She met his blue eyes. "If I agree to this, and I'm not saying that I will, I'm not lying to people. I won't tell them that you and I…that we're anything more than friends."

"And I wouldn't ask you to."

"Then I'll give you my answer tonight."

She turned and walked away before he could say anything else. She had enough things to consider. She didn't need him adding anything else. Once in the office, she turned off the ringer on the phone. She'd get to the messages shortly. She just needed a moment to breathe.

As she sat there and stared off into space, Alex's words came back to her—he was doing what he must to protect his family and heritage, much like she was trying to protect the patchwork of people whom she now considered her family. They weren't as different as she'd originally thought. The love for those they considered family came first. And this trip would help both of their families.

She really didn't have that much to consider after all. If her mother was able to handle the inn, she would be boarding a plane tomorrow. But when she thought of slipping on that ring and stepping in front of the cameras on Alex's arm, her insides quivered. Thankfully she'd have Alex to lean on. With his dream smile and charming ways, surely he'd be able to distract the paparazzi. He'd have them believing anything he told them.

But what about her? Would she be able to remember that this trip was nothing more than a fantasy and that they were each playing a part? How would she protect her heart from the charming prince?

The big moment had arrived.

A black limousine with diplomatic flags rolled to a stop by the airport entrance.

Alex took a deep breath, wondering if he'd been right to drag Reese into this game with the paparazzi. Still, he couldn't imagine anyone else playing the part of his girlfriend. He had absolutely no desire to hold anyone else's hand or to stare longingly into their eyes—for the media's sake, of course. Oh, who was he trying to bluff? Reese's kisses were as sweet as Mirraccino's juiciest grapes and held a promise of what was to come next.

He glanced over at Reese's now pale face. He hated that their departure had to be made such a public affair. She was wearing the newly repaired little black dress that had done him in the other night when they'd visited Rockefeller Center and he'd at last held her close.

He knew that any attempt to kiss her now would be rebuffed. Reese might have agreed to help him, but things had changed. She even looked at him differently, as though she didn't quite trust him. And he couldn't blame her.

None of this had worked out the way he'd wanted. His gaze slipped to her arm. "How's the arm feeling?"

"What?" She glanced at him with a questioning look.

"The arm—how is it today?"

"Don't start coddling me. My mother did enough of that when she got home yesterday from my aunt's."

He knew to tread lightly around the subject of her mother. Even though all of the staff at The Willows had offered to pitch in extra to help her mother run the place while they were in Mirraccino, Reese was still uncomfortable with the decision. He couldn't tell if it was leaving her mother or if it was letting go of the control she had over the inn, but either way this trip would do her some good. A well-deserved vacation.

"Make sure and tell me if the pain gets worse. We have some of the finest doctors in Mirraccino. They'll see that you're healing properly."

"Did you see all of those reporters and fans out there? Some are even holding signs."

"Don't worry. We have security. Those people won't be able to get to you."

"Is it always like this when you travel?"

"Not this bad. But I had to swirl up sufficient gossip

about my love life to gain the paparazzi's attention." With each passing moment it was getting more difficult to remember what was real and what was fake.

"I'd say it's working." She fidgeted with the hem of her dress. "So do you like all of this fuss?"

"Gaining positive press coverage is part of my duty as prince. A large part of Mirraccino's revenue comes from the tourism industry."

She inhaled a deep breath and lifted her chin to him. "Then let's get this over with."

"But first you will need this." He removed the black velvet box from his pocket and opened it.

She glanced at the ring and then back at his face. There was something in her expression, a tenderness—a question—and in a blink it was gone. Perhaps he'd just imagined it.

She held out her hand for the ring. He could just place it in her palm, but he wanted an excuse to touch her—to recover some of that closeness they'd shared before reality had pulled up the blind on their relationship and left all of the flaws visible under the bright light.

He took her hand in his, noticing how cold her skin was compared to his. Was she truly cold? Or was it a bad case of nerves? Did she also find this moment a little too real?

He slipped the ring on her finger and pushed it over her knuckle. It fit perfectly. And more than that, it looked perfect. He'd picked it out especially for her when this idea had started to take shape. Of course, working with his jeweler back in Mirraccino over the internet had been a bit of a risk, but the ring had turned out better than he'd hoped.

"Perfect."

"What?"

"The ring. It fits perfectly."

She glanced down at her hand, and he wanted to ask

what she was thinking, but he refrained. Was she having second thoughts? With them about to face the press, it was best just to let her be. He didn't want to say anything to upset her further.

When she lifted her gaze to meet his, there was such turmoil in her eyes—such agony. His resolve crumbled, spreading like snowflakes in a blizzard. He couldn't just sit by and not at least try to comfort her. He reached out and pulled her close. Her head willingly came to rest on his shoulder. Her silky hair brushed against his neck and the delicate scent of her floral shampoo teased his senses.

"You don't have to worry. I'll protect you." He meant it with every fiber of his being.

She lifted her head and looked at him. "You'll be my Prince Charming and ride to my rescue?"

"Yes." His gaze dipped to her lips. They were full and berry-red. Like a magnet, they drew him in and his head dipped. His mouth brushed her trembling lips.

It took him every bit of willpower to keep from devouring her lips. She tasted sweet and smelled divine. When she didn't back away, he continued his exploration. He'd never known a kiss could be so intoxicating. She tasted sweeter than the finest Mirraccino light pink Zinfandel.

This act of being a devoted couple was becoming more and more desirable with each fleeting second he held her close. He couldn't imagine ever letting her go. He wanted this kiss to go on and on. And if they hadn't been in the back of a hired car with the paparazzi just a few steps away, he'd have liked to find out where this heated moment would lead.

As it was, he was grateful for the tinted windows. There were certain things he must share with the world. This wasn't one of them. This was a very private moment that had nothing to do with providing cover for his family.

His hand slid up her arm and cradled her neck. Her pulse thumped against his palm, causing his heart to beat out a similar staccato pounding. This moment was something he would never forget. Everything about Reese was unforgettable. How in the world was he going to let her walk away when the time came?

A tap on the car door signaled that everyone was in place for them to make their grand entrance into the airport. Reese jerked back, her eyes wide and round.

"It's okay." Alex gave her arm a reassuring squeeze. "They won't open the door until I signal them."

Her fingers pressed to her now bare lips. They were slightly swollen. And her cheeks had taken on a rosy hue. He smiled, enjoying that he'd been the one to make her look ravished.

"I can't go out there now. I must look a mess."

"You look beautiful."

She reached for her purse. "I need to fix my makeup."

His hand covered hers. "Leave it. You can't improve on perfection."

Her questioning gaze met his and he pulled her hand away from her purse.

"Shall we go?"

"Wait! I—I've never done something like this. What if I make a mistake? What if I say or do the wrong thing?"

"Is that all you are worried about?" His face lifted into a smile. Relief flooded his body.

She nodded and stared at him as though not understanding his reaction.

"You'll do a wonderful job. The paparazzi are already enthralled with you."

"But I don't know how to be a prince's girlfriend."

"You're doing an excellent job." He sent her a certain look, hoping to steady her nerves. "And I don't plan to let you close enough to the press to speak to them. This is more about teasing them and letting them wonder about you and me."

Her shoulders straightened and she blinked away the uncertainty in her eyes. "You really think I can help you do this?"

He nodded. "I wouldn't have asked you otherwise."

She reached for his hand, lacing his fingers with hers.

He gave her a reassuring squeeze. "Ready?"

She nodded.

"Don't forget these." He handed her a pair of dark shades and a big black hat with a wide brim to shield her face from the cameras. "Make the paparazzi work for a close-up of you."

"Part of the cat-and-mouse strategy?"

"Exactly."

She settled the glasses on her face, hiding her expressive eyes. Next he handed over the hat, which she angled off to the side. And last, he helped her turn up the collar of her black wool coat.

"There. All set." Alex signaled the driver.

In seconds, the back car door swung open. For the first time, a natural smile pulled at his lips as he faced the cameras. He was proud to have Reese on his arm.

Alex knew it was dangerous to get too comfortable with this arrangement. Soon the final curtain would fall on their show. The thought niggled at him. Was this all just a show? Or was he more invested in this situation than he was willing to admit?

CHAPTER FOURTEEN

So this was paradise?

Reese stared out the window as the private jet flew over Mirraccino, headed for the private landing strip used by the royal family. Alex's family. She couldn't believe that they'd gone from a gray, snowy day to clear blue skies. The sandy beaches captured her attention. She tried to restrain her awe over the islands' beauty, but she couldn't help herself. As the plane dipped lower, she had an even better view. Never had she seen such picturesque land— from the tropical gardens to the white beaches.

"This place is amazing."

"I'm glad you think so. Just wait until you see it all up close and personal."

She tore her gaze from the window to look at him as panic set in. "But I forgot my camera. My mother is never going to believe this place."

"I have a camera at the palace you can use." He leaned back in his seat. "Now you see part of the reason I want to protect it. The subversives have in mind to rip up the protected land surrounding the beaches and turn it all into exclusive resorts and condos. They can't see that they'll be destroying a national treasure."

"And that's what the revolt is over?"

"No. There's much more to it, but it boils down to a very

unhappy man who has an ax to grind with my papa about something from their childhood. I have never been privy to the details, as the king says that it is not worth repeating. Either way, I've met the man and he's hard, cold and revels in controversy."

"So if this man learns about your brother's marriage, he'll have more ammunition to use against your family."

"Yes. And over the years he has gained a following of troublemakers who think that they can manage the country better than the king and the governing body. But don't worry yourself about it. You have other things to think about. Like enjoying yourself and smiling—a lot."

She should know more about what was expected of her while she was here. "What exactly will I have to do while I'm here?"

"What would you like to do?"

"I'd like to tour the islands, especially the beaches. They look amazing. Maybe go swimming, except I forgot to pack my swimsuit."

"There's something you should know—"

Her body stiffened. "Not more bad news."

"No, nothing like that. I only wanted to warn you that though it is sunny out, the temperature is cool. So swimming in the sea wouldn't be advisable. However, there's a private pool within the palace walls that you're free to use at your leisure. As for clothes, you don't have to worry. I'll have someone stop by with an assortment for you to choose from."

"But I couldn't. I don't have the money."

"It's a perk of the job. You have to look the part of a prince's…um, girlfriend."

She didn't like the thought of taking handouts. But he was right. Her wardrobe was either supercasual, jeans and T-shirts, or business suits for hosting weddings and events.

With her recent lack of a social life, she hadn't needed anything else.

But ever since Alex had dropped into her world, things had changed drastically. In fact, it was just settling into her mind that she would be staying in a palace. An honest-to-goodness palace. This trip had some truly amazing perks—besides the devastatingly handsome guy beside her, who could make her insides melt when his lips pressed to hers.

Her gaze settled on Alex. He leaned back in the leather seat and attached his seat belt as the pilot came over the intercom to instruct them to prepare for landing. This was it. She was about to step into a fairy tale. This would be a story she could tell her children one day—if she ever found that one man she could trust.

Things moved quickly after the plane's wheels touched down. The Mirraccino palace with its enormity and beauty left her speechless, and that didn't happen often. The palace's warm tan, coral and turquoise tones glistened in the sunlight. It reminded her of fine jewelry. Its graceful curves and stunning turrets were regal while reflecting an island flair.

She pointed a finger at the magnificent structure as she struggled to find her voice. "You…you live here?"

His eyes lit up and his lips lifted at the corners. "Yes. I was born here. The whole royal family lives here. In fact, I need to check in on my papa and brother as soon as we get inside. I hope you don't mind."

"Not at all. I know you've been worried about them. It's really nice how close you are with your family."

Alex cleared his throat. "We're just your average family."

She couldn't help but laugh. "Not quite."

Nothing about Alex was average. Not the Learjet they

flew in on or the magnificent palace he called home. But there was more than just the physical elements of Alex's life that stood out. There was his need to look after her when she got hurt. And his need to fix her apartment.

But then there was the other side of this man—the side that withheld the truth about himself. How did she get past that? And should she even want to? After all, this whole game of charades was temporary. She had to be careful not to forget that this whole trip was nothing more than to benefit the paparazzi.

A man in a dark suit stepped out of the palace. He didn't smile or give any indication that he even saw her. The man's focus was on Alex. Something told her that he wasn't there to retrieve their luggage—not that she had much. She turned a questioning look to Alex.

His demeanor turned stiff and unreadable. "I need to deal with something. If you want to wait inside, I'll be right in."

"No problem." She didn't have to be asked twice. She was eager to see the interior of this amazing palace.

This all has to be a dream.

Reese resisted the urge to pinch herself.

She entered the grand entryway. Her high heels clicked over the marble floor. She craned her neck, taking in the splendor of the walls and high ceiling. She was in awe of the spaciousness and the sheer elegance of the interior, which included a crystal chandelier. And if that wasn't enough to make a girl swoon, standing before her was a man almost as handsome as Alex—in fact, they looked a lot alike. The man filled out a navy suit with the top two buttons of his blue dress shirt undone.

His hair was a deeper shade than Alex's. But it was the man's eyes that held her attention. They were blue, but there was something more—something she couldn't quite define. Perhaps it was loneliness or pain. Whatever it was her heart went out to him.

He spoke in a foreign language.

She held up her hands to stop him. "I'm sorry. I don't understand what you're trying to say."

"No, it is I who am sorry. I forgot that you're American. Welcome to Mirraccino." His voice was deep like Alex's. "I'm Demetrius. You must be Alexandro's friend."

"Ah, yes, I...I'm Reese." She clutched her purse strap tighter. "Alex is talking with someone outside. He'll be right in."

As if on cue, Alex stepped up behind her and placed his hands possessively on her shoulders, as though they belonged together. "Sorry about that. There's a problem down at the port. But nothing that can't be dealt with later. I see I am too late to make the introductions."

Demetrius stepped forward. "This will give me a chance to say this once. Thank you both for everything you've done to keep the paparazzi from making this difficult situation even worse."

Reese wasn't sure what to say to the crown prince. Should she just say *you're welcome?* Or offer her condolences on the dissolution of his marriage?

Alex rode to her rescue when he stepped around her. "Is everything resolved?"

Demetrius's shoulders slumped. "She's gone."

"It's for the best." Alex's matter-of-fact voice startled Reese. "You have a duty to Papa. To the nation. That must always come first."

Demetrius's pained stare met his brother's unflinching gaze. How could Alex be so emotionless? Reese obviously didn't know him as well as she'd thought. She struggled to keep the frown of disapproval from her face.

As it was, the room practically vibrated with emotion.

With bated breath she waited to see if the brothers would come to blows.

Demetrius's hands clenched at his sides. "That's the difference between us, little brother. I don't believe that duty is the be-all and end-all of life."

"And look what that thinking cost you. You look terrible and this whole episode was taxing on Papa."

"Just because you can live without love doesn't mean that I can." Demetrius's eyes narrowed. "And don't think I'm the only one who has his future drawn out for them. You have no more freedom than I do. And we all know that you're the good son who'll marry whoever they choose for you—"

"Enough." Alex's voice held a hard edge. "I know this is a hard time for you, but we have a guest."

Demetrius's gaze moved to Reese. "I'm sorry you had to witness that. Just be glad that you're here doing a job and you didn't actually fall for my brother. He can be heartless at times."

Before she could even think of a response, Demetrius stormed out of the room.

She turned a startled look at Alex. "How could you say that to him? Couldn't you see the pain he's in?"

"He has to remember what's at stake. Living here—" he waved his hands around "—comes with responsibilities others don't think of. My brother can't afford to forget that his decisions affect far more than just himself. He'll get over that woman."

Reese's mouth gaped open. "I was wrong. I'm not the grinch around here. You are."

"What's that supposed to mean?"

"Read the book, you'll find out. And maybe you'll learn a lesson, too."

His forehead wrinkled. "I don't need a child's book to

tell me that there's no room for romance when it comes to the future of this nation."

"And you had to remind your brother of that right now when you can plainly see that he's brokenhearted?"

Alex raked his fingers through his hair. "You're right. I didn't handle it very well."

"That's an understatement." There was one more thing that she had to know. "Is he right? Will a wife be chosen for you?"

Alex's gaze met hers. "My family has plans for me to make an advantageous marriage to a woman from an influential family. We are a small nation and in these uncertain times we can't have enough allies."

Reese's heart sank. "Will you go through with it? Will you marry who they choose?"

He sighed and raked his fingers through his dark hair, scattering the strands. "I don't know. I have more to consider than my happiness. If my marriage can benefit Mirraccino, I must take that into consideration."

All of a sudden this scenario was beginning to sound all too familiar. What was it about men putting everything ahead of love? Did they really think you could sustain a meaningful relationship without it?

She glared at Alex, letting her anger mask her disappointment. "You're just like Josh—"

"What?" Hurt reflected in Alex's eyes. In a blink it was replaced with a hard wall that locked her out. "I can't believe you'd compare me to him."

"Both of you are out to have relationships with women you think can help you. It doesn't matter if you care about them or not. All that matters is what you can get from them."

"That's not true. I'd never lead a woman on."

"True." He definitely wouldn't do that. "You'd tell them up front what you wanted."

Alex reached out to her, but she backed away. "You're tired after our long trip and you're letting my brother get you worked up. We can talk about this later."

He was right. She was getting worked up. But she refused to let another man hurt her—betray her. And the thought of Alex belonging to another woman hurt more than she wanted to admit—even to herself.

"Go after your brother and make things right."

Alex's eyes widened as though he wasn't used to being ordered around. "You're serious?"

"Yes. Go."

"I'll send someone to show you to your room. Later, I'll give you the grand tour."

She nodded her approval. "I need to call my mother and check on things."

Armed with the knowledge that Alex would have a bride chosen for him, she'd have to be careful going forward. She didn't want to get swept up in paradise with a sexy prince and lose her heart. Because in the end, she'd be going back to New York.

Alone.

CHAPTER FIFTEEN

IT WAS JUST the two of them, at last.

Alex stopped next to Reese in front of the glass doors leading to the garden. He hoped a good night's sleep had put her in a better frame of mind. She had to be overcome with exhaustion to accuse him of being anything like her ex-boyfriend. He was nothing like that jerk. He'd never intentionally use a woman. She just didn't understand how things worked when you were born into royalty.

"How are things between you and your brother?" Reese asked, drawing him from his thoughts.

"Getting better. You were right. He really cared about that woman."

They stepped onto the patio and Reese glanced up at him with those big brown eyes. "Does this mean you now believe in love at first sight?"

Alex smiled, amazed by her persistence. "I'll take it under advisement. Perhaps there's more to this love thing than I understand."

She smiled, too, and he had to resist the urge to plant a kiss on her upturned lips. He didn't want to press his luck. At least today she was speaking to him and not glaring at him as though he was the enemy.

They descended the sweeping steps to the edge of the sculpted garden. The sun was high overhead. He enjoyed the fact that she had on a teal dress that he'd personally picked out. When he'd first laid his eyes on it, he'd known it would look spectacular with Reese's long auburn hair.

"You look beautiful."

"Thank you. I don't even want to think how much this dress must have cost you. Did you know that it has a designer label?"

He smiled, enjoying the enthusiasm in her voice. "All that matters is that you like it and you look beautiful in it."

She ducked her head. "I considered not wearing it. It has to be so expensive. I didn't want to do anything to ruin it. But then I realized that I don't own anything suitable to wear here. And I didn't want to embarrass you."

"You could never do that." And he meant every word. He was proud to be seen with a woman who was just as beautiful on the inside as out.

She stopped in front of him and turned. Her shoulders straightened and her chin tilted up. "Tell me about her."

"Who?"

"The woman your family wants you to marry."

He resisted the urge to roll his eyes. "You don't want to hear about Catherine."

"Catherine. That's her name?"

"Yes." He didn't like where this conversation was headed. "There are some flowers over here that I think you'll like."

Reese didn't move. "This Catherine. What does she think of you being in the papers with me?"

"I—I don't know." He hadn't thought about it. Perhaps he should have let her in on the plan, but they'd never made a point of being a part of each other's lives. "We don't talk very often."

"But you're supposed to marry her."

"It's what our families have arranged. It's what is expected of us."

"But neither of you has agreed to the arrangement?"

Was that a glimmer of hope in Reese's eyes? Was she hoping there was room in his life for her?

"Catherine and I have never talked about marriage. We're friends and we spend time together when our families visit."

"Do you love her?"

At last, the question he'd been certain would come up. "Catherine is a wonderful friend. And a very sweet person. But no, I'm not in love with her."

Reese's mouth settled into a firm line as she glanced away, leaving him to wonder about the direction of her thoughts. He'd rather she get it all out in the open, but instead of prodding her, he remained silent. She was at least still here with him. He shouldn't push his luck.

Reese set off down one of the many meandering paths in the sprawling garden. It amazed him how fast she could move while wearing those silver high heels—but boy, was it a sight worth beholding. As she turned a corner, he realized she was getting away. He set off after her.

He'd just caught up to her when she came to an abrupt halt. It was all he could do to keep from running into her. His hands came to rest on her shoulders as he regained his balance. He was just about to ask what she thought she was doing when his gaze settled on the king.

His papa had stopped in front of them. "I didn't know anyone ever took the time to stroll through the gardens."

Alex glanced at Reese's wide-eyed stare and immediately knew that she was intimidated by not only his papa's title but also his booming voice. "I was just showing Reese around."

"There's lots to see. Your mama firmly believed that

it was necessary to pause every day and smell the roses. Your mama knew what was important in life. Sometimes I wonder if she'd approve of my choices, especially with you boys."

Alex was rendered silent, unused to seeing his papa in this state of contemplation concerning his family.

Reese cleared her throat. "I think you've done a great job with Alex. He's kind and thoughtful. You should be proud of him."

"I am." The king's tired face lit up. For a moment, he studied Reese. "Perhaps I am worried for no reason. Now, make sure my son shows you the yellow roses. They were his mama's favorites. If you'll excuse me, I've got to get back to work."

As his papa walked away, Alex was struck by how much his papa still vividly loved his mama. Alex wondered what it must be like to experience such a profound love. But was it worth the risk of ending up alone like his papa—

"Did you hear me?" Reese sent him a puzzled look.

"I'm sorry. What were you saying?"

"I wanted to know which direction led to the roses."

He led her along the wide meandering path edged with low-cut hedges that formed various geometric planting spaces. Each section was planted with just one type of flower, fruit or vegetable. Even though he'd lived here his whole life, he still found the vibrant colors beautiful, but today he only had eyes for Reese.

"With all of these gorgeous flowers, it's like paradise here. You're so lucky."

He looked around the vast garden. He definitely saw it in a different light after living in Reese's world for a few weeks. And though he was blessed financially, Reese was much better off. Her life contained priceless things such as the wonderful relationship she had with her mother, who obviously loved her very much. And even the people who worked for Reese were totally devoted to her.

His guards were devoted to him to the point of laying down their lives to protect him, but it wasn't out of love. It was a duty—an allegiance to a greater good. He wondered what it would be like to have a warm relationship with those around him like Reese had with her staff.

She glanced at him. "You seem to have a lot on your mind."

"I was thinking that until now I've never considered myself lucky. Sure, I appreciate the fact that I lead a privileged life, but sometimes I wake up and wish I had a normal life."

"You can't be serious. You'd really want to give all of this up?"

He shrugged. "Sometimes. When the rules and duties dictate my entire life."

Her forehead wrinkled. "You mean like now, when you had to drop everything and fly to New York?"

"Actually, that's something I'll always be grateful for." He stopped walking and turned to her. "It gave me the opportunity to meet you."

"Are you flirting with me?"

"I don't know. Is it working?"

A hint of a smile pulled at her rosy lips. "What do you think?"

His heart thumped against his ribs. The sun glistened off her auburn hair and her eyes sparkled. He was drawn to her as he was drawn to none other. His fingers stroked her cheek and she leaned ever so slightly into his touch.

His royal duties and the knowledge that Reese would never fit into the king's idea of the proper wife fled his mind. In this moment, the only thing that mattered was the woman standing before him with longing in her eyes—such beautiful eyes.

His head dipped down and her soft lips were there meeting his. He moved slowly at first. Like a bird to nectar, he didn't want to startle her. But when she matched him move for move, his heart pounded harder. Faster.

An overwhelming need grew in him for more of this—more of Reese. His arms encircled her waist, pulling her flush to him. He'd never experienced a kiss so tantalizing, so sweet. And he'd never wanted someone so much in his life. Not just physically. Her very presence in his life was like a smoothing balm, easing away the rough edges. It was as if he'd donned a pair of glasses and could see things so much more clearly.

A gentle moan swelled in his throat as her fingers threaded through his hair. He wanted more, oh, so much more. He needed to move them out of the garden. Someplace where they wouldn't be under constant supervision of the security detail—someplace where they could see where this would lead.

There was the sound of hurried footsteps followed by someone loudly clearing his throat. Alex knew the sound—it was time to get back to work. Damn. Why did duty call at the least inopportune times?

With great reluctance he released Reese. "I must go. I've been waiting on an important call."

It was as though he could see the walls rising between them in Reese's eyes. He couldn't blame her for wanting to come first in someone's life. The men in her life had relegated her to an afterthought and collateral damage. She deserved so much better. Not that he was the man to give her all the love she deserved.

As he walked away, he inwardly groaned. His common

sense and emotions warred with each other. When it came to Reese, she had him reconsidering everything in his life.

Reese was in dangerous territory.

And though she knew that Alex could never have a future with her, she couldn't resist his sultry kisses. Or keep her heart from pounding when his fingers touched hers.

She needed some space—a chance to clear her mind and remember that this was just a show for the press. But there was no time for getting away. There was no chance for her to be alone except at night in her room. They had a job to do—keep the press concentrating on them while his brother pulled himself together and the last of the legal negotiations were handled.

And this morning, Reese and Prince Alexandro were about to have their first press-covered outing. Alex's long, lean fingers threaded through hers as they strolled along the palace drive on their way to tour the nearby village of Portolina. His grip was strong and she drew comfort from it as she was about to be paraded before the cameras.

This public appearance didn't require big sunglasses or hats to hide behind. Instead Reese had selected a pair of dark jeans, a navy blazer and a white blouse. Alex had advised she dress casually. She hoped her choice in clothes would suffice.

Reese gripped Alex's hand tighter. When he glanced her way, her stomach quivered. But it had nothing to do with the reporters waiting for them on the other side of the palace gates. No, the fluttering feeling had everything to do with the man who had her mind utterly confused between her want to continue the kiss from yesterday and her need to protect herself from being hurt when this fairy tale ended.

Alex leaned over and whispered in her ear, "Trust me. You'll be fine."

She let out a pent-up breath and nodded. They approached the gate as it swung wide open. She faced the paparazzi's flashing cameras and smiled brightly.

"When will the formal engagement announcement be released?" shouted a reporter.

"Is there a ball planned to celebrate the impending nuptials?"

"When's the wedding?" chorused a number of voices.

"The palace has no comment." A spokesman stepped forward as planned to field the questions. "Prince Alexandro and Ms. Harding are out for a stroll about the village. If there are any announcements to be made in the future, my office will notify you."

Security cleared the drive for them. Reese wasn't sure her legs would support her—her knees felt like gelatin. As though Alex understood, he moved her hand to the crook of his arm for additional support and then covered it with his other hand.

As they made their way toward the small village, he leaned over and whispered in her ear, "You're doing great. Now they'll never guess your deep dark secret."

She turned to him and arched a questioning brow.

He leaned in again. His minty-fresh breath tickled her neck, sending delicious sensations racing to her core. His voice was low but clear. "That you're a bit grinchy. And that beneath that makeup you're really green."

She laughed and the tension in her body eased. "You looked up the story I told you about."

He nodded and returned her smile. So he really did hear what she said. Her lips parted as her smile intensified.

With the paparazzi trailing behind, Alex gave her a walking tour of Portolina—a small village near the palace. If not for the festive red-and-green decorations, it would not seem like Christmas—at least not the cold, snowy Christmas that Reese was accustomed to in New York.

The stroke of Alex's thumb against the back of her hand sent her pulse racing as she tried to keep her attention focused on this fascinating town. It was teeming with history, from the old structures with their stone-and-mortar walls to the stone walkways. She even found the doorways fascinating, as some were rectangular and others were arched. Beautiful old brass knockers adorned the heavy wood doors. This place definitely had a unique old-world feel to it. She could see why Alex and his family weren't eager to bulldoze this place and modernize it with condos.

Some people rode scooters but most villagers walked. Many of them smiled and waved. Some even came up to Alex—their prince—and greeted him like some returning hero. But most of all, she could feel their gazes on her. Of course, Reese couldn't tell if they were curious about her or the caravan of reporters. She noticed how Alex barely gave the paparazzi much notice. He merely went about his day and she tried following his lead, enjoying the sights and sounds.

The paths he led her on ebbed and flowed through the village, sometimes between buildings and sometimes under passageways. It was so different from her life in New York City. With the camera Alex had lent her, she took dozens of photos—eager to remember every moment of this amazing trip.

They sat down in a coffeehouse that had been closed to the public. Alex lifted her hand and kissed it. "What's bothering you, *bella?*"

Her heart stuttered as she stopped and stared at him. His reference to her with such an endearing term caught her off guard. But before she let herself get caught up in the moment, she reminded herself that this was all an illusion. She pulled her hand away. He was playing his part—acting like the ardent lover. Nothing more.

But if that was the case, why was he doing it when there was no one within hearing distance? Reese could feel her last bit of resolve giving way. And as he once again reached across the café table to her, she didn't shy away. His warm hand engulfed hers reassuringly. She could feel her resistance to his charms crumble even further.

"You can tell me anything." His voice was soft and encouraging.

Glancing around just to make sure they were in fact alone, she lowered her voice and said, "They expect us to get married. This is what I was worried about. They've jumped to the wrong conclusion. I'll have to call my mother and warn her not to believe anything she reads in the paper."

Reese glanced down at the ring causing all of the ruckus. She wiggled her finger, enjoying the way the light danced over the jewels. It truly was the most beautiful ring she'd ever seen.

Alex waved away her worries. "Don't worry about it. Just enjoy yourself." There was a pause and then he added, "You are enjoying yourself, aren't you?"

"Yes. But when this illusion ends, everyone will think it's my fault."

"*Bella,* you worry too much. After all, you are forgetting that I control what information is fed to the press. On my honor, I promise your good name will remain intact."

She wanted to smile and take comfort in his words, but she couldn't. They weren't the words she was longing to hear. She wanted him to say that she mattered to him. That this illusion was real to him. That it wasn't going to end.

After their extensive lunch was served, the waiter brought them espresso to wash it down. Reese, not used to such a large meal, wasn't sure she had room for it.

Alex took a sip of the steaming brew. "I have some meetings this afternoon that I must attend, but feel free to finish touring the village."

"I think I'll do that. I still have my Christmas shopping to do."

"I promise to return as soon as I can."

"Don't rush on my account. I know that you have important issues to attend to."

"Nothing is more important than you." His warm gaze met hers and her insides melted. "You're my guest and I want you to be happy here. I hope the paparazzi's attention has not been too much for you."

"Actually, your staff has done a great job of keeping them at a distance. And I think the people of Portolina are amazingly kind. You're lucky to live here. I'll never forget my visit."

Her heart pinched at the thought of one day waking up and no longer bumping into Alex. She didn't know how someone she'd only met recently could become such an important part of her life.

She brought her thoughts up short. This was ridiculous. She was falling for her own PR scam. They weren't a couple. And he wasn't someone that she should trust, but with each passing day she was finding her mistrust of him sliding away.

Maybe like the Grinch, Alex's heart was starting to grow. Which gave her a great idea for a Christmas present. There was a small bookstore just back a little ways. She would get him a copy of *How the Grinch Stole Christmas*. Perhaps it wasn't too late for him to see life differently.

CHAPTER SIXTEEN

How could it be more than a week since they'd arrived in Mirraccino?

Alex's body tensed as he realized there was no longer a need for Reese to stay—except for the fact that he wasn't ready to let her go yet. He'd spent every available moment with her, and he still hadn't gotten his fill of her. He'd never had this sort of experience with anyone before.

They'd toured Mirraccino's finest vineyards and taken a trip to the bustling port on the other side of the island. The outings allowed her to rest her arm and the bruises time to begin to fade. And best of all, her frosty demeanor had melted beneath the bright sunshine.

He knew as Prince Alexandro, he should end things here and now. But the plain, ordinary Alex didn't want to let go. He couldn't imagine Reese being gone from his life. How did one return to a dull and repetitive life after being shown a bright, sparkling world full of hope?

Alex had made his decision. No matter what the king said, it was simply too soon for Reese to leave. His brother, the crown prince, was simply not in good enough spirits yet to deal with the press. It wouldn't take much for them to notice the crown prince's melancholy expression. He wore it like an old war wound, reminding his whole family of what he'd lost in order to uphold his royal duty.

Thanks to Reese, Alex was starting to believe his brother's feelings for the woman had run much deeper than he'd originally thought. The price of being royal could cut quite deep at times. He was about to pay his own dues when Reese left for the States. He wasn't relishing that impending day. In fact, he refused to think of it today.

Christmas Day had at last arrived and the paparazzi had fled for their own homes, leaving everyone at the palace in peace—at least for one day. And now that the official photos had been taken, the gifts opened and the extravagant lunch served, he had a very special surprise in mind for Reese. He'd been working on it all week and now he was anxious to surprise her.

"I can't believe the size of your Christmas tree." Reese's voice was full of awe as they strolled back to their rooms, which were in two different wings. "It's a good thing I remembered to have you take my picture next to it. My mother never would have believed it was, what— twenty feet tall?"

"I don't know." He smiled over the things that impressed her. "If you want I can inquire."

"No. That's okay. The picture will say it all. You did get the whole tree in the picture, didn't you?"

"Yes. Now I have a question for you." He sensed her expectant look. "After we change clothes, would you join me for a stroll along the beach?"

"I don't know." Her gaze didn't meet his. "I'm kind of tired. It's been a really long day."

He wasn't going to give up that easily. This was far too important—he had a very special surprise for her. "Or is it that you stayed awake all night waiting for Santa?"

There was no hint of a smile on her face. "Something like that."

"I was only teasing you."

"I know." She continued staring at the floor.

His finger lifted her chin. Sadness reflected in her eyes. "Reese, talk to me. I'll make it better."

She shook her head. "You can't. No one can."

His voice softened. "Sometimes talking things over can make a person feel better."

She leaned her back against the closed door and pulled at the short sleeves of her midnight-blue dress. "Do you really care?"

His fingers moved some loose strands of silky hair from her face and tucked them behind her ear. "You know I do. I care very much."

Reese glanced up and down the hall as though to confirm that they truly were alone. This must be more serious than he'd originally thought.

"Why don't we step into your room?" he suggested.

She nodded and turned to open the door. Inside, she approached the bed, where she perched on the edge. With the door closed, no one would bother them. Alex's mind spiraled with all of the intimate possibilities awaiting them. Perhaps this hadn't been such a good idea for a serious talk.

Reese lifted her face. Her shiny eyes and pale face stopped his wayward thoughts in their tracks. He sat down beside her and took her hand in his.

Her voice came out very soft. "I was up last night thinking about how my life has changed since my father died at Christmas two years ago."

The news smacked into Alex, stunning him for a moment. "I had no idea."

"I didn't want to make a big deal of it. It was Christmas Eve, to be exact. He was leaving…leaving me and my mother to meet his longtime lover." She swiped at her eyes. "He didn't even have the nerve to tell us to our faces. He wrote a note. A note! Who writes a note to tell the people that he is supposed to love that their lives were a lie and he doesn't love them and he wants out?"

Alex didn't have a clue what to say. Her rigid back and level shoulders sent keep-away vibes. So he sat there quietly waiting for her to get it all out.

"He hit a patch of black ice and went over an embankment. They say he died on impact. He didn't even have the decency to stick around to say goodbye. There was no time for questions—and no answer to why he'd destroyed our family. It was all over in a heartbeat."

"I'm so sorry he did that to you and your mother."

Reese swiped at her eyes. "At the time, I thought I had Josh to lean on. He was there for the funeral. He was the perfect gentleman, sympathizing with me and my mother." A hollow laugh echoed from her chest. "He had the nerve to condemn my father for his actions. And yet when it came to light that the savings had been drained off and the mansion had been mortgaged to pay for my father's new life, Josh couldn't get out the door fast enough."

Her shoulders drooped as she got the last of the sad story out. It was as though without all of the anger and pain, she deflated.

Instead of words, he turned, drawing her into his arms. She didn't resist. In fact, she leaned into his embrace. Maybe his plan for today wasn't such a good idea after all.

Reese inhaled a shaky breath. "Now you know why I've been so hesitant to trust you—to trust anyone."

Alex lifted her chin with his thumb. When her brown gaze met his, he said, "You can trust me. I promise I won't abandon you and I won't betray you."

He leaned forward, pressing his lips gently against hers in a reassuring kiss. Her bottom lip trembled beneath his. He didn't know how anyone could take her for granted. Reese was everything he'd ever wanted in a woman and more.

She pulled back and gave him a watery smile. "Thank you. I didn't mean to put a damper on the day."

"And if I had known what a tough day this would be for you, I wouldn't have tried to talk you into an outing."

"The truth is, I'll never be able to relax now."

"Are you saying you want to go?" He didn't want her to do anything that she wasn't up for.

She nodded and wiped away the moisture on her cheeks. "Just let me get changed."

"I'll meet you back here in ten minutes."

"Sounds good. Thank you for listening and understanding." The smile that touched her lips this time was genuine, and it warmed a spot in his chest.

On second thought, maybe his plan was just what she needed to push away her not-so-happy past and replace it with new, happy memories. Yes, he liked that idea. Reese deserved to be happy after the way she went out of her way for the people in her life—he wanted to be the one who went out of his way for her.

In that moment, he realized something that he'd been avoiding for a while now. He had feelings for Reese—deep feelings. He knew it was a big risk with his heart. Thoughts of his heartbroken father flashed through his mind. But in the next breath, he envisioned Reese's face.

He didn't have a choice.

Somehow, someway, she'd sneaked past his defenses. He cared for her more than anyone else in his life. But he didn't know what to do with these feelings. He was a prince. There were expectations he must fulfill for the good of the kingdom.

As he headed for his suite, he realized it was time he called Catherine. They needed to meet after the holidays were over. In light of his genuine feelings for Reese, he couldn't let the lingering questions surrounding the anticipated royal engagement drag on.

Although with all that hinged on the engagement, breaking the news to Catherine would have to be handled face-to-face and very carefully.

Reese's mouth gaped.

Gripping the red beach bag hanging over her shoulder and with Alex holding her other hand, she stood on the sand utterly speechless. Her gaze searched his smiling face before she turned back to the towering palm tree all decked out with white twinkle lights. The scene belonged on a postcard. It was picture-perfect…just like Alex in his khaki pants and white shirt with the sleeves rolled up and the collar unbuttoned.

Alex gave her hand a squeeze. "Do you like your surprise?"

"I love it." She nodded and smiled. Her gaze roamed around, trying to take it all in. "Is this all for me?"

His eyes lit up as he gazed at her. "It's my Christmas present to you."

The wall around her heart that had been eroding all week completely crumbled in that moment. She was totally vulnerable to him and she didn't care. "But you've already given me so much that I can never repay."

"That was all about our deal. This, well, this is because I wanted to do something special for you." He shifted his weight from one foot to the other. "And I know how much you enjoy the little lights, so I ordered enough to decorate the bungalow inside and out. Do you like it?"

She nodded vigorously. "No one has ever done anything so thoughtful for me. Thank you."

She lifted up on her tiptoes and without thinking of how

their diverse lives would never mesh, leaned into him and pressed her lips to his. She heard the swift intake of his breath. They'd been building toward this moment since their first kiss at Rockefeller Center. With each touch, look, kiss, she felt a heady need growing within her. The electricity between them had crackled and arced ever since they met. And now beneath the darkening Mediterranean sky, it had the strength of a lightning bolt. Her insides warmed with undeniable anticipation.

She swallowed hard, trying to regain her composure. "Are you going to show me the inside?"

He blinked as though he, too, had been thoroughly distracted by the kiss that promised more to follow. "Um... yes. Lead the way."

She easily made it up the stone steps that meandered up the embankment and led to a wide-open terrace with a white table and matching chairs. An arrangement of red poinsettias was placed in the center of the table, where a burning white candle flickered within a hurricane lamp. She wondered if his attention to details extended to all parts of his life.

She stopped on the terrace and turned to Alex. This night was so romantic, so perfect. Her heart thumped against her ribs. He'd done all of this for her. With every passing moment it was becoming increasingly difficult to remember that she was only playing a part for the sake of his nation's national security.

And then her chest tightened. Her palms grew damp. And she bit down on her lower lip. In that moment, she remembered how much it hurt when happy illusions shattered and reality ran up and smacked her in the face. She'd promised herself she wouldn't set herself up to be hurt like that again. It was just too painful.

Needing to add a dash of reality to this picture-perfect

evening, she asked, "Have you thought about how we're going to end all of this?"

Alex's brow creased. "Why would I think about something like that when we're having such a wonderful time?"

He had a good point, but fear overrode his words. "But eventually you're going to have to tell the press something when I go back to the States without you."

His fingers caressed her cheek. "Just for tonight, forget about the future and enjoy the moment."

She wanted to, more than he knew. But this just wasn't right. They'd gotten caught up in the show they were putting on for the public. In reality, there was another woman in Alex's life.

The sobering reality propelled her away from him— needing a little space to resign herself to the fact that this evening, as beautiful as it was, couldn't happen. If they made love—if she laid her heart on the line—she couldn't bear to walk away from him. As it was, stepping on the plane now would be torture, but to know exactly what she'd be missing would be unbearable.

She stepped up to the rail to gaze out over the ocean as the sun was setting. Pink and purple stretched across the horizon as a big ball of orange sank beneath the sea. The breeze tickled over her skin while the scent of salt filled her nose.

When she heard his footsteps approaching her, she tried to act normal—whatever that amounted to these days. "I've never seen anything so beautiful."

"I have." Alex's hands wrapped around her waist. "And I am holding her."

His compliment made her heart go tap-tap in her chest. She turned in his arms. "I'm sure you've been with much prettier women. What about Catherine? Shouldn't she be the one who is here with you?"

His brows gathered. "No, she shouldn't."

"But you're supposed to marry her."

"Is that what's bothering you?" When she nodded, he added, "Then stop worrying. I've called Catherine."

He did? Her heart took flight. "You told her about me?"

"Yes—"

Reese launched herself at him, smothering his words with a passionate kiss. Excitement and relief pumped through her veins. Her arms wrapped around his neck, pulling him close. There was nothing more she needed to hear. He'd told Catherine that they were together now. How could she have ever doubted him?

Reese hadn't known she could ever be this happy. The rush of feelings inside her was intense and they were fighting to get out. The time had come to quit holding back and trust him with her heart. Because if anyone was a good guy, it was Alex.

She pulled back and looked up at him. "Sometimes fantasies really do come true."

"Yes, they do."

He drew her back to him, the heat of his body permeating her dress. His lips pressed to hers. This time there was no hesitation in his touch. There was a deep need and a passionate desire in the way his mouth moved over hers. It lit a fire within her that mounted in intensity with each passing second.

Someone cleared his throat.

Reese jumped, pulling away from Alex's hold. She didn't know why she'd automatically assumed that they were alone. And that Alex had planned this as a romantic getaway for two.

Heat scorched her cheeks as she turned to face their visitor.

The butler stood at attention. "Sir, we need to know if you would like us to set up the meal inside or out."

Alex glanced at her. "It's your choice. Where would you like to dine?"

"Without the sun, the temps are dipping." She rubbed her arms, which were growing cold without his warmth next to them. "Would you mind if we eat inside?"

"Not at all. Would you like a fire lit?"

She glanced through the glass doors at the stone fireplace. The idea of sitting next to a crackling fire with Alex sounded perfectly romantic. "Yes, please."

Once the butler and small staff set about laying out the meal, Alex approached the fireplace mantel and retrieved a red plush Santa hat. "I think this will help set the mood."

She let him place the hat upon her head. "I guess it depends on what sort of mood you're creating."

"I'll let you wonder about that for now."

She spied another Santa hat on the mantel and decided that the prince needed to have some fun with her. She tossed her beach bag on the couch and raced over to the mantel. With the other Santa hat in hand, she turned to Alex.

A smile lit up his face as he started shaking his head. "No way. I am not wearing that."

"This evening is all your creation. I think that you're more Santa today than I am. I'll be Santa's elf."

He stopped shaking his head as his eyes lit up with definite interest. "My elf, huh? I guess that means that you have to listen to me."

"I don't think so." She backed up but he followed her with a devilish look in his eyes. "Don't go getting any wild ideas."

He grabbed her by the sides and started tickling her. His fingers easily found her sensitive spots. She could barely breathe from all of the laughter. Though his magical fingers had stopped moving, he continued to hold her close. It felt so natural to be in his arms. Her arms draped over his shoulders as she leaned into him, trying to catch her breath.

His gaze met hers. "You know Santa left some packages over there under the tree for you."

She leaned her head to the side to see around his hulking form. "I can't believe I didn't see those before." She glanced back at him. "Are you sure they're for me?"

"I don't know. Were you a good girl this year?"

She nodded.

"Are you sure?"

She nodded again. "Can I open them now?"

"Not quite yet." When she stuck out her bottom lip, he added, "Surely you can wait until after dinner."

"But that's not what I'm pouting about. I only have one gift for you." She pulled away from him to move to the couch and reached in her beach bag. She removed a package all neatly wrapped in white tissue paper with a shiny red bow.

"You didn't have to get me anything."

"That's what makes it special. I wanted to. But I must warn you that it's nothing expensive or impressive."

"Anything you give me will be a thousand times more special than the most expensive wines or sports car."

"A sports car? So that's what you wanted Santa to bring you?"

He reached out for her hand and drew her to him, pulling her down on his lap. "Everything I want is here. You didn't have to get me a gift."

"I would have given it to you this morning at the gift exchange with your family, but I knew your family wouldn't understand the meaning behind it. And I didn't want to do anything that might be misconstrued by your father."

"That you don't have to worry about. Did you notice how well he's taken to you?"

"I know. What was up with that?"

"I told you that you had nothing to worry about by coming here. He really likes you—they all do. Most especially me."

By the glow of the firelight, they enjoyed soup and antipasto. Neither of them was that hungry after the large Christmas luncheon. This light fare was just perfect. And Alex was the perfect date as he kept her smiling and laughing with stories of adventures from his childhood.

"You were quite the daredevil back in the day," Reese surmised as she settled down on the rug and pillows in front of the fireplace. "Something tells me that the adventurous part of you is still lurking in there behind the prim and proper prince."

"You think so." He popped a bottle of Mirraccino's finest sparkling wine and the cork flew across the room. The contents bubbled over the top and he sucked up the overflow before it could make a mess.

"My point is proven." She laughed.

He poured them each a flute of the bubbly golden fluid and then held one out to her. She accepted it with a smile. This whole trip had been amazing and she had no doubt where the evening was headed.

"To the most beautiful woman I have ever known. May all of your wishes come true."

Their glasses clinked and before Reese even held the crystal stemware to her lips, a fluttery feeling filled her stomach. Her gaze met his hungry one. She took a sip of the sweet wine, but she barely noticed it as the cold liquid slid down her dry throat.

"You do know that we're all alone now?" He set aside his glass.

She set her wine next to his. Her gaze slipped down to his lips. They looked quite inviting. "Does this mean that I get my Christmas present now?"

His voice came out unusually deep and gravelly. "That depends on what present you want to unwrap first."

She leaned toward him. "I think I'll start right here."

In the next breath her lips were covering his. When his arms wrapped around her, pulling her close, she could no longer deny that she had fallen for her very own Prince Charming. She loved Alex with every fiber of her being.

His hands encompassed her waist, pulling her to him. She willingly leaned into him. The sudden shift of her weight sent them falling back against the stack of pillows. She met him kiss for kiss, touch for touch. The fire crackled as Alex nuzzled her neck, causing her to laugh. She couldn't remember ever feeling so alive—so in love.

CHAPTER SEVENTEEN

A KNOCK SOUNDED.

Alex woke with a start. He squinted as the bright morning sun peeked in through the windows, catching him in the eyes. He glanced over finding Reese still breathing evenly as she lay snuggled beneath the pile of blankets. His thoughts filled with visions of her being in his arms. It had been the most amazing night of his life.

One kiss had led to another. One touch had led to another. And at last they'd ended up curled in front of the fireplace. He recalled how Reese's face had lit up with happiness. The sparkle in her big brown eyes had been his undoing. Her joy had filled a spot in him that he hadn't even known was empty.

He turned away from her sleeping figure and ran a hand over his hair, trying to will away the fogginess of sleep. This wasn't supposed to have happened. He hadn't meant for them to get in so deeply. Not yet. He still had so much to set straight with his family. And yet he couldn't deny that he cared deeply for Reese.

Another knock had him jumping to his feet. The fire had died out hours ago and a distinct chill hung in the air. He rushed to throw on his discarded and now wrinkled clothes. He moved silently across the hardwood floor to the front door.

His personal assistant stood at the door. The older man's face was creased with lines, but nothing in his very proper demeanor gave way to his thoughts of finding Alex in an awkward moment.

"Good morning, Guido." Alex kept his voice low so as not to wake Reese, since they'd gotten very little sleep. "What can I do for you?"

"I'm sorry to interrupt, sir." He also kept his voice to a whisper. "There's an urgent matter you must deal with at the palace."

Alex's chest tightened. He didn't like the sound of that. Thoughts of his papa's health and his brother's latest fiasco raced through his mind. "What is it?"

"There's another problem with a shipment at the port. I don't know the details. Only that you are requested to come immediately. I have a car waiting for you."

"Thank you. I'll be along soon."

"Yes, sir."

Alex closed the door gently. One of the problems with being a small nation was that the government was much more hands-on. He didn't understand why all of a sudden they were having endless problems at the port. And it didn't help matters that the problems seemed to concern a fleet of cargo ships owned by Catherine's father, who had been less than pleased with the last problem, involving a falsified manifest and a very greedy captain.

Alex didn't even want to guess what the harbormaster had uncovered this time. Dread coursed through his body. Still, there was no way around it. The only thing he could hope was that it was another shipping company.

"Who was at the door?" Reese's sleepy voice was deeper than normal and very sexy.

If only Alex didn't have important matters to tend to, he'd spend a leisurely morning with her. But duty came first.

"It was a message from the palace that my attendance is needed."

Reese's eyes widened. "Is something wrong?"

"Nothing for you to worry about. Just a problem at the port." He slipped on his loafers and collected his things. "Take your time. There is food in the kitchen."

"But our presents. We didn't open them—"

"I'm sorry. There's no time now." He glanced at the fanciful packages beneath the tree. "It'll give us something to look forward to later."

"Unless we get distracted again." Her voice was still deep from sleep.

The sultry sound made him groan with frustration. "We'll get to them…eventually."

Her cheeks beamed a crimson hue, but that didn't stop her from teasing him. "I can't promise you that it'll be any time soon. I have plans for you."

"I'll hold you to your word." He leaned down and gave her a lingering kiss that made it almost painful to tear himself away from her. "I'll send the car back for you, but I have no idea how long I'll be."

How could someone be so unhappy when surrounded by such beauty?

Reese paced back and forth. It wasn't so much that she was unhappy…more like bored. Frustrated. Agitated. There was a whole dictionary full of words to describe her mood.

Sure, her palace suite was beautiful, from the high ceiling with its white, blue and gold polychrome tiles to the huge canopied bed. It was like sleeping in a very elegant museum—in fact, the entire palace was like something people only viewed in glossy magazines. It made her hesitant to touch anything for fear of breaking something.

She strolled over to the large window overlooking the sea. The sun was shining and the water was tranquil, unlike her mind, which could not rest. Her thoughts continually drifted back to Alex, as they had done so often since their very special evening together. Her cheeks warmed at the memory of how sweet and loving he'd been with her. It had been a perfect evening. So then why had Alex been gone the past twenty-four hours?

The only message she'd received from him had come the prior evening, when he'd extended his apologies for missing dinner, claiming he had work to do. The note only made her even more curious about his whereabouts. What was so important? And why couldn't he deliver the message in person?

Unable to spend another lonely moment in her opulent suite, she threw on some old comfy jeans and a pink hoodie with a navy-blue New York logo emblazed over it. The clothes certainly weren't anywhere close to the fancy ones she'd been wearing since she'd arrived in Mirraccino, but she didn't feel a need to put on a show today. Besides, where she was headed there wouldn't be any paparazzi. And if there were, she was in no mood to care.

She headed for the private beach, hoping to clear her head—to figure out where she and Alex went from here. The sun warmed her back and helped her to relax. As for Alex, things there were complicated. It wasn't like being in a relationship with the guy next door. But she couldn't just walk away, either. The other night had drastically changed things. She'd given her heart to him.

A smile tugged at her face as she thought of Alex and how far they'd come. When she'd met him, she hadn't wanted a man in her life. She'd been unhappy, even though she hadn't realized it at the time. She'd had her eyes closed to her mother's progress, but Alex had helped her see things that were right in front of her. She'd learned to trust him and that she didn't have to be in control of everything all of the time. In fact, her daily calls to her mother revealed that The Willows was prospering without Reese's presence.

Her steps were light. It was as if she were tiptoeing along the fluffy white clouds dotting the sky. She was humming a little ditty to herself as she strolled down the beach, and then she spotted Alex. He was dressed in blue slacks and a blue button-up shirt with the sleeves rolled up. The breeze off the sea rustled his dark hair, scattering the strands. She was just about to call out to him when she got close enough to notice someone at his side. A woman. She was much shorter, with long dark hair that shimmered in the sun. They leaned toward each other as they laughed about something.

A sick feeling settled in the pit of Reese's stomach. She took a step backward. So this was why he'd been too busy to see her?

No. Alex wouldn't do something like this to her. He'd promised that she could trust him. And she'd given him her heart.

She dragged in a deep breath, hoping to calm her rising heart rate. She was jumping to conclusions. After all, he wasn't her father. He'd never leave her bed to go to another woman. *Have faith. Alex will make this right.*

Reese leveled her shoulders and forced her feet to move in the direction of the man she loved. She refused to be childish and jealous. There was a simple explanation to this. One that would make her feel foolish for jumping to conclusions. Maybe she was his cousin. Or the woman his brother had married. That must be it. He was comforting the woman and passing along a message from his brother.

"Good morning." Reese forced a smile on her face.

They both turned to her. Alex's brows lifted and the woman's eyes lit up as her gaze moved from Alex to Reese and back again. The woman's painted lips lifted into a smile.

Reese's radar was going off loud and clear, but she insisted on giving Alex a chance. "Beautiful morning, isn't it?"

Alex nodded. "Um…yes, it is." The surprise on his face slid behind a blank wall. "Reese, I would like you to meet Catherine."

"It is good to meet you." The woman's voice was warm and friendly. "You are the one helping, no?"

Catherine's English was tough to understand behind a heavy accent. "Yes…yes, I am."

But there was so much more to their relationship. Why did the woman seem a bit confused? Alex had said he'd told Catherine about her. An uneasy feeling settled in her stomach. She'd once again let her naivety get her into trouble. She should have asked him exactly what he'd told the woman. Because it obviously wasn't that he loved Reese. That much was clear.

Catherine smiled and held out her hand. "I would like us to be friends, no?"

Reese didn't have much choice but to force a smile and extend her hand. The sunshine gleamed off the pink sapphire, reminding her of the heated kiss she'd shared with Alex when he'd given it to her. What would Catherine make of the ring?

She searched the woman's face for some hint of hostility or jealousy, but she didn't detect any. The woman truly appeared to be kind and outgoing. What was Reese missing? Had Alex duped them both?

Not understanding any of this, she turned a questioning look to Alex. But his gaze didn't meet hers. Except for the slight tic in his cheek, there was nothing in his outward appearance to let her know that he was uncomfortable with this meeting.

Oblivious to the undercurrents running between Alex and Reese, Catherine said, "You help Alex with paparazzi, no?" The woman's voice was soft and gentle. When Reese nodded, the woman continued to speak. "You are a good woman. He is lucky to have you."

What could she say to that? Though it killed her to exchange pleasantries when all she wanted to do was confront Alex, she uttered, "Thank you."

Alex cleared his throat. "Catherine and I were headed back inside. I have a meeting to attend. Would you care to join us?"

There was no warmth in his voice. No acknowledgement that they were anything more than casual acquaintances. Just the cool politeness of a politician.

"Yes, join us. I want to know about you and New York." Catherine's eyes reflected her sincerity.

With determined reserve, Reese maintained a cool outward appearance. "I think I'll stay out here. I'd like to stretch my legs. One can only be cooped up for so long."

Reese turned to Alex and bit back an impolite comment. There was no way she could be rude to Alex in front of this woman. As much as she wanted to dislike Catherine, she couldn't; she appeared to be a genuinely nice person. In another universe, Reese could imagine being fast friends with Catherine. But not here—not today.

Reese could only presume that the woman didn't know what had transpired between her and Alex the other night. And there was no way she would be the one to tell her. That was Alex's problem.

What she had to say to him—and there was a lot—would have to wait. She didn't need this woman knowing what a fool she'd made of herself, falling for a prince far outside her league.

A look of relief crossed Alex's face. "Then we'll leave you to enjoy the day."

He extended his arm to Catherine, who turned to Reese. "Nice to meet you. We talk later."

"Nice to meet you, too." Reese couldn't believe how hard it was to say those words without choking on her own tongue.

She stood there watching the departing couple. Catherine's head momentarily leaned against Alex's arm, as though she knew him well—very well. The thought slashed into Reese's heart. She was the odd man out.

It wasn't until they turned the corner and headed up the steps toward the palace that Reese realized she'd been holding her breath. She was afraid to breathe out—afraid the balled-up emotions inside her would come tumbling out. She blinked repeatedly, clearing her blurring vision. She wanted to believe that this was some sort of nightmare and she'd wake up soon. Because it just couldn't be possible that she'd been duped into being the other woman.

Her stomach lurched. Her hands wrapped around her midsection as she willed away the waves of nausea. After all of the days and nights of wondering how her father's lover could have carried on an affair—now Reese was in those very uncomfortable shoes. And she hated it.

She started walking down the beach with no destination in mind. Her only thought was to get away. Her steps came faster. Throughout the whole drama with her father's death and finding out that he'd siphoned off their savings, she'd had a hard time believing her mother hadn't known anything about it. How could she not?

Looking back on it, there had been so many clues—so many things that didn't add up. She'd ended up harboring angry feelings toward her mother for allowing all of that to happen to them by turning a blind eye to her father's activities. But now Reese had more compassion for the situation her mother had been in. When you love someone, you trust them.

Reese stopped walking, drawing one quick breath after the other. She glanced around, realizing she'd ended up back at the bungalow. She hadn't realized she'd wandered so far down the beach.

Her legs were tired and her face was warm from the sun, but it was the aching loss in her chest that had the backs of her eyes stinging. She refused to dissolve into a puddle of tears. She wouldn't stop living just because she'd once again let herself be duped by a man. The memory of Alex and Catherine arm in arm and with their heads together, laughing, was emblazoned on her memory. How could she have trusted him?

With renewed anger, she started off for the palace. This fairy tale had come to an end. And like Cinderella, it was time to trade in her gowns for a vacuum and a day planner.

She'd reached the bottom of the steps up the cliff when she spotted Alex sitting there. He didn't notice her at first and she paused, not sure she was up for this confrontation. Still, it was best to meet it head-on and get it over with. She didn't want any lingering *what if*s or *should have*s. This would end things cleanly.

Leveling her shoulders, she headed straight for him. When he saw her, he got to his feet and met her halfway. Lines bracketed his eyes and his face looked as though he'd aged a few years. Was he that worried that she'd blow things for him with Catherine? She took a bit of satisfaction in knowing that he was stressed. It was the least he could feel after he'd used her without any thought to her feelings.

"Reese, you had me worried. You didn't tell anyone where you were going."

She crossed her arms and narrowed her gaze on him. "I'm sure you were too busy to be worried about me."

"That's not fair. You know I care."

"Was Catherine the reason you took off after we spent the night together?" *Right after I'd given you my heart. When I'd at last trusted you.*

"No. I told you there was a problem at the port."

Reese crossed her arms and hitched up a hip. "So what's she doing here?"

"She knew I wanted to speak with her, and since a problem had arisen with one of the ships her father owns, she flew in. I knew nothing of her arrival until last evening."

Reese wasn't about to assume anything this time around. "Does Catherine know how you spent the other night?"

V-shaped lines etched between his brows. "Of course she doesn't know. What kind of man do you think I am? I don't go around discussing personal things."

"The kind who likes to keep a woman on the side like a spare suit or an extra pair of shoes." Her voice quavered with anger. "Is that what I am to you?"

"No, of course not." His blue eyes pleaded with her to believe him, but she was too worked up to be swayed so easily. "But you don't understand. I can't just blurt out to Catherine that I have feelings for you."

"Why?"

He glanced down and rubbed the back of his neck. "Because I won't hurt her like that. She deserves better."

Reese heard the words he hadn't spoken, louder and clearer than anything else. He cared about Catherine. Those powerful words blindsided Reese. They knocked into her full force, stealing the breath from her lungs. She stumbled back.

He had real feelings for Catherine.

Reese's teeth sank into her lower lip, holding in a backlash of anger and a truckload of pain. How stupid could she have been? Catherine oozed money and culture. The woman was a perfect match for a prince. Reese glanced down at her faded jeans and worn sweatshirt. She'd laugh at the comparison, but she was afraid that it'd come out in sobs. She swallowed down her emotions.

"We don't have anything left to say to each other. You should go to her—to your future fiancée."

"You're spinning this out of control. Catherine has nothing to do with you and me."

"Yes, she does. She has everything to do with this. You care about her."

Not me!

A sob caught in the back of her throat. A piercing pain struck her heart, causing a burning sensation at the backs of her eyes. She loved him, but he didn't feel the same way. She clenched her hands, fighting to keep her pain bottled up. She refused to let him see just how deeply he'd hurt her.

"Let me explain. We can work this out—"

"No, we can't." Her nails dug into her palms as she struggled to maintain her composure. "Do you know how much this hurts? It's killing me to stand here. To be so close to you and yet so far away."

He lifted his head and stared up at the blue sky for a moment, as though coming up with a rebuttal. "You don't understand. I do care about her. But I don't love her."

Reese heard the sincerity in his voice and saw the pleading look in his eyes. Maybe he hadn't set out to make her the other woman, but that didn't change the fact that three was a crowd. And she wasn't going to stick around to make a further fool of herself.

"I'm leaving."

Alex reached out, grabbing her arm. "Don't leave like this."

She spun around so fast his eyes widened in surprise. "Why not? What reason do I have to stay?" Her throat burned as the raw words came tumbling out. "Did you end things with Catherine? Did you tell your family the marriage is off?"

He held her gaze. "It's not that easy. Her father is very influential. If he pulls his business from Mirraccino, it'll have a devastating ripple effect on the country's economy. But you must know that I have never made any promises to her. It's all a business arrangement—my duty."

"You're forgetting I saw you two together. You aren't strangers."

"You're right. Catherine and I have been friends since we were kids. But I swear it has never gone further than that—"

"Stop." She wasn't going to let his smooth tongue and convincing words confuse her. "The fact is you can't have us both. It's time you choose between your duty and your desires."

She stood there pleading with her eyes for him to choose her—to choose love. But as the strained silence stretched on, her hopes were dashed. She had no choice but to accept that his duty to the crown would always come first. She might have fallen in love with him, but obviously it was a one-way street.

A tear dripped onto her cheek and she quickly dashed it away. "I—I have some packing to do."

She pulled her shoulders back and moved past him with determined steps. It was time to make a hasty exit before she dissolved into a disgusting puddle of self-pity. And she couldn't let that happen. Her heart was already in tattered ruins. The only thing she had left was her pride.

Alex jogged over to stand in front of her. "Give me time to sort things out."

"You can have all of the time in the world. I'm leaving." Then as an afterthought, she slipped off the pink sapphire and tossed it at him. "And I won't be needing this any longer."

She turned and strode up the beach...alone.

CHAPTER EIGHTEEN

ALEX PLACED THE STORYBOOK Reese had given him for
Christmas next to his suitcase.

He probably shouldn't have opened it without her. But
after she'd left he'd been so lonely without her that he
needed a tangible connection.

He stared down at the hardback copy of *How the Grinch
Stole Christmas*. Was she sending him a message? Did she
really think his heart was three sizes too small? Probably.
And he couldn't blame her for thinking so. He'd made a
total mess of things.

Since the day she'd left him standing on the beach,
he'd barely slept. He couldn't wipe the devastated look on
her face from his mind. For all of his trying to stay aloof
and objective, he'd fallen head over heels in love with her.

It wasn't until he'd tried explaining his relationship with
Catherine and his family's expectations for him to Reese
that he realized he'd spent his entire life being the perfect
prince and honor bound to the crown. And he just couldn't
do it any longer—not at the expense of his love for the
one woman who made him want more than his position
within the monarchy, the woman who made him believe
that without love, he had nothing.

Now the time had come for him to make his needs a
priority, even if they didn't coincide with the family's view

of an acceptable life for a prince. At last, he fully understood what his brother had gone through with his brief marriage. And from the look of Demetrius, he really did love that woman. Now Alex wondered if his brother would ever have a chance at true happiness.

However, Alex wasn't the crown prince. He wasn't held to such high standards. He'd made his decision and now he didn't have time to waste. After a few phone calls to make the necessary arrangements, Alex went to meet with the king.

Papa was having breakfast with his brother and Catherine. Alex came to a stop at the end of the formal dining table, more certain than ever that he was doing the right thing.

"You're late." The king pointed at a chair. "Join us."

"I don't have time. I have something urgent I must do."

"I would think Catherine's presence would be your priority."

Alex glanced at Catherine. He'd spoken to her last night and explained how he had planned to do his duty, no matter what was asked of him, but somewhere along the way, he'd lost his heart to a beautiful firecracker from New York. And he just couldn't pass up his one chance to be truly happy. Catherine was happy for him. She had a secret of her own. She was in love with someone, too, but she had been reluctant to do anything about it. Now both Catherine and he could be happy.

She nodded at him, as though giving him encouragement to keep going. He hoped someday he, Reese and Catherine could all be friends. But he had to win back Reese's heart first.

"Catherine and I have spoken and we're not getting engaged. Not now. Not ever."

The king's gaze narrowed. "Alexandro, we've discussed

this and it has been decided that you'll marry Catherine. And it's high time that you do it."

Alex shook his head. "From now on, I'll be making my own decisions about who I marry." He made direct eye contact with the king. "I'll not let you bully me into giving up the woman that I love like you did with Demetrius."

The king's fork clattered against the plate. "I did no such thing. Your brother and that woman decided to part ways of their own accord."

Alex didn't believe it. Demetrius was too distraught to have dumped his wife. But when Alex turned to his twin, his brother nodded his head.

"It's true. Papa didn't split us up."

The king sat back and crossed his arms. Alex wasn't about to give up. This was far too important—Reese was far too important.

Alex continued to stand at attention the way he used to do when he was young and in a world of trouble. "You should also know that I'm not going to drop everything in my life to cover for the latest scandal to strike the family. I have my own life to lead. And my priority is seeking the forgiveness of the woman I love. I've put my duty ahead of her since the day I met her. Now it's time that she comes first."

His brother's mouth gaped. Too bad he hadn't been able to make such a bold move. But the crown prince didn't have as many options.

Everyone grew quiet, waiting for the king's reaction. What would he say? Alex didn't honestly know. The breath caught in his throat as he waited, hoping the king wouldn't disown him.

His papa made direct eye contact with him. "I've done a lot of thinking these past few weeks. Though there are legitimate reasons for a strategic marriage, perhaps there's another way to strike up the necessary allegiances. Who am I to deny my sons a chance to know love like your mother and I shared?"

Alex had to be certain he'd heard the king correctly. "You approve of Reese."

The king's silver head nodded. "When you are in New York, make sure you invite your new princess to the palace for the winter ball. It will be the perfect place to properly introduce her to everyone."

Alex truly liked the idea of escorting Reese to the ball. He just hoped she would find it in her heart to forgive him. "I'll most definitely invite her."

Alex didn't spare any time making his way to the private airstrip. With the king's blessing, he knew that he could now have his family and the woman he loved—if she would forgive him.

CHAPTER NINETEEN

THIS HAS TO WORK.

Alex stared blindly out the car window. Large, fluffy snowflakes fell, limiting visibility. Aside from the snow, his return to New York City was so different than his last visit. This time he was surrounded by his security detail and instead of a wild taxi ride he was settled in the comfortable backseat of a black town car with diplomatic tags. There was no looking over his shoulder. This time it didn't matter who knew he was in town.

His only goal for being here was to win back Reese's trust—her love.

The car tires crunched over the snow. He glanced out the window at the passing houses. They were getting close. His gut tightened. Normally when he had an important speech, he'd make notes and settle most of what he'd say ahead of time. This time, he didn't know what he'd say. He didn't even know if he'd get past the front door.

The car tires spun a bit as the car eased into the driveway. Alex pulled on his leather gloves. Before the car pulled to a full stop, Alex had the back door open. He took the porch steps two at a time.

His foot had just touched the porch when the door swung open. It was Reese. Her long hair was swept back in a smooth ponytail. Her bangs fell smoothly over her forehead.

Her eyes widened as she took in his appearance. "What are you doing here?"

He might have been prepared for the winter weather, but he wasn't prepared for the hard edge in her voice.

"Hello, Reese. You forgot your Christmas presents."

Her eyes grew round. "You flew all the way here to give me some presents?"

"And I thought we should talk—"

"No. Take your presents and go away. We said everything that needed to be said." She waved him away. When he didn't move, she added, "We were a publicity stunt. Nothing more. Now go home to Catherine."

He refused to be deterred. One way or another, she'd hear him out. "I am here on a matter of great importance."

"That's too bad. I'm on my way out. I don't have time to talk."

"Then let me give you a ride." He moved aside so she could see his hired car. Other women he'd met would swoon at this opportunity. But Reese wasn't other women. She wouldn't be easily swayed. But she was most definitely worth the effort.

When he sensed she was about to turn him down, he added, "Either let me take you or expect to see me waiting here when you return."

"You wouldn't."

He arched a brow. There was hardly a thing he wouldn't do to win her back.

She sighed and rolled her eyes. "Fine. If this is what it takes to get rid of you, let's get it over with."

Her pointed words stabbed at his chest. He knew he'd hurt her, but he'd been hoping with time that she would have become more reasonable—more understanding. So much for that wishful thinking. He would have to do a lot of pleading if he was ever going to get her to forgive him.

And he wasn't well versed in apologies. Good thing he was a quick learner.

He waved away the driver, getting the door for her himself. Reese was one of the strongest people he knew. She'd held together her family after her father's betrayal. Not everyone could do that. Now he had to hope that she had enough compassion in her heart for him—to realize that he'd learned from his mistakes.

Reese gave the driver a Manhattan address before turning to Alex. "I hope you really do have something important on your mind. Otherwise you're wasting both our time."

"Trust me. This is very important." She arched a disbelieving brow at him, but he didn't let that deter him. "Do you mind me asking where we're headed?"

"An art school. I've enrolled and this is the first class of the semester. I'm working on my graphic art."

"But what about The Willows? How do you have time to do everything?"

She leaned her head back against the black leather upholstery and stared up at the ceiling. "When I got back from Mirraccino, I found that you were right." Her face contorted into a frown as she made the admission. "I'd been hovering over my mother too much. While I was gone, she handled this place. She regained her footing."

"That's great news. And now you can follow your dreams."

Reese nodded. "It seems my mother and Mr.—erm, Howard are officially dating, too."

"And how does that make you feel?"

She shrugged. "Happy, I guess. After all, it isn't like she owed anything to the memory of my father. So if Howard makes her happy, I'm good with that. Now what brings you here?"

He removed an official invitation with the royal seal from the inner pocket of his black wool coat. He held it out to her. When their fingers brushed, a jolt rushed up his arm and settled in his chest. She quickly pulled back.

He cleared his throat. "Before you open that, I have a few things to say."

She glanced out the window into the snowy afternoon. "Make it quick. We're almost there."

"Reese, I want you to know how sorry I am for not being more up front about my situation with Catherine. I had mentioned you to her on the phone, but I didn't bring up that we were intimately involved. I wasn't sure of Catherine's feelings and didn't want to announce that I wasn't going through with the engagement over the phone."

Reese nailed him with an astonished stare. "So it was better to keep your fiancée in the dark?"

"She was never my fiancée. Not like you're thinking. I never proposed to her. I never loved her. We are friends. Nothing more. In fact, when I told her that you and I were involved, she told me that she was happy to be released from the arrangement because she had fallen in love with someone."

Reese's brows rose. "You're serious."

"Yes. Catherine was as relieved as I was to call off the marriage."

"I bet your family didn't take it well."

"The king respected my decision."

Reese twisted around to look at him face-to-face. "You're really serious? You stood up and told everyone about us?"

"Yes, I did. I realized that I'd let my sense of duty take over my life. I told them that I wouldn't be on call twenty-four-seven to cover up any scandals. You had to come first."

Her eyes opened wide. "You really said that?"

He nodded, reaching out to take her hands in his. "Please believe me. I know I messed up in the past, but I won't let that happen again. No more secrets."

His gaze probed hers, looking for some sign that he was getting through to her. But in a blink her surprise slid behind a solid wall of indifference. Was he wrong about her? Didn't she feel the same as him?

Before he could think of something else to say to convince her to give him another chance, the car pulled to a stop in front of a building.

She grabbed her backpack from the seat. "This is where I get out."

"Can I wait for you? We can talk some more. I know we can work this out."

"No. You've said what you've come here to say. Now please go."

She got out of the car and closed the door with a resounding thud. His chest ached as he watched her walk away. He raked his fingers through his hair and pulled on the short strands as he fought off the urge to go after her.

What had she just done?

Panic clutched Reese's chest. She rushed over to the building, heedless of the coating of snow on the sidewalk. She yanked open the door of the arts building and hustled inside with no real destination in mind. It wasn't until she was away from the wall of windows and out of sight of the car that she stopped and leaned against the wall. It was then that she let out a pent-up breath.

Had she lost her mind?

Had she really just turned down an honest-to-goodness prince?

But it wasn't a royal prince that she loved. It was plain Alex—a living, breathing, imperfect human—the same person who'd hurt her. Alex just happened to come with an impressive title and hung his coat in an amazing palace. But those physical things weren't enough to sway her decision.

The backs of her eyes stung and she blinked, refusing to give in to tears. He'd said all of the right things. Why couldn't she let down her guard? Why couldn't she give him another chance?

She glanced at the large metal clock on the far wall. She had five minutes until her class started. She'd been hoping that going back to school would fill the empty spot in her life—help her forget—but nothing could wipe away the memories of Alex.

Part of her wanted to run back out the door and into his arms. The other part of her said it just wasn't right. Something was missing.

She glanced down at the envelope he'd handed her in the car. Her name was scrolled over the front of the heavy parchment. The royal seal of Mirraccino was stamped onto the back. Curiosity poked at her.

Her finger slipped into the opening in the flap and she ripped along the fold. Inside was an invitation that read:

King Ferdinando of Mirraccino formally invites you to the Royal Winter Ball. The grand fete will take place at the royal palace on Saturday, the seventh of March at six o'clock. The honor of your presence is requested.

Reese stared at the invitation for a moment, stunned that she was holding an invitation to a royal ball. A deep, weary sigh passed her lips. When she went to put the invitation in her purse, it slipped from her fingers and fluttered to the floor.

She bent over to snatch it up when she noticed some handwriting on the back of the invite. She pulled it closer.

Reese, I love you with every fiber of my being. Please be my princess at the ball.
Alex

He loved her!

Those were the words she'd been waiting to hear.

Her lips lifted and her heart pounded. In that moment, the pieces all fell into place. She loved him and he loved her.

In the next breath, the smile slipped from her lips. She'd sent him away. Was it too late? Was he gone for good?

She took off running for the door. He had to be there. He couldn't have left yet.

Please let him still be here.

Practically knocking over a couple of young guys coming through the door, she yelled an apology over her shoulder and kept moving. She stepped onto the sidewalk and stopped.

The black town car was gone. For the first time ever, Alex had finally done as she'd asked. Why now? Tears pricked her eyes.

And then she saw it. The black town car. That had to be the one. It was approaching the end of the block and had on its turn signal.

She had to stop him. Not worrying about the ice or snow, she set off running after the car. She couldn't give up. She was so close to having the man she loved.

The car came to a stop at the intersection. She called out to Alex, not that he would hear her. Then the brake lights went out and the car surged forward. Reese's chest burned as she called out one last time to him.

Then the bright brake lights flashed on and Alex emerged from the back. He sent her a questioning look before he set off toward her with open arms. She rushed toward him with the intention of never leaving his embrace.

After he held her for a moment, he took a step back so they could make eye contact. "I don't understand. What changed your mind?"

"You did."

"But how? When you got out of the car, you were so certain."

She held up the invitation. "What you wrote here said everything I needed to know."

His eyes closed as he sighed. "I was so worried about apologizing that I totally forgot to tell you the most important part. Reese, since I've known you my heart has grown three sizes because it's so full of love for you. I promise I'll tell you every day for the rest of our lives."

She smiled up at him. "Why don't you start now?"

"I love you."

"I love you, too."

EPILOGUE

Two months later...

PRINCE ALEXANDRO CASTANAVO stared across the hallway at Reese. He'd never seen anyone so beautiful. She stole his breath away. And the best part was she was beautiful inside and out. After they'd spent the past couple of weeks at the palace, no one in Mirraccino could deny that Reese would make a generous and kind princess.

Tonight's ball was for the residents of Mirraccino. With it being between growing seasons, this was the nation's chance to celebrate the past year and the royal family's chance to mingle with the citizens—to bring the island together.

And it was Alex's chance to introduce them to the queen of his heart. They were going to love her as much as he did—well, maybe not that much, but pretty close.

He approached and offered his arm to her. She smiled up at him and his heart thumped. How had he ended up being the luckiest man alive?

"May I escort you into the ballroom?"

Reese grabbed the skirt of her royal-blue-and-silver gown and curtsied. Her eyes sparkled with mischief.

"Why yes, Your Highness."

"You know, I like the sound of that." He couldn't help but

tease her back and he put on a serious expression. "Perhaps I'll have you address me as Your Highness all the time."

Reese's mouth gaped. "You wouldn't."

He smiled. "I'm teasing you. I love you the way you are, strong and feisty. I'd never try to change that about you."

Before he could say more, they were summoned inside the ballroom to be announced.

"His Royal Highness, Prince Alexandro Castanavo, and Her Ladyship, Miss Reese Harding."

Before they could be ushered into the crowd, Alex held up his hand, pausing the procession. "If you all will allow me a moment, I have something very special to share."

A hush fell over the crowded room. He fished a black velvet box from his pocket. He was surprised the box had any material left after he'd looked inside at least a couple hundred times trying to decide if it was the right ring for Reese. In the end, he couldn't imagine her with any other ring.

He dropped to one knee and heard Reese's swift intake of breath. He lifted his head and smiled at her, hoping to reassure her. Still, she sent him a wide-eyed gaze.

He took her now trembling hand in his and he realized that perhaps his idea to share this very special moment with everyone he cared about had been a miscalculation. But he was on bended knee now and the room was so quiet that he could hear the beating of his own heart.

"Reese, would you do me the honor of being my princess today and for all of the days of my life?"

Her eyes sparkled with tears of joy as she vigorously nodded. "Yes, I will."

He stood tall and removed the ring from the box. His hands weren't too steady as he slipped the five-carat pink sapphire surrounded by sixty-four diamond side stones onto her finger.

"You kept it." She held up her hand to look at it.

"I thought the ring had a special meaning for us. You aren't disappointed, are you?"

She held up her hand to admire the engagement ring. "I love it!" Her warm gaze moved to him. "But not as much as I love you."

* * * * *

Vanessa's Bucket List

1. Learn to ride a horse
2. ~~Go to Disney World~~
3. ~~Visit Australia~~
4. ~~Learn to scuba dive~~
5. ~~Kiss a cowboy~~ Kiss Jonah Dalton!
6. Go skinny-dipping!
7. Dance in the rain
8. See an active volcano
9. Fall in love…forever…

* * *

Montana Mavericks:
20 Years in the Saddle!

THE LAST-CHANCE MAVERICK

BY
CHRISTYNE BUTLER

MILLS & BOON

Published in Great Britain 2014
by Mills & Boon, an imprint of Harlequin (UK) Limited,
Eton House, 18-24 Paradise Road, Richmond, Surrey, TW9 1SR

© 2014 Harlequin Books S.A.

Special thanks and acknowledgement are given to Christyne Butler for her contribution to the MONTANA MAVERICKS: 20 YEARS IN THE SADDLE! continuity.

ISBN: 978-0-263-91323-1

23-1014

Harlequin (UK) Limited's policy is to use papers that are natural, renewable and recyclable products and made from wood grown in sustainable forests. The logging and manufacturing processes conform to the legal environmental regulations of the country of origin.

Printed and bound in Spain
by Blackprint CPI, Barcelona

Christyne Butler fell in love with romance novels while serving in the United States Navy and started writing her own stories six years ago. She considers selling to Mills & Boon® Cherish™ a dream come true and enjoys writing contemporary romances full of life, love, a hint of laughter and perhaps a dash of danger, too. And there has to be a happily-ever- after or she's just not satisfied.

She lives with her family in central Massachusetts and loves to hear from her readers at chris@christynebutler. com. Or visit her website, www.christynebutler.com.

Prologue

Carrollton Cancer Center, Philadelphia, PA
Eleven months ago

"Okay, read it to me…" Adele's voice faded for a moment as she struggled to speak against the plastic mask covering her nose and mouth that supplied her with fresh oxygen. "…again. We need to finish our list."

Vanessa Brent swallowed hard against the lump in her throat that refused to go away. Every time she walked into this room—as plush and beautiful and unlike a hospital room as a sun-filled space could be—she had the same physical reaction and it stayed with her until she'd left again.

One would think after three months of being here on a daily basis she'd be used to the sight of her best friend fighting a battle they'd recently accepted she wasn't going to win. That she'd be able to sit here, hold Adele's hand and do as she asked.

"All of it?" Glad her words managed to find their way around the obstacle in her throat, Vanessa glanced at the aged piece of paper she held in her hand. Titled "Adele and Vanessa's Bucket List, created July 4, 2001, Secret Clubhouse, Vanessa's Attic, Chestnut Hill, PA," the well-creased, lined sheet of notebook paper was covered with two distinct styles of handwriting, one belonging to her twelve-year-old self and the other a more mature scrawl. "Or just the things we've added?"

They'd discovered the childhood list one day while going through some forgotten boxes in Vanessa's loft apartment. Back when they'd thought Adele had once again beaten the childhood cancer that returned at the tender age of twenty-five, but then went into remission after treatment.

That had been just before Easter. By early June Adele was back in the hospital, but during those few precious weeks they'd managed to check off some of the items on their list.

"Start at the beginning." Adele turned to look at her, the bright red silk scarf protecting her sensitive scalp brushing against the pillow. "Let's review…what we've done…so far."

Taking a deep breath, she started reading. "Number one—dance beneath the Eiffel Tower. I did that back in college the year I studied abroad," Vanessa said, thankful she had a photograph to honor the event as she technically didn't remember doing so thanks to generous amounts of wine that night. "Number two—swim in the Pacific Ocean. You did that when you were in college."

Adele smiled, but remained silent.

"Number three—get a tattoo." Letting go, she flipped her hand and laid it side by side next her friend's, their matching interlocking heart tattoos visible on their inner wrists. "Number four—see a Broadway show. By ourselves."

They'd done both on a last-minute road trip to New York City that Adele had insisted on in May not long after they'd found their long forgotten list.

"Shouldn't have taken us…until age twenty-five to accomplish—" her friend rasped "—either of those."

"Considering how unhappy your mother was with us for taking off without telling her, not to mention our permanent souvenirs, we're lucky she didn't ground us when we got home like she used to do when we were kids."

"I think my mom was more worried because of me being in remission. Your father never said a word."

Vanessa wasn't even sure her father had even realized she'd left the city, much less inked her body. "Okay, let's see. We did go to Disney World on our senior class trip so that counted for number five. I was lucky enough to visit the White House and shake hands with the president during an art exhibit a few years back. Number six. I attempted to learn to scuba dive while visiting Australia the summer before my mother—well, before she got sick, so that covers numbers seven and eight."

"That's right. So you swam in the Pacific Ocean, too."

"Well, technically, it was the Tasman Sea. It doesn't count. So, other than the first eight, we haven't managed to accomplish the rest of the 2001 list." While Vanessa was sure that flying among the clouds (and not in an airplane!) was a childish wish that would never come true, she guessed moving out west, learning to ride a horse and the last goal, kissing a cowboy, were still possible. At least for her.

She swallowed hard again, but the unfairness of it all kept the lump firmly in place. "You know, judging from the last few items, I think we watched too many old Westerns back when we were twelve."

"I always liked John Wayne. The strong, silent type," Adele said. "So how many…do we have so far now? With the new ones included?"

"The original twelve and the eight we added while in New York." Vanessa read through the rest of the list. When her friend had insisted on updating it with new goals that weekend, they'd truly believed both of them would have time to accomplish things like going skinny-dipping, being part of a flash mob or dancing in the rain. Knowing now that her friend was never going to be able to accomplish any of them… "I think twenty is a good number."

"No. Need four more. Twelve old and twelve new."

"Well, number twenty is to see an active volcano. I don't know how we're—" Vanessa's voice caught again, but she pushed on. "How we're going to top that."

"Number twenty-one—take a bubble bath…with a man."

She couldn't help but smile at her friend's words as she propped her sketchbook on the edge of Adele's bed, using it as a base to write on. "How do you know I haven't done that already?"

"Because you would've told me. Best friends tell each other everything."

Vanessa nodded. "You're right. And I think that might top the volcano experience."

"Number twenty-two—kiss…Prince Charming and number twenty-three…" Adele's voice fell to a whisper, barely heard over the steady beeping from the row of machines on the far side of her bed. "…have a baby. Or two. Or three."

Vanessa blinked rapidly against the sting of tears, struggling to see clearly enough to add them to the list. Adele's words brought back the memory of how each of them, being only children, had always wished for younger siblings. That shared secret, revealed on the day they first met when Adele's mother had come to work for Vanessa's as a social secretary, had sealed their lifelong friendship. She still remembered the afternoon she'd returned from a ballet lesson and found a scrawny girl, her flaming red hair in braids and wearing a hand-me-down dress with dirt on her knees, sitting on the silk tufted bench in the grand foyer of Vanessa's home reading *Little Women*.

"And number twenty-four…fall in love forever."

Vanessa's fingers tightened on the pen until she was sure it would break. She tried to write the last goal, but the page was too blurry.

Then Adele's fingers brushed against the back of her hand. She latched onto her friend's cool touch and pressed Adele's hand to her heated cheek. "That's… that's quite a list."

"It's not a list. It's a life. Your life." Adele's voice became strong and clear, more than it has been in days. "It's time for you to get back to it."

"Adele—"

"You've been with me constantly over the last year. I'm surprised you've found time to get any painting done, not that I want you to jump back into your crazy work schedule." She paused for another breath. "And I know it's you I have to thank for being as comfortable with this outrageously expensive hospital room. My mom and I are so grateful—"

"Oh, shut up," Vanessa admonished her friend gently, her gaze still on the blurred list. "You know I would pay anything—*do anything*—to have you well again."

Adele jiggled on Vanessa's hand, signaling she wanted her attention. Vanessa brushed away the tears before looking at her friend who'd tugged the plastic mask from her face.

"What's that saying? We only have one shot at life, but if we do it right once is enough? You know better than most—especially now—how quickly life can be taken away," Adele said, her voice low and strained. "Don't get so lost in your art after I'm gone that you forget about all the wonderful things waiting out there for you."

"I still have three pieces to finish," Vanessa said, the familiar argument returning once again. One that had started years ago between them when she'd spent her thirteenth birthday working on a painting instead of attending a school dance. "You know how I get before a show. This is an important one, too. People are coming from Europe, the Far East—"

"You've been painting since you were a kid," Adele cut her off. "You were a star in the art world at seventeen and we both know that's because you buried yourself in your art after your mom died. Please don't do that again. Thanks to your gift and your trust fund, you're set for...life. It's time to live it."

"You make me sound like a nun or something."

"You're not too far off. What happened to that fun-loving girl you were a few years ago?"

Vanessa's memory flashed back to her time in Paris. "That was college, Adele. Being foolish and wild was part of the curriculum back then. Now, it's about my work."

"There's more to life…than work. Than art."

Vanessa had heard all of this before. Adele had always been supportive of her career, especially during the darkest moment in her life after her mother died when Vanessa was only sixteen, but she also constantly reminded her there was more to the world than her beloved brushes and paints.

"Art *is* my life, Adele. It's what got me through the pain and the heartache last time." She pulled in a deep breath, but her eyes filled again. "I'm counting on it to help me again…. Oh, how am I going to…"

Adele tightened her hold. "Please, don't be sad…for too long. We've talked about this. That's why I insisted we finish our list. I want you to go out there and experience all the things we've dreamed about. I want you to put check marks by every single one of those items."

The fact that her friend was spending her last days thinking of her made the constant ache inside Vanessa fracture a bit more, sending icy tentacles deeper and further, their frozen tips scraping at her heart. The feeling was a familiar one, felt for the first time since almost a decade ago.

The time from her mother's diagnosis to her death had been less than eight months, barely any time for them—her or her parents—to come to terms with the illness that would take her life. While her father had thrown himself into his work after the funeral, Vanessa had done the same, her art allowing her a way to express her pain and grief.

Back then she'd poured all her fears onto the canvas in the back of her mind, she too worried that she might die young. Though genetic testing reassured her she was unlikely to develop the same disease, and her time in her studio produced magnificent pieces of abstract art that made her famous, for years, Vanessa had been unable to shake the feeling that something bad was about to happen to her.

She'd never dreamed it would be the loss of her best friend.

It was Adele who'd helped her pick out a prom dress, who came to visit her at art school, who got her to laugh again when the someone she'd thought was her true love had broken her heart. Even more than her father, Adele and her mother, Susan, had become Vanessa's lifeline. They'd been there for every birthday, every holiday and now...

"Come on...promise me."

Adele started to cough and quickly shoved the oxygen mask back into place. Vanessa shot to her feet and bracing herself on the bed, gently laid her hand over her friend's, making sure the device was working properly. "Hey, take it easy."

Adele held up her hand, fingers curled in a fist except for the last, her pinky finger extended into a hook. She looked up, her deep green eyes locking with Vanessa's. "A solemn vow between best friends."

Vanessa saw a lifetime bond that went beyond friendship in her friend's gaze. Adele was the sister she'd never had. They knew each other's secrets, fears and dreams. They'd shared late night whispers, dried each other's tears and laughed together more times than she could count. "You make it sound like this is my last chance to have a life."

"No, but maybe it's a second chance. How many do you think we get? Just promise you'll work hard to be happy...to fulfill our list."

Vanessa wrapped her pinky finger around her friend's and dropped her forehead to rest against Adele's as both squeezed tight and held on. "I promise."

Chapter One

Present Day
Rust Creek Falls, Montana

Vanessa wasn't sure she'd heard Nate Crawford correctly.

A rushing noise that reminded her of the crazy bumper-to-bumper traffic on Philadelphia's Schuylkill Expressway filled her ears, except it was the beautiful mountain scenery around her that went a bit hazy as she choked down a mouthful of hot tea. Blinking hard, she focused on the disposable cup in her hand, noticing for the first time she'd grabbed two different flavored tea bags which explained the chocolatey-orange taste burning her tongue.

Even though she'd *remembered* arriving early enough for this morning's meeting to grab some refreshment at the canteen here on the job site—not to mention watching the breathtaking Montana sunrise through the two-story, floor-to-ceiling windows that filled the back wall—maybe it had all been a figment of her imagination.

Maybe she was still tucked beneath her goose-down comforter in that amazingly oversize Davy Crockett–style bed in her cabin, dreaming...

"Are you all right?" Nate asked, getting her attention. She looked up in time to see him rock back on his heels, a slight frown on his handsome face. He then glanced at his fiancée, Callie Kennedy, a nurse who helped run the local clinic, who'd placed a hand on his arm.

"Yes," she gasped, "yes, I'm fine."

No, that was a lie. Vanessa was definitely *not* fine despite the fact she stood in the cavernous lobby and main entertaining space of a log mansion that Nate, a local businessman and member of one of the town's founding families, was converting into a year-round resort.

The gorgeous view of the Montana wilderness was at her back while a stone fireplace big enough to stand in filled the opposite wall. And then there were the rest of the walls. All empty. Her gaze honed in on one of them—freshly painted if the scent tickling her nose meant anything, above the oversize, hand-hewed, carved desk where guests would check in once the resort officially opened.

"You want to hire me—" Vanessa asked, knowing she had to hear the words again. "—to do what?"

"Paint a mural," Nate repeated, gesturing at the large blank space. "I thought it would be a great tribute to the people and places that mean so much to this town, to Montana. Rust Creek Falls has a connected history with both Thunder Canyon and Whitehorn and I'd like see all three towns honored here at the resort."

Her gaze followed, trying to see the vision the man's words created, but nothing came to her artist eye. Zero. Zilch. Her stomach cramped at the now conditioned sensation. How many times had she experienced that same feeling over the past year?

"I think he surprised you, didn't he?" Callie asked.

"Ah, yes." Vanessa glanced down at her cup again. "Maybe I should've gotten something a bit stronger to ensure I was fully awake for this."

"And maybe we shouldn't have asked you to meet us here so early, but we both have to be down in Kalispell for most of the day. Nate didn't want to wait, and you did say—"

"Ah, no, early is fine. I'm usually up before the sun, anyway." Looking up at her friend, she waved off Callie's concern. "But I'm still a bit confused. You're asking me to do this because…"

"Because I was quite amazed." Nate paused and took a step closer, his head bent low even though the three of them were the only ones around, "and pleased when I found out the Vanessa Brent who's running an after-school art program at the community center and V. E. Brent, world-famous abstract expressionism artist, were one and the same."

Nate's soft-spoken words took her completely by surprise.

Not that she went out of her way to hide who she was or what she did with her life before moving to Rust Creek Falls back in July. When asked, she'd only said she'd worked in the creative arts, but was currently on a time-out, rethinking her career plans. She'd then change the topic of conversation because deep down, the explanation had more than a ring of truth to it.

Or more simply put, she hadn't painted anything in almost a year.

Oh, she'd thought about her craft often, obsessed about it, really. At least until she'd moved out here. Lately, she'd begun to dream about it again, like she'd done as a child. But even though she'd brought along all of her supplies, the white canvases that lined one wall of the cabin she'd rented a few weeks after arriving in town were still blank. Her paints and brushes lay untouched, her heart and her mind as vacant as the walls that surrounded them now.

"Ah, yeah, we're the same person," she finally responded to the expectant looks on Nate's and Callie's faces. "I mean, yes, I'm V. E. Brent, but I haven't… been involved with the art world for quite some time."

Even now, Vanessa was still surprised at the deep depression she'd sunk into after Adele's death last year. Or the fact that she hadn't been able to fill the void with her art.

Adele had hung on until just before Thanksgiving and the day of her memorial service had been the start of an arctic winter that had settled in Philadelphia, and most of the country. Vanessa, too, had become locked in her own personal deep freeze. For months she'd mourned, but unlike when her mother died, she failed to find the same solace and comfort in her work. No matter how hard she'd tried, no matter the techniques or tools she employed, her gift had faded into a vast wasteland where nothing flourished.

Even after she'd finally broken out of her self-imposed grieving this past spring, thanks to an intervention led by Adele's mother, the ability to create was still dormant and she'd decided something drastic was needed to shake her back into the world of the living.

Number ten: move out west.

Vanessa had been reading a weekly blog by a big-city volunteer coordinator who'd moved to Rust Creek Falls to help the town recover from a devastating flood the year before and ended up falling in love and marrying the local sheriff. Soon the idea to move to this little slice of cowboy heaven planted itself in her head and wouldn't let go. So she'd sublet her loft apartment, refused to listen to her father's halfhearted attempts to change her mind and bought a one-way plane ticket to Big Sky Country, placing the first check mark on her and Adele's bucket list in months by arriving just before the July Fourth holiday.

"But you are involved in art," Callie said, breaking into Vanessa's thoughts. "You're great with the kids at the community center."

Vanessa smiled, remembering how she'd gotten roped into helping with a summer day camp that'd showed up at the center looking to entertain a group of kids on a rainy day. "That's pretty much finger painting, playing with clay or simple watercolors. Other than that I'm not…"

Her voice cracked and she looked away, that familiar lump back in her throat. Damn! She walked across the vast space, her gaze centered on the empty fireplace. "I'm not…well, let's just say that side of me—V. E. Brent—she isn't painting. At all."

"Oh, please don't think we've invaded your privacy." Callie hurried to her side. "We haven't told anyone else who you really are. Nate came up with this idea before we even knew thanks to your beautiful sketches."

She looked back at them. "My sketches?"

"Yes, the ones you've been doing of the locals around

town. They're amazing. I love the portrait you did of me when I was tending to a scraped knee at the playground. I never even realized what you were up to until you gave it to me. I've got it hanging in my office at the clinic."

A few weeks after her kids program took off, Vanessa had started to once again carry a sketch pad and colored pencils in her oversize bag.

Something she hadn't done in months.

At first, the blank pages seemed to mock her whenever she opened the pad, but then she'd forced herself to do quick exercises, simple pen-and-ink sketches of whatever might catch her eye.

Surprisingly, it had been people.

The citizens of Rust Creek Falls had become her test subjects, either in the park, the community center or while sitting tucked away in a corner of a local business. Sometimes she asked for permission, but usually the sketches were done so quick the focus of her practice exercise didn't even realize what Vanessa was doing until she'd rip out the page from her sketchbook afterward and offer it to them.

So far, no one had been upset with her. She'd figured most had just been tossed away, but she had spotted a few, like Callie's, posted around town. Evidence that her creativity was trickling back little by little.

"The drawing you did of my mother working the counter at Crawford's Store is now matted, framed and holds a place of honor in my father's study," Nate said. "Callie and I were there for Sunday dinner and that drawing got me thinking about the mural, the resort and you."

Surprised at that, Vanessa's gaze was drawn back to the empty space over the desk, looking very much like the oversize blank canvases in her cabin. Nate's request caused her fingers to itch, a familiar sign they wanted to be wrapped around a paintbrush again. But Vanessa knew what would happen. As soon as she'd pull out her paints…nothing. Sketching a few random subjects was vastly different than taking on a commissioned work, where the nuances she'd have to capture in oils required planning and a delicate touch.

Things that were still beyond her reach.

Moving far away from home and memories of Adele had been her way to start her life again, and deep down, hopefully restore her spark, her inspiration for her craft. Except for those rare moments when she tried to paint and still failed, Vanessa was enjoying her time in Rust Creek Falls. She'd been lucky enough to find a great place to live, joined the Newcomers Club—a social group of women new to Rust Creek Falls—made some great friends and explored the area. The art program at the center kept her busy, she'd gone on a few dates with some of the local cowboys and made a point to appreciate each day of her new life.

Number thirteen: stop and enjoy sunrises and sunsets.

Another check mark on her list, made the first morning she woke up in Montana. Adele had been right. Concentrating on her life, and using their list as a guide, had helped her to find joy again.

Which made this idea of Nate's downright scary. What if she said yes and her creative block kept her from putting anything on the wall? And her work was abstract in the truest sense of the word. Powerful color compositions with no reference of any kind to anything recognizable. What Nate was describing was much more detailed, and in a way, more personal.

Still, she found herself wanting desperately to take on the challenge.

Maybe this mural was a chance—her last chance— to find her talent again.

Jonah Dalton breathed in the cool morning air, holding it for a moment in his nose and mouth, like he used to do as kid. The air had a bite to it—like the fresh tartness of a Granny Smith apple the moment you first sink your teeth into it—that couldn't be matched anywhere but here in the wilds of Montana.

He'd missed that taste more than he'd been willing to admit.

The air in Denver, his home for the past eight years, had a flavor that was a mix of excitement and culture, but that was to be expected in a sophisticated city of over 600,000 people, he guessed.

He released his breath, watching the white puffs disappear. He stood on the large circular drive outside of Bledsoe's Folly, soon to be known as…well, whatever Nate Crawford decided to name his as-yet-unopened resort. All Jonah knew was that when the chance came to restore and revitalize this twenty-year-old log mansion into a state-of-the-art, and hopefully popular destination for year-round vacations, his architect's heart wouldn't let him turn down the project. Not when the initial construction of the castle-like mansion had fueled his love of architecture and design all those years ago.

So he'd taken a leave of absence from his job with one of the top firms in the country and worked pretty much nonstop on the plans and blueprints for the necessary renovations.

And now he was here.

Even though he'd been less than thrilled about Nate's

condition that he be onsite for the last three months of the project in case any problems arose, Jonah had always enjoyed seeing his designs come to life. At work, he forgot everything else. And that's just how he liked it.

He figured he could do the same thing here, even if it meant coming home. And he had to admit he was looking forward to the quiet and slow pace of his home town, especially after all the craziness—professional and personal—he'd left behind in Denver. He'd arrived late last night after driving fifteen hours straight and hadn't made it past the living room couch at his parents' place.

Yet, here he was at the job site first thing the next morning, anxious to see his dream turned into reality.

His shiny Cadillac Escalade looked a bit out of place in the parking lot crowded with older-model cars and trucks, but Jonah took the number of vehicles present as a good sign that the crew was already hard at work. He grabbed his white hard hat and turned to head inside, surprised when his older brother Eli pulled up the long winding paved road in a battered pickup.

"What are you doing here?" he asked.

"Good morning to you, too, little brother." Eli waved a piece of paper at him. "Hey, I found your note on the kitchen counter as I was heading out. Decided to stop by and—"

"What are you doing with that?" Jonah cut him off. "I left that for Mom, warning her I plan to stay out at the cabin and not to worry about getting my old room ready."

"I know, I read it. Here, take this." Eli handed over a travel mug stamped with the brand of the family's ranch, The Circle D. "Jeez, you're just like the rest of the family, a bear without your morning cup of joe.

Nice to know some things haven't changed. Oh, and welcome home."

The enticing aroma filled Jonah's nose and his blood cried out for caffeinated bliss. Not wanting to wake his family, he'd only grabbed a quick shower and dressed, figuring he'd see everyone tonight at dinner. He'd guessed there'd be a canteen set up inside for the crew, but this was better.

Jonah took the cup. After Eli shut off the truck and climbed out to join him, he grabbed his brother's outstretched hand and allowed Eli to pull him into a quick hug that ended with a strong slap to his back. "Thanks, it's…ah, it's good to be back, but I still don't get why you took my note."

"You can't stay at the cabin." Eli stepped back and righted the dark Stetson he wore so much Jonah had often wondered if his brother slept with the darn thing. "It's been rented."

Surprised filled him. "You rented out my cabin?"

"Technically, it wasn't me. It was Mom. And it's not your cabin."

"I designed it. I built it. It's on the acreage Grandpa and Dad set aside for me." Jonah held tight to the mug as the memories that went along with the one bedroom cabin he'd forged with his own hands came crashing back to him. After eight years one would think he'd be over it by now. "Why would Mom rent my cabin to a stranger?"

"I guess because nobody knew when you planned to show your face in town again." Eli turned and headed for the main house. "This place must still have working bathrooms, right?"

Jonah sighed and followed his brother toward the oversize double front doors. Yes, he'd missed both

Thanksgiving and Christmas, the two times he made a point of returning home over the past few years.

"I couldn't be here because I was out of the country most of last year working on a major project," he said as he and Eli stepped through the rustic mahogany-and-iron entryway that was original to the building.

"And when you got back to the U.S. you still didn't visit."

"But I did call. I do have a life, and a job in Denver, you know."

"I know that and you know that. Mom? Not so much. She and Dad were really excited to find out you were the lead architect behind the redesign of this place. The fact they had to hear about it from your boss didn't go over so well."

Jonah had planned to tell his folks about working with Nate Crawford, but his life had been going non-stop since he'd agreed to take on the project. "Well, I'm home now and since I'm going to stick around until at least Christmas I'd like to stay at my cabin."

"Why? You never stayed there before."

Because he hadn't actually finished the darn thing until a couple of years ago, working on it whenever he was home. Besides, it was time to get rid of some old ghosts, but Jonah wasn't going to share that.

"There must be plenty of available housing from those who left town after the flood last year." Including his ex-wife, he thought, taking a long sip of the strong brew despite the steamy vapors. "Mom can tell the renter they have to move. Or I'll tell them. It's my place so technically I'm the landlord."

"Great. Here's your chance."

His brother pointed out Jonah's boss across the room. Nate Crawford stood near one of the room's best features, the original stone fireplace, with two women. One was his fiancée, whom Jonah had met when she'd come with Nate to Denver for one of their many meetings and the other was a stunningly beautiful brunette.

A powerful jolt raced through his veins and Jonah immediately blamed the mouthful of java he managed to choke down. He took in her dark brown hair, a mass of curls that just touched the wide neckline of a bright purple sweater that hung down far past her hips, but still managed to display feminine curves in all the right places.

Or maybe it was her black skintight, sorry excuse for pants that did that.

He couldn't make out what she was holding in her arms, but then she reached up and pushed a handful of those curls off her face, releasing a jangle from the stack of bracelets that slid from her wrist to her elbow as she turned in a slow circle, her gaze seemingly locked on the empty walls of the room as her ankle-high boots clicked on the newly finished reclaimed barn wood floor. Then Nate's fiancée touched her arm and the two started to talk.

Staring was rude, gawking like a teenager was worse, but for whatever reason Jonah was helpless to look away.

"Yeah, that's the typical reaction." Eli reached around and waved his hand in front of Jonah's face. "Not hard to tell Vanessa isn't from around here, huh? Which is why she needed a place to stay. Like *your* cabin."

As if she heard them, or maybe because Callie was now pointing in his direction, the beauty looked over and caught him watching her. Jonah snapped out of his dazed state and pushed his brother's hand away, realizing at that moment the woman he'd been transfixed by was the one sleeping in his bed.

Whoa! Nope, not going there!

Yeah, he'd also built the king-size log bed that took up most of the one bedroom in the cabin, but still…

"She's the renter?" he finally asked, turning his back on her, and his boss, to face his brother again.

"That's her," Eli said, then chuckled. "Can I stick around and watch you go all Scrooge-like?"

"Don't you have someplace to be? Like the men's room? Or the ranch?"

"I'm going, I'm going." Eli grinned and backed away. "Gee, all the Daltons under one roof again. Not sure how Derek is going to feel about that, but the twins and the folks are going to be in heaven."

Jonah scowled, watching his brother stop and chat with a few workers before disappearing around a corner. He should go over and let Nate know he'd arrived, but his unexpected reaction to— What had Eli said was her name?

And why did he care?

The cool touch to her arm jolted Vanessa out of her self-imposed trance. She dropped her hand to her side, noticing for the first time that the interior of the resort had gotten busy as members of the construction crew moved from room to room, the noise of their chatter and work tools filled the air while she'd been trying to conjure up something—anything—for the mural.

At some point during her daydreaming she'd handed off her cup of hot chocolate and pulled a sketch pad from her oversize leather bag, but other than grabbing a trio of pens and holding one-handed in a familiar pretzel twist of fingers, she had…

Nothing.

"I hope your silence is a sign that you're already brimming with ideas for the mural," Callie said. "I think Nate's suggestion is wonderful."

Despite the panic ricocheting inside of her, Vanessa's smile came easy. One of the first people she'd met after moving to Rust Creek Falls had been Callie, who was also considered a newcomer in town after she left Chicago back in January. "You think Nate is wonderful."

Callie's eyes were bright as she glanced at the tall man next to her talking with a member of the construction crew. "Yes, I do. It's funny, but from the moment I saw him—oh, look, there's Jonah."

Vanessa's gaze followed Callie's pointed finger and amazingly the panic over her creative block quieted, replaced with a warm glow that surprised her as much as the way the handsome man stared at them.

At her.

Did she know him? He looked vaguely familiar, but Vanessa was sure they hadn't been introduced before. No, she'd have remembered if she'd met this man.

Unlike the majority of the men here at the resort and in Rust Creek Falls with their broken-in jeans, T-shirts and flannel button-downs in every plaid pattern and color combination imaginable, he was dressed in black business slacks and a dress shirt.

He was tall, over six feet she guessed, and his slightly mussed brown hair showed hints of gold when the sunlight caught it as he turned away. Her gaze lingered over the way his shoulders filled the expensive cut of his dark gray suit jacket that she'd bet her last pair of Manolos was cashmere. The only thing that made him fit in was the hard hat he held in one hand.

"Who is that?"

Callie smiled and Vanessa realized she'd spoken the question aloud. "I mean, I haven't seen him around town." She paused, catching the capped end of one of her pens between her teeth. "At least I don't think I have."

"Well, you've certainly dated enough of the single men in town to know."

Vanessa flipped her wrist and pointed her pen at Callie. "Hey! Six dates in three months isn't that many."

"Six dates with six different guys."

"Five." Vanessa had made the mistake of going out twice with the same cowboy. There wouldn't be a third time. "But who's counting? Besides, not everyone believes in love at first sight. I'm more of the 'you only live once, so enjoy yourself' kind of girl."

Unlike half of the women in the town's Newcomers Club, it seems.

Besides Callie, two other members—Mallory Franklin and Cecelia Clifton—had also found happily-ever-after in the past few months and were sporting pretty engagement rings, even though Mallory claimed she hadn't specifically moved to Rust Creek Falls for the great "Gal Rush" as many of the locals called the arrival of females over the past year or so. She'd initially come to town to raise her orphaned niece, the little girl her sister and brother-in-law had adopted from China. Then she fell in love with former playboy rancher, Caleb Dalton.

"Hey, Jonah!" Nate called out, "Come over and join us."

The man hesitated, but then spun back around and headed across the room toward them, the hard hat now perched on his head with a rakish tilt. Callie backed up a few steps toward her fiancé and sent Vanessa a quick wink. She grinned in response and followed, happier now that the conversation had shifted away from the mural she still hadn't officially agreed to do.

"Welcome home." Nate held out his hand. "When did you get in?"

"Late last night." He switched his travel mug from one hand to the other and shook Nate's. "Very late. Hence, the need for coffee."

"There's always a need for coffee." Nate released him and turned to her and Callie. "You remember Callie?"

He nodded. "It's good to see you again."

"You, too, Jonah. I bet you're glad to be home."

A shuttered look filled his gaze for a moment bringing Vanessa's attention to his green-gold hazel eyes. Tired eyes. The man looked like he could use a good night's sleep and it was barely eight in the morning.

"Yes, it is," he said, then turned back to Nate. "Sorry I'm a day late. I know I said October first, but I got stuck on business—"

"Hey, one day doesn't matter. Did you read my latest email?"

"I meant to, but yesterday was all about tying up loose ends and a long drive. Did I miss something important?"

"Yes, but I think this is better, anyway. Remember when I said I had a great idea for the lobby?" Nate waved his hand toward Vanessa. "Well, here she is."

The stranger turned his gaze to her, the expression on his face as blank as the walls—as her imagination. Well, blank when it came to the mural. Suddenly she was coming up with some great ideas for her and this handsome guy.

Vanessa forced out a quick laugh, thankful it sounded so relaxed and stuck out her hand. "Gee, you make me sound like a pole dancer or something. Hi, I'm Vanessa Brent."

"Jonah Dalton."

He took her hand in his and heat engulfed her fingers. Where had the tingling come from that turned the heat up to volcanic level?

The widening of his eyes told her he felt it, too, and he quickly released her, tipped his mug again and took a long gulp. It was then she noticed the logo on the side. "Dalton…are you related to either of the Daltons here in town?"

He nodded, tugging the brim of his hard hat a bit lower. "Charles and Rita Dalton are my folks."

"Oh, my goodness! What a small world!" Vanessa hugged her sketch pad to her chest. "Your parents are the sweetest people. I mean, your whole family is so nice. I'm renting a cabin on the Circle D Ranch."

"You don't say."

"Do you know the place? When I was looking to move out of the boardinghouse in town, you mom insisted she had the perfect cabin and she was right! The living room has this one wall that's a huge single pane of glass—" she waved a hand at the windows that filled the other side of the room "—nothing like that, of course, but the views of the ranch and the mountains are amazing. I'm still learning how to work the woodstoves, the nights have been getting chilly, but the best thing is the claw-footed tub in the bathroom." Vanessa closed her eyes for a moment a sighed. "Oh, fill that baby with foamy bubbles, give me a good book and I'm soaking for hours up to my—"

The sound of choking had her eyes flying open in time to see Jonah thumping at his chest with his fist. "Are you okay?"

"Yeah." One more thump and then he cleared his throat. "Last mouthful of coffee went down the wrong way. Yes, I know the cabin. I grew up on the Circle D Ranch."

"So, are you a cowboy like your brothers?" It wasn't hard to picture him in a classic Stetson instead of the hard hat he wore. "Although, I'm guessing from your current chapeau you're working here on the renovation?"

Both Nate and Callie laughed, reminding Vanessa she wasn't standing here alone with this long lost Dalton son she'd now recognized from the numerous family photos in the main house on the Dalton's ranch.

"Yes, Jonah is working on the resort. He's the lead architect on this project," Nate explained. "All the innovative building techniques we're putting into this place to turn it into a premier resort are his. He's also the lead on all of the interior design so you'll be working for him. In a way."

"She will?" Jonah asked, clearly confused. "As what?"

"An artist," Nate said. "I've commissioned Vanessa to paint a mural over the registration desk in the front lobby."

"You have?" The confusion on his face gave way to something closer to annoyance. "When?"

"Just today," Vanessa chimed in. "But I haven't agreed to anything yet."

"Well, that's good."

Hmmm, interesting response. One arched eyebrow from her told him he was free to continue.

"No, that came out—what I meant was we've already got the designs for the interior furnishings in place." Jonah's gaze darted from Vanessa to Callie and back to

Nate. "I mentioned earlier this week that Rothschild—the firm in Denver we hired—is sending a representative in a few weeks to give the team a final presentation on everything from furniture to curtains to…well, artwork."

An emotion that hovered between resentment and relief filled Vanessa's chest. It seemed Nate and his architect weren't on the same page when it came to this so-called mural. Good. While the idea of taking on the commission scared her more than anything had in years, she'd admit she had been leaning toward saying yes, confident her talent hadn't deserted her completely.

Now it didn't seem to matter.

Chapter Two

"Are you telling me you honestly didn't know Nate had hired Vanessa to paint a mural in the resort?" Eli asked.

They'd managed to find an empty table with a couple of tall stools—one with a trio of half-finished drinks still sitting there—in the back corner of the Ace in the Hole, the local bar that catered to everyone from cowboys to bikers. Between the cracking of the pool balls against each other to the country music blaring from the jukebox for the dancers on the crowded parquet floor, the place was loud and noisy and Jonah had to lean forward to hear his brother. "No, I honestly didn't know."

Eli looked at him with one eyebrow raised.

"I didn't." Jonah dropped his gaze and fixed it on the icy longneck beer he turned in slow circles against the table top. "Not that it matters now."

"Why's that?"

Because Vanessa had walked out this morning with

Callie following close behind, leaving Nate to make it clear the mural was going to happen and since the man owned fifty-one percent of the resort, he was going to get his way.

"I missed the email explaining Nate's vision," Jonah said. "Add the fact the rest of the investors had already approved the idea and it's a done deal."

"So your vote wouldn't have made any difference?"

"No, but that doesn't mean—" Jonah looked at his brother again. "Wait, what makes you think I had a vote on the subject?"

Eli's mouth rose into a half grin. "You're one of the investors, aren't you?"

Jonah glanced around. No one seemed interested in their conversation, but he kept his voice low. "Why would you think I'd be—"

"Give me some credit, little brother. You've been in love with that old place from the moment it was built back when we were kids. You used to ride all the way from the ranch just to watch it being constructed. Even when it sat empty for years, you'd sneak in and hang out there. Remember that night with the football players from Kalispell?"

It took him a moment, but then Jonah smiled. "Yeah, we just about had them out of there, convinced the place was haunted, until Derek tried to steal their beer. That was a heck of a fight."

"Only because that one guy had a can of spray paint aimed at one of the walls. You took him out with a flying karate leap and the fists started flying."

It'd been him, his two brothers and three cousins—the Dalton gang as they'd been known back then—against the entire offensive line from the nearby high school, but they'd won. At least until word got back to the town sheriff and their folks. "I never shoveled so much horse manure in my life as we did that fall."

"Anyway, I figured a rich and famous architect would have plenty—"

"I'm not famous." Jonah cut off his brother and sat back in the tall stool, the heel of his steel-toed cowboy boot caught on the bottom rung. "Or rich."

Eli toasted him with his now empty bottle. "You better be tonight. You're buying and I could use another beer."

Jonah watched his brother turn away and attempt to flag down a waitress. He never confirmed Eli's suspicions, but the man was right. When Nate had contacted him about his plans for the forgotten log mansion and he'd found out about the investor team Nate was putting together, Jonah had insisted on buying in, easily parting with a healthy chunk of his savings.

Still, would he have voted along with the majority for the mural?

Probably, since after talking with Nate and finally reading the email, he liked the idea and what the painting would represent, even though it meant added work for the interior-design team when it came to including the painting in the overall plan. It seemed this Vanessa Brent was a pretty famous artist from back east. He hadn't had a chance to do any research on her yet, but obviously she, and her work, had made an impression on Nate.

Just the sight of her had done something to Jonah that hadn't happened in a long time.

Made him curious.

What was she was doing in Rust Creek Falls? Was she here as part of the influx of females influenced by an online blog about life in the Wild West his mother and sisters had talked about at dinner? According to his dad and brothers there'd also been a fair amount of single men and families who'd come to town as well over the past year, thanks to jobs created by both the recovery work from last summer's flooding and more recently, the resort. They'd even hired on a few new hands at the ranch, putting the bunkhouse to use again for the first time in a long time.

Along with his cabin.

He couldn't help but wonder what Vanessa might have done to the empty slate he'd left behind after she'd moved in. Were the few pieces of furniture he'd put in still there? Including the bed he'd handcrafted and now refused to picture her sleeping in?

And that flash of anger in her golden-brown eyes when he'd shot down the idea of a mural... Why had it changed to relief just before she'd walked out?

Stifling a yawn, Jonah drained his beer and chalked up his interest in Nate's artist to his being dead tired.

Coming to the bar his first full day back in town hadn't been part of his plan for tonight. A quick meal and then crashing headfirst into a soft bed had been more of what he had in mind, but the talk at dinner had quickly turned from the town's population boom to him. His job, his travels and after one too many questions from his mother about his personal life, Jonah had willingly agreed to Eli's idea they'd grab a beer or two to celebrate his homecoming.

Two more beers arrived and Jonah swore this would be his last as he twisted off the cap. It was then he heard a familiar laugh from a nearby table. He turned and looked at the group of men playing a lively game of poker, recognizing one of them right away. "Didn't

Derek rush through dinner because he had a big project to do in the barn?"

"Yeah, so?"

Gesturing toward the table, Jonah saw Eli's gaze shift until it landed on their younger brother who sat with his back to them.

"Guess he finished early," Eli said. "Or else he got tired of listening to mom's excited chatter about your many accomplishments."

Jonah's face heated. "I was getting tired of that, too."

"Hey, she's proud of you. Dad, too. You're the first one of us kids to make it big with your fancy Denver penthouse, traveling the world designing everything from skyscrapers to celebrities' homes, not to mention dating a famous ballerina."

"How did you know about that?"

"Mom cut out a picture of you two attending a charity event—nice tux, by the way—from some magazine. She had it hanging on the refrigerator for months until we all got so sick of seeing it she finally moved it to her sewing room."

He groaned. "Please tell me you're screwing with me."

Eli grinned. "She was hoping you'd bring the lady home for a visit."

Not likely. He'd returned from a business trip and walked in on her entertaining a fellow dancer—a ballerina—in her apartment. Hey, he was all for a person being true to themselves, but he wasn't going to be her stand-in. Especially after the way she'd hinted about the two of them getting married. "I haven't dated Nadia in a year. That was over before I left for Brazil."

"Whatever happened to that sexy architect from your

office I met when I visited a few years back? Before Nadia?"

Yeah, getting involved with a coworker he'd collaborated with on a couple of projects, moving their relationship from the office to the bedroom had been a mistake, too. He didn't realize that until she decided to move up in the world and left him to marry a partner in a rival company, when he made it clear that he and marriage were not a good fit. Not anymore. "I wasn't rich *or* famous enough for her."

"Well, I guess mom's just getting antsy for one of us to finally settle down," Eli said. "Again. You're the only one who's tried the marriage bit. As much as she and dad were against you becoming a husband while still in your teens, I think she's ready now for some grandchildren to spoil."

This time the memory flashed in Jonah's head before he could brace himself.

The pregnancy test found in the trash. His joy at becoming a father after what he'd thought had been four years of wedded bliss. Lisette's stunned silence. His mistake in thinking her reaction was because he'd ruined the surprise.

Yeah, she surprised him all right—

"Hey, you okay?" Eli clicked the bottom edge of his bottle against Jonah's, pulling him from the past. "You grip that beer any tighter and it's going to shatter in your hand."

"Yeah, I'm fine. Just tired." He must be. He hadn't thought about that night in a long time. It was almost like it'd all happened to someone else. Someone he used to be. He forced his fingers to relax. "It's been a long few days. Months, actually."

"Well, you'll get a good night's sleep tonight. Back in your childhood bedroom."

Same room, but thankfully the furniture had been updated. There was no way he'd be comfortable in a twin-size bed. "Very funny."

"So, I'm guessing you decided not to kick Vanessa out?"

After the way her eyes lit up and hearing the excitement in her voice as she described the cabin, Jonah knew he couldn't ask her to leave. It wasn't her fault he'd come back assuming the place would still be empty. "The subject never came up, but no, I don't plan to ask her to move."

"She got to you, huh?"

"What's her story?" Jonah avoided his brother's question with one of his own. "What do you know about her?"

"Not much." Eli shrugged. "I hadn't met her until Mom had her over for dinner one night back in August and announced she was renting your cabin. I didn't even know she was an artist until you mentioned it. She's nice, always with a smile on her face and rarely at a loss for company, from what I've heard. But hey, my days usually run twelve to fourteen hours taking care of the ranch. I don't have time for much else, which should show my brotherly love in saving your butt tonight by coming here. Why are you asking?"

"No reason. Just curious about who's living in my place and who I'll be working with for…well, for however long it takes her to paint a mural." Jonah tipped back his beer for a long swallow.

"Maybe you should ask Derek. Seeing how he promised to teach her to ride a horse. Convenient, huh?"

The cold liquid caught in the sudden tightening of

his throat. Jonah tried not to cough, but failed and did his best to hide it as he wiped at his mouth. "Derek's chasing after her?"

"You know our brother."

Yes, he did. Derek had been popular with the ladies ever since he'd figured out the difference between boys and girls somewhere back in elementary school. Derek did his share of chasing, but usually it was the ladies who went after him, most winding up with nothing to show for their trouble but good times and a broken heart when they got too serious.

A fire burned in his gut at the idea of Derek messing with Vanessa that way and damned if he knew why. He'd only met the woman today. Just because she'd stirred his curiosity, among other things, didn't mean anything.

Neither did the sparks that crackled between them the moment he'd taken her hand this morning. Maybe he'd just been alone for too long. There hadn't been a woman in his life—or his bed—in a long time. Hell, there hadn't really been anyone since his ex-wife destroyed their marriage eight years ago and just about destroyed him along with it.

"Boy, you really must be tired."

Jonah blinked, realizing he'd been so lost in his own thoughts he'd missed whatever his brother had said. "Yeah, I am. You must be, too. Maybe we should head home."

"Oh, don't leave now." A soft feminine voice spoke. "The party's just getting started."

Jonah and his brother turned in unison and found three ladies standing there. His gaze immediately went to the brunette with bouncy curls who stood head and shoulders taller than the two petite blondes flanking her.

Vanessa.

She reached for the glasses on the table, handing one each to her friends. Keeping the wineglass for herself, she sent him a wink over the rim when their eyes clashed. A quick glance at all three ladies' slightly disheveled appearances and apparent thirst at how they finished off their drinks, made him realize he and Eli had taken their table while they'd been on the dance floor.

"Sorry, didn't mean to steal your seats." His brother quickly came to the same conclusion and slid off his stool, but instead of stepping away—as in heading for the exit—he just moved to make room. "It's pretty crowded tonight. Do you mind if we share?"

"Only if you're buying the next round." One of the blondes spoke while the other giggled.

Yeah, actually giggled.

Vanessa smiled, remembering what it felt like to be barely legal enough be in a bar. Not that at twenty-six she was that much older than her new friends, but there were many times she felt much older than her actual age.

And woefully out of shape.

Grabbing at the front of her sweater, she yanked it back and forth, enjoying the slight breeze against her heated skin. Thursday nights were busy here at the Ace and the dance floor was crowded. She was finally getting the hang of the steps, dips and sways that went along with country line dancing, but boy, she wished she'd thought to change her outfit before coming tonight.

She had, in fact, almost stayed home, but then she'd seen the reminder on her calendar and once again thought about the list.

Number sixteen: learn how to line dance.

She'd arrived early but the bar had filled up quickly, so she'd offered to share her table with the two girls she'd just met tonight who managed somehow not to look the least bit sweaty or have a lock of their flowing golden manes out of place.

"Of course, I'm buying." Eli readily agreed and offered to escort the ladies to the bar. He started to walk away, but then stopped and pointed back at Jonah and her. "No need for introductions, right? You two remember each other?"

She sidled a look in Jonah's direction. Oh, yes, she remembered him.

In fact, Vanessa hadn't been able to think about much else but Jonah Dalton all day, even when she should've been concentrating on the design for the mural that after much more prodding from Nate and Callie was back on.

"Yep, I think we'll be fine." Ignoring the stool he'd vacated the same time as his brother, Vanessa moved closer to the table and set her empty glass down. "Hello again, Mr. Dalton."

"Please, call me Jonah."

There they were again. She'd thought she'd imagined the tingling that felt like a thousand tiny pinpricks dancing along her skin at the smooth tone of his voice the few minutes they had talked this morning, but now he'd only spoken four words and they were back. Like gangbusters.

Maybe she should just peel off this darn sweater. It's not like she didn't have anything on beneath it. In fact, she wore a double-layer tank top—

"What can I get for you at the bar, Vanessa?" Eli asked. "Another glass of wine? Maybe a bucket of ice water?"

His question caused her to stop her frantic moves,

her hand now still against her chest. "Oh, an ice water would be great. Just a glass."

Eli smiled, then looked at his brother. "Jonah? Another beer?"

"Yeah, sure. Why not?"

Hmmm, four more words but with an edge to them this time. Eli and the girls disappeared into the crowd. Vanessa leaned against the table, elbows propped along the edge and her beloved bracelets jangling as they landed on the smooth surface. "So, are you having fun…Jonah?"

"I'd rather be in bed."

Five words this time and boy, the heat level rose again. That's it. She straightened and eased behind Jonah, as he stood between the table and the back wall, one hand already under the bottom edge of her sweater. "Do you mind?"

"Mind what?"

He started to look back over one impossibly wide shoulder, but she nudged him forward with her elbow. "Just give me a minute, I need to…"

A quick tug and one arm came free. After a tussle with both her bracelets and oversize hoop earrings, she deftly pulled the garment over her head. The cool air lapping at her damp skin felt wonderful. "Ah, so much better."

Running her fingers through her hair would be a lost cause, the wayward curls did whatever they pleased, but she did it anyway and then adjusted her bra straps to make sure they didn't show.

"Are you finished back there?"

The confusion laced in Jonah's question made her smile. That and the fact he was still using five-word sentences.

"Thanks for being my screen." She stepped back around to the table, laying her sweater over the closest stool. "I don't think anyone noticed."

Ha! Now *she'd* done it. Twice!

"Noticed what?" Jonah asked, looking at her. His gaze stilled, locked somewhere around her mouth before it slowly traveled the length of her body.

The slow appraisal caused those pinpricks to rise into goose bumps along her bare arms. She quickly blamed it on the bar's air-conditioning, but her girly parts enjoyed his perusal so much her toes curled inside her favorite suede ankle boots.

"You—ah, you changed." Jonah's words came out in a low whisper. He lifted his beer to his mouth, ready to tip it back, but then noticed the bottle was empty and set it back down.

"Actually, I just took off a layer." She tugged the edges of the tank top down over her hips, but it barely covered the pockets on her leggings where her phone, driver's license and cash were safely tucked away. "All that dancing made me hot."

"Yeah, I can see that."

Vanessa smiled and leaned against the table again. "Hmmm, I'm not sure if I should take that as a compliment."

Jonah started to reply, but before he could, Vanessa's gaze caught on something—or should she say someone—on the other side of the room.

Without stopping to think about what she was doing, she laid a hand over Jonah's and said the first thing that popped into her head. "Hey, architect, want to be a hero?"

His gaze dropped to their hands for a moment, and then he looked at her again. "Excuse me?"

"There's a cowboy—tall, big shoulders, plaid shirt—heading this way."

Jonah quickly looked around the bar. "You do realize you've just described about every man in here?"

"This one's wearing a hat like your brother's…I know, a lot of men are, but he's standing on the other side of the third pool table and stealing glances at me with a determined look on his face."

This time Jonah glanced to his left and Vanessa watched as the two men made eye contact. Oh, boy, she hoped this was a good idea.

"Is that bothering you?" He turned back to her.

"Well, ever since I told him I don't kiss on the first date, he's been angling to get me to go out with him again."

Jonah's hazel eyes darkened. "For a second date?"

"Third, actually. I didn't kiss him the last time, either," she hurried to explain, wanting him to understand. "I just wanted to get to know him a bit better, but no sparks, ya know? I told him it would be better if we were just friends, but the guy won't take no for an answer."

At that moment Eli returned, setting two beers and her glass of ice water down with a noisy clank before pushing their drinks across the table. "Your friends decided to stop by the ladies' room—drinks in hand—so who knows if we'll see them again. Hey, look at you. Getting more comfortable?"

"Much." Vanessa reached for her glass, enjoying a long sip of the cool liquid. She didn't know if her throat was so dry because of the dancing or this crazy idea of hers. "Oh, I so needed that."

Jonah took a long swallow from his beer. "Yeah, me, too."

"So, what do you say?" She set the glass back down, and gave him a gentle squeeze. "Help a girl out?"

Eli's gaze bounced back and forth between them, before it landed on her hand on Jonah's wrist. "Ah, did I miss something?"

"I just need a favor from your brother."

"Jeez, I'm the one who bought the lady a drink."

Jonah shot his brother a dark look, then turned to her again. "What do you want me to do?"

Now that he was agreeable, Vanessa realized she was at a loss for ideas. Boy, what else was new?

Was it enough they were standing here, practically holding hands? Maybe she should slide a bit closer? Press up against his shoulder?

Biting down on her bottom lip, she tried to come up with something when the jukebox switched songs and a classic country music ballad came on.

"Dance with me," she said.

This time Eli laughed. "Oh, you've picked yourself the wrong rescuer, Vanessa. If there's one thing Jonah doesn't like to do, it's dance."

Okay, maybe it would be enough if she just stood next to him. Surely, her admirer wouldn't cause any trouble if it was clear she was here with someone else, and now that Eli was back...

"How presumptuous of me. I'm sorry." She released her hold, her fingers lightly sliding back across his skin. "I guess I've got to learn that I can't assume every man in town is a cowboy or likes to two-step. Never even thought—"

Jonah surprised her by capturing her hand in his. "Come on, let's dance."

Chapter Three

Jonah ignored the shock on his brother's face, especially when it morphed into a smirk. He instead concentrated on the surprise—turned delight—on Vanessa's. Her asking him to dance was just another way she'd surprised him since she'd walked up to their table tonight. Her table. Hell, since he'd walked into his resort and found her standing there.

"Are you sure?" she asked.

He shot a glance at Vanessa's admirer, who looked vaguely familiar and was heading their way. Releasing her hand, he gestured toward the already crowded dance floor. "After you."

She rewarded him with a bright smile and then turned on one heel of those sexy boots. Moving in close behind her as they maneuvered around the tables, he placed a hand at the small of her back. Her top felt slightly damp and the heat of her skin easily melted through the soft cotton material to warm his fingertips.

Damn, there went those sparks again, just like the glowing spatter from a welder's torch to steel, these figurative sparks would burn just as easily of he got too close.

Maybe this wasn't such a good idea.

His brother was right. Jonah had never been a big fan of dancing and he couldn't remember the last time he'd done any two-stepping, slow speed or otherwise. And since she'd stripped off that sweater and wore nothing but a flimsy tank top that showed off toned arms and sexy cleavage, how was he going to hold her in his arms and not—

They reached the parquet floor and instead of waiting for an opening crowded outer circle of couples, Vanessa moved into the fray, spun around and assumed the position.

He moved in, placing one hand just beneath her left shoulder blade and lightly took her right hand in his. Two quick steps, one slow and—

"Oh!" Her booted foot knocked right into his. "Sorry about that."

"That's okay. It's takes a few minutes to get into the swing—" She did it again and ending up bumping into the couple behind her when she tried to back away and find her rhythm at the same time.

"Sorry about that, folks," he said to the man when he turned and glared at him over his shoulder, then focused again on his dance partner. "Vanessa, do you know how to two-step?"

Her nose scrunched up. "Not really. I've been watching the couples when I'm here at the bar and I want to learn, even though it's not on my—" She stopped and bit down on her bottom lip for a moment. "I've been concentrating on line dancing."

Jonah glanced to his left and found the center of the dance floor filled with couples, but moving much slower. He stepped out of the ring of couples and pulled Vanessa in closer.

"Hey, what are you doing?"

"Dancing." He turned to face her again, this time sliding his hand to the small of her back, holding her in place—much closer this time—as he started to move in an unhurried circle. "Isn't that what this is called?"

"Ah, yes." Her stiff posture relaxed as she smiled, moving her hand up to circle his neck while aligning her body with his from his chest to his knees. "I believe it is. You know, I always wondered why couples would gather out here in the center of the floor and slow dance."

The press of her soft curves reminded Jonah again of how long it'd been since he'd held a woman in his arms. "Maybe because one of them doesn't know how to two-step."

"Or maybe they want to be able to talk and get to know each other a little better."

"They can't do that while sitting at a table?"

She laughed softly, her puffs of breath enticingly warm against his throat. "Probably wouldn't be as much fun."

He couldn't argue with that.

"When was the last time you did any dancing?" she asked. "Country or any other style?"

It took him a minute as he thought back. The charity event in Denver where that photograph of him and Nadia had been taken. "It's been over a year."

"Don't get out much?"

"I've been working quite a bit. Got back from a year

in Brazil in the spring and started working on the resort project in August."

"Well, you know what they say about all work and no play, architect."

Yeah, many probably considered him a dull guy, but dedication to his work was what got him through the hardest time of his life.

Not wanting to go down that path, Jonah figured he and Vanessa probably should get to know one another better since they were going to be working together, but first things first.

He tightened his grip on her hand before bringing it in to rest against his chest. "I owe you an apology for my rudeness this morning."

She leaned back and looked up at him. "I take it finding out about me and the mural was a surprise?"

Boy that seemed to be the word for the evening. "Yes." He waited a moment and then added, "But a nice one."

A tilt of her head told him she wasn't sure if she believed him. "Why do I get the feeling a certain architect doesn't like surprises."

That had been more of a statement than a question, so Jonah remained silent. The truth was he hated them. Always had. Even as a kid, he liked knowing what was happening, what was coming down the road and when.

Birthdays and Christmas mornings were only made better once his folks took his detailed lists of gift ideas seriously. His brothers had messed with him a time or two over the years, but once he got into high school his life revolved around his studies and the girl he'd started dating his freshman year.

The only girl for him until everything changed eight years ago.

"No apology is necessary," Vanessa continued, cutting into his thoughts. "I'm happy you're on board with the idea now."

Glad she wasn't upset with his behavior, Jonah wove his way back to his original intent. "Very much on board. I'll need to get our interior-design team in the loop on this, sharing any preliminary drawings and color choices you have for the mural with them."

Vanessa dropped her gaze from his. "Yes, of course, you will."

"I'll admit I don't know much about your work or even how a mural is painted. Do you have any ideas or sketches yet?"

"I just found out about Nate's idea this morning, as well." Her shoulders stiffened and her feet once again became tangled with his. "Oops! Sorry about that. Ah, it's going to take me some time to come up with…a plan, a design."

Jonah wondered how much time, the analytical side of his brain already making plans as he mentally reviewed the upcoming schedule.

"The main hall where you'll be working is pretty much finished except for the furnishings and such, so you won't have to worry about any construction mess getting in the way," he said. "Of course, we'll have to build you scaffolding depending on the size and scope of the mural."

"Yes, I know, but—"

"And find a way to give you as much privacy as you need, but then again, it is a construction site so I hope you can work with noise and people. Do artists tend to prefer quiet?"

"Yes, s-some do. I usually work alone, but I'm sure I'll be able to manage."

Jonah picked up on the hesitation in her words. "Did Nate tell you the grand opening of the resort is planned for the Christmas holidays? That's less than twelve weeks away. Does that time frame work for you? I hate to have the project half finished—"

"Wow, has anyone ever told you that you talk too much?"

Vanessa's question cut into his sentence, silencing him for a moment as he gave it serious thought. "Yes, actually, it has been mentioned a time or two. Especially when it comes to work."

"So, let's not talk about work. Or talk at all." She trailed her fingertips across the back of his neck, just along the edge of his shirt collar. "Just enjoy the music, the dancing…the moment."

She was right. They had plenty of time to talk about the mural and resort later. It'd been a long day and while dancing was the last thing he'd ever thought he'd be doing tonight, he had to admit it felt pretty damn good to hold her in his arms.

Pressing his cheek to her hair, he pulled in a deep breath and a fresh, flowery scent filled his head. He relaxed for the first time since he'd come home.

As the song ended and another began, Vanessa didn't make any move to step away. In fact, she seemed to cling tighter. Her lush curves felt great, especially since the last woman he danced with was so thin and delicate he'd often wondered if she'd break if he held her too tight.

"Not going anywhere," he whispered.

The tension eased from her body and they danced through that song and a third one before the music selection changed and things got lively again.

"Let me guess," Vanessa stepped back when he

stopped moving. "You're not interested in doing any line dancing."

"You've guessed right."

She smiled, moved out of his embrace and headed off the dance floor. Jonah fell into step behind her as they made their way through the crowd, almost bumping into her when she suddenly stopped.

"Ah, hello, Tommy."

Jonah looked over her shoulder and found the cowboy she'd been trying to dodge standing right in front of them. Taking a step closer and to one side, he again placed a hand at the small of her back, and moved in next to her.

"Jonah." She turned, a look of relief on her face. "This is my friend, Tommy Wheeler. Tommy, this is Jonah Dalton, my…um, my…"

"Date." The word popped out of his mouth before he could think about it, but the dazzling smile of Vanessa's was worth the white lie. "Nice to meet you, Tommy."

The cowboy pushed up the brim of his hat and offered Jonah a long look before finally taking his outstretched hand. "Dalton," he said. "You related to Anderson Dalton?"

"My cousin, why?"

"Just curious." Tommy finished the handshake. "I've worked on the Daltons ranch for the last ten years or so."

Okay, so maybe that's why he looked familiar. "They're a good outfit. Right up there with The Circle D."

"You don't work for your family's ranch."

It wasn't a question. "No, I'm back in town to work on the renovation of the new resort."

Tommy only responded with a nod of his head, and

then turned his attention back to Vanessa. "So, how about a dance?"

"No, thanks. It's getting a bit late."

He glanced at his watch. "At ten o'clock? You and I have been out later than this, darling."

Was it his imagination or did Vanessa just lean in a bit closer to him?

"Yes, but that's all in the past now," she said, her fingers playing with the numerous bracelets on her wrist. "And I think it's time I head home."

"We." Jonah corrected her, again surprised when the word came out of his mouth. Not bothering to think as to why, or maybe he was just too tired, he drew her against his side and slid his hand around to cup her hip. "We're heading home."

They were?

Vanessa felt like a tennis ball, bouncing back and forth between Tommy and Jonah, but she never expected him to say that.

Heck, hearing him call himself her date had weakened her knees. Or was the sensation from how amazing it'd been to be in his arms as they danced? Or the way he held her right now?

"We are?" Her gaze collided with his for a second and she read understanding in Jonah's dark hazel eyes. She turned back to Tommy and smiled. "Ah, yes, we are. So, I'll—ah, we'll see you later."

With Jonah's hand pressing against her back—oh boy, that felt good, too—she walked past Tommy and headed back to their table. Eli Dalton still sat there alone, but the bottles and glasses had multiplied, indicating he had company at some point while they were gone.

Jonah dropped his hand from her hip, putting some distance between them just before Eli looked their way.

On purpose? Probably. A few dances and a few fibs to an ardent admirer didn't make them a couple.

Far from it.

They were…coworkers, she guessed, for lack of a better description, from the many questions he had about the mural. Questions she didn't have any answers to.

Yet.

But she would, she hoped.

She also hoped to get better acquainted with Jonah because she liked him. More so than any of the first dates (or seconds!) she'd gone on since coming to Rust Creek Falls. She'd been waiting for the right cowboy to come along. Could Jonah Dalton be the one?

"Hey, congratulations, Vanessa." Eli said, toasting her with a raised beer. "You not only got my little brother on the dance floor, you managed to keep him out there. What's your secret?"

She glanced at Jonah, already deciding she wasn't going to share that he'd actually been the one who offered to stay for more than one song.

"I'm not sure." She grabbed her glass, which was now just water as the ice had long melted. "Once he figured out I'm still a newbie at two-stepping I'm lucky he didn't go off and leave me standing there."

"I wouldn't do that."

Jonah's soft words caused her to look at him again. "I know that."

He dropped her gaze, focusing on the table for a moment before looking up at his brother. "I guess all of this means you aren't ready to head home? Or are you having a party of one?"

"The blondes returned. They're on the dance floor now and no, I'm not ready to leave." Eli tipped his head toward the poker table. "Besides, Derek's still playing. I thought I'd stick around. You know, just in case."

She wasn't sure what he meant, but Jonah seemed to understand the message. "Any chance you can get a ride home from your new friends? I'm ready to get out of here."

"I'll take you." Vanessa spoke before Eli could open his mouth. "I mean, that's what we said…" Her voice trailed off for a moment. "We're both heading back to the same place. You to the ranch house, me to the cabin. You are staying with your folks, right?"

"Oh, yeah, he's staying at the big house." Eli grinned.

"You okay to drive?" Jonah asked his brother.

Eli nodded. "This is my last one. I'll be fine."

"Okay, then." Jonah turned to her, picking up her sweater and holding it out in her direction. "I'm ready if you are."

They said their goodbyes, but when Jonah started for the front entrance of the bar, she grabbed his hand and motioned toward the back. He followed and soon they were outside in the cool evening air. Cool enough that Vanessa stopped and tugged on her sweater, wishing she'd remembered her jacket, once again fighting with her jewelry after she managed to get it over her head.

"You must really like those." Jonah said, pointing at her captured wrist.

"Yes, I do." She freed her hand, shaking her wrist to enjoy the noise her precious collection made. She then tugged the ends of the sweater down over her hips. "Some are made of beads or crystals, but my favorites are the individual metal circles that expand when you press on them. Each holds an individual charm."

Her favorite one, purchased during her and Adele's last trip to New York City, caught her eye. She looked down at it, gently rubbing her thumb across the raised heart engraved there.

"Gifts from friends and family?"

"Some." Vanessa blinked hard so the tears would be gone when she looked up at him. "A few I purchased myself. When I couldn't resist one that caught my eye, especially while trolling the internet in the wee hours of the morning."

Jonah seemed to be studying her and she was glad for the dark shadows in the parking lot. Digging out her keys from her pocket, Vanessa pointed toward the first row of vehicles. "I'm parked down in front. A perk of getting here early."

She started across the gravel lot and Jonah fell into step next to her. The music and noise from the bar filtered out through the open windows reminding her again of the huge favor he'd done for her tonight.

"Thank you. For dancing with me…and everything else back there," she said as they walked. "Hopefully Tommy was smart enough to pick up on the pretending we were doing."

"I think he got the message."

"Let's hope no one else noticed or else we'll be the topic of the local gossip mill come morning."

Jonah halted at her words. She turned, watching as he heaved a deep sigh and closed his eyes.

"Did I say something wrong?"

"No." He opened his eyes again, shook his head and started walking. "I'd just forgotten what a small town this is. Of course, knowing my brother, I'll be getting grief from my family before my morning coffee over the dancing."

She couldn't help but smile at that. "Should I apologize as well as say thank you?"

"No, neither is necessary. I had a good time, was glad to help and I appreciate the lift home." He stopped when she walked to the driver's-side door. "In this? This is your car?"

"Actually, it's a pickup. I'd think a cowboy would know the difference."

Jonah looked over her vehicle with a speculative eye. "I haven't been a cowboy in a long time and this thing has got to be at least twenty years old."

She liked that she had once again surprised him. "Not what you were expecting, huh? And be nice to Big Bertha, she's just celebrated her thirty-first birthday."

"The guy who runs the gas station used to have a truck he called Big Bertha."

"One and the same." She unlocked her door. "I had a rental for the first month I was here, but then I figured I needed something more permanent to get me through my first Montana winter. She's reliable, decent on gas and has never given me a lick of trouble. Head on around. I'll let you in."

Only after she jiggled with the passenger-side door for a few minutes while Jonah waited outside did Vanessa give up and get back out. She hurried to his side of the truck, unlocked the door and it opened right away.

"I think maybe you hurt her feelings," she said, offering a quick smile.

"Then I'm sorry."

Not sure if he was apologizing to her or her truck, Vanessa decided it was best not to ask as she headed back to the driver's side while Jonah climbed in.

"Did you know your inside light's not working?"

She looked up before closing her door. "Yep, you're right. The bulb must've just gone out."

Hooking her seat belt, she waited for a moment while

Jonah did the same, once he moved the hardback book away from the locking mechanism. "What's this?" He peered at the cover. *"Harry Potter and the Goblet of Fire?"*

She nodded, starting the engine and heading out the parking lot. "Great book."

"Exactly how old are you?"

She glanced at him, happy to see a smile when they passed under a street light. "Very funny. I'm twenty-six, but that doesn't matter. Harry Potter is for everyone. Besides, I never read the series when it first came out back when I was a teenager. Now, I'm up to book four."

"What made you decide to read them now?"

Number fifteen: read all the Harry Potter books.

Adele had devoured each of the books as they were released, often standing in line at bookstores at midnight to get the first copy. She couldn't understand why Vanessa had never taken time away from her art to do the same. She'd insisted the item be added to their list when they had revived their list.

"Vanessa?"

"Oh, sorry. I got lost in thought there." It only took a few minutes to clear the town limits and soon they were on the back roads heading toward the ranch. She found she liked the darkness of the rural countryside that surrounded them. "One day I saw a display of the books and assorted merchandise in a bookstore and decided it was time. Let me guess? You've read them all."

Jonah nodded. "My twin sisters loved the books from the very beginning. I used to read them until…well, until I moved out."

"When was that?"

"When I was eighteen."

Jonah stayed quiet after that and she wondered for a

moment if she should turn on the radio, but the silence was nice after the mayhem back at the bar. Soon they reached the turn off for the ranch, but still had a few miles to go before getting to the main house.

An idea suddenly came to her and before she could chicken out, she said, "Hey, do you have any plans for tomorrow?"

"Tomorrow's Friday," Jonah said. "I'll be working. Everyone works on Fridays."

She had to admit she was a bit disappointed by his oh-so-practical tone. "Hmmm, you're one of those, huh? Okay."

Silence filled the interior of the truck again as they bounced over the dirt road until he finally asked, "Why?"

"Ever been to BearTrap Mountain?"

"The ski resort?"

Vanessa nodded. "It's about an hour from here, right?"

"Yeah, but if you're looking to ski it's still a bit early. Don't let that snow on the mountaintops fool you. Barring an early storm, it'll be another month before the ski trails get enough cover."

"Oh, I wasn't looking to ski." There was no way she was going to tell him the real reason she wanted to go. She had a hunch Jonah might be a bit too straitlaced for what she had in mind. "Just wanted to check it out."

The headlights of her truck cut across the land that had belonged to the Dalton family for over a hundred years. She loved listening to Rita Dalton, Jonah's mother, talk about the family history whenever she'd go to Sunday dinners at the house. So unlike the quiet dinners when she was growing up when it was usually just her and her parents.

After her mother died, her father often ate in his office or was out on business so she'd either had the housekeeper or more often than not, Adele and her mother to keep her company.

"You can drop me around the corner, back by the kitchen door."

Jonah's words were soft as she turned into the drive and continued on past the front door and the porch that ran the length of the house. Pulling around the side, she eased to a stop just outside the glow coming from the kitchen window.

"Nice to know Mom still leaves the light on for us wayward kids." He released his seat belt. "Thanks again, Vanessa. For the company tonight and the ride home."

"You're welcome. I had a good time, too. Glad you ended up at my table."

Jonah returned her stare for a long moment and just when Vanessa wondered if he was going to lean in closer, a nonverbal request for her to do the same, he turned and reached for the door handle.

"Oh, it's hard to open from the inside. You need to jiggle it to the left three times, up twice and then down while pulling on it."

Jonah followed her directions, but the door wouldn't budge.

"No, three times to the left."

"I did go left."

She sighed and released her belt. Moving her book out of the way, she scooted closer. Propped on one hip, she leaned across his lap. "Here, let me. You just need the magic touch."

"Is that right?"

His words were soft against her hair, his lips right

at her ear taking her back to when they'd danced and he'd reassured her he wasn't ready to leave the floor yet. That dizzying feeling came back again and needing to brace herself, she put one hand on the closest surface, which turned out to be his muscular thigh.

Well, it was either that or between his legs, so this was probably best.

"Yes, that's right. Just give me a second…" She continued to play with the handle, reciting the steps silently to keep her mind occupied and away from the fact she was practically in his lap.

The door finally popped open. "There!" Pleased, she moved back, turning her head toward Jonah at the same time. "All it took was the right…"

Her words disappeared as their mouths brushed, lips clinging until someone, and for the life of her she didn't know who, moved. Soft and tender, the pressure barely felt until their breaths combined.

She backed away, realizing she now had both hands on his legs, but it wasn't enough. Her elbows gave way, but he reached for her shoulders, keeping her in place.

"Why did you do that?"

He looked at her. "Do what?"

Was he serious? "Kiss me."

"I didn't kiss you." His gaze left hers and settled on her mouth. Even in the dark she could see banked desire there. "You kissed me."

A shiver of indignation skirted down her backbone. "I already told you I don't kiss on the first date."

"This isn't a date."

Vanessa started to protest, but he was right, despite how he'd labeled himself back at the bar. "Point taken."

His mouth hitched up one corner. "So, that makes it okay that you kissed me?"

"I didn't! Believe me, architect, if I'd kissed you, you'd have known—"

The rest of her words disappeared once again as his mouth came down on hers.

Chapter Four

Boy, this cowboy can kiss.

A silly thought to be sure. Jonah had made it clear he hadn't been a cowboy in years, but it was the first thing that raced through Vanessa's mind when he interrupted their "who went first" argument by kissing her.

And he kept on doing so.

His mouth was firm when it first crashed down on hers, but it softened when she made it clear she was fully on board with what he was doing by opening her mouth, her tongue darting out to sneak a taste of him.

Heavenly.

A low groan escaped from him as he angled his head, pulled her closer and settled his mouth against hers again. Deepening the kiss, his tongue glided against hers, stealing her breath and when it returned it was a soft moan to let him know how much she was enjoying this.

She hadn't been kissed in a long time and the way he explored her mouth, teasing and tasting, along with a hint of urgency that overrode any hesitation she should be feeling, told her just how much she'd been missing.

Instead, she wanted to test that resolve, wanted to see just where he would take this if she released the tight grip she had on the solid muscles of his thighs and simply crawled into his lap and wrapped her arms around his neck.

The thought of doing just that seemed to melt her every bone, or maybe that was the heat from his body as he held her close, just like when they were dancing.

But then he broke free and drawing in a ragged breath, he slowly set her back on the seat before releasing her. "Ah, that was…"

His husky whisper trailed off and even though he was looking at her, shadows covered most of his face.

Except for his mouth.

The perfection of his still-wet full lips was only inches away, open as if he had more to say, but he stayed silent.

She fought back the temptation to be the one to initiate round two of surprise kisses that came out of nowhere—or would that be round three?—and instead said, "Yeah, I didn't…"

Whatever else she'd planned to say vanished from her head like bubbles popping in midair. Hmmm, guess he wasn't the only one at a loss for words.

She swiped her tongue across her parched lips and he dropped his head a fraction of an inch. Her breath caught, certain he was going to kiss her again. But then he moved and seconds later stood outside, the open door allowing the night's cool breeze to displace the warm sultry air that had filled her truck.

"Thanks again…for the ride home. Good night."

She expected him to shut the door and walk away, but he remained standing there.

Waiting for her to respond? What was she supposed to say?

"Good night."

Yes, that was a clever comeback, but before she could say another word he stepped back and gently closed the door, double-checking that it was shut. He then turned and headed up the stairs until all she could see of him was his legs from the knees down as he stood on the porch.

It took her a moment to realize he was waiting for her to leave. The idea raced through her head of crawl- ing out from the driver's side and joining him, just to see how he'd react, but this was his family's home and heck, he'd been the one to end their impromptu make- out session.

She slid back behind the wheel, put the truck into Drive and slowly pulled away. Not looking in the rear- view mirror was impossible as her gaze automatically went there. Jonah remained on the back porch until she could no longer see him as the road twisted away from the main house.

It only took a few minutes and she was parking next to the cabin. The lights she'd left on, both inside and the porch lamp, welcomed her home. She slipped in- side, thinking about Jonah doing the same thing back at his place. Despite the distinct warmth that still flooded her insides thanks to those amazing kisses, she noticed the chill in the air as she locked the door behind her.

Shutting off lights as she headed to the bedroom in the back of the cabin, she went to the small woodstove in the corner. Rita Dalton had been the one who'd shown her how to start a fire and keep it going, but even with written instructions it sometimes took her a few tries. Things went perfectly this time and as she watched the kindling ignite, her thoughts drifted back to the night's events.

It'd been clear that Jonah hadn't expected to see her at the bar, much less for her to ask him to dance. Yes, she should've told him that her two-stepping skills were sorely lacking, but he'd been so sweet in taking her out to the middle of the dance floor instead of heading back to the table. So understanding about her need to avoid an overamorous cowboy.

She liked talking to him, getting to know him better.

At least until he mentioned the mural.

The minute he'd gone all businesslike and started asking detailed questions, she'd felt the dread surge to life deep in her stomach.

"Maybe agreeing to do that mural wasn't your best idea," she said aloud as she placed a couple of larger logs inside the stove. "Not that your block is anyone's fault but yours. Still…"

Her voice trailed off as she stared at the flames, fingers outstretched for the warmth. She studied her hands and thought about how they'd never let her down before. Not once in all the years she'd been painting.

"You've done it before, you can do it again."

Closing up the stove, she then grabbed her pajamas and headed for the bathroom. A hot shower was just what she needed before going to bed. Standing beneath the steamy spray she relived the moments in the truck, still not sure who'd kissed who first.

But she knew for sure that second kiss was all Jonah and for someone who claimed not to like surprises, he'd certainly pulled a rabbit out of the hat the moment his lips touched hers.

She washed away the night's sweat and smells from the bar, but also the rich, spicy scent of Jonah's cologne that filled her head, clung to her skin and made her weak in the knees every time she got close to him.

A few minutes later, she was tucked beneath the covers in the coolest bed ever after making sure the woodstove had enough fuel to keep the room toasty until the morning. She clicked on the radio that only seemed to pick up two stations, country music and a national news show. Soft strains of an old Patsy Cline ballad played as she reached for the sketch pad and the leather case that held her pens and pencils, her gaze catching on the folded piece of paper on her nightstand.

She gently opened it, smoothing it out with her hands. Grabbing one of her pens, she trailed a finger down the list, remembering the moments last year with Adele when they added to their childhood agenda for a happy life.

Number twelve: kiss a cowboy.

When she told Jonah she didn't kiss on the first date, she meant it. A personal rule since she was a teenager. Despite dating quite a few cowboys since coming to town, she hadn't kissed a single one.

In fact, the last time she'd been kissed was well over two years ago after her last relationship ended, thanks to a cheating boyfriend who'd managed to keep both her and a girl in Boston in the dark about each other for over a year.

Heck, she hadn't even dated since then, throwing herself into her art. Just like Adele had said. So when she'd moved here she'd been determined to meet new people. Do new things. Find the joy and happiness missing from her life.

Find someone new to kiss. Find her lost talent.

And she liked to think she had at least started on those goals, even if her gift was only coming through in practice sketches.

She'd made friends, and yes, being as small of a town as Rust Creek Falls was, people tended to know each other's business and felt compelled to offer unsolicited advice at times, but they cared about each other. Cared about their town.

And when it came to kissing…

Well, she knew now why none of the men she'd dated had tempted her to break her rule.

They weren't Jonah.

Technically he was more city boy than cowboy now, but she'd bet her custom-made sable paintbrushes the man could still saddle a horse and ride off into the sunset.

Kissed Jonah Dalton!

She scrawled the words next to number twelve and placed a checkmark there, as well. Another mission accomplished. One she wouldn't mind repeating.

Out of the sixteen remaining goals on their list, she'd completed five so far. Well, she was still working on the Harry Potter books, but she was halfway through them so that goal got a checkmark, as well.

She looked over the list again, her heart giving a little jolt when she read one of the goals they'd written down when they were twelve.

Number nine: Fly among the clouds (and not in an airplane!)

Impossible? Maybe not.

She'd come up with an idea and in a spur-of-the-moment flash, probably still in the clouds from being held in the man's arms, she'd thought maybe Jonah would—

"Nope, don't go there." Vanessa folded up the list and tucked it back between the lamp and a framed collage of pictures of her and Adele through the years.

"Don't ruin how great tonight ended." She then turned back to her sketch pad. "Okay, let's make some magic for this mural."

She opened to a blank page, switched out her pen for a pencil and held it over the stark whiteness in front of her. Waving the pencil back and forth, the tip hovering over the paper just enough not to leave a mark, she waited for…

Something.

Anything to come to mind that would represent a mural honoring the special place and people that meant so much to this town and its residents.

And yet again, there was nothing.

Her head was as blank as the paper before her.

Sighing, she closed her eyes, shut out the unadorned sheet and focused on the Tim McGraw ballad that filled the air, one of the songs she and Jonah had danced to tonight.

Forcing the pencil to make contact, to glide across the page, stroke after stroke, she allowed the music to guide her, already knowing what she was sketching. When the song ended, she looked and the rough outline of dark eyes, slightly mussed hair and a strong jaw looked back at her.

Jonah.

She tossed the sketchbook and pencil to the empty side of the bed, turned off the light and snuggled deep beneath the covers, determined not to think about the man she'd only met this morning—and kissed tonight!—and get some sleep.

Sleep. Who was she kidding?

Jonah pulled into the parking lot of the Grace Traub Community Center, the town's newest building, built just this past spring.

He checked his watch. Just after four o'clock.

Usually he'd still be putting in at least three more hours of work before calling it a day, but the foreman had pointed out construction was ahead of schedule and recommended starting the weekend a bit early. Jonah had agreed and when the last worker pulled out of the parking lot, he wasn't far behind.

Because of Vanessa.

When she mentioned last night how the town's gossip mill would probably make them dancing together a hot new topic, Jonah had figured it would start this morning at breakfast, but he'd been wrong. Only because both Derek and Eli made the walk of shame as they showed up still wearing the same clothes they'd had on the night before, so all three Dalton boys were on the hot seat.

Their mother had stayed quiet when the two of them walked in the back door at the same time, and all Dad had wanted was for them to shower and eat so they could get started on the workday. Even though she was well aware that all of her children were adults now, it still amazed Jonah how their mother had the ability to express her emotions without saying a word—and she wasn't happy.

That is, until Eli had pulled out the often used diversionary tactic from their youth and asked Jonah about his ride home.

Once Jonah had cleared up the confusion by admitting he'd gotten a lift from Vanessa, his mom had talked nonstop about their tenant. When he'd mentioned Nate had commissioned her to paint a mural for the resort, she'd shown him a pencil sketch Vanessa had done of his father while sitting in the barn one afternoon, drawing as he worked without the old man realizing she'd been there.

The piece was stunning.

She'd captured his father's weathered, yet still handsome features. The deep grooves around his eyes from years of working outdoors, laugh lines he called them, saying they came from being happily married to their mother all these years. The cowboy hat perched back on his head as he concentrated on whatever job he'd been tackling.

Jonah was impressed with her talent and wanted to see more of her previous work, especially since he hadn't done an internet search on her last night when he'd gotten home like he planned.

Not after the way she'd kissed him.

He kissed her.

They'd kissed each other.

The first time had been purely by accident. Although the way she'd leaned across his lap to mess with the door handle—her hand on his leg, her hair in his face, knowing that she only had to turn his way—so yeah, the thought had crossed his sleep-deprived mind.

But the cute way she'd insisted it hadn't been her fault, not to mention the dare she'd practically thrown down made him cut off her protest with a searing kiss.

It was only when he'd pulled her even closer and thought about dragging her onto his lap so they'd both be more comfortable, that he'd put a stop to the craziness, got out of her truck and said good-night.

Before it was too late.

His brothers had used their mother's focus on Vanessa and her artwork to slip out of the kitchen, so thankfully they hadn't seen his mental stroll down memory lane, but his mother had picked up on his quietness. When she pushed, he claimed he was still tired from the long drive from Denver the day before, but agreed that the sketch was terrific.

That was how he'd found out Vanessa been doing similar sketches of many of the locals and about the afternoon program she ran here at the community center on Mondays, Wednesdays and Friday afternoons.

He knew they had to talk about what happened last night and he'd waited all day for her to show up at the resort, but she hadn't. Some of the crew had given him some good-natured ribbing about being in the bar last night with Vanessa, so maybe that's what she was trying to avoid?

Glancing at his watch again, he rubbed at his jaw feeling the day's growth of his beard and wondered if he should've gone home first to shower and shave.

Then he wondered if he was too early, maybe the class lasted longer than what his mother had said, but the front doors of the center opened and a stream of kids and adults came out.

He waited until most had either driven or walked away before getting out of his truck. He headed up the front steps, his architectural eye appreciating how the building fit in so well with the rest of the businesses here on North Main Street. A few of them, like Crawford's General Store on the opposite corner, had been around almost since Rust Creek Falls was first founded back in the late 1800s.

There was an office off the lobby, but it was empty. Straight ahead was the main room, a large space with a stage that could be used for any community event, which was the purpose of the building he guessed, but no Vanessa.

"Excuse me." He spotted a teenage girl in the corner of the room, doing something with a large bulletin board. "Can you tell me where I can find Vanessa Brent?"

"Sure." She pointed with one hand, never taking her eyes off her project. "Go back out to the main hall, head for the right side of the building and follow the music."

"Okay, thanks." He turned, but then thought about what she'd said. "Wait, did you say music? I thought she taught an art class."

"She does. Trust me, listen for the tunes and you'll find her."

Following her directions, Jonah started down a long sun-filled hallway, passing a number of closed doors before the strains of a Frank Sinatra song caught his attention.

He came up to the large windows that allowed visitors to see inside the room, spotting Vanessa right away. With her back to him, she rocked her hips back and forth in time with the swing tune as she moved around a bunch of pint-size tables, picking up art supplies and pushing in miniature chairs.

She was again wearing those same stretchy leggings that had captured his attention yesterday, this time a bright blue color. The same ankle boots were on her feet while an oversize man's dress shirt splattered with every color of the rainbow covered her past her backside, but the sleeves were rolled back showing off her jewelry. Her hair was a wild array of curls, but held back off her face with a hair band the same color as her pants.

The same kick in the gut he'd felt when he'd first saw her—hell, every time he'd run into her yesterday—nearly knocked him over again. When he reached the open doorway, he paused and leaned against it, using the time to get his breathing under control and enjoy the show.

She moved around the room with ease, singing along with Old Blue Eyes questioning what really was a lost last love, as she stacked papers, tossed garbage and filled a nearby sink with dirty paintbrushes.

When she dropped something, she didn't just bend over and pick it up, but twisted to the floor, her hips never stopping as her boots easily moved across the tiled flooring. She rose and spun around in one motion, coming to a complete stop when she finally spotted him.

"Jonah!"

He smiled, liking that this time he was the one doing the surprising. "Sorry, didn't mean to startle you, but I didn't want to interrupt your duet with Frank."

"Jeez, you heard me?" She placed the stuff in her hands on the counter and turned down the portable electronic device sitting between a set of miniature speakers. "Please tell me you just showed up."

"No, and I think the whole building heard you."

Instead of being embarrassed, she only laughed. "Boy, I need to remember to close the door and drop the blinds once the kids head out."

"You play swing music while the kids are here?"

"Sure do. And anything else that comes up on the playlist. We've got everyone from Bon Jovi to Katy

Perry to The Muppets. All preselected and screened for young ears."

He straightened and entered, noticing the area in the back of the room was floor to ceiling bookcases, some with doors and others open shelving, filled with every kind of art supply imaginable. Another wall was an oversize corkboard where the prized artwork of her students was on display. "Wow, this is quite a setup you've got here."

"Thanks, I'm pretty proud of it." She looked around, her expressive face reflecting her words as she moved to the sink and turned on the water. "They let me totally redo the room once I explained what I needed for the class. Hard to believe this used to be a stuffy conference room with wall-to-wall carpeting and a kitchenette."

"It's good they had room in the budget."

"What?" She squirted liquid soap, filling the sink with bubbles. "Oh, no, I paid for it."

He looked around the room again, easily adding up the cost of the work needed, never mind the kid-size furniture. "You paid for the entire renovation? What about the ongoing supplies needed?"

She shrugged. "It was my idea for the class in the first place." She smiled and waved a soapy finger at him. "Be careful what you volunteer for."

Here she was surprising him again. He stared at her, his gaze taking in all of her from her curls to her boots, the few feet separating them suddenly made her seem far away. "That's very generous."

She returned his appraisal, then abruptly turned and faced the sink. "I've got connections for great discounts on the art stuff. So, what brings you to the community center this afternoon?"

He crossed the room, joining her at the counter.

"You. I was hoping— I thought I'd see you at the resort today."

She kept her gaze on the items she'd washed, rinsed and set to dry on a nearby rack. "Why? I told you last night I haven't even started on the design for the mural yet."

"And you said you had plans for today." He remembered her asking about the nearby ski resort. "Did you make it over to BearTrap Mountain?"

"No, I didn't even get out of bed until almost noon." She shook back her curls and finally looked at him. "I had a tough time getting to sleep last night."

Pulling in a deep breath, he took in the tangy odors of clay, paint, wet paper towels and the same flowery scent of hers he'd discovered while they danced. While they kissed. "Yeah, me, too."

"Really?"

He nodded. "I wanted to see you today so I could apologi—"

"Don't say that." His words disappeared when she slapped a soapy hand over his mouth. " Don't you dare apologize for any part of last night."

He pulled her hand away and wiped at his mouth, the taste on his lips made him cringe, reminding him of a few times in his childhood when the threat of washing out his mouth with a bar of soap truly came to pass.

Vanessa's eyes grew wide. She snatched her hand back to her chest. "Oh! I'm so sorry! There's a water fountain in the back."

He found it quickly, having to bend almost in half to reach it, but rinsed away the residue with the cool liquid. Rising back to his full height he found Vanessa standing there, fresh paper towels in her hand. "Thanks."

"I really am sorry. I didn't think…"

He grinned after wiping at his mouth. "Yeah, I figured that out pretty quickly."

"So now I'm the one apologizing to you, but only for my soapy mishap." She took a step closer, and laid a hand on his chest. "Not last night. I'm glad you showed up at the bar, glad you danced with me, let me take you home and—"

This time he silenced her, but with just one finger pressed to her lips. She could've stepped away and continued talking, but she went still beneath his touch.

"Even though you don't kiss on the first date?" he asked.

"It wasn't a date."

He dropped his hand, the apology he'd practiced in his truck on the way here listing all the reasons why the kiss they'd shared had been wrong—how tired he'd been, they were working together, he wasn't looking to get involved—vanished from his thoughts.

"Are you busy tomorrow?" he asked instead.

She shook her head.

"Would you like to check out that resort? We could head over in the afternoon—"

"How about ten a.m.?"

He smiled. "Okay, ten o'clock. I'll drive."

A mock look of hurt crossed her pretty face. "Are you saying you don't like my truck?"

"I'm saying I want to make sure we get there in one piece. And why so early?"

She beamed a bright smile at him. "Oh, there's an… exhibition there I want to check out."

"Anything I might be interested in?" he asked.

She offered a casual shrug as she stepped back, but he caught a mischievous sparkle in those big brown eyes. "Maybe. How do you feel about flying?"

Chapter Five

She had to be kidding. Zip-lining? That's what Vanessa had been talking about yesterday when she quizzed him on flying?

They had arrived at BearTrap Mountain, a no-frills ski resort an hour's drive north of Kalispell, fifteen minutes ago. Wandering through the main lodge, a simple structure of glass and concrete that was surprisingly busy for an early October Saturday, they found the ski lifts were operating, taking leaf peepers up to the summit to view the beautiful fall foliage. There were also plenty of signs pointing to hiking and mountain biking trails.

When they reached the large open area of the lodge that would be swamped with skiers in another month or so, Jonah had been busy comparing the space to what the resort in Rust Creek Falls would need, not noticing Vanessa had wandered off until she returned with a piece of paper, claiming she needed his signature.

"I have to sign a waiver in order to do this?" he asked.

"Of course. They take safety very seriously, but still…"

"Are you sure you want to try this?" He pushed when Vanessa's voice trailed off.

"Are you kidding? To feel like you're flying among the clouds? Look at the video and the pictures." She pointed at a desk area that showed the adventure that awaited them in full color. "Doesn't it look like fun?"

Jonah sighed, still not believing he'd allowed her to rope him—literally—into this. "Okay, let's go."

Giving a little squeal of delight, Vanessa lifted on her tiptoes and planted a quick kiss on his cheek before she headed for the sign-up desk. Jonah followed her, wondering if that was considered a real kiss, especially since she'd made it clear that was something she didn't do on first dates.

After sitting through a discussion on safety and equipment procedures, they were given helmets and got fitted in a harness with straps that made certain parts of his anatomy a bit uncomfortable. Thank goodness he'd worn jeans and boots today.

They were put in a group with a family with three young boys, a duo of teenagers and a honeymooning couple around about the same age as him and Vanessa.

"How long have you two been together?" the recent bride asked as they sat in the back of a tram that would transport them up to the mountain for the start of the tour.

"Oh, we're not—"

"This is our first date." Jonah leaned forward, cutting off Vanessa as he grabbed her hand. "Her idea."

The couple grinned at them. "First time zip-lining, as well?" the husband asked.

When the two of them nodded, he said, "Well, if you can make it through this, anything after will be a breeze."

"Thanks a lot." Vanessa turned to look at Jonah, concern on her face for the first time.

"Hey, you wanted to do this." Jonah reminded her with a grin. "I was just about to suggest a nice, smooth ride up on the ski lift."

They reached their starting point and headed off into the woods, their guide pointing out the local flora and fauna as they hiked. Soon they reached the first sky bridge, where Vanessa surprised him by agreeing to be the first one in line after the lead guide. Jonah moved into place behind her as they walked across, tethered to a safety cable. He had to admit the scenery was beautiful.

As long as one kept their eyes on the trees and not the ground below. The platform was sixty feet up in the treetops.

"Oh, wasn't that the most amazing thing ever?" Vanessa said as they waited for the rest of their group to join them.

"I think I'll save amazing for what's next. The first zip line." Jonah pointed at the metal cable to their left. "You going first again?"

"Unless you want to," Vanessa said, her eyes bright with laughter.

"Oh, no. Ladies first."

"Chicken," she said, teasing him.

"No, I'd rather you not be here to see me lose my man card when I have to shut my eyes before taking the initial step off into nothingness."

"Don't worry." She leaned in close, her hand giving his biceps a quick squeeze. "Your manhood status is guaranteed with me."

And right then he wanted to kiss her—personal rules be damned—but the platform was crowded as everyone had made it across the bridge.

The boys wanted to be first down the zip line, so he and Vanessa went after the family, with Vanessa again going ahead of him. She stepped right off and let out a "yee-haw" all the way down. Jonah was so impressed with her spirit, he did the same, enjoying the rush as his body zoomed through the trees.

The rest of their two-hour tour went quickly, with everyone taking turns at being the first ones to go at each new station. The last zip line was a dual line, and it was Jonah and Vanessa's turn to go last. The newly-weds went just before them, with the bride declaring it a race just before she stepped off ahead of her husband.

"If winning makes her happy, then I'm happy," he said, waiting a second more before heading down.

Jonah watched as Vanessa stepped up to the platform next to his, both of them clipping on their harnesses at the same time.

"So, are we going to race, too?" he asked.

"I don't know. What does the winner get?"

Jonah had quite a few ideas, but he just shrugged and said, "Whatever they want."

Her answering smile could only be called sassy. "Oh, game on."

Damn, his body ached from his eyebrows to his feet.

Dropping his tools, Jonah stood and stretched, raising his arms high over his head, feeling the aching protest of muscles he hadn't worked in years.

Whoever said weekends were for kicking back and relaxing hadn't been from his hometown. He'd been on the go since yesterday morning. First, a day on a mountain with Vanessa, and today he was working alongside his brothers mending a fence line until…

Well, until later.

During the past three hours of backbreaking work, which included replacing damaged posts, untangling and stretching yards of barbed wire and replacing missing staples, Jonah and his brothers had fallen into a familiar rhythm. They stayed focused on their work, talking only when it was related to the task at hand. But he could tell both of them had been chomping at the bit to get at him.

About Vanessa.

"You know, I bet spending the afternoon doing ranch work is nothing compared to daily trips to some fancy, expensive gym."

And there was the first volley.

Derek's voice came from behind him. Jonah lowered his arms, turned around and found his brothers had stopped working and were at the truck, taking a break. He yanked off his gloves and rubbed at the red spots on his hands where new calluses were sure to form.

"You're right." Shoving the gloves into a back pocket, he walked over to them. "Eight miles a day on a treadmill and lifting weights is fun, but this is real work. And you two are as good—no, better—at it than I remember."

His younger brother seemed amazed by Jonah's praise. He meant every word. His ass was dragging and they still had at least two more hours to go. Still, he was glad to see the two of them were as sweaty and dirty as him.

"You've got a right to be tired." Eli filled a plastic tumbler with water from the cooler sitting on the tailgate and handed it to him. "You hit the ground running the moment you got home three days ago. Even working on Saturdays? I noticed your truck was gone most of the day."

Jonah froze, the refreshing liquid halfway to his mouth. He had gone over to the resort yesterday afternoon for an hour or so after his adventurous day with Vanessa. Did that mean his brothers thought he'd been there all day?

"Don't let him fool you, man. His truck headed east past the barn yesterday morning before he eventually left the ranch. There's nothing down that way except cattle, horses, the creek." Derek paused, as if deep in thought. "Oh, yeah and his cabin. Or should I say Vanessa's cabin."

"Really?" Eli grinned and winked at him. "So, does your artist know she's sleeping in your custom-made bed yet?"

"If she didn't before, she probably does now," Derek deadpanned, grabbing one of the sandwiches their mother had packed for them.

Jonah lowered his drink, still having not taken a sip. "Is my spending time with Vanessa a problem for you?"

"Why would it be?" Derek said. "If I was interested in her I would've made that clear when the two of you were getting cozy at the Ace the other night."

His brother looked him straight in the eye when he spoke and Jonah believed him. But it bothered him that he'd never given what Eli had said about Derek offering Vanessa riding lessons—and if that meant anything—a second thought.

Not when they danced.

Not when he kissed her, and not for one moment yesterday.

"So what did you two end up doing all day?" Eli tossed him a sandwich. "Please tell me you really weren't working."

Jonah took his time finishing off the water, enjoying the coldness on his dry throat. He wondered if his brothers were baiting him, already knowing but trying to get him to say the words aloud.

Not sure, he purposely took his time setting the empty tumbler down and then opened his sandwich, waiting until his brothers had both their mouths full before he spoke.

"We went zip-lining on BearTrap Mountain."

In unison, both men choked, but at least Eli managed to keep his mouth shut. Derek ended up spitting out the water he'd chugged a second ago all over his boots.

Jonah laughed at their stunned expressions, which probably matched his yesterday when he and Vanessa got to the ski resort and she finally explained what her cryptic comment about flying had meant.

"Are you kidding me?" Eli finally asked, after swallowing his food and pounding a coughing Derek on the back so hard, the kid hopped off the truck to get away from him. "You? Zip lining?"

"Yes, me." Jonah grinned, giving a casual shrug. "It was something Vanessa has wanted to do for a while, not that I was aware of her plan until we got there.

"Sounds like you had a good time," Derek said.

Jonah nodded. "Zip lining has become really popular over the last few years. Not to mention it's a great way for a ski resort to earn money in the off season. The place was packed yesterday, and not just because it was the last weekend for the activity. The guides said they'd been swamped all summer long."

It was then his brain had gone into high gear. "I'm planning to talk to Nate Crawford about including something similar at the resort once we get started on the outdoor recreation portion—"

"No, that's not—" Derek cut him off, shaking his head. "Jeez, you're a moron."

Confused, Jonah stared at his brother. "Come again?"

"I'm not talking about business. It was gorgeous outside yesterday. What was it like on the mountain with the sun on your face and the wind in your hair?" Derek moved closer, invading Jonah's personal space. "Did you step right off like those kids with a loud 'hell, yeah' coming out of your mouth all the way down the first time? Or were you so scared you could've wet your pants, but hey, there was no turning back?"

Silence filled the air for a long moment as Jonah stared at his brother.

"I think what he's asking is if you, and Vanessa, had fun yesterday," Eli added drily, as he started cleaning up their mess. "But I'm just guessing."

"Yes," Jonah said. "It was fun. *We* had fun."

"I'd say from that smile of yours, you had a lot of fun," Derek said. "Good to know you still have it in you."

Still had it in him? Jonah stared at his brother. "What's that supposed to mean?"

"It means this is the first time you've been out on a date with someone who lives in this town. It means it's nice to see you being social. You know, instead pulling that hermit act like you usually do whenever you come home."

"I have a social life in Denver."

Derek remained silent, returning his stare for a long moment. He then shook his head before pulling on his gloves and heading back for the fence line.

"You've got to admit, he's got a point." Eli jumped down from the back of the truck. "Yeah, we know you've dated some since your divorce, but like you said, that's in Denver. We don't expect you to find true love here again, but whenever you come back for a visit you'd either be at the cabin or sticking close to the ranch working on whatever architect stuff you'd brought with you."

"Finishing that cabin was important to me," Jonah said. At least it had been over the almost six years it took him to complete it. "For a lot of reasons, and I can't just walk away from my work obligations while on vacation."

"Either way, you were never interested in having any fun. Hell, you hardly cracked a smile most times." Eli shrugged and continued to clean up. "It's like you shut down as soon as you crossed the town line. I was surprised when you agreed to get a beer with me the other night."

His brothers were right.

He'd always kept to himself whenever he'd come home.

His mom had often tried to talk to him about it over the past few years, to get him to open up about the end of his marriage and how much he'd changed. Jonah had only reassured her he was doing okay, and proved it by working even harder on the cabin, only accepting help from his family when he had to tackle a job that required more than one person.

But the cabin was done now. It had been for almost two years, sitting empty before Vanessa rented it.

Now that his brothers had pointed out his changed

behavior, Jonah had no answer as to why things were
so different this time around.

Was it because of a certain brunette who'd captured
his attention his first day back?

That same vivacious and gorgeous woman he had
a second date with tonight after accepting an invitation for dinner.

At the cabin she still didn't know belonged to him.

This was his place.

Vanessa stood in the small, but efficient kitchen, having just put the chicken breasts into the oven while keeping an eye on the two pots simmering on the stove top,
still unable to believe what she'd learned earlier today.

This was his place and he'd never said a word during their adventure yesterday.

Excited that Jonah had accepted her invitation to
come for dinner tonight, she'd made a quick trip to
Crawford's General Store earlier today.

She'd decided to make him a favorite dish of hers,
so she'd hoped to find a few necessary ingredients, or
else she'd have to make the drive to nearby Kalispell.

But as surprised as she'd been at finding angel-hair
pasta and garlic cloves in the same place that also sold
just about everything from flannel shirts to children's
toys to enough hardware to build an ark—or a cabin—it
paled in comparison to what she'd overheard while debating which bottle of wine to pick up for the evening.

She'd first heard her and Jonah's names spoken by
a couple of females in the next aisle, and then how the
two of them were not only seen dancing the other night,
but also spotted together at nearby BearTrap Mountain.

Grinning over the fact she was now officially a part
of the town's gossip mill, Vanessa had started to step

around the corner to actually confirm their stories when one of women mentioned how cozy it all was.

Seeing how she was renting *his* cabin.

A cabin Jonah actually built by hand.

It supposedly had taken him years to complete it, according to one of the busybodies. He'd worked on it only when he came home for visits, refusing to allow anyone to help him. Apparently it had stood empty once he completed it.

Until his mother rented it to Vanessa, that is.

She looked around the open space that made up the kitchen, separated from the combined dining and living room by a V-shaped island. A woodstove, the same style as in the bedroom but a bit larger, stood on the other side of the island, providing heat for the entire area.

The walls were filled with windows that opened up to views of the beautiful Montana scenery and the decking that surrounded the cabin on three sides. There were automatic shades that could be lowered after the sun went down, which it was in the process of doing right now.

She found the remote and pressed the button, watching as the shades silently lowered into place. It wasn't cool enough yet for a fire, so she turned on a few lights, including the intriguing antler chandelier that hung over the dining-room table, and lit some of the candles she had sitting out.

The glow of it all reflected off the pale logs and filled the space with a warm radiance.

It was beautiful.

She'd fallen in love with the place the first time she'd seen it.

Moving into the dining room, she fussed with the table settings, upset again that she'd left the store without picking out a bottle of wine, the news about Jonah and the cabin ringing in her ears.

As soon as she'd arrived home, she'd gone on a cleaning frenzy, wanting it to look perfect when he saw it again, remembering how he seemed transfixed by the place when he'd picked her up yesterday morning.

Now she knew why.

She'd been waiting outside for him, so excited about their day, so he hadn't actually been inside yet. The only thing he'd commented on had been the twin country-red rocking chairs she'd put on the front deck. She'd told him about finding them in Crawford's and how it just didn't seem right to split up the pair.

Looking around the interior, she wondered what he would think of what she'd done to it.

There'd only been a few pieces here when she moved in. The dining-room table with two chairs and that fabulous light fixture overhead, an oversize leather couch that had seen better days, but was oh so comfortable to stretch out on, and the king-size bed made from hand-hewn logs in the bedroom.

Jonah's mother had offered to look around the main ranch house for some stuff and despite Vanessa's assurance that it wasn't necessary, she'd come by the next day with a set of dishes and cookware for the kitchen.

From there, Vanessa had enjoyed filling the place with whatever necessities she needed or any impulse buys that reflected her personal style. She shopped for everything from furniture to artwork to sheets for that glorious bed—

A knock came at the door and Vanessa jumped.

Then she laughed.

"Oh, girl, you are being so silly." She fluffed her

wavy hair, tugged her sweater down over her hips and headed for the front door. "Coming!"

That must be Jonah.

He probably didn't care two figs about this place. If he had, he would've said something to her before now. Maybe building it had been part of his job. The man was an architect, after all. He obviously had his own apartment or house in Denver where he lived full-time.

"You're obsessing about this because you're nervous," she whispered to her reflection in the small, ornately framed mirror that hung next to the entrance. "It's just dinner. A second date. Nothing special."

She smiled, checked her teeth as she'd been sampling her cooking, and opened the door.

Jonah stood on the other side, looking impossibly handsome dressed in jeans, a Western-cut shirt and boots. In one hand he held an oversize bouquet of gerbera daisies, a riot of neon yellows, oranges, pinks and greens. In the other hand a bottle of pinot grigio wine.

"Hey there." He held out the wine first. "I didn't know what you're cooking for us, but I remembered your wine at the Ace had been white. I hope this is okay."

He remembered that? She'd downed the remains of her wine within the first minute of finding him at her table.

"And the flowers?" she asked, her words coming out much softer than she planned. "What's their story?"

"Ah, I hope they're not too corny," he said with a sheepish grin as he offered them to her, as well. "As soon as I saw these beauties I knew there was only one woman who'd appreciate them."

She smiled and reached for the flowers, their fingers brushing when he released them to her. "Nothing wrong with corny, which these are not. They're lovely. Thank you."

"So, does that mean I can come in?" He leaned to one side, his gaze darting around the room. "Something smells great."

"Of course. Yes, please." She stepped back, allowing him to enter. "Welcome home."

His footstep faltered for a moment, but then he moved inside and closed the door behind him, his gaze never leaving hers.

"You know, don't you?"

She nodded. "That the cabin belongs to you? Yep. What I don't know is why you didn't tell me."

Chapter Six

"How did you find out?"

"The old-fashioned way." She headed into the kitchen, turning the pots on the stove down to the lowest possible setting before grabbing a vase for the flowers. "I overheard a couple of gossipy old ladies in Crawford's today. I think you and I are the latest hot topic."

"No surprise there."

His tone was sarcastic, but she heard humor there, too.

Turning from the sink so she could put the flowers on the dining-room table, she found him still standing near the front door.

He was looking around, as if he were seeing the place for the first time. Rita had said it'd been finished almost two years ago, but she was the first person to live here.

Was this his first time back since completing the cabin? He seemed to be studying the place. Did he like what she'd done to it?

"There's a corkscrew in the top drawer next to the sink," she said, thinking maybe he needed something to do. "Glasses are in the cabinet above if you want to open the wine."

He nodded and walked behind the leather sofa, his free hand trailing along the back of it for a moment. "Good idea. I could use a drink."

That makes two of us.

Surprised at how nervous she truly was, Vanessa busied herself with rearranging the table to fit the flowers in the center. She then noticed Jonah holding back the blind that covered the large window over the sink. He stood transfixed, staring, the corkscrew forgotten in his other hand.

Unable to stop herself, she joined him, curious as to what caught his eye. Standing close, she could feel the heat from his body as his familiar spicy cologne filled her head. It took some effort, but she managed to tear her gaze from his profile and look outside.

She smiled. Another amazing Montana sunset.

The last rays of daylight washed over the breathtaking scenery while a scattering of clouds seemed to slowly swallow the last remnants of color, the darkness spreading across the copper-colored sky.

How could she have forgotten to take a moment to enjoy this? "Beautiful, isn't it?"

He dropped the blind back in place and turned to her. She waited a moment, her heart pounding in her chest as she felt his gaze on her, but then she looked at him.

"Yes, very beautiful." He studied her for a moment longer, and then turned his attention back to the wine bottle. "You know, I'm surprised my mother didn't mention this place was mine when she rented it to you."

"Maybe she did, but I don't remember. I just know

I fell in love with the cabin the moment I saw it." She took the half-filled glass he held out to her. "As soon as I walked in, the first thing I noticed was how it felt so…" She paused, searching for the right word.

"Empty?" He offered.

"Lonely," she said instead, leaning against the counter. "A beautiful house, obviously crafted by someone with a great attention to detail—"

"Thank you."

She looked at him, smiling at his interruption. "But it was like she was waiting for someone to give her a chance to be a home. You know, make her pretty, make her useful. Give her some style."

"Well, you've certainly done that. This place is nothing like it was the last time I was here."

She liked that once again a gentle wit laced in his tone. "You know, those ladies also said it took you a long time to build this place, and that you did it alone." She took a sip of her wine. "How old were you when you started?"

"I got the land from my grandfather when I was eighteen, and played around with the design for a few years." He suddenly seemed very interested in the contents of his glass. "But I didn't start the building process until I was twenty-one."

"Was it a school project? I'm guessing being an architect requires a college degree."

"Yes, the drawings had been part of my schooling, but it was a place I'd wanted to build for a long time. It wasn't easy to find the time, between my school and work schedule—I was working full-time down at the local lumber mill back then. Of course, I guess it should've bothered me that my ex-wife didn't seem to care about the amount of time I was spending out here."

Shock raced through Vanessa at his words, her stomach dropping to her feet. "You were married?"

Jonah nodded, taking a healthy swig from his glass. "Yep."

"You were so young."

"Graduated high school and got married in the same weekend. We were both eighteen and had been together for four years."

Wow, thanks to her devotion to her art she hadn't gone on a date until she was seventeen. "How long were you married? If you don't mind me asking."

"Four years, almost to the day. Got my college degree and signed the divorce papers in the same week. Poetic justice, huh?"

Vanessa was desperately curious as to what happened, who was at fault, but when he remained silent, so did she.

Then she had another thought. Had he built this cabin for his ex-wife? Obviously they'd been divorced long before he completed it, but it could've started out as something—

"This might be none of my business," she blurted out, "but were you building this place for her? For the two of you?"

Jonah smiled, shaking his head. "No. We had a tiny, two-bedroom house in town that her folks owned. Lisette refused to live on the ranch. In fact, she never saw this place even when it was nothing more than a foundation and framing. She actually dreamed of getting out of Montana altogether. Said she was sick of the winters."

"I'm guessing she doesn't still live in town?"

"She did up until a year ago, moving after the massive flooding last year. I was the one who left town when I got a job offer from a firm in Denver not long after the divorce." Jonah took another swallow as he moved back into the main room, making his way to the tall built-in bookcases in the far corner.

"I would work on this place whenever I came home to visit. Never wanted any help." He shook his head, as if he couldn't believe what he was saying. "How crazy was it that I was determined to finish it on my own? But my dad and brothers pitched in when more than one set of hands was needed. Took me six years but I finally got it done."

"It really is beautiful." She followed him, watching as he looked over her vast array of books. Scattered among them were the half dozen Chinese bamboo plants she managed to keep alive and her collection of crystal miniature turtles, started when her mother gave her one as a birthday gift when she turned ten. "Why didn't you tell me any of this before?"

He turned to face her. "Probably because before I even met you I had plans to kick you out."

"Kick me out?" She started to ask why, but then it hit her. "Because you wanted to stay here."

He shrugged. "That was the plan, but then you started gushing about the cabin when we met at the resort—"

"I wasn't gushing!"

He grinned. "Yeah, you were. Besides, I'm only going to be in town until the resort opens in December. I figured it was unfair to ask you to move, seeing how neither you or my mother knew about my plan. And now that I've seen what you've done to the place, I can't imagine anyone else living here."

Yes, Jonah was only here for a few short months, wasn't he?

Well, that fit perfectly in her new "live for the moment" lifestyle. Her move to Rust Creek Falls was about finding joy and happiness, two things she felt a lot of whenever this guy was around.

"Well, thank you. Would you like a tour of the rest of the place? We've got time before I need to finish dinner."

"Sure."

She spun around, gesturing with one hand toward the open space. "Well, as you can see, I kept the few pieces of furniture that came with the cabin. Did you know about those?"

Jonah nodded. "The leather couch was a castoff from my uncle's law office when my aunt Mary was redecorating it, but I like the pillows and that blanket you've got laying over it."

"Hey, that's a cashmere throw."

"Oh, excuse me." He grinned, and walked to the only other place to sit, a Bergère armchair that had been reupholstered in a faded patchwork quilt. "And where did you get this beauty?"

"At an antique store in Kalispell."

When she saw his gaze sweep the room again, she waited, wondering if he would say anything about the stuff in the far corner. Deciding she didn't want to talk about that, she took a few steps back toward the kitchen. "And the dining-room table?"

"A hand-me-down from my folks," he said, walking with her. "I'm pretty sure it was a hand-me-down to them first."

"You're mom gave me some dishes and stuff, the rest I picked up here and there. Oh, and I love the antlers over the dining-room table."

"Have you told my father that?" Jonah asked with a smile, reaching up to tap one of the lower antlers. "He bought it for the main house, but my mom refused to hang it. The poor thing languished in the attic for years. I asked about it one time and the next time I came back I found it installed."

"Ah, so that's why your dad was so happy." Vanessa winked. "The first time I had Sunday dinner with your family I couldn't stop talking about it." She started walking backward into the tiny hallway that separated the back of the cabin from the front.

Jonah followed, peeking into the closet near the back door. "Nice to see the folks put in a washer and dryer."

"I'm sure I'll appreciate them even more come winter." One more step and she'd be in the bedroom. With Jonah. Not that it meant anything. She was the one who'd offered the tour, but still it was a rather intimate place to be with a man she'd kissed after knowing him less than a day.

And didn't kiss at all yesterday during their ziplining adventure.

The thought had crossed her mind a few times— okay, more than a few times—but then she'd decided to enjoy the day and just see what happened.

Same plan for tonight.

But that didn't mean she wouldn't mind being in his arms again and having his mouth on hers.

"And last but not least, the master suite."

Ignoring that glorious bed, she clicked on a small lamp and then headed for her second favorite feature of the cabin. Okay, third after the claw-footed bathtub. "I think I mentioned my love for this tub, right?"

Jonah followed her into the bathroom. He gestured toward a pale green bottle. "Yeah, and bubbles and Harry Potter. I remember."

She smiled, recalling that moment back at the resort,

as well. She then pointed overhead. "But *that* is hands down the coolest thing I've ever seen."

Jonah's gaze followed, a big grin on his face. "You like that?"

Like it? She loved it.

The only window in the room was high overhead, cut into both the roof and the side wall of the cabin. Half of the glass was horizontal across the ceiling and the other half came down about two feet, allowing a bird's-eye view of the world outside.

"The sunlight that fills the room during the day is amazing," Vanessa sighed. "But at night, with just some candles lit, I lie back in this tub and watch the stars."

Jonah dropped his gaze from overhead, his eyes locked with hers. "Just what I was picturing when I designed it."

Was he now picturing her just as she described? Naked, hair pinned up haphazardly, covered in bubbles up to her neck?

Number twenty-one: take a bubble bath...with a man.

One of the last items she and Adele had added to the list raced through her mind.

Instantly she saw not only herself lying in the tub, but this incredibly sexy man right there with her, holding her as she leaned back into his chest while hot, soapy water splashed around them—

Jonah pulled in a sharp breath, then looked away before closing his eyes.

Oh, no. Did I just say that out loud? Vanessa bit back a groan. Jeez, no pressure for a second date, huh? "Ah, are you okay?"

"Yeah, it's just that…" His voice trailed off as he waved his glass in the air. "Ah, the scent in here…it's very—"

"Strong? Yeah, I'm sorry about that." Vanessa sniffed, but it smelled the same as always to her. Like her. "My shampoo, body wash and lotion all come from the same line. It's a mix of gardenia and white flowers with hint of coconut oil and lime. I think it's very fresh and summery and—"

"Sexy." Jonah opened his eyes, his gaze on her again as he closed the distance between them with one step. He took one of her curls and gently pulled it through his fingers. "That's the word I was going for. It's very sexy."

Hmmm, she liked that. Almost as much as she liked being this close to him, and the way he tugged on her hair made her think about closing the space between them, but there was food cooking…

"Thanks. I think maybe we should get back out into the kitchen. Dinner is blackened chicken, but we don't want to do that literally."

Jonah laughed and took a step back. "After you."

She walked out of the bathroom, her eyes once again going right to that bed. It was probably tempting fate, but she had to ask. "The bed was the only other piece in the cabin when I moved in. It's beautiful. Where did you get it?"

"I made it."

His simple statement had her spinning around. "You *made* it?"

Jonah nodded, the pride evident on his face as he looked it over. "Handmade by yours truly from felled trees found right here on the ranch."

"Oh, Jonah. It's beautiful."

"Thanks."

"No, I mean it." She laid a hand on his arm, waiting until she had his full attention. "Really. It's a work of art."

"That's high praise coming from an artist like you." He clicked his wineglass to hers. "By the way, I noticed you don't have any Vanessa Brent originals hanging in the cabin."

She tried to swallow the lump that filled her throat, but it wasn't budging. A healthy sip of wine did nothing to help. "Ah, that's right. I don't."

Vanessa muttered something about getting the pasta ready, and headed back for the kitchen.

Jonah followed her signature scent that filled the bathroom and now filled his head, not to mention the images his vivid imagination was creating after her words about that damn tub and the innovative skylight he'd put in the room.

Yeah, those images were going to haunt his dreams tonight.

He watched her work at the stove for a moment and he had to admit the smells coming from the kitchen were good.

Almost as good as the one in the bathroom which had made him want to pull her into his arms and start off this second date with a second kiss.

"Hey, how about I get a fire started?" he asked, wanting to do something—anything—to keep busy and take his mind off of...other things.

She looked at him, the gleam in her eye telling him they'd already done that.

"In the woodstove," he added. "It's supposed to get chilly tonight."

"Sure, that would be great." Refilling her wineglass, she held out the bottle with a silent question. He put his glass on the island and pushed it toward her and headed for the wood stacked on the bottom shelf of the bookcase.

Walking up to the front door earlier tonight, he'd been planning to tell her about the cabin belonging to him. But it only took a simple phrase from her for him to figure out she knew that already.

Then again, talking about his ex-wife hadn't been part of his plan.

It wasn't as if he was hiding the fact he'd been married, back when he'd been young and dumb enough to believe in forever, but it seemed once a woman knew he'd been hitched before she became a firm believer that was what he wanted again.

No, thank you.

He was glad Vanessa hadn't asked a lot of questions about his past, but instead went back to the safer topic of the cabin, which he had to admit looked better than he'd even thought it could.

Not surprising, considering she was an artist.

There was color and texture and life in here now. All things he probably never would've thought to add if he'd moved in as planned. To him, it had been just a place to crash until he got the resort finished and went back to Denver. Vanessa had made it her home.

Except for her art.

He glanced around the room again, his gaze catching hold of the easel, standing alongside what appeared to be stacks of blank canvases in the far corner of the room.

Interesting. No slash of paint on any of them.

"I'm going to use the bathroom," Vanessa said, heading toward the back of the cabin again. "I'll be right back."

"Okay. I'll just wash up in the kitchen sink once I get this going."

Turning his attention back to the task at hand, it only took a moment for the flames to catch. He had these same style woodstoves in his penthouse in Denver and used them quite often.

Standing, Jonah held back a groan as his muscles protested. He'd spent an hour under the hot spray getting ready for tonight, but after a long day working along-side his brothers, he was going to be hurting tomorrow.

He walked to the kitchen, washed his hands and then reached for his wineglass just as a painting he hadn't noticed earlier got his attention.

It wasn't large, but it was colorful with splashes of purples, reds and blues and a big drop of yellow in one corner. Unframed, the stretched canvas seemed to hang suspended on the corner wall in the dining area.

Was it one of hers?

He'd moved closer, studying it, remembering what he'd found on the internet about her earlier tonight.

Yes, it seemed Vanessa Brent—the adventurous vol-unteer art teacher and country dancing wannabe—was a big deal in the art world. Her works fetched hundreds of thousands of dollars and were coveted by collectors all over the world.

And it'd been that way ever since she was a teenager.

"No, that's not one of mine."

Jonah turned and found she'd returned and was once again busy with pots and pans that contained something that looked as good as it smelled. "At first I thought it might be," he said, "but it looks a little…primitive, com-pared to your work."

She went still for a moment, then went back to pre-paring two dinner plates.

"A friend of mine did that many years ago."

"I like it."

"Yeah, what do you like about it?"

Jonah turned back and studied the painting again. "It's uncomplicated, as if the artist didn't care what anyone thought. There's a hint of anger in there, but the pop of yellow says all is forgiven."

He looked back over his shoulder and found Vanessa standing at the table, two dinner plates in her hands, staring at him. "What? What'd I say?"

She blinked and shook her head, setting the plates down. "Nothing. That was very...insightful."

Maybe too much so?

Jonah turned away from the painting and headed for the table. "Can I do anything to help?"

Vanessa shook her head again and went back to the kitchen counter for her wineglass and a basket of rolls. She returned and gestured for him to sit, but he waited until she did so first.

"This looks amazing." He looked down at the meal. "What did you say it was again?"

"Blackened chicken with creamy angel-hair pasta."

The food was terrific, but Jonah couldn't get the painting behind him—and Vanessa's reaction to his words—out of his head.

"Can you tell me more about your friend's painting?"

She looked at the art over his shoulder, her face taking on a very faraway expression. "It was our senior year of high school. I had passed on going to my prom because I was up to my eyeballs getting ready for a show. My friend wasn't happy about that, but she came by the next day—still dressed in her prom finery—and found me a bit loopy as I'd pulled an all-nighter."

Vanessa paused and took a sip from her wineglass. "I

wasn't happy with anything I had worked on all night, so sure that no one would want to even look at my pieces much less buy one."

"And nothing your friend said could convince you otherwise?"

This time she looked at him. "That's right. So, she grabbed a blank canvas, some paint and a brush and whipped up that beauty. She then handed it to me with a great flourish and told me I was now the proud owner of a rare, one-of-a-kind piece and if I ever found myself destitute I could sell it."

She smiled, light coming back into her eyes as she grabbed her fork again. "We both burst out laughing and I felt a hundred percent better. So I make sure I keep it somewhere where I can see it…and remember."

"So, if that's true, why, then, are your own canvases blank?"

Chapter Seven

Could he have said what was on his mind in a worse possible way? Yeah, probably. He could've just come right out and accused her of being a fraud.

Of course, they both knew that wasn't true.

Jonah had found out more about her, and her career, just by looking around her space, than during a twenty-minute internet search and the images of her work he'd seen online were impressive.

Bold and colorful and full of life. Just like her.

But none of that passion was reflected in the empty canvases sitting on the other side of the room.

Vanessa slowly lowered her fork back to her plate. "What did you say?"

The hurt in her voice caused his insides to twist. He should backtrack, apologize for saying something stupid. Then again, he had a feeling Vanessa wouldn't let it go that simply and for reasons he couldn't explain, he didn't want to let it go, either.

"I couldn't help but notice your artist's corner seems a bit too neat and clean," he said. "No soiled brushes, no paint-covered rags, no…"

Spine straight and shoulders pushed back, she appeared almost regal, uncomfortably so as she looked at her plate, jabbing at the food. "No paintings."

He let his silence tell her she'd correctly finished his sentence.

"Maybe I don't like living in a mess." Her focus remained on the pasta and bits of chicken she nudged with jerky movements. "Maybe I cleaned up before you came over."

Both explanations could be true, but Jonah knew they weren't.

Yes, the cabin was neat and beautifully decorated, but it was lived in.

Magazines were scattered on a turquoise colored side table next to the chair, her boots laid forgotten by the front door and the couch pillows were messy, almost as if she'd been lying there, waiting for him.

"Maybe," he finally said. "But I don't think so."

She jerked her head up to look at him, indignant fire in her eyes. "And maybe it's none of your business."

The fight in her wasn't a surprise. He was glad to see it. "True, but when I asked you said there weren't any of your paintings here in the cabin."

"That's right."

"Which I took to mean you didn't bring any of your completed works with you when you moved from Philadelphia—yes, the internet told me where you're from, but does that mean you haven't done any painting since you moved to Rust Creek Falls?"

She held his gaze for a long moment. Jonah had a

feeling he already knew what her answer would be, but he waited, wondering if she would answer him.

Or maybe she'd just toss him out of here on his ass. "No."

The simple reply seemed to take the life out of her.

Vanessa sank deeper into her chair, her shoulders slumped and her chin almost to her chest, her body free of the bravado from a moment ago.

He wanted to go to her, pull her into his arms and tell her everything would be all right. The strength of that wanting surprised him, kept him glued to his chair.

"When did you last paint something?" he finally asked.

"It's been…a while."

She gave up playing with her meal. Resting her elbows on the edge of the table, the numerous bracelets slid down her arm, her fingers so tightly laced together the tips were turning white. She stared across the room at her art supplies, a painful longing evident on her face.

"A long while," she continued, her voice barely above a whisper. "Almost a year."

Jonah didn't know much about art, but for any person to be away from their work for that long…

There must be a reason, which didn't explain why she'd accepted Nate's commission. "Why did you agree to paint a mural at the resort, then?"

The longing disappeared as she turned to face him again, a bit of that rebel still flickering in her gaze. "Are you asking as my boss?"

"I'm not your boss." His tone left no room for argument. Still, he softened it when he said, "I'm asking as a friend."

She sighed, and relaxed her grip, wiggling her fingers for a moment before untangling them to tuck a few wayward curls behind one ear.

"I took the job for a couple of reasons," she said. "One, because Nate was so persuasive in what he was looking for and why he wanted a mural that I really wanted to be a part of his vision for the resort. And two, I thought doing a commissioned piece—with a deadline—might be just what I need to get over this…"

"Block." Jonah finished her sentence when her voice trailed off. "Is that how you've overcome a situation like this in the past?"

"I've never experienced anything like this before. Never been cut off from my gift before. I used to be able to get lost in my work, paint for hours on end. Almost in a subconscious way, but now…" Vanessa's voice trailed off, as if she was lost in her own thoughts.

Then she offered a small smile while righting herself in her chair, her posture back in place. "Boy, that's the first time I've actually admitted that aloud. Not sure how I feel about that."

Relief swept through Jonah at the curve of her lips, even if the gesture didn't quite reach her eyes.

Perhaps asking about her work—or lack thereof—had been a good thing after all. "It happens to everyone, you know."

She dug back into her meal. "Even you?"

"Well, no, not exactly." Jonah admitted, taking a forkful of meat and pasta, as well. "I've been pushing hard, working pretty much nonstop for last eight years. Starting at the bottom, but with no plans to stay there, I had to pay my dues in my chosen field. Work my way up. I didn't have time to be blocked."

"Sounds like you had something to prove."

Considering what he'd already shared tonight about

his failed marriage, she was right on target. "I did. To myself and a few others who thought my dream of being an architect was just the wishful thinking of a kid who preferred Legos and Erector Sets to horses."

He shrugged. "Maybe a part of me still feels that way. I've succeeded in what I set out to do careerwise, enough so that I could take a leave of absence to work on the resort."

"Whereas I just fell into my success before I was even a teenager."

Jonah wasn't sure he liked where this was heading. "Hey, I didn't say that. From what I read you've worked very hard for your achievements."

"I know you didn't mean it that way." She waved off his words, then stilled, her gaze focused on both of her outstretched hands. "Yes, I have worked hard since finding out I could paint, continuing to study and practice my craft. So to have it just up and disappear after fourteen years…is a bit scary."

She dropped her hands, grabbed the basket of rolls and held it out to him. "And how is it you've never been stuck creatively? There's got to be more to your line of work than planning, designing and constructing."

"There is, namely, the customer." Jonah took one of the soft and still warm buns. "Very rarely am I given total free rein to design whatever I want. In fact, the last thing I did that was purely my own from start to finish was this cabin. There are a whole lot of discussions about what the customer wants and needs—be it a private home, factory or a twenty-story high-rise, not to mention all the rules, regulations and red tape that go along with any project, before creativity comes into play."

"So tell me more about how creative you got to be

with the resort." She gave him a quick wink. "From what little I've seen so far the place is going to be magnificent."

He knew what she was doing.

Getting him to talk about his work would keep him from asking her any more questions. Okay, fair enough. He'd spoken out of turn. Even if that ended up being a good thing, if she wanted to lead the discussion in another direction, he'd let her.

They resumed eating while he shared his plans and ideas for renovating the old log mansion. He talked about the environmentally friendly steps they were taking to bring the structures into the twenty-first century while maintaining the rustic charm that would be the resort's biggest selling feature. It was a favorite topic of his.

She ooh'd and ahh'd in all the right places, even giving him a big smile when he mentioned adding zip lining to the resort's summertime activities.

Still, that didn't stop Jonah from thinking about what she'd revealed to him a few minutes ago.

He wanted to ask her what—if anything specific— had caused her to be unable to paint. She'd said it'd been almost a year. Had something happened back in Philadelphia? Was moving to Rust Creek Falls this past summer a way of reviving her creative juices?

If so, that had been three months ago. Why hadn't it worked?

They finished their meal, and the bottle of wine, and when they took their dishes into the kitchen, Jonah decided a peace offering was in order.

After all, she was right. Her painting was her business, not his.

"How about I do the dishes?" he asked. "You can

consider it payment for sticking my nose in where it didn't belong."

She filled the sink with dish soap, reminding Jonah of her doing the same thing just a couple of days ago at the community center.

"How about we let them soak for a while?" she said, taking his plate and utensils from him to add with hers. "But if you really think restitution is in order, I've got an idea."

Jonah took a step back when she aimed the water spray at the sink, never quite sure what crazy idea she'd come up with next. "What did you have in mind?"

She turned off the water, grabbed a dish towel and dried her hands as she headed for the bookcases. Seconds later a classic Garth Brooks song filled the air.

"Teach me to dance." Vanessa walked back to where he stood. "Country-style two-stepping, to be precise."

Jonah grinned, moving out of the kitchen into the dining room. There might be enough room if they pushed back the leather sofa and the antique chair. "Right here?"

"Nope."

She brushed past him and headed for the oversize, floor-to-ceiling windows behind him. Running her hand down the left side of the middle glass, she found the hidden latch and the window—which was actually a door—opened, pivoting toward the deck outside.

"Can you believe I lived here for almost three weeks before I figured this out?" She turned to him, a light breeze coming in through the opening and ruffling her curls. "Your mom was so impressed when I showed her."

"I'll bet." He glanced down at her bare feet, having done his best not to stare at the bright-blue-polished toes until this moment. "If we're going to do this, maybe you should get your shoes on."

Vanessa looked down. She was barefoot.

How in the world had she'd spent the past hour and a half with this man and not realized that?

"That's probably a good idea. Be right back."

She hurried to the bedroom, grabbing a pair of socks and her favorite ankle boots. Sitting on the edge of the bed, she pulled them on, and then took a moment to check her hair. Pushing a few curls into place, her hand stilled when she saw her and Adele's picture on the nightstand in the mirror's reflection.

He'd noticed Adele's artwork, the evidence that she wasn't painting and how she tried to change the topic of their dinner conversation.

She got the feeling not much got past Jonah.

Not when he came right out and asked about the blank canvases.

For a moment during dinner, she'd toyed with brushing off his questions, and even though he hadn't come right out and asked her why she wasn't painting, he'd been the first person other than her agent to talk about it.

No one among her family and friends had dared to question her lack of producing anything new. Granted, they'd been worried about the deep depression she'd gotten herself into the past year. But even when she'd finally come out of that there were no inquiries about a new collection.

She'd only told the firm who represented her work that she was taking a break for the unforeseeable future, which ironically had driven up the value of her older pieces in the past few months.

Deep inside, she often wondered if maybe what she'd created in the past fourteen years was all there was.

Nope, not going there.

Giving herself a mental shake, Vanessa backed away from the mirror. "You've got a sexy architect out there waiting to hold you in his arms. That's more than enough to keep you occupied tonight."

She hurried back out to the main room and saw Jonah had stepped out on the deck. Flipping on the outside lamps to give them a bit more light, she joined him. The night was cool, but that didn't seem to bother Jonah as he folded back his shirtsleeves until the cuffed material stopped just below his elbows.

"Gearing up for battle?"

He turned around, a smile on his face. "Good thing I wore my steel-toed cowboy boots."

She faked a pout. "Oh, I'm not that bad."

He offered one raised eyebrow in response.

"Okay, but it's because of lack of practice." She clapped her hands together. "So, what's first?"

Jonah stepped forward, reaching for her and she easily moved into his arms. "You seemed to get the necessity of the framework—the placement of our hands—and the need to keep some distance between us, especially when you're first learning."

Yeah, not as much fun as the intimate way he'd held her when they danced at the bar.

That night their bodies had been touching completely, her soft curves against his muscles as they moved in slow circles—

"Vanessa?"

The huskiness of Jonah's voice made her leave the memory to look up at him. The light from the open door spilled out on the deck, but only on one side, leaving the rest of his face in shadow.

Not enough that she couldn't see the heat in his gaze as his fingers closed around hers while the muscles in his shoulder constricted where she'd placed her right hand.

Was he remembering, too?

"Did you hear me?" he asked.

She blinked, then nodded. "Frame and distance. Got it. It's more of the 'quick, quick, slow, slow' and remembering to start off with my right foot that throws me."

"Just remember what women have been saying since time began," he said. "You're right. About everything, including which foot to start off with."

She smiled. "Very funny. True, but still funny."

"Try to remember to put your weight on your left foot when you get into the ready position so you're all set to step off with the other foot."

Hmmm, that made sense. "Okay, I'll try."

"Oh, and even though the female might be 'right' in this situation," Jonah dipped his head closer, his voice now a whisper, "there is a leader and a follower when it comes to two-stepping. The man is the leader."

Oh, she'd follow his lead anywhere.

One corner of his mouth rose into a grin and she wondered again if she'd spoken aloud something that definitely needed to stay inside her head.

"You're in charge." She schooled her features into an expression of innocence, tossing in a few battered eyelashes at him for good measure. "I'm here to do your bidding, sir."

Jonah straightened, clearing his throat. "And look at me." He locked his gaze with hers when she did. "At your partner. No need to see what your feet are doing. That's only asking for trouble."

They got into position and with Jonah counting off the steps in a low tone, they began. Easily shuffling to the end of the deck near the back of the cabin, where it was much darker even with the outside lighting.

Then came the dreaded turn and she tumbled right into his arms. And onto his feet.

Jonah laughed, but quickly showed her the correct steps for a smooth turn and they were off again, making their way around the entire perimeter twice without a mistake.

"You see, you're doing fine."

"Shhh, don't talk unless you're chanting." She shot back, afraid she'd lose count. "You'll throw me off."

Jonah's laugh was a low chuckle, but he went back to reciting his instructions. When they were on their fourth circuit, dancing to Billy Currington's song about a woman who's got a way with him, Vanessa realized Jonah had gone silent and they continued to move in a natural rhythm.

Even she had stopped saying the words in her head and simply enjoyed dancing and being in Jonah's arms. "I think I've finally got the hang of it."

Jonah nodded. "It's a bit harder in a club or bar where you're surrounded by other couples, all moving in the same direction, but as long as you focus on what you and your partner are doing, you'll be fine."

"This is so great. Wait until the next time I go dancing at the Ace. I'll be fighting off the men who'll want to partner with me."

Jonah stumbled and almost fell backward, but kept the two of them upright by pulling her close. Her hand automatically moved higher up on his neck as he wrapped his arm around her waist, his hand spread wide against her back, anchoring her against him.

Just like Thursday night at the bar.

"Ah, sorry about that." Jonah spoke into her curls. "The deck must be getting slippery."

The warmth of his words against her forehead felt wonderful. So wonderful she'd missed what he'd just said. "What?"

"Vanessa, it's raining. Hadn't you noticed?"

She tipped back her head. A light mist appeared in the glow from the lamps and landed on her skin. She'd been so involved with the lesson she hadn't realized she and Jonah were dancing in the rain.

Oh!

Number nineteen: dance in the rain.

Without any planning or intention, she'd checked off another item on her list. Closing her eyes, Vanessa sent a silent thank you to the heavens and a shiver raced through her in response.

"Are you cold?"

Jonah's hand was warm against her neck, and she opened her eyes to look at him. She shook her head, and when his thumb gently moved back and forth across her lips, she couldn't stop herself from tasting him.

"Vanessa."

He whispered her name, his thumb still against her lips, before his mouth covered hers. His hand tunneled into her hair, pulling her closer.

A hot flush exploded over her as she welcomed his kisses. Wrapping her arms around his shoulders, she held on as a yearning, passionate and deep, raced to every part of her before it returned to settle deep inside her heart.

She'd wondered if her reaction—both physical and

emotional—to the kisses they'd shared a few nights ago was due to time and distance, but she'd never felt this sweet pull before.

She'd never been seduced by just a man's kiss before. Wanting it to go on forever, but desperate to see what might happen next. He tasted sweet and spicy as his mouth continued to move against hers, causing another tremor to attack, the intensity of it making her shake in his arms.

He lifted his lips from hers then, but before she could say a word he picked her up in his arms and carried her back inside the cabin. Pausing for a moment, he gently kicked at the door and it swung closed. Walking farther inside, she wondered for a moment if he was going to take her back to the bedroom, but he crossed to the leather sofa and sat, still cradling her in his embrace.

His mouth was back on hers as he pressed her back into the softness of the pillows. She grabbed his shoulders, and tugged, making it clear she wanted him to join her.

He hesitated, breaking free, his eyes dark and questioning.

"Please, Jonah."

He stretched out over her, levering himself up on one elbow as he placed soft, wet kisses the length of her neck from ear to her shoulder where her sweater had slipped off.

His one arm was caught beneath her, but with his free hand he caressed her, his fingertips brushing over the swell of her breasts.

Wanting desperately to touch him, too, she tugged at his shirt, finally freeing it and working her hands to the heated skin beneath the damp cotton material.

He groaned when her fingers met bare skin, a sound

that went even deeper when she arched her body, pressing her center to the hard ridge of his erection that told of his need for her.

"Vanessa...I want..." His words disappeared as he claimed her mouth again in a way that spoke of the pleasures to come, but then they changed.

Softened. Slowed. Stopped.

He was pulling away from her, cooling the fire that burned between them even if their bodies refused to comply. Confusion filled her and she wondered if she'd done something to make him think she didn't want—

Wasn't ready—

To make love with a man she'd known less than a week.

A man she'd spent time with every day for the past four days. A good man. An honest man. She knew that about him with every fiber of her being, but did that mean she was ready to be intimate with him?

Yes.

The certainty surprised her, but since so much of her life had been unreliable and crazy over the past year, it felt good to know for sure what she wanted.

"Your brain is racing as fast as your pulse." Jonah placed a kiss at the base of her throat, his tongue tracing over her collar bone for a moment before he pulled away and got to his feet.

"So is yours."

He stood with his back to her, his hands braced on his hips. "Yeah? How can you tell?"

"Because you stopped."

Her words caused Jonah to pull in a deep breath, his shoulders expanding as he did. He remained silent, except for his rushed exhale that she was happy to hear carried a bit of frustration with it.

She got to her feet, one hand hovering at the center of his back for a moment before she touched him. "Are you okay?"

A rough laugh came out of his mouth as he turned to face her, grabbing her hand in his. "Yeah, I'm great."

"Hmmm, why don't I believe that?"

He rubbed his thumb across her knuckles, much like he'd done with her mouth, and the desire fanned to life again. "Look, I should try to explain. I haven't been with…haven't been involved with anyone in a long time."

She nodded, but stayed silent.

"I didn't want to assume…" he continued, but stopped again. "I'm only in town until the holidays, then I'm headed back to my life in Denver. Getting involved with someone while I was home was never part of my plan."

"Hey, if I've learned anything over the last—" Vanessa stopped her words by biting down on her bottom lip. She then took a step closer to Jonah, looked up at him and laid a hand against his cheek. "*Involved* is a complicated word. As long as what's happening between us is right for us—right now—that's okay by me. No demands, no labels, no expectations. I like you, Jonah Dalton, and I'm pretty sure you like me, too."

He smiled, his gaze dropping to the front of his jeans. "Yeah, that's pretty evident, I think."

She laughed, glad to see his playful side had returned. She dropped her hand from his face. "Well, I've enjoyed every moment I've spent with you and I'd love to do more of the same. If you're okay with that."

He cradled her head with the palm of his hand, placing a quick kiss on her lips. "Very okay."

Ignoring the faint twitch in her heart, she smiled. "Good."

"It's getting late and I need to be at the site early tomorrow, but how about I tag along as your date for dancing at the Ace on Tuesday?"

Now, there was a silly question. "I'd love it."

He nodded, dropped his hands from her and started to head backward toward the door. "And maybe you could come by the resort tomorrow or Tuesday. I'll give you a grand tour of the place."

Unable to stand there while he got farther away from her, she joined him at the front entrance. "I'd like that, too."

"Maybe it'll knock some chinks in that wall you've got built around your talent." He leaned in again, and pressed his mouth to hers one more time. A chaste kiss, but neither of them seemed interested in ending it.

"Your work is terrific, Vanessa," he whispered. "The resort would be lucky to have your talent on display for years to come."

She nodded her thanks for the compliment as he slipped out the door and disappeared into the darkness toward his truck. Not wanting to watch him drive away, she closed the door and leaned up against it.

Well, it seemed the one place both she and Jonah would be involved with was the new resort.

That is if she ever found a way to either climb over, around or blast through that damned wall that she suddenly suspected didn't just surround her talent, but was also firmly entrenched around her heart.

Chapter Eight

"You want me to do...what?"

Vanessa eyed the dark blue bandanna Jonah held out to her with a dubious expression on her beautiful face.

She'd been waiting for him on the front deck of the cabin, sketchbook on her lap, when he'd pulled up. He hoped that was a good sign, especially considering his plans for them this evening.

Tucking the pad into her oversize tote, she'd climbed into his truck and had given him a quick kiss hello. He'd waited until she clicked her seat belt into place before he'd made his request.

"Come on," he cajoled, adding a grin to sweeten his request. "Turn around and let me put this on you."

"Over my eyes?"

He sighed, dropping his hand. "Yes, over your eyes."

She tried for a suspicious expression, but failed. Or maybe it the small giggle that escaped that sweet mouth of hers that gave her away. "Why?"

"Because I have a surprise for you. One I don't want you to know about." He paused and smiled again, thinking about all the hard work he'd done this afternoon. "Until I'm ready for the big reveal."

Her own smile came easy as she studied him. Just the sight of her looking so relaxed on this beautiful yet cool Sunday afternoon did wonders for his timeworn attitude.

As did the kiss she'd given him.

A simple one, but laced with ever present hunger just below the surface, too. A hunger he shared, but still wasn't sure he should act on.

Especially now as he was worried he might be overstepping when it came to his big surprise for today.

They'd seen each other a few times since last Sunday, but things like delayed equipment deliveries, a failed inspection on three of the resort's fireplaces and an onsite injury that thankfully wasn't serious, had added up to a crazy week with him putting in twelve- to fourteen-hour days at the job site.

It'd started on Monday when he'd tried to give her an extended tour of the resort, happy when she'd shown up after he suggested it the night before.

But they'd been interrupted numerous times with issues that needed his attention. He'd finally had to forgo the tour and go back to work after getting a promise from her that she'd let him show her the rest of the place another time.

Then again, if he was being honest, his own personal craziness had started Sunday night when he'd allowed his good sense to override a burning need to make love to this woman.

Even after she'd said she was okay with the fact

he wasn't interested in anything long-term, he'd still walked out and returned home to an empty bed.

And he continued to do so every time they were together.

Which made no sense at all. She wanted him, he wanted her. What the hell was wrong with him?

"Okay, go ahead." Vanessa turned away, giving him her back as she brushed her curls away from her face. "I put myself in your hands."

He scooted closer, the cool October air clung to the denim jacket she wore, but his head was filled with that sexy, summery fragrance of hers.

"Hmmm, I like the sound of that." He whispered against at her ear, enjoying the shiver that raced through her.

He quickly folded the material into a long rectangle and placed it over her eyes, tying the ends snugly at the back of her head. "How does that feel? Not too tight?"

"Nope, feels fine."

"And you can't see anything?"

She turned back to face him, her chin tilted upward. "I've got my eyes closed beneath this, I promise."

He fought against the temptation that was her mouth. It would be so easy to take their relationship to the next step. It wasn't as if he'd lived the life of a monk since his divorce.

What was it about Vanessa that made him hold back when he wanted her in a way he hadn't felt in years? Maybe ever. He'd been a teenager when he first married, had loved and desired his ex with the mindset of a kid. Now, as a man, he was experiencing a need for this woman that was brand-new to him.

"Jonah?"

He shook off his thoughts and slid back behind the steering wheel. "Okay, let's go."

"I hope this surprise includes a meal. I'm starving."

Sure enough, Vanessa's stomach rumbled as if to confirm her words.

She laughed and pressed a hand to her middle. "See what I mean?"

"Don't worry, I'll feed you." He headed down the road that led off the ranch. "And I'm sorry about being late. Again."

"That's okay. I'm sort of getting used to it."

Jonah heard the teasing in her words, but she was right.

When she'd mentioned during their private dance lesson how popular she'd be at the Ace in the Hole, there was no way he wanted anyone else being her partner. So he'd joined her twice this past week for dancing at the bar, but he'd run late both times, driving directly from the job site to meet her there.

They'd had a good time, but when she'd invited him back to the cabin that first night after sharing a few sweet kisses in the parking lot, he'd begged off claiming exhaustion, even though it'd barely been nine o'clock.

Two nights later, he'd been tempted to invite himself back to her place, especially when their parking lot goodbye had turned into an old-fashioned make-out session in his truck—something he hadn't done since high school.

Thankfully he'd parked in the far back, dark corner of the parking lot, but he'd once again been the one to slow things down.

Right before he'd asked her out for dinner and a movie.

All the while trying to do up the snaps on his shirt she'd tugged open, with gusto, minutes before.

They'd had a great time Friday night, and when he'd taken her home he'd accepted her invite to come inside. Passionate kisses and heated touches on the living-room couch soon followed until she'd excused herself to slip into something more comfortable.

And he'd passed out cold before she'd returned.

He'd awakened from a sound sleep around dawn, at first having no idea where he was. When it all came back to him, he'd gotten up and gone to where she was asleep in the bedroom.

But instead of crawling into bed next to her, he'd just stood there and watched her sleep for a few minutes. He'd left her a note apologizing for last night and told her he had to get to the job site, but would call her later.

He had, asking her for tonight's date after the idea for a way to help her overcome her artistic block came to him while running errands.

"I could've sworn we were heading toward town, but you've made so many turns I'm truly lost."

Vanessa's comment pulled him from his thoughts as he made another turn, this one very familiar. He eased into a space in the empty parking lot and shut off the engine.

"We're here?" she asked, reaching for the blindfold.

"Yes, but the bandanna stays put for the moment." Jonah grabbed her hand, stopping her. "As do you. I'll come around and help you out of the truck."

When he got around to the passenger side, she'd released the seat belt and had grabbed her tote. Placing his hands at her waist, he helped her down, making sure she had her balance before closing the truck door behind her.

"You know, I was going to lead you," Jonah said, placing her hand at his shoulder before bending to lift her into his arms. "But I think this way is much safer."

Vanessa squealed in surprise, grabbing at his shoulders. "Hey! Put me down."

"Nope, this is easier." He started to walk. "Even if your bag adds another ten pounds for me to carry."

"It's not that heavy. Besides, I've got something I want to show you," Vanessa said. "Once I'm allowed sight again."

"Yeah, what's that?"

"I…" She paused, tightening her hold on him for a moment, causing him to glance at her in time to see her pull in a deep breath. "I think I've had a breakthrough in the mural design."

Her news caused a hitch in his step. "Really?"

"I was sitting on the deck, enjoying the beautiful scenery when I closed my eyes and grabbed three colored pencils. Blue, brown and green." Vanessa's words spilled out in a rush. "The next thing I knew I was shading the three colors on the page, one right below the other. A few drops of water on my fingertips washed the edges of the colors into each other and I realized I'd matched the sky, mountains and land right in front of me. I added some definition, putting the falls that the town is named after, right in the center. I think it'll be the perfect backdrop for the mural, a reflection of the beauty of Montana with a cobalt-blue sky, the rugged darks of the mountains and the earthy tones of the land."

He managed to get them inside without putting her down while she chatted away, doubting she noticed they'd moved indoors.

Walking past one part of his surprise, he continued

into the large space, glad they'd arrived while there was still plenty of light coming in through the windows.

"Of course, I went completely blank when it came to the next step, but at least I've got something to work from. I hope I do, anyway." Vanessa sighed. "So, what do you think?"

"I think it sounds great." He stopped and eased her back to her feet. "I can't wait to see your sketch, but first things first. Stay here and don't move."

"Hey, are we inside somewhere?"

"Yes." He backed away from her, careful of where he stepped. "Now, wait for just a few more minutes."

"Jonah, this is driving me crazy. What are you— Is that—" She sniffed the air. "Okay, I smell something spicy and delicious, but also a hint of— Did you just light a match? And why are our voices echoing?"

Jonah smiled as he hurried to get everything into place. He should've known once he took away her sight, her other senses would be on high alert. "Patience isn't really your thing, is it?"

She smiled. "What are you up to?"

Giving the area one last look and satisfied with what he saw, Jonah went to her and slipped her bag from her shoulder. He then cupped her face in his hands, tipping her head back and lowered his mouth to hers.

She sighed again, opening to his kiss. Her hands went to his waist, holding tight as he groaned beneath his breath. He worked hard to keep the kisses light and easy, but a few slipped along the edge of desperate.

A desperation he felt down to his bones, along with a thirst he hoped soon to quench.

Easing back, he gently pushed the bandanna up and away from her eyes, smiling when she kept her eyelids closed.

"You can look now."

She opened her eyes, blinked a few times and then looked around. "Hey, we're at the resort, but why…"

He liked how her words disappeared as she caught sight of the picnic he'd set up in front of the grand fireplace, where the first official fire was catching hold of the kindling and logs he'd placed there.

Using a couple of old quilts, a handful of small pillows he'd taken from the main house and a couple of lanterns standing by for when it got dark, he'd set up their dinner.

Nothing fancy, just a meal package from the local wings place in town, but he'd brought real china and silverware, and a bottle of chilled wine.

"Oh, Jonah, this is wonderful." Delight shined in her eyes as she looked at him again. "What made you think of this?"

"I'll explain in a minute, but first—" He reached for her tote again. "How about showing me your artwork?"

She took the bag and held it close to her chest. "It's not that big of a deal, just a watercolor sketch."

"I'd still like to see it."

Nodding, she pulled her drawing pad out and flipped past some pages until she found what she was looking for. She tucked the other pages behind the drawing and then turned it to him. "It's not much."

He studied it for a moment.

"Yes, it is. It's beautiful," he said, easily seeing the influence of the view outside of the cabin in the drawing. "It's perfect."

Vanessa looked down at her drawing and shrugged. "Well, the background, anyway. Nate said he wanted to honor the people and places that mean so much to this town, to Montana. I'm still drawing a blank on what to do next."

"I have an idea." Jonah's gaze flickered to the wall behind her. "If you're interested."

"Sure, but can you tell me while we eat?"

He shook his head. "No, I think showing you would be best."

Taking her by the shoulders, Jonah turned Vanessa around just as the setting sun came in through the over-size windows lighting up the wall over what would be the resort's registration desk.

Vanessa gasped, swaying a bit when she saw what he'd done.

Jonah gave her arms a gentle squeeze, one part reassurance and one part to hold her upright. He looked at the blank space, seeing it with the background Vanessa envisioned, and much more.

"What—what have you done?"

He guessed she wasn't talking about the scaffolding he'd had a crew put into place that ran the length of the wall and would allow her access all the way to the ceiling.

No, she was referring to the more than two dozen pen-and-ink sketches—her sketches—that he'd spent most of the day collecting from people in town, and tacked them to the wall. Including the one she'd done of his father.

"There is your inspiration, Vanessa." He pulled her back against his chest, wrapping one arm around her waist when she leaned into him. "You've already captured what makes Rust Creek Falls so special. The people. The people who live here and call this place home."

"But those are just practice sketches. They're not real art."

"They are real because the people are. I know your previous works are abstract contemporaries with intense, broad strokes of color, but the details in those simple portraits up there are just as powerful."

She remained silent, shaking her head as if she couldn't—or wouldn't—believe him.

"Okay, maybe the mural won't include Charlie, who owns the gas station or Daisy from the donut place, or Gage, the town sheriff. Maybe Nate is looking for more historical figures, not to mention places, but that's just research." Jonah pushed, hoping she understood what he was trying to show her. "You *can* commemorate those special people and places because you've already done it. On a very basic level, maybe, but it's an important one. At least to the people who've kept and displayed your work."

When she still didn't say anything, he decided to go all in. Spinning her around, Jonah gently pressed against her chin until she looked up at him, the distress and anxiety in her gaze breaking his heart.

"Maybe your talent isn't blocked, per se. Maybe it's changing, at least for this project. You talked last week about how you'd get lost in your art. You can't do that this time. You're going to have to get up close and personal with every person, every place you include in the mural. You're going to have to be all in, one hundred percent involved."

Doubt filled her beautiful eyes. "I don't know if I can."

He motioned to all the drawings on the wall. You already have. Believe in yourself, Vanessa. In your gift." He pulled her into his arms. "I know you can do this."

She looked over her shoulder again at the wall. "They do look pretty good up there, don't they?"

Jonah grinned. "You bet they do."

A long moment passed as she studied her work. He waited silently, not wanting to push her any more than he already had.

"I'm just about there," she finally said, turning back to face him again. "But I think I know what will convince me one hundred percent..."

"Yeah? What's that?"

She smiled. "At least a half dozen of those tangy, spicy wings sitting on that blanket over there."

Jonah laughed. "I love a woman who's not afraid to eat. Okay, Ms. Brent, let's have some dinner while you let my reasoning percolate inside that pretty head of yours."

They moved to the blankets. Vanessa sat and started serving up the food while Jonah lit the lanterns as the sun was already starting to set. He joined her and poured them each a glass of wine. They ate, and he waited until Vanessa was halfway through her stack of wings before he approached a subject that had him curious.

"When did you first start painting? I mean, I read about you coming onto the art scene when you were just a teenager. Had you been painting for a while by then?"

"I took my first art lesson when I was in the second grade. It was either that, ballet or swimming. I wasn't crazy about being up on my toes or putting my face in the water, so I picked art." She licked at her fingers, a natural side effect of eating wings, and then wiped her hands on a napkin. "I think my mother wanted me to be a dancer."

"Are either of your parents artistic?"

She shook her head, a shadow falling over her eyes. "No, they are—were—very smart, analytical people.

They were both financial wizards, met and fell in love while working for the same brokerage firm before opening their own. My mother became a stay-at-home mom after I was born to concentrate on her charity work and me, especially after I was discovered. She died ten years ago, when I was sixteen."

Jonah's heart ached for the pain he heard in Vanessa's voice. "I'm sorry. I shouldn't have asked."

"No, it's okay."

"Was she ill?"

Vanessa nodded, her gaze focused on the plate in her lap. "Yes. Breast cancer. It was less than eight months from her diagnosis to her death. My father, who'd always been a distant presence in my life, chose to handle his grief by throwing himself into his work, while I found solace in my painting. It was a way for me to express my pain and my grief."

"That must've been a tough time for you." He reached out and took her hand, not surprised when she held tight to him.

"It was, but I had good friends and people who were there to take care of me. And my art. The pieces I produced after I lost her were the ones that really put me on the map as an artist."

"All while still being a teenager?"

She nodded and took another sip of her wine.

"Is your father still living in Philadelphia?"

"Yes. He wasn't crazy about my idea of moving out here, but I think he's finally accepted that I'm happy with my new life."

Jonah wondered how the man could be distant from such a wonderful woman as his daughter. "Not the life he pictured for his little girl?"

"Well, when I dumped my cheating ex-boyfriend

a couple of years ago, who just happened to be one of his star executives—and yes, my father set us up—he thought I was making too much of a fuss. As proud as he claims to be of my art, I think he would prefer if I lived a different lifestyle."

Pushing aside his anger at the man who'd hurt her, Jonah found it hard to believe Vanessa was as casual about her estranged relationship with her father as she seemed. Maybe because his relationship with his parents was so tight. Still, if her life, and his, had taken different paths, who knows if they ever would've met.

"Hey, do you hear that?" Vanessa released her hold on him to turn and gaze out the floor-to-ceiling windows on the far side of the room. "It's raining. I love that sound."

Jonah listened as the tiny clicks against the glass told him Vanessa was right. "Very soothing. My favorite is the hiss and crackle of a fire. Hey, I've got an idea."

He pushed aside their dinner and stretched out on the quilt, piling the pillows beneath his head. Holding on his hand, he beckoned her to join him. "Come on, let's lie here and just listen to the rain come down and the fire burn."

She smiled and his heart gave a little lurch, almost as if it was trying to tell him something. She crawled across blanket to him.

Resting her head on his chest, she put an arm across his stomach and cuddled up next to him. "This is nice. Thank you, Jonah…for everything."

He found he had more he wanted to ask her, more he wanted to know. About her hopes, dreams and plans. But there was time for that later.

Right now, being with her like this was enough.

Chapter Nine

"And then Jonah turned me around and there on the wall were my sketches."

Vanessa sat in one of the folding chairs scattered around the meeting room in the community center. It was Wednesday night and she was here for the Newcomers Club meeting.

Most of the members were female and the club was a way to make friends and help the recent transplants adjust to their new lives in the rural town.

"I'll admit I was really worried about being unable to paint for the last—well, for a long time, before I even moved to town," she continued, stirring her coffee.

She hadn't planned on sharing that side to her story, but once she'd started talking, everything came out. "But now, thanks to Jonah, I've been sketching like a crazy woman for the past few days, even though I'm not sure who or even what will be included in the mural.

It just feels so good to have the creative juices finally flowing again."

"Hold up, I'm still back at Jonah blindfolding you. That's something Nick hasn't done to me." Cecelia Clifton, who was originally from Thunder Canyon, had moved to town a year ago to help in the flood recovery, following in the footsteps of her then best friend, now-fiancé Nick Pritchett. She took the seat next to Vanessa, a saucy grin on her face. "At least not yet."

"Not to mention Jonah whisking you away for a romantic picnic at the resort, complete with a roaring fire and listening to the rain," Callie added, joining them. "Now, that's creative."

"And after seeing the way the two of them get all wrapped up in each other while dancing at the Ace, I'd say he's already got her juices flowing," Cecelia added.

Vanessa laughed along with her friends. It felt good to be surrounded by smart and funny women who looked out for each other. A tiny pang centered in her chest, and she quickly rubbed it away, accepting it for what it was, a reminder that while the sisterhood-like bond she'd shared with Adele could never be repeated, she was lucky to have found new friendships since moving to town.

"Ladies, I'm talking about the mural," Vanessa insisted, "and the fantastic resort being built outside of town. Is all you want to talk about is my love life?"

"Yes!"

Her friends answered in unison, joined by Mallory Franklin, who was now engaged to one-time local playboy Caleb Dalton. Another newcomer, Mallory worked for Caleb's father, the town's only lawyer.

"Boy, this doesn't sound like the Jonah Dalton I've

heard about," Mallory added. "Caleb described his cousin so differently over the last few months."

Vanessa turned to her. "That's right. Your husband and Jonah are family, aren't they?"

Mallory nodded. "Caleb said he and Jonah were more than cousins growing up, they were best friends. He was even Jonah's best man at this—oh, you do know he was once married, right?"

Taking a quick sip of the still-too-hot coffee, Vanessa hoped the cup's rim hid her mouth when her smile slipped. "Yes, I know."

Not that Jonah had shared any more details about his ex-wife—or the reason for their divorce—with her. She thought they might talk about it during their picnic, especially after the way she'd opened up to him, but that hadn't happened.

She was curious, but he'd made it clear his stay in town was only temporary and he wasn't looking to get involved, so Vanessa worked hard to keep their times together fun, easygoing and firmly entrenched in the present.

Even if doing so was a bit harder on her than she'd thought it would be.

She loved spending time with him, be it dancing or movies or the horseback-riding lessons he promised her.

But after he'd surprised her with his take on the new direction her talent was heading and how much he believed in her, she'd finally accepted a tiny corner of her heart would always belong to him.

Even if he continued to hold himself just a little bit apart from her.

"Caleb made it sound like Jonah hadn't been seriously involved with anyone since his divorce," Mallory continued. "At least, not anyone in town."

That made sense considering what Jonah had told her about sticking close to the ranch and concentrating on working on the cabin during his previous visits home.

Was it wrong that she was secretly thrilled no one else had caught his attention before? Or maybe that was because he had someone back in Denver?

No, he'd told her he hadn't been involved with anyone in a long time. How long was long? Weeks? Months?

"Well, he doesn't live in Rust Creek Falls full time," Vanessa said, realizing her friends were staring at her as if waiting for a reply. "He's only in town through Christmas, just until the renovations on the resort are complete and it opens for business."

"Oh, that's too bad," Cecelia said. "You two make such a cute couple."

"We're having fun and enjoying each other's company." *Living for the moment,* she added silently, because as she'd learned all too well, sometimes that's all we have. "Nothing more."

Nothing but wonderfully fervent kisses, generous touches and a simmering sexual hunger that she'd been sure they would've satisfied Friday night if the man hadn't fallen asleep on her.

"Hmmm, now why don't I believe you," Cecelia said with a grin. "That's quite a devilish gleam you've got in your eyes, Vanessa."

"Do I?" She feigned innocence, wanting to keep her and Jonah's private affairs just that. Private. "I have no idea what you mean."

Callie laughed. "Oh, I feel sorry for the hordes of lonely cowboys bemoaning their lost chances with you. You're definitely off the market. At least for the next few months."

Yes, Vanessa considered herself taken, for as long

as Jonah was in town. When she found herself wishing things might last longer, she stopped, reminding herself that being with him now was better than not at all. "Well, there are plenty of ladies to go around for them to concentrate on."

"Could we talk about something else, please?"

Vanessa and her friends turned around and found another member of their club, Julie Smith, standing there.

As close as the rest of the women were, Julie always seemed to be a bit aloof. Not in a snobbish sort of way, but more as if she wasn't sure she belonged in the group although everyone had been friendly to her.

"Is something bothering you, Julie?" Vanessa rose from her seat and went to the girl, who barely looked old enough to be out of college, especially because she always wore her long blond hair pulled back into a high ponytail. "Have we upset you?"

"No, it's just…" Julie's voice trailed off and she sighed, looking down at the plate of cookies in her hands. "It's silly, but all this talk of men and dating and the invasion of females looking for love…I wish— I mean, no one's even asked me to…"

Vanessa understood, sharing quick glances with the others when Julie's voice faded away.

Yes, her friends liked to tease her about her numerous first dates since coming to town, but it seemed Julie was having the opposite problem.

"You know, I'm sure between all of us ladies we can do a bit of matchmaking," Vanessa said. "Find you a nice guy."

"Oh, no, I'm not—I mean, I don't want—" Julie shook her head, sending her ponytail flying. "Don't worry about me. I'm fine."

Vanessa wasn't so sure, but their conversation was

over for the moment as Lissa Christensen, the columnist whose blog put Rust Creek Falls on the map after the Great Flood, had arrived to talk about the big holiday party in the works to celebrate the grand opening of the new resort, to be held on Christmas Eve, of course. Everyone hurried to take a seat as the ideas began to fly.

After the meeting wrapped up, Vanessa had stuck around to help clean up. She had to admit, the idea of her art being such a big part of the resort was still a bit scary.

She loved what Jonah had done to convince her to see her talent in a new light, but what she really needed was to do some research. Perhaps someone at the mayor's office could assist with getting her some history on Rust Creek Falls and the other towns Nate had mentioned.

"Yes, seek and you shall find the answers you need."

Vanessa whirled around, the voice startling her.

There stood an elderly woman dressed in bright colors, a couple of mismatched shawls wrapped around her shoulders. Her weathered face and gray hair, worn in a braid wrapped around her head, spoke to her age, but Winona Cobbs had kind eyes and a warm smile.

Originally from Whitehorn, Montana, Winona had come to town a couple of months ago to give a talk here at the community center about trusting your inner psychic. As a nationally syndicated advice columnist, she was also well known for her special gift.

"How do you know I'm searching for something?" Vanessa asked.

"We are all searching, in our own way, our own time." Winona then offered a smile as she moved slowly toward a seating area outside the center's main office. "The heart knows what it wants."

Vanessa grabbed her tote and followed the old

woman. "What I'm looking for is information. It has nothing to do with my heart."

"Of course it does. Your gift comes from your heart, your soul and your brain." Winona sat, her hands folded in her lap. "All must be in harmony so you can share that gift in your painting."

Oh, this could be just the person she'd been looking to find!

Taking the other empty chair, Vanessa leaned forward. "I'm guessing you're quite knowledgeable about some of the prominent families and their histories of Montana's past?"

"The things I know of…things connected to the past," she answered slowly, "and to the future are great indeed."

"I would love to sit and talk with you, to get some ideas for the mural. Would that be okay?"

Winona nodded. Vanessa opened her tote and pulled out her sketchbook. Opening to an empty page, she grabbed a pen and waited.

"Jeremiah Kincaid, of the Kincaid Ranch in White-horn, was a rancher. His granddaddy was one of the first settlers of that town, but it was Jeremiah who made Whitehorn his town."

Vanessa hurried to take notes. "Who else might I include?"

"Have you ever heard of the 'Shady Lady' of Thunder Canyon?" Winona asked. "Miss Lily Divine ran a respectable saloon, but, of course, there were those who were sure the bar was just a front for its true business—a house of ill-repute. Miss Divine covered it well, but there were always rumors. Like with most things."

Vanessa jumped once again when this time the old woman reached out and laid her hand on her arm. Winona's fingers were cool, her grip strong. "The trick, my dear, is in knowing where to look for your answers… and to be sure you're ready for what you find."

"Are we still talking about the mural?"

Winona smiled. "Unless there is something…or someone else you wish to discuss?"

Jonah walked out of his uncle's law office and headed across the small parking lot, debating whether he should head back to the job site or not.

It was still early, not even seven o'clock. Vanessa had said something about a meeting tonight so she was busy.

Which was probably a good thing.

Ever since their picnic on Sunday evening Vanessa had been talking nonstop about the mural. It was as if a fire had been lit inside of her. She glowed with excitement and energy and Jonah found himself wanting to be near her, to be with her, in every way possible.

Vanessa wanted to be with him, too. He was smart enough to know that. He just wished he knew what it was that kept him from making that happen.

Maybe he wanted more than—

A shuffling noise—feet being dragged against the pavement—caught his attention, interrupting his thoughts.

Jonah looked around, spotting a man walking toward him. Shoulders stooped with a headful of scraggly gray hair that shot off in every direction, his gaze fixed on the ground before him.

Jonah moved out of the man's way, otherwise the old-timer would've walked right into him. He wasn't someone he recognized, but so many new people had moved to town in the past year he wasn't surprised.

"You okay, fella?" Jonah asked when the stranger

suddenly stopped, head jerking up and his wide blue eyes darting around even though there was no one around but the two of them.

"Homer Gilmore," the man said, his voice scratchy.

"Is that your name?" Jonah asked. "Homer?"

The elderly man nodded, his head bobbing quickly.

"Is there something I can help you with?"

"The past is the present," he rasped. "The present is the past."

"I'm sorry?"

The old man repeated the same cryptic phrase as he slowly backed away.

Jonah stepped forward, wondering if he should direct the old-timer to the sheriff's office at the end of the block. He looked as if he could use a hot meal and decent night's sleep.

A quick glance at a patrol vehicle parked out front told him someone was in the office, but when he turned back the old man was gone.

Okay, that was weird.

Jonah looked around again, but the man had vanished. He shrugged off the odd encounter and dug his keys from his pocket.

"Hey, stranger. It's about time I saw your ugly face."

Grinning this time at the familiar masculine voice, Jonah looked up. "Careful, boy, we're related. That makes you as ugly as me."

"Naw, my side of the Dalton clan got the beauty and the brains." Caleb Dalton stood next to Jonah's truck. "But I'll admit you've got a sweet ride here."

Jonah laughed and when his cousin grabbed him and yanked him into a quick embrace, complete with a hearty slap to the back. He did the same. "Damn, it's good to see you."

"Tell me about it." Caleb took a step back. "You've been back in town—what? Two weeks now and this is the first time we've seen each other?"

Guilt filled Jonah. Out of everyone in town, he'd always made a point of meeting up with his cousin whenever he returned home. "Yeah, sorry about that. I've been really busy."

"I know. I heard."

"Things have been a bit rough at the job site, but that's to be expected with a project this big," Jonah said. "Especially since we're in the final stages, but I planned to give you a call once—"

"I'm not talking about the resort," his cousin said, a big grin on his face. "I'm taking about your busy social life. Dancing, zip lining, a good old-fashioned dinner-and-movie date night."

"What the hell? Is this published somewhere?" Jonah shook his head. "Jeez, small towns."

"You free to grab a beer down at the Ace and catch up?" Caleb asked. "I've got some time before I need to pick up Lily at a friend's house."

Jonah frowned. "I thought your fiancée's name was Mallory."

"It is. Lily is her daughter." Caleb's shoulders squared up proud. "And as soon as we get married and I put through the necessary paperwork, she'll be my daughter, too."

Jonah offered his friend congratulations and the men parted, each getting into their own trucks. Minutes later, they'd were seated in a corner booth at the Ace in the Hole. Thankfully the place wasn't busy yet, with the jukebox off while the Colorado Avalanche battled against the Boston Bruins, already down two goals, on the televisions hanging over the bar.

Jonah waited until the waitress dropped off their beers before he spoke, knowing he had something to say to his friend.

"I'm sorry, man."

Caleb stared at him. "What for? You bought the first round."

"I'm talking about back in August when you called looking for some advice." Jonah leaned forward, cradling his beer in one hand. "You were trying to figure things out between you and Mallory, and me telling you to cut and run was pretty useless."

"Yeah, you weren't exactly helpful that night." Caleb took a swig from his beer.

"I was under a lot of pressure playing catch-up with work, having just returned the previous month from being out of the country for the last year," Jonah explained, even though his friend already knew that. "Then Nate and his resort fell into my lap and my life was all about the renovations, twenty-four seven. Giving relationship advice was the last thing on my mind. Not to mention, just about the least thing I'm qualified to do."

"You know, I was stupid enough to follow what you'd said for a few days." Caleb's smile was easy, but Jonah could see the painful memories behind it from the man's eyes. "Good thing I got some better insight from another source on what it means to be in love."

His parents, maybe? Jonah's aunt and uncle had been happily married for over thirty-five years. Much like his own folks. "Some fatherly wisdom?"

"Nope. Kid wisdom. Lily was the one who set me straight on how I was acting and how much I was hurting Mallory."

Jonah grinned—although his mouth had to stretch

tight to do it—and held out his beer. "And they all lived happily-ever-after."

"Amen to that." Caleb lightly clinked the long neck of his beer bottle against Jonah's. "And speaking of happy, you seemed to be in a far better mood than you were a couple of months ago."

"I am."

"So, is it just from working your dream job on that resort?" Caleb pushed. "I know you've loved that old log mansion ever since we were kids."

"Yeah, having free rein on the renovations and turning that place into what will be a world-class vacation spot is one of the best things I've ever done in my career."

"And dating Vanessa Brent?"

Jonah paused for a moment, but then said, "Yeah, dating Vanessa is part of it, too."

"I got to admit, I didn't believe it at first when I heard you were spotted dancing right here in the Ace with her," Caleb said. "The last time we talked you weren't too gung ho on the female species."

"Vanessa is one of a kind."

"She must be. The last girl you spent any time with in town was Lisette."

His ex-wife was the last person Jonah wanted to talk about. "That's been over for a long time."

"I know, but she worked you over pretty good. After what you went through, most guys would be a bit hesitant about getting involved again."

"We're not involved."

Caleb only offered a raised eyebrow at that statement.

"Okay, we're dating, but one of the reasons it's easy to be with Vanessa is because she hasn't made any emotional demands," Jonah explained. "She knows I'm divorced, but she didn't pry into what went wrong."

"And you haven't told her."

"The past is in the past, it's got nothing to do with what's happening now. Besides, I made it clear I'm only in town temporarily and left the ball in her court. She was very up-front about not wanting to put any expectations or labels on what we're doing. She's a free spirit who lives for the moment."

"And that's exactly what you're looking for?"

It was, but that didn't explain why Jonah still hadn't taken their relationship to a more intimate level. Every cell in his body wanted her, wanted to make love to her.

So what was he waiting for?

Vanessa was getting tired of waiting.

She paced back and forth along the scaffolding, looking at the background she'd finished up just this morning.

The colors matched perfectly with the smaller sketch she'd done. Using a grid format, she easily transferred her vision to the large wall. Both the mountains and the land needed more details added, as did the waterfall, but the essence of her vision was there.

It took her a few false starts to loosen up, but once she did the work flowed. What a great way to end the work week.

Now, if she could just get Jonah Dalton to loosen up on the chivalrous attitude.

Climbing down, she grabbed her sketch pad before backing up a few steps so she could see the entire wall.

Busy with writing down notes about which areas of the mural needed work before the next phase started—talking with Winona Cobbs had given her a great place to start and she now had a list of people and places that were going to be included—she didn't notice anyone had approached her until a hand landed on her arm, making her jump.

"Hey, it's just me."

Nate Crawford stood in front of her, and a handsome man with enough of the same features—tall, dark brown hair, but serious deep blue eyes—as Nate's that he must be his brother, at his side. "I wanted to stop by and tell you how impressed I am with what you've done so far."

"Well, it's not much, but it's a start." Vanessa smiled at the men. "Things are going to get interesting soon. The devil is in the details, as they say."

"You'll do fine."

Vanessa kept smiling, hoping it hid her nerves. "You have to say that. The paint is already up on the wall."

The man with Nate had turned and studied the wall for a long moment before he looked back at her. "I agree with my brother. Very impressive." He held out one hand. "Hi, I'm Jesse Crawford."

"Vanessa Brent." She put her hand in his and right away she felt at ease with this man. "And thank you. Do you know anything about art?"

He shook his head. "Nope, and even less about people. I prefer the company of horses than most humans I know."

She couldn't give a reason why, but Vanessa felt like Jesse had spoken those words with just a hint of quiet resignation.

After Jesse and Nate said their goodbyes, Vanessa went back to working on her notes, once again getting lost in her thoughts.

Especially when those thoughts turned to Jonah.

Which happened quite often.

As happy as she'd been since moving to this small town, Vanessa now truly felt more alive than she had in a long time. Thanks to Jonah. Yes, he reignited her passion for art, but just being with him made her feel good. Special. Wanted. And it was the simple things that did it. Eating lunch together, except when he had a meeting scheduled or was off site, like today. Dancing and being with friends at the bar, enjoying cozy nights in front of the woodstove watching either action movies he prefered or the chick flicks she liked.

Her feelings for the man were growing deeper by the day and she wanted to share that with him in every way possible—

"Wow, you're kicking butt on this mural."

Another interruption, but when Vanessa looked up, she found Cecelia, who worked on the site as a construction assistant, standing there. "Thanks."

"I don't know where you get the energy." Her friend sent her a wink. "Must be all those pleasurable hours spent after work with Jonah, huh?"

Vanessa sighed. Her friend's innocent question reminded her again at how much she missed Adele. She so wished she could talk to her best friend about Jonah and where things were—and weren't—going between them.

"Is everything okay?" Cecelia asked.

"I could use some advice."

"Hey, what are girlfriends for? Ask away."

Before she did, Vanessa grabbed her friend's wrist and dragged her to a corner of the room. Despite the fact hardly anyone worked in this section of the resort, and if they did they'd be at lunch at the moment, Vanessa wanted as much privacy as she could get.

"Actually, Jonah and I haven't...well, we haven't

taken things to the next level," she confessed in a low whisper before she could think about if she should. "Yet."

"Oh." Confusion filled Cecelia's face for a moment, but then understanding dawned. "Oohh! But why?"

Vanessa blew out a frustrated breath, sending the curls dangling over her forehead flying. She'd been asking herself the same question over the past few days.

It wasn't like Jonah was a virgin, for heaven's sake. Their make-out sessions had been toe curling, heart pounding and downright wonderful, but he always seemed to pull back before things went too far.

Was he doing it for her? Did he think she wasn't ready to take the next step? Physically, she was. Emotionally? Well, that was something else entirely. Jonah was quickly finding a way into her heart. Would making love to him cause her to fall for him all the way?

"Maybe his former marriage has something to do with him holding back. Maybe he's trying to protect my feelings." Vanessa spoke her thoughts aloud. "Perhaps a little extra push in the right direction is what he—what *we*—need."

"Well, if anyone can do the pushing, my money's on you," her friend said.

"You know, I could surprise him with a few candles, a great bottle of wine, me wearing something sexy…" Vanessa's voice trailed off as she warmed to the idea. Yes, she needed to show Jonah just how much she wanted him, wanted the time they spent together to be even more special.

Even if it meant putting her heart on the line.

Chapter Ten

Jonah Dalton Designs. J. Dalton Designs. Maybe simply JD Designs?

Yeah, he liked the sound of that.

Over the years—heck, ever since he was a kid—he'd dreamed of what he'd name his own architectural design firm one day.

Today he'd been asked three times about his business. *His* business, his firm. Not the place where he was still employed despite his current three-month leave-of-absence.

His calendar had included an onsite meeting with Nate and a businessman who had a property north of Seattle along the coast. He wanted to redo the place into a getaway resort and had heard about the work being done in Rust Creek Falls.

There were also two unplanned phone calls from former clients. Both were interested in what he and

Nate's team had accomplished in renovating the old Bledsoe place and in Jonah's environmentally friendly design plans.

Nate had joked that Jonah should grab one of the resort's offices and hang out his shingle. He'd brushed off the comment, but since his ride home took him into town to pick up a bottle of wine for tonight, Jonah couldn't stop the thought from returning.

A thought that blew up into a crazy idea as he'd passed an old Victorian house on the corner of Falls and Commercial Street that caught his eye every time he drove by. Now, tonight, as he headed back to the ranch to meet Vanessa for dinner, he couldn't resist swinging by that house again, just for a fast look, he promised himself.

From the outside, the empty home looked a little worn, but a coat of fresh paint and a clearing of the yard would make her shine again.

The front porch took a sharp turn and continued down the side. The large windows were numerous, including two that projected out from the front of the house bow-style, one right over the other. He guessed they were for a dining room with a bedroom overhead on the second floor. Either would make a perfect sun-filled office—

Whoa! Getting a little ahead of yourself, aren't you?

Jonah stopped halfway to the door of the cabin, wine bottle in hand. Yeah, it'd been flattering this afternoon to find so much attention centered on his work, but he'd had accolades and compliments for previous projects.

Why was he suddenly considering now was the right time to be heading out on his own?

And here in Rust Creek Falls?

The idea of moving back had never crossed his mind in the past eight years.

As much as he loved his family and the stark beauty in this part of his home state, there'd always been too many bad memories here. Memories that had kept his visits short and solitary.

Not this time, though.

He'd dreaded the idea of being home for three months from the moment Nate had said it was a required part of the job offer.

Now, just a couple of weeks into his stay—two weeks after meeting Vanessa—he was feeling more relaxed and at the same time more...alive than he'd felt in years.

Because of Vanessa?

His fingers tightening on the wine bottle, he pushed that thought firmly from his head, and continued walking. The outside light came on automatically as the sun had gone down almost an hour ago and dusk had fallen over the distant hills.

Determined to think only about the evening ahead, he reminded himself the good thing about a Halloween party two weeks before the actual holiday was that costumes weren't necessary. At least not according to Vanessa, who'd tracked him down this afternoon between meetings to ask if he was interested in going to a party with her tonight.

Still, she'd had a mischievous gleam in her eyes when she talked about their plans that he found very sexy.

Hell, everything about Vanessa was sexy.

Eager to see her, even though it'd only been just a few hours since they'd been together at the resort, he knocked on the door.

"Come in."

The words came faintly from the other side and stepped inside, quickly closing the door behind him to shut out the cool night air.

"What the…"

His voice faded as his senses were attacked from every angle.

First was the pale purple radiance that filled the room. Mixed with the firelight from the woodstove and flicking candles perched on every surface imaginable, the inside of the cabin glowed.

The scent of sandalwood and vanilla surrounded him, but the familiar flowery essence that was all Vanessa was there, too. He inhaled deeply, enjoying the mixture while soft jazz music played in the background.

His gaze then took in the spider webs, jack-o'-lanterns, miniature ghosts and skeletons scattered around the room before being drawn to the colorful silk floor cushions that rested on top of a plush, faux, white bearskin rug. All the elements combined to give the room the appearance of a haunted gypsy encampment or harem.

"'Step into my parlor,' said the spider to the fly."

Her soft words shifted his focus to the bewitching creature that stood on the other side of the room.

Vanessa.

Leaning against the doorway that led to the back of the cabin, she was in the shadows. There was enough light to see she wore something lacy and silky and looked so damn beautiful his breath caught in his throat.

She smiled and turned a bit to one side allowing the flowing material to sensually slide open, revealing a bare leg from her toes to her hip.

Any plans for breathing vanished.

Of course, other parts of his body were working just fine and responded instantly to the sight before him, including his brain, which quickly put two and two together and came up with an amazing night ahead.

He'd been thinking about being with her like this for a while. Hell, from the moment they'd met. It finally hit him today that he'd been using his past relationships, including marriage—and how poorly they'd ended—as a barrier between himself and Vanessa. Which wasn't fair to either of them. He cared about this woman, enjoyed being with her. Vanessa felt the same. Tonight was proof of that. He should've known that when he balked at making the first move, Vanessa would take matters into her own hands.

In spectacular fashion.

"Please tell me the party is here tonight," he said, grateful for the ability to speak. "And that it's just the two of us."

"You don't mind?"

One corner of his mouth rose into a grin. "No, I don't mind."

"Why don't you put that in the kitchen and then join me back here." She stepped farther into the room, gestured at the forgotten wine in his grip. "I've already got dessert waiting."

He was looking at dessert. The sweetest concoction known to man.

Jonah had forgotten all about the bottle, surprised he'd managed to hold on to it all this time. He did what she asked, unable to tear his gaze from her while walking into the kitchen.

When she moved into the light from the woodstove, the lace on the top half of her slinky outfit turned into intricate tattoo-like images on her skin. She then sat on the rug and the material pooled around her legs.

His blood turned to fire. Anticipation filled him and he found himself glad he dressed casually, leaving his shirt untucked as his ability to hide his body's response to her was gone.

He left the wine on the counter and headed back into the living room. Stepping in front of the quilted chair, he noticed for the first time a tray resting on the couch that held a plate of fresh cut fruit and bowl of whipped topping.

This was getting better and better.

"Why don't you take those off before you sit down?" Vanessa gently tapped one toe of his cowboy boots with the end of an empty wineglass. "You'll probably be more comfortable."

Sitting in the chair, he did as she requested, again unable to take his eyes off her as she filled two glasses from a chilled bottle of wine on the floor next to her.

He joined her on the rug, his back to the woodstove and one hand braced just past her hip, his knee almost touching hers.

She twisted back to face him and held out a glass, the liquid sloshing around inside gave away the slight trembling of her fingers.

Glad he wasn't the only one feeling some nerves here.

Instead of taking the drink, he leaned forward and rested his fingertips against her neck, feeling her pulse jump at the base of her neck.

"Aren't you thirsty?" Vanessa asked.

Her question had his gaze locked on her mouth.

"Parched." His thumb moved to her lower lip, lightly brushing back and forth.

A low moan slipped past and he gave into temptation. Capturing her mouth with a gentleness he labored for when all he wanted was to consume her, body and soul, the way she'd done to him, he kissed her.

When she met the pressure of his lips by opening hers and slanting her head to one side, he slipped his hand farther into her hair, fisting her curls. Groaning as their tongues slid against each other, he tasted the softness, heat and unspoken promise of an unforgettable night for the both of them.

He held his desire in check and enjoyed her taste, warm and minty. Finally, he pulled back, reluctant to part from her as he pressed lingering kisses to her mouth, chin and lastly the tip of her nose.

Vanessa remained perfectly still, wineglasses in her hands, eyes closed. "Hmmm, that was nice." Her voice was slightly breathless.

Jonah relieved her of one of the glasses while he took the time to study her attire up close. The pale pink of her negligée looked almost translucent against her skin, except for where the dark shadows of her nipples pressed against the fabric.

He took a sip of wine to soothe his very dry throat. "I agree."

She opened her eyes. "You hungry?"

A light blush filled her cheeks as she read his answer in his gaze. "I mean for dessert," she added.

He nodded.

Vanessa turned back and grabbed a strawberry, dipped it into a bowl of whipped cream and then held it out to him.

Jonah opened his mouth and she placed it inside. The cool, tart juiciness of the fruit mixing with the topping reminded him of the beautiful woman in front of him.

He swallowed the tasty morsel and said, "My turn." Reaching past her, he brushed her bare shoulder, his hand lingering against her warm skin for a moment as he studied the plate. "Have a favorite?"

"Surprise me."

He grinned and picked up one of the green slices and followed her example.

"Ah, kiwi." She spied the offering when he held it in front of her. "Why's that?"

"Because it's the most unique. Just like you."

Vanessa smiled, and then opened her mouth. He placed the fruit on her tongue. She closed her lips, capturing his thumb and lightly sucking away the dollop of cream there.

Every muscle in his body tightened as she lightly nipped at the end of the digit before letting him go. He thought about leaning in for another kiss, but the rumble from her stomach stopped him.

"Is someone hungry?" he asked when Vanessa slapped a hand to her middle. "Maybe we should bring the food over here before you waste away to nothing."

"No chance of that, but yes, I skipped dinner."

Jonah put down his wine and then moved the fruit plate and the bowl of whipped cream, setting both between them on the rug. "Dig in, darling. You're going to need your strength."

"Am I?"

He read a hint of uncertainty in her eyes. His past behavior when they'd been this close, this intimate, the cause. "Oh, yeah. No one's leaving early or falling asleep tonight. Unless that's what you want."

Vanessa grinned, the playfulness returning. She grabbed a hunk of watermelon. "Then perhaps you should build up your energy, as well."

He liked the sound of that.

They ate, feeding each other and themselves, until most of the dessert was gone and they were each on a second glass of wine. There were lots of kisses and laughter and Jonah found he liked the slow pace of the evening.

Both of them knew where this evening was heading. The slow build of anticipation only whetted their appetite for each other. He was so aware of her, the delicious heat that hummed in his veins made him tight and hot every time he caught her looking at him.

When she lifted a hand to his chest, her fingers playing with the snaps on his shirt, he remembered how she'd tugged them open in his truck, before pulling him down over her as she laid back against the seat....

The sound of the first snap coming undone sent an arrow of pure desire straight to his groin. Her feather-light caress and the scrape of her nails against his skin as she opened a few more rocked him to his core. By the time she reached the last one, the back of her hand was tantalizingly chafing the hard ridge pressing against the button fly of his jeans.

Unable to resist any longer, he brushed his fingertips along the tiny strap holding the lacy material against her breasts. Following their path downward, he palmed her fullness, his thumb rubbing lightly over one rigid nipple, causing her to shiver and ease from his touch.

He dropped his hand. "You cold?"

She shook her head, drawing her hand away from him, as well. "No, although I am slightly less clothed than you."

Yes, she was and even with his shirt now fully open, he was burning from the inside out.

Still, he asked, "Should I add another log to the fire?"

She bit down on her bottom lip for a moment. "If you want."

Jonah rose and tended to the woodstove, thinking maybe Vanessa was looking for a moment or two alone.

To rethink her decision?

Stopping now would just about kill him, but he meant what he said earlier. She was calling all the shots tonight. It wasn't like this was the last chance they'd have to make love.

There was plenty of time to take things to the next level. They had until the holidays before the project was finished and he left again.

Ignoring the sudden tightening in his chest, Jonah returned to where Vanessa sat and saw she'd moved the dishes and wineglasses back to the tray on the couch and was reaching toward the lamp on the end table.

Still standing, he leaned over her, snapped off the light, extinguishing the purple glow that he guessed came from a special lightbulb. Their hands bumped, knocking over a wicked-looking witch, complete with a tiny broom and a pair of what looked like monkeys with wings.

"Oh, jeez, could I be any more a klutz?"

"Nope, my fault," he said, straightening her things before joining her on the floor again. "I'm guessing decorating this place took up most of your afternoon."

"I think I bought out the craft store in Kalispell." She looked around the room. "Halloween has always been my favorite holiday. Do you like it?"

He again let his gaze slowly travel the length of her body, taking in every lace- and silk-covered curve laid out before him.

He half growled, half laughed. "Oh, yeah, I like it."

Her laugh was sexy and sweet at the same time as she returned her focus to him. "I was talking about the decorations."

Reaching out, he wrapped a finger around the silk cord that held together the sheer lace panels that me~

at the dip in her cleavage. One gentle tug and the loop would disappear.

He managed not to test that theory. Yet. "So was I."

"I want you, Jonah." A dark heat filled her eyes. "I guess that's pretty evident, from everything that's happened so far, but did I go overboard? You know, with planning all of this? Did I push too much?"

Jonah's need for her slammed into his chest the moment she said aloud she wanted him. He'd been a fool not to take everything she'd offered before this night. The fact that she was worried she'd overstepped somewhere along the way made him determined to make everything from this moment on, perfect for her.

"How about you let me take over the pushing from here?"

Oh, that sounded good to her.

Vanessa had been second-guessing herself from the moment she started placing each pumpkin, spiderweb and candle. Not to mention the sexy nightie she'd been so sure was perfect after buying it in a mad rush of shopping this afternoon.

The room did look great, exactly as she pictured it in her head when she'd come up with this crazy idea. When Jonah had finally arrived, she'd stood quietly, watching his reaction.

As hard as she'd worked toward this new "be bold, be happy" lifestyle, there was a part of her that was still the introverted artist who found comfort in being alone.

His surprise at the cabin's decor had turned to sensual awareness the moment he'd spotted her. The naked longing in his gaze gave her a boost of confidence that lasted through dessert. It allowed her to be brave get him a bit closer to being as undressed as she was when she easily unsnapped his shirt, revealing his chest, lightly dusted with fine curls and an impressive six-pack of abs.

But then she'd given into the nagging doubt that maybe she'd gone a bit too far with her plan. Did she seem desperate? That maybe, despite his obvious arousal, he was only here because…

Of what?

The man had come right out and said he wanted to be with her and he'd been the one to kiss her first—

"Boy, you've got a lot of thinking going on up here." Jonah pushed back her curls, his fingers lightly massaging her temple. "Want to share?"

She smiled, hoping it concealed her confusion. "Are you kidding? I can't even make sense of the craziness in my head. I wouldn't want to put you through that."

"Maybe we should leave the thinking for another time, then." He whispered the words against her lips.

When she nodded in agreement, he kissed her.

This time he devoured her mouth in a way that was wet and deep, powerful and seductive. He leaned into her, his hand moving to the back of her neck, offering support as he pushed her gently backward.

She grabbed onto his shirt, fisting the two sides as she returned his kisses, arching her body until her lace-covered breasts met the heat of his skin.

He groaned, his mouth breaking free to move along her jaw to her neck, nibbling and kisses here and there as he gently lowered her to the softness of the rug.

Wanting nothing between them, she reached for the knot between her breasts that would allow the material covering her to fall away, but Jonah's hand was already there.

He pulled and tugged and then cool air flowed over

her skin before it was replaced with the heat of his mouth closing over her nipple.

She hissed, dragging in the outdoorsy scent that clung to him deep inside her, tunneling her fingers into his hair to hold him in place as his lips and tongue moved over her.

A deep pang of longing filled her, a sharp edge of pleasure that drove straight to her core making her wet and ready for him. She moved against his jean-clad leg where it laid between hers.

"Jonah."

Yanking his shirt down over his wide shoulders, she was impatient to have it gone completely, but he ignored her, moving from one breast to the other, licking and sucking and teasing, his fingers stroking the dampness left behind.

His hand then moved, slowly trailing over her belly until he cupped her, brushing back and forth across the lace that covered her, but couldn't conceal the damp evidence of what he was doing to her. His fingers slipped inside her panties, touching her while his mouth never left her breast.

"Jonah, please."

She felt him smile against her skin as he slowly moved both his hand and his mouth away, but only for a moment as he pushed the silky material of her nightie to either side, baring her completely to him. Then his mouth returned, his tongue leaving a wet trail behind, pausing when he reached the edge of her matching panties.

Vanessa waited, wondering if he would see, ready to show him how easy it would be, but then she felt his mouth against her hip. The bow on the side releasing as he tugged the string holding it in place with his teeth.

The material fell away and then he was at the center of her, nudging her to open wider to him as he dipped his head. He kissed, stroked and teased as one finger, then two, dipped inside her.

She gasped, already feeling the tightening deep within as her passion rose, right on the edge. He loved her in ways she'd never experienced before, ways that told her just how much he meant to her, in her heart where it truly mattered.

A part of her wanted to push him away, wanted them to be together when each of them reached that moment. Then, as if he read her thoughts, Jonah pulled back, rising to his knees. She watched as he yanked off his shirt. He then got to his feet, making quick work of his jeans and briefs and socks, his eyes never leaving hers.

But hers did move away. She wanted to see all of him, his wide shoulders, lean hips, the proof of his desire for her. He stood in the glow from the fire, the hard planes of his body as strong and sure as the mountains right outside. Then she returned to meet his stare, so powerful when he gazed down at her it caused a sting to bite at the edges of her eyes.

Naked, he retrieved a condom from his wallet, and quickly rolled it down his sex before he joined her again, stretching out over her.

She rose to meet him, eyes closed to hide her tears as she cradled his face in her hands while they kissed. He thrust into her, filling her completely and she welcomed him home. Clinging to him, she chanted his name again and again as he buried his face in her neck.

"Vanessa," he whispered against her skin, as he kissed her there.

He rocked his hips, moving back and forth, pressing deep and holding before retreating and then doing it all over again. He lifted one hip, angling her to give her more. Giving and taking back all she offered as she matched his desire.

"Yes. Oh, please…yes."

Vanessa pulled him closer, the perfection of this moment washing over her as she pressed her heart to his. The truth deep inside spilling free as she spiraled upward and then exploded into a million pieces as Jonah went rigid, straining with his own release as he groaned her name.

She loved him. She loved Jonah Dalton.

In that moment both the deepest joy and powerful heartbreak filled her soul, knowing she'd never experienced emotions this devastatingly profound in her life.

And after tonight, she never would again.

Chapter Eleven

The morning sun filled the cabin with a warm glow, but thankfully the still-pulled shades kept out any piercing shafts of light.

Vanessa stirred on the plush rug in the living room, stretching, feeling the soreness of muscles that hadn't been used in a long time. The softness of the aged quilt moved against her skin while the scent of freshly brewed coffee filled her head. The aroma awakened her senses, even though she usually greeted the day with an oversize mug of her favorite chai tea.

"Good morning, sunshine."

She froze. Jonah's greeting came from behind her, the low tenor of his voice sending her heart thumping in her chest.

Memories of their wonderful night together came rushing back.

They'd made love twice more, the final time long

after midnight once she'd slipped away to blow out the candles and banked the fire in the woodstove. Thinking he'd fallen asleep, she'd grabbed a quilt from the couch and moved to lie next to him again, unfolding the faded patchwork material over the two of them.

It was then that Jonah grabbed her, pulling her on top of him, silencing her squeal of surprise with a kiss. A kiss that led to many more and they'd made love again. That time she'd straddled him as he held tight to her, allowing her to set the pace until he sat up, pulled her to his chest and claimed her mouth again as they both exploded in a mutual release.

And each time, when their passions cooled and he held her closely tucked to his side, she'd waited.

Waited for the never-before-felt kaleidoscope of joy and ecstasy and love careening around inside her to settle down. To fade away.

It didn't.

If anything, the emotions grew even stronger. And so did the niggle of fear that came along with them.

The night had been wildly romantic. They'd been working their way to this moment since they met. Of course, things would change once their relationship became physical. They were both young, healthy and each had made it clear it'd been a while since they'd been involved with someone.

That's all it was. Compatibility.

Fun. The next step in their…friendship.

Great sex. Great sex with a guy who was smart and funny and caring and creative—

"Hey, are you not awake yet?"

His question cut into her thoughts. Good thing, too. She refused to allow herself to believe that any of the crazy feelings bouncing around inside of her meant anything more than—what had she called it again?

Yes, compatibility. Not love. She had to have been mistaken last night.

Accepting that, she finally replied, "I'm awake. I'm just not used to talking to anyone before I shower."

Hmmm, that sounded mean.

Surprised that any words managed to make it past the tightening of her throat, Vanessa rolled to her back and opened her eyes to find him standing over her. "Sorry. No offense. I meant to say good morning."

"None taken."

"What time is it?" she asked.

"Almost ten o'clock."

"Ten?" She bolted upright, clutching the blanket to her chest. "Are you serious? Ten? Oh, I missed the sunrise!"

"No, you didn't. Don't you remember? We watched it together."

That's right, they had.

Her internal clock had made sure she was up just before the first light broke over the mountains. She'd slipped from Jonah's embrace, wrapped herself in a blanket and made her way to the oversize glass door, raising just the one shade so as not to disturb his sleep.

Vanessa had watched the world awaken and offered a silent greeting to her friend, thanking her once again for insisting it'd been past time for Vanessa to take a chance and dare to live a different life.

If she hadn't, she never would've met Jonah.

Moments later, she'd jumped when he'd stepped in behind her, wrapped his arms around her and placed a gentle kiss in the wild mess that was her hair.

He'd then asked if she was all right.

She'd lied and told him yes.

But that hadn't been a lie. Not fully. Being with him had been more than all right. It'd been wonderful.

Then she'd made up some excuse about being an early riser even on the weekends, but not a morning person. When Jonah had suggested she get back beneath the quilts while he got the woodstove going, she'd readily agreed and must've fallen back asleep.

"Here." He sat on the edge of the couch and held out a mug to her. "Maybe this will help welcome you back to the land of the living."

She took his offering, pleased to see he'd remembered her preference for tea, thanks to their morning breaks at the job site. After the first sip, she then noticed that unlike her, he was fully dressed, right down to his boots.

He was leaving?

She had to admit she hadn't thought about the morning after when she'd planned their private party for the previous evening. The truth was she hadn't been completely sure of its success, never mind him staying all night.

"Yeah, I have to go," he said, having picked up on her perusal. "Derek texted me about twenty minutes ago asking if I still planned to help him and Eli today on another section of fence that needs mending."

"Ah, okay."

Jonah took a sip from his own mug, and then grinned at her over the rim. "If I wasn't too tired, that is."

That meant his brothers, if not his entire family, knew he'd spent the night here. She wondered how long it would be before the entire town knew.

Not that she was ashamed of being with him. Those who knew them probably already assumed they were sleeping together, but Jonah didn't seem to like the gossipy side of living in such a small town.

"But we're still on for lessons this afternoon," he added. "I'll see you at the barn around four?"

Number eleven: learn to ride a horse.

The item from her list flashed inside her head, as did Jonah's offer last night to again teach her when he'd shared stories about growing up on the ranch.

She'd mentioned Derek's offer for lessons and how he hadn't been able to find the time other than the first afternoon. Then the lesson had been cut short when he'd been called away, before she'd even gotten in the saddle.

Jonah had insisted if she was still interested in learning, *he'd* be the one to teach her. She'd liked that his tone had held just a hint of jealousy, even though she'd never thought twice about his brother in that way.

She'd never thought—or felt—about anyone the way she did toward the man in front of her.

And that scared the bejeebers out of her.

"Oh, I don't want to take you away from anything important." She pulled her knees to her chest, keeping the blanket firmly in place as she drank a bit more of her tea. "We can do the lesson another time. After all, you're not going anywhere for another couple of months. Right?"

Wow, where had *that* come from?

Jonah's brows dipped into a sharp V over his forehead. "You won't be taking me away. I want to do it."

"Okay, I'll be there."

He got to his feet, walked into the kitchen and poured the contents of his mug in the sink. "What are your plans for today?"

"I don't know." She shrugged. "Working on sketches for the mural. Cleaning up this place."

Jonah joined her again, dropping to one knee so they were eye level. "Don't clean too much." He placed a finger beneath her chin and tipped her face up to look at him. "I think Halloween is turning into my favorite holiday, too."

And just like that, her heart was gone again.

Something was wrong.

Jonah couldn't say exactly what, but Vanessa had been acting strangely for the past week. Ever since their first night together, in fact.

Which had been incredible. As was every moment he'd spent time with her since, both in and out of bed.

Being with her had made him feel like a new man. She was passionate and fun in her lovemaking, just as she was in life.

But his gut was telling him she was bothered by something.

She'd cut their horseback-riding lessons short the following afternoon claiming she had to get back to work on her sketches, but considering his sisters and his mother had tagged along for the trail ride, he couldn't really blame her.

Not that they'd said anything to her about him spending the night. At least she'd claimed they hadn't. His brothers had been quick to inform him when he'd finally joined them that the entire family was aware his truck had been spotted outside the cabin.

All night.

Still, he'd invited her to dinner with his family for the following day. His mother had pointed out that Vanessa hadn't been to the main house since he'd come home, but when he called to ask, she'd been out at the resort working and hadn't wanted to stop her creative flow.

They'd gotten together later that night and he'd stayed over again on Monday and Tuesday as well, making love to her in the bed he'd built for the cabin after they'd gone to the Ace in the Hole to dance.

She'd been just as spirited and lively as always, surrounded by a crowd of people, and while he'd enjoyed being there with her, all he'd wanted was to get her alone.

To ask her to come to Denver for a few days.

He'd gotten a last-minute phone call from his office Tuesday evening and due to a couple of issues on a job there that needed his attention, he was heading back to the city for a few days the following morning.

At first, he'd been surprised when the idea of inviting Vanessa to go along with him had popped into his head, but the more he thought about it, the more he wanted her with him.

Wanted to show her his penthouse, his office. Take her to his favorite steakhouse for dinner. Squeeze in a visit to the Denver Art Museum if they had time.

She'd turned him down.

Her eyes had lit up when he first brought up the idea on the drive back to the cabin. He'd been so sure she was going to say yes, but then she looked away for a moment before telling him there was no way she could be away from the mural for that long.

He'd tried to convince her, but in the end he'd gone alone. Due to a bad storm, he hadn't gotten back to Rust Creek Falls until late last night. As tempted as he'd been, he hadn't gone to see Vanessa when he got back to the ranch.

And today, they'd only exchanged a few text messages as she was working again on the mural. On a Saturday. Not that he had a right to complain. He'd worked plenty of Saturdays and today was no exception.

"You did good today."

His father's voice cut into Jonah's thoughts, causing the brush he was using to rub down Duke, a buckskin stallion he'd gotten for Christmas his senior year in high school, to tumble out of his hands.

He quickly scooped it off the ground, glad he was done with the animal's grooming as it meant he was due to see Vanessa in a couple of hours. "Thanks, Dad."

"Things went a lot faster with you helping out." His father stood in the open doorway of the stall. "Your brothers might not say it, but they liked having the extra set of hands around. As for me…"

Jonah fed the horse the treat he'd taken from the tack room refrigerator, but his gaze was on his father.

Charles Dalton had been a rancher all his life, like his father before him. The years of hard work showed, but he was still strong and tough and worked his land right alongside his sons and their crew.

Two of his sons, anyway.

"I appreciate you chipping in."

His father was a man of few words and that was as close to a thank you as Jonah was going to get.

He gave his horse one last slap on the rear that sent the animal out into an outside corral before he exited the stall. "I enjoy ranch work. I always have."

"Just not enough to make it your life's work."

Jonah stopped to look his father in the eye. "No, not that much."

The two men walked together toward the front of the barn, Eli and Derek nowhere to be found. Jonah wondered if this was going to turn into another lecture on family legacy. It'd been a while since his father had pulled out his "you're a Dalton and Daltons are ranchers" speech.

Jeez, at least five years or so.

They stepped out into the afternoon sun and headed for the corral with a few horses roaming around, including Duke. Stopping at the railing, they each propped their hands on the highest slat. It'd been a beautiful fall day, but there was a nip in the air now and it was expected to drop below freezing tonight.

A good night for two people to stay in and—

"You know, it meant a lot to me when you asked for your birthright."

His father's words again jolted Jonah and he tucked away any thoughts of Vanessa to concentrate on what the old man had to say about the acreage promised to each of his sons. "Even if I used the land to build one of my designs?" he pointed out.

"I didn't care what you did with it— No, that's not true. I did care, I do care. I was glad to see you building a home there." His father kept his gaze locked on the horizon, the brim of his Stetson pulled low on his forehead. "Glad to have you back on the ranch. Knew it meant you were coming back. Even if it was only for a few hours a week."

"Dad, I was busy with school and work—"

"And your wife, I know." A wave of the old man's hand cut him off. "But it felt like the moment you married and moved to town, you turned your back on your life here."

"I was living my own life."

"And you had someone who supported your dreams, which is more than I did back then."

Despite the fact he had two sons already involved

with running of the ranch, Charles Dalton had wanted all of his boys to work the land with him.

"You paid for my college."

"That was your mother's doing. She insisted, no matter what studies you were working toward. Same with your brothers and sisters."

Jonah nodded, but stayed silent not sure where this conversation was heading.

"We had hoped that you and Lisette planned to move out here, once you graduated college and finished that place." This time his father glanced at him. "Thought maybe she'd changed her mind about ranch living."

Jonah shook his head. No, that had never happened and his marriage had ended only four years after it had begun. Of course, that had nothing to do with the ranch and everything to do with the choices Lisette had made.

"Did you know I almost screwed things up with your mother?"

Jonah looked at his dad this time, but the man was once again staring straight ahead. He had no idea what his dad was talking about. His folks had been happily married for well over three decades.

"We met in high school, too, like you and Lisette, but I was a couple of years older. After graduation, I told her—and my folks—that I wanted to rodeo professionally, so off I went."

Jonah and his siblings had heard this before. His father's trophies and awards from his bronc riding days were in his study.

"And she stuck with me. Of course, she was still in school for the first two years. So I'd go off and do my thing, get injured, come back here to heal and work for your grandpa until it was time for me to head out again. Sometimes we were together. Sometimes we weren't."

His father paused, his rough-as-leather hands laced together tight out in front of him. "After about five years of this she told me she was tired of waiting on me to make up my mind. I didn't believe her and we had some real knock-down, drag-out donnybrooks over breaking up or staying together. Until the time I came home and she said I had one last chance to get it right or she was gone."

Jonah knew what the answer was, but he asked, anyway. "What happened?"

"I finally told her the truth. I was scared I'd end up like my dad. A man who couldn't honor his wedding vows no matter how much he tried. Lord knows, with three marriages to his name, the man tried hard. Told her I'd already messed around while we were apart, told her everything. You know what she did? She asked me to marry her."

Jonah smiled. "And you said yes?"

"Hell, yeah, I said yes." He returned Jonah's grin. "I might've been dumb back then, but I wasn't stupid."

No, he wasn't that.

"The point to this story is I may not know all the details, but I do know that girl hurt you bad when she ended your marriage." His father's tone was serious now. "And you've been running from your home, your family and this town ever since. Your work on that resort has finally brought you back and a special lady is making you happier than you've been in a long time. Maybe it's time for *you* to think about what it is you really want out of life."

Jonah remained silent, letting his father's words sink into his head. It was spooky how much they matched his own thoughts over the past few nights as he'd laid alone in his bed in Denver.

Missing Vanessa.

"Are you saying this is my last chance?" he finally asked.

The old man stepped back from the railing. "Last chance, second chance. Who knows? Maybe it's just time for a little honesty."

With that his father gave him a quick clap on the back, turned and headed for the main house. Jonah watched him go.

He made a lot of sense, and not just because Jonah had been doing a bit of self-examination lately, being back here in town.

Exploring the past, thinking about his future.

Especially since the first time he'd made love to Vanessa and felt something deep inside that he'd never felt before with anyone, not even Lisette.

Maybe it was enough that he was finally concentrating on something besides what had consumed his life for the past eight years, his work.

Unable to wait a moment longer, Jonah dug into his pocket for his cell phone.

Chapter Twelve

Vanessa barely heard the special ringtone she'd given to Jonah's phone number over the sound of rushing water. She hurried to turn off the tub's faucets. Gallons of hot water awaited her with enough bubbles to last for the hour she planned to soak, along with a glass or two of wine.

All to be enjoyed in anticipation of seeing Jonah again for the first time in three days.

And yeah, that was her fault.

She could've gone to Denver with him, but it was harder to keep things simple and casual between them. It had taken daily self-talks and a bit of distance—emotional and physical—even though they had spent the night together three more times in the past week—to keep up the appearance.

Spotting the reminder on her phone's calendar that her best friend's birthday was fast approaching, and the fact she'd completely forgotten about it in the midst of "living for the moment," helped to remind her that nothing in life was certain.

Catching a glimpse of his life in Denver would've only been a reminder of that uncertainty because Jonah had made it clear he was heading back there when his stay in Rust Creek Falls ended.

Yes, staying behind had been the right decision.

Still, her heart pounded in her chest when she grabbed her phone from the dresser in the bedroom. She swiped her thumb across the screen and forced a lighter tone to her voice when she said, "Hey there, cowboy."

"What are you doing?"

Hmmm, short and to the point. She glanced at her reflection in the mirror, taking the silk bathrobe she wore and her curls, pinned up and out of the way. Should she tell him?

Live for the moment. "I'm about to ease into a steaming hot bubble bath. You?"

His sharp intake of breath could be heard clearly through the phone. She waited, wondering what he'd say now.

"Need someone to wash your back?"

Vanessa smiled. Just what she'd hoped for.

Because she missed him.

Missed seeing him, talking with him, kissing him. She could at least admit that much if to no one else but herself. "Come on down."

"I need to grab a shower first."

She laughed. "Doesn't that negate the hot soapy water available at my place?"

"I've been working on the ranch all day, darling. I smell like dirt, sweat and horse."

Okay, she'd been in Montana too long because all of that sounded wonderful. At least it did on him.

"Okay, do what you need to," she said instead. "I'll leave the front door unlocked, but don't take too long. I could be asleep by the time you get here."

"I'm sure I can come up with some way to wake you."

She was sure he could, too.

They ended the call and she stood there, the phone pressed to her chest, the happiness inside of her warring with the truth.

She loved Jonah. No matter how she'd tried to talk her heart out of it, the truth was there. And that love scared her.

Even more than thinking about how it would feel when he moved on with his life. The real fear came from planning for a future she wasn't sure she should have, deserved to have.

She had no idea what was coming down the road and wasn't that for the best?

Take life as it comes.

If the events of *her* life had taught her anything it was that nothing was certain. It was better not to make any hard and fast plans. Life could change in a heartbeat.

Or end just as quickly.

Putting the phone down, her gaze caught on the folded sheet of paper tucked into the corner of the mirror.

Her and Adele's bucket list. She opened it and read it again, even though she knew it by heart.

Number twenty-one: take a bubble bath...with a man.

She grabbed a pen, placed a check mark next to the item and again wrote Jonah's name on the paper.

Just like she'd done five times before.

So far she'd completed nine of the remaining sixteen goals since her friend's death almost a year ago. Jonah had played a part in six of them.

Was it a good thing or not to see so many of her goals were connected to one man? He'd made it clear from the beginning he was only in town for a short while.

His life wasn't in this place that Vanessa had come to love in the past few months. But hers was, and it was so different from what she'd known in Philadelphia. The only thing that city held for her anymore was a distant father and unhappy memories. Even Adele's mother had moved on, following her husband to Florida before Vanessa had even made the decision to head out west.

She felt at home here, enjoyed her new friends, and the new direction in her art had her excited in ways she hadn't been in years.

Again, thanks to Jonah.

Yes, she'd accomplished a lot in the past few months, but did any of that matter? What right did she have to pursue these dreams when her best friend never had the chance?

"No, not going to think about that now." She shook off the sadness before it could take hold. "Enjoy today."

Minutes later, with music playing and candles lit, Vanessa climbed into the tub, oohing at how delicious the silky, hot water felt on her skin as it rose almost to her shoulders.

Lying back, she tried to picture Jonah in here with her and although the tub was certainly big enough for two people, that would probably mean some of the water had to go.

Did he really plan on stripping down and climbing in?

She wasn't sure—maybe she shouldn't have been so

quick to make that check mark—but she adjusted the water level, anyway. Now, there was nothing to do but wait. Less than fifteen minutes went by—she'd been watching the clock—when the faint click of the front door told her he was here. Listening to his boot heels on the hardwood floor, he came toward the bedroom.

"Vanessa?"

Okay, how silly was it his voice caused her to jump, sending bubbles flying?

Where else would she be? Did he not believe her when she'd told him her plans for this afternoon?

"In h-here."

He entered the bathroom and the first thing she saw was his beautiful smile. Then she noticed the single yellow rose he held in his hand.

Darn, her heart just gave itself to this wonderful man all over again. How many times could that happen before it belonged to him forever?

She blinked hard, hoping it would be enough to hold back the tears. Cupping a handful of soapy froth, she blew them in his direction. "Hi."

"Boy, you look good in bubbles."

He walked to the tub, bent down and covered her mouth in a kiss before handing her the rose. He smelled fresh and clean, his familiar cologne tickling her nose. He'd showered after all.

"I've missed you," he whispered.

"Me, too." The words slipped out before she could catch them. She lifted the rose to her face, inhaling its sweet fragrance. "I mean, I missed you, too."

He smiled and straightened, his hands already tugging the ends of his Henley-style shirt from the waistband of his jeans. "Want some company?"

She nodded, unable to speak as he reached back behind his head and easily pulled his shirt off his body. Hmmm, same wide shoulders, lean hips and flat stomach she'd seen many times since their private party last week, but her body still responded in a rush of heat at the sight of him.

Next came balancing on one foot, then the other, as he removed his boots, then his socks. Finally, his hands went to the button on his jeans, but he only undid the top one before his smile turned into a suggestive grin. "Is this where I should start dancing?"

She laughed. "You don't hear me complaining, do you?"

Jonah chuckled, but it faded as he undid the next few buttons. Even with the overhead light dimmed, the half dozen candles gave off plenty of light that played across the perfection of his body.

By the time he got to the last button her fingers had tightened on the stem of the rose so much she almost broke it in half. She tore her gaze away and looked around, wondering what she was going to do with—

"Here, let me take that."

Jonah lifted the rose from her hand and walked out of the bathroom. He returned a few minutes later with the bloom safely tucked into a tall, half-filled drinking glass. Setting it on the bathroom counter, he then proceeded to quickly strip down to nothing.

Vanessa's breath disappeared.

He walked to the tub and she had enough brain power left to scoot forward so he could climb in behind her. The heat from his body as he sat, his legs stretched out on either side of her, enveloped her as the water rose up over her breasts.

For reasons she couldn't explain—probably because

her brain had stopped working—she remained sitting forward while cradled between his powerful thighs.

He leaned in close, one large hand coming around to rest against her belly and she jumped again.

"Hey, you okay? It's just me."

His whispered words flowed over one shoulder before he placed a slow kiss on her neck.

She closed her eyes, loving the way his fingers gently spread out over her skin. "I know. It's just that I've... well, I've never..."

Jonah waited as her voice trailed off, a bit surprised at her admission.

Her fresh, citrusy and sexy scent had filled his head from the moment he'd walked into her bedroom. He'd called out, wanting her to know he was close by and the slight hesitation in her voice now made him pause.

Then he reminded himself she'd accepted his offer for help washing her back. He just hoped that meant he'd be doing it while in the tub with her.

The delight in her eyes at his simple gift made him glad he'd snagged one of the roses from the bouquet his sister Kayla had brought home. The way that emotion changed into pure desire as she watched him undress had his body responding before he'd gotten anywhere close to her.

Now that she was in his arms, but still kept her distance from him, despite his kiss and his arm wrapped around her had him finishing her sentence. "You've never taken a bubble bath with anyone."

Vanessa nodded, still not looking back at him.

"Me neither."

"Really?"

He smiled at her amazement. He kissed her again,

same spot, but his lips lingered a bit longer. "I'm glad my first is with you."

His admission was enough for her to relax and she eased back against his chest. The length of the tub was no match for his long legs so his knees rose a bit above the water line. A perfect resting spot for her hands.

She followed when he leaned back and he waited until she laid her head at his shoulder before he gently turned her face to his, a soapy hand at her chin, and kissed her.

She welcomed him, twisting in his arms to allow both of them to deepen the connection between them.

"Hmmm, have I mentioned how much I've missed doing that?"

He spoke the words against her lips, even though they weren't needed. She probably guessed that much with the hard evidence of his arousal pressed against her hip.

"No, you haven't," she said, then she turned to face front again and gave a little wiggle as she got comfortable. "Not in so many words."

He groaned. She giggled.

He fell in love.

As simple and as complicated as that, Jonah finally allowed his heart and his mind to accept what had been obvious from the moment he met this amazing woman.

He loved Vanessa.

For the second time in his life and for the first time as a grown man, he was in love. Vanessa's passion for life, and all the wonder and excitement it held, had awakened him from the lifeless existence he'd been staggering around in for the past eight years.

Yeah, he had a kick-ass career that was getting better by the day, but he'd poured so much of himself into his work, there'd been nothing left for anyone or anything else.

Until now.

He wanted to shout it from the rooftops, whisper it against her skin. Was this the right moment to tell her? He hadn't said the words in such a long time.

Dropping his head, he again kissed the back of her neck, making his way up to her ear.

"So, you've never bathed with a woman before?"

Her question surprised him, but it was the perfect lead into what he hoped wasn't going to be a difficult story to tell. She deserved to know about his past before they could talk about the future. "A shower, but not in a bubble bath, and that was after my divorce."

She went still for a moment, then continued to trail her fingers back and forth across the tops of his thighs. "You and your wife never... I mean, not even showered together?"

"We were so young, just kids when we got married. Of course, you couldn't tell us that back then. Eighteen and so sure we were ready."

The memories of that time, both the good and the bad, came flooding back. He rarely thought about his ex, but he needed to tell Vanessa how his marriage had ended.

"Lisette was such an innocent. So was I, actually. We were each other's first loves, first lovers. We dated over two years before we had sex for the first time."

"Let me guess. Prom night?"

"Cliché, but true. Our junior year. I proposed six months later, to both our parents' dismay. I already told you we were married the day after we graduated from high school."

Vanessa nodded, but remained silent.

"We lived in a house owned by her family and went to college while working. Thankfully both her folks and mine had money set aside that they didn't hold back despite their feelings about our marriage. When Lisette got her degree in paralegal studies, she went to work for a law firm in Kalispell while I worked at the lumber mill and continued my classes. We were happy. At least, I thought we were."

"So what changed?"

"I was a few months from graduating, knowing I needed more schooling in order to be an architect. Seattle or Denver would've worked," he paused, the memories returning as fresh as the day it happened.

"We'd always talked about starting a family after I got my degree, but Lisette had been dismissing the subject whenever I brought it up those last few months. I knew how much she wanted out of this town and I thought if I could just get us away, she'd be happy. Well, I came home early one day, excited about a job opportunity in Denver. Lisette wasn't home and I still can't remember how it happened, but I found a home pregnancy test in the kitchen trash.

"I was so excited, thinking all our plans were coming together. All that changed when she got home. She told me she'd been seeing one of the lawyers at the firm where she worked. She wasn't sure who her baby's father was."

Vanessa gasped. Her hands dug into his knees as she held tight to him. He welcomed the pressure, liking the grounding it gave him, especially for what he still had to share with her.

"As you can probably guess, her announcement didn't go over very well. There was a lot of yelling about getting tested and filing for divorce. Then I did a real mature thing, took off for a camping trip in the mountains with my brothers. They were smart enough to leave me alone, but it gave me a lot of time to think and make some decisions.

"I returned home and told Lisette I wanted to make our marriage work. For the sake of the child. I knew there was a chance the baby wasn't mine, but in the eyes of the law I'd be the child's father."

"Obviously things didn't work out that way."

He shook his head. This part of the story still stung, but not as strong as it had in the past. Maybe the woman listening was the reason?

"She had divorce papers waiting. I signed them and moved back home with the understanding she'd get tested to find out who's child she was carrying. Shortly after that, Lisette lost the baby. I never found out if the child was mine or not."

"But you mourned the loss just the same."

Yeah, he had. Except for confiding in his cousin and best friend, Jonah had never told anyone the real reason behind his divorce.

Everyone assumed they'd just grown apart. Maybe that was true. His ex had turned into someone he barely recognized the last year of their marriage. Maybe he had, too. He'd been so occupied by school, work and clearing the land for the cabin that they rarely saw each other.

"Thankfully, the job I'd lined up in Denver was still open. I left town and never looked back, and I've only rarely been back, for holidays and such."

"And to work on this amazing place."

Jonah pulled in a deep breath, feeling better than he had in years. Maybe time did heal all wounds. Or maybe, it was just what he'd thought...the beautiful woman in his arms accounted for him being able to share the worst moment of his life with her.

And come out of it realizing he'd done the best he could've back then.

Had he been the perfect husband? No, but who was? He'd done his best by Lisette and it hadn't been enough for her. But all of that was in the past. It was time to start looking toward the future.

His future.

"Thank you," he said, gathering her into his arms, loving how easily she fit there.

"For what?"

"For listening."

"I didn't mind." She traced a soapy pattern on his forearm where he held it over her breasts. "But I'm sorry you had to go through all that."

"Me, too," he agreed, suddenly wanting to talk about something else. Anything else. "But that's in the past. I think we need to leave it there and concentrate on the more recent past. And the future."

Vanessa's fingers kept moving, but he detected a slight tension in her shoulders.

"What do you mean?"

"Well, I've got to admit being back in Denver, even for a few days, felt really strange. It was too noisy, too crowded." Jonah gave her a gentle squeeze. "I found myself missing the wide-open spaces and peace here in Rust Creek Falls. Missing you."

"Well, maybe you're just a country boy at heart."

"I never used to think so, but lately everything I thought I knew, *believed,* is now upside-down and twisted inside out." Jonah chuckled again. "I'm finally ready to move forward. Damn, after eight years, it feels good to say that."

"I bet it does."

He laid a hand along her cheek and lightly turned her face until she looked at him. "You're a big part of that, too."

Her beautiful brown eyes widened. "Part of what?"

"Of some decisions I need to make." He dropped a kiss to her lips. "Plans for the future."

She pulled away from his touch, twisting in his arms so she could reach forward to flip the switch that held in the water before she stood, the bubbles sliding off her beautiful curves. "Ah, as interesting as that sounds, my only plans for the future are getting warm and rinsing off these bubbles."

Jonah sat there, watching as she got out of the tub and tiptoed across the room to the oversize tiled stall shower. Seconds later, the water inside came on and it only took a moment for the glass door to steam over.

The abruptness of her move floored him and all he could do was sit as the water inside of the tub slowly emptied.

Then the door opened again and Vanessa popped her head out. "Hey, sexy. You going to stay over there or join me?"

He smiled, his body relaxing again, and got to his feet. Okay, now this was more like it.

Chapter Thirteen

Vanessa almost made it past the main ranch house when she spotted Rita Dalton in a pretty burgundy dress, perfect for Sunday-morning services, waving at her from her front porch.

When Jonah had left the cabin this morning, he'd asked about her plans for the day—mentioning again his mother's standing invite for Sunday dinner—but she'd managed to sidestep answering him.

Much like she'd done for most of yesterday.

When he'd shared the reason for his marriage ending during their bath, Vanessa had worked hard to stay composed when all she'd wanted to do was rail against the hurt and injustice his ex-wife had put him through.

But then he started talking about looking forward, about the future. After her own internal battle about being worthy of even being alive an hour before, she'd bolted from the tub using the cooling water as an excuse to change the subject.

And the location. He'd joined her in the shower and after that, she'd kept him too busy to talk.

When his cousin Caleb had called soon afterward and said he and Mallory were looking for company for a late dinner, she'd jumped at the chance to go.

All because she was frightened of what he might say. Or ask.

Which was crazy, of course.

One would think a person would be excited if the man she loved started making plans—especially if those plans included her. But she now knew it wasn't the unknown when it came to her relationship with Jonah that bothered her as much as the fact she wasn't sure she had the right to even think about the future.

A belief confirmed by a voice mail left for her while she and Jonah had been making love in the shower.

She'd listened to it while Jonah had been making plans with his cousin, surprised at first when she heard Adele's mother's voice, but with Adele's birthday coming up soon, she guess she shouldn't have been. What the woman had said left her dumbstruck.

Easing her truck to a stop as Rita hurried down the steps, Vanessa glanced at her own paint-splattered jeans and old sweater. It was obvious she wasn't heading to church this morning.

No, she was hoping to get lost in her painting.

She'd gotten used to working on the mural with an audience around and the interruptions weren't too bad. People were genuinely interested in the images that were slowly coming to life and she'd gotten a few requests to turn her simple pen-and-ink sketches into full-color portraits.

Still, she found she missed the solace and peace in being alone with her art.

Vanessa put the truck into Park, but left it running. It was then she noticed the box Jonah's mother held in her hands as she came down the walkway.

An icy blast roared through Vanessa that had nothing to do with the cool morning air coming from her now open window.

No, not yet. She wasn't ready.

"Good morning, Vanessa. I'm glad I caught you."

Rita's greeting came with a warm smile, but it did nothing to thaw the deep freeze Vanessa was encased in. She tried to speak. Her mouth opened, the words ran through her head, but there was nothing.

"Vanessa?" Jonah's mother reached through the window and placed a hand on her shoulder. "Are you okay, honey?"

She blinked hard and fought though the aching hurt, amazed at the power it still had over her.

Even after all this time.

She'd been so lost for so long in the sorrow that engulfed her when her friend died. To be so easily pulled back into that dark place was frightening.

"Ah, yes, I'm fine." Vanessa forced out. "I'm sorry. I was lost in thought for a moment."

"Well, this is yours." Rita held up the box, the return address from Florida clearly visible. "Marcie dropped it off yesterday afternoon during her postal rounds since she was driving by the ranch."

Vanessa nodded and reached for the package, surprised at how much it weighed. She held it to her chest for a moment, but when her eyes started to burn she quickly set it on the seat next to her. "Ah, thank you."

"You know, we do need to get an official address for the cabin, instead of using ours. Not that I mind collecting your mail for you," Rita quickly added. "But I totally understand a person's need for privacy. Even if we do think of them as family."

"Rita, I'm not—"

"Oh, I don't mean to push, but you should know how happy we are that you and Jonah have found each other." The woman cut off her protest. "He's needed a special someone in his life for a long time. Someone to keep him grounded while supporting his dreams. I think maybe you need that, too, dear."

Not knowing how to reply to that or if she'd be able to and not break down in tears, Vanessa only thanked Rita again, and drove away.

She made it to the main road, before she reached down and rested one hand lightly on the box.

"Hello again, dear friend."

"…and before I knew it, I'd agreed to buy the whole block. Well, not the actual block. Just one section, from street corner to street corner. Can you believe that? Vanessa? Hello?"

Vanessa looked up from the salad she'd been pushing around with her fork instead of eating. The resort's main dining area was currently being used by the contractors and construction crew as both a meeting place and a lunch room. At least, until the fancy furniture arrived.

The kitchen wasn't operational yet, but the oversize refrigerators worked so many brought their noontime meal with them to work.

Including Vanessa, when she took the time to eat. Her clothing already felt looser.

She'd refused to take a break from the mural the past couple of days, mainly because she was struggling again. And that scared her.

Her vision for the massive painting wasn't quite so

strong, the colors not as bright and clear in her head as they had been. She was second-guessing the work she'd already completed, both the faint outlines and the finished portraits, and there was still so much— so many important people and places—that needed to be added before the deadline that was less than two months from now.

When Jonah had found her today sitting on the edge of the scaffolding, staring off into space, he'd insisted she join him for lunch. She'd hardly been able to argue, especially when her empty stomach had loudly rumbled in agreement.

Knowing what she had to do later on today, eating had seemed like a good idea at the time.

"Vanessa?" Jonah repeated her name, a look of concern and frustration on his face.

"I'm sorry," she said. "What did you say?"

"Where are you?" he asked.

Was that a trick question? "I'm right here."

"No, you're not." He dropped the remains of his sandwich to the paper it'd been wrapped it. "You've been lost in your own little world for the last three days. What's going on?"

She looked away, her gaze back to her barely touched food, not wanting to have this conversation. Again. Jonah had picked up that something wasn't right with her when he'd come by the cabin Sunday evening, but she'd waved off his questions claiming to be tired.

She wasn't ready to talk about it. Not with him, not with anyone.

And not today of all days.

Her stomach clenched, the lettuce and cut vegetables she'd managed to eat now sitting like rocks deep inside. Coming in today had been a mistake. She should've stayed home until she found the strength to complete her task.

"Nothing is going on," she said, filling the silence between them. "I was just thinking…about work."

"So much so that you didn't hear a word I said about buying four houses in town this morning."

Surprise filled her. "You did what?"

"Yeah, I'll admit I even shocked myself." He grinned now. "My meeting with the Realtor was just supposed to be about looking over the properties, getting information. Actually, there was only one house I was really interested in, but the four of them—all on the same side of Falls Street, all empty, built around the same time with good-size yards in between each one—they're perfect."

Okay, now she was really confused. "Perfect for what?"

"Model homes. I told you I've been looking into ways of taking certain design aspects from my work here at the resort and scaling them down to be used in the private sector, especially the environmental elements. Remember?"

Yes, she remembered. Sort of.

Trying to keep her distance from Jonah was harder than she'd thought. Not physically. That part of their time together was wonderful, but it was the "getting to know you, share your dreams, plans for the future" conversations that were difficult.

Which didn't make any sense.

Most people would want to have those talks, especially with the man you were in love with, but Vanessa just couldn't do it.

She couldn't let herself believe in the future.

"Yes, I remember," she finally answered him. "But

you never said you planned to do that work here in Rust Creek Falls."

His smile slipped. "Is that a problem?"

"No, but that's a lot to put on your plate, what with all the work that still needs to be done around here."

Jonah looked around the room, pride in his gaze. "I know we're going to be busy right up to the grand opening at Christmas, and afterward, with the expansion plans for phase two I'm working on. And yeah, buying property in town was impulsive, but it's a good investment for the future. For my future." He took her hand and gave it a squeeze. "Dare I hope to say…our future?"

Suddenly unable to breath, Vanessa yanked her hand free and pushed back her chair. She stood, mindful that people were staring, but needing…needing to get away.

Now.

"Vanessa? What's wrong?"

Ignoring Jonah's question, she hurried from the room. Never breaking her stride, she marched past the scaffolding and kept on going until she was outside with the fresh air hitting her face. Even then, she didn't stop until she reached her truck.

"Hey, hold on."

A strong hand took her arm. Jonah. He'd followed her. Of course, he followed her. Squeezing her eyes shut, she kept her head down as he gently turned her to face him.

"Talk to me, honey," he pleaded. "Please. Tell me what's going on."

She shook her head, her watery gaze focused on the asphalt beneath their feet. "Nothing's going on."

Jonah cupped her cheek, his fingers pressing on her jaw until she had to look at him, her eyes brimming with tears.

"What can I do to help? Just tell me and I'll do it."

Angry at herself for letting it get this far, Vanessa again shook her head and brushed the wetness from her eyes. "It's nothing."

"Don't say that." Jonah put his hands on her upper arms, keeping her in place. "You've been—I don't know, pulling back, pulling away…putting distance between us ever since we slept together that first time."

She should've known he'd pick up on what she'd tried to do. "And here I thought you were having a good time in my bed."

"Being in your bed, or anywhere with you, is great. Wonderful. Perfect. So perfect, I want to be there for a long—"

Vanessa laid her fingers to his mouth, stopping him.

How had she gone from being worried that all he wanted was something causal to being terrified that he wanted more?

"Please. Don't."

He pulled her hand from his face, but held tight to her fingers as he now grasped both her hands. "Every time I've dared to mention the future—for us—other than what we might be doing in the next day or so, you cut me off. Change the subject. Why?"

"You were the one who was worried about getting involved, remember? You were only going to be in town for a short while. I assured you no demands, no labels and you seemed happy with that." She took a step back, but he still wouldn't let go. "We've known each other less than a month, Jonah, and here you are making plans for me…for us."

"Is it too soon?" He finally released her. "Are you saying you're not thinking about us that way? You're not interested in a future—"

"I'm saying it's not a good day for this discussion. I have to— You don't understand."

"I can't understand if you won't explain it."

"It's not that simple." She dug into her pocket for her keys. "I have to go."

"Go where?"

Jamming her key into the lock, she twisted and then yanked the door open and climbed inside. Jonah stepped into the space, crowding her, keeping her from pulling the door shut.

Tunneling his fingers into her curls, he crushed his mouth to hers. She pushed at his chest and he softened the kiss, but it was the slight trembling of his lips against hers that did her in. She fisted his flannel shirt, pulling him closer, deepening the kiss, desperation clogging every pore in her body.

Both of them were now demanding and greedy, giving and taking in a white hot rush of desire that burned deep inside of her. She loved this man, loved him with her entire being—but something was stopping her from taking that next step. From believing, from taking a chance.

The need for air had them finally breaking free, their breathing ragged and hot as he pressed his forehead to hers. "Don't leave, Vanessa."

His words came out a harsh whisper, a plea that involved so much more than this single moment in time. He was asking her not to leave…him. She blocked out the inference, shaking her head. He stepped away without another protest. She closed the door, started the truck and pulled out of the parking space.

Driving away, she refused to let her gaze go to the rearview mirror knowing he stood there, watching her do exactly what he'd asked her not to. Leave.

Chapter Fourteen

Forty-two minutes.

Jonah checked his watch again. Vanessa had been gone almost an hour. He had no idea where she'd gone and she wasn't answering her phone.

Enough. He wasn't sure where she'd gone, but he'd tear this entire town apart until he found her.

After replaying what happened between them earlier over and over in his head, he still didn't have any answers, but one.

It was time for them to be honest with each other.

He should've told her he loved her.

Maybe that would've kept her here. Allowed her to open up to him. To share whatever it was that had her scared.

He thought back to the few times she'd shared bits and pieces about her past.

She'd warned him she held things deep inside. That being an artist went hand in hand with being an intro-

vert and it took a long time for her to let people in. That
the loss of her mother while still a teenager, a distant
father and being cheated on by her ex-boyfriend had
taught her to rely on herself.

She needed to know she could rely on him, as well.

His first stop was the cabin. Jonah's truck rounded
the corner, disappointed that hers wasn't here. Where
else could she be?

Pulling into the spot where he usually parked, he
started to turn around, but something about the front
door caught his eye. He put his truck in Park and hopped
out, the engine still running.

The door was open.

He went inside, calling for her even though he knew
she wasn't there. Had she come here after leaving the
resort?

He looked around. Everything seemed okay. Taking out his phone, he called her again, but again he got
nothing. Not even her voice mail. Determined to keep
looking, he started back for the door when something
on the leather couch caught his eye.

A piece of paper. Maybe she left him an explanation.
He grabbed it. His name was written over and over, but
it wasn't a note. Instead he saw a series of checkmarks
some with Jonah's name scrawled next to them.

What the hell was this?

He went back to the top, noting the crease lines that
showed how often the paper had been folded and re-
folded.

A bucket list? Vanessa's? And who was Adele?

There were quite a few things listed, the majority of
them having been checked off, but he focused on the
ones where his name was written.

Fly among the clouds (and not in an airplane!).

Learn to ride a horse.
Kiss a cowboy.
Learn how to line dance.
Dance in the rain.
Take a bubble bath...with a man.

All the crazy and wonderful things he and Vanessa had done together over the past few weeks.

What did this mean? Had she been using him? And why was she suddenly checking off each item she could find? What was the big rush? Vanessa was still a young woman.

The questions whirled around inside his head. Then he saw the small notation written at the bottom of the page and his blood ran cold.

List updated September 23, 2013. Carrollton Cancer Medical Center, Philadelphia, PA.

No. That couldn't be. Vanessa wasn't—

Jonah shoved the list into his jacket pocket, refusing to let his mind go there. He went back outside and got in his truck, then spotted Eli coming over the hill on horseback.

He waved his brother down and the two met in the middle of the road.

"If you're looking for your lady love, she's been here and gone."

Was that good news or bad? "You saw Vanessa? Did you talk to her?"

Eli shook his head. "I watched her drive up from the far hill. After she got out of her truck, she paced back and forth on the outside deck for a few minutes, waving her hands around."

"Was she on the phone?"

"I don't know. I was too far away, but like I said, her hands were flying, almost as if she were having an argument with herself." Eli pushed up the brim on his Stetson. "I was just about to head down to see if she was okay when she went inside."

"Did you see her leave again?"

"Yep. She came back out a few minutes later carrying a package or something. Then she took off, tires spinning and gravel flying," Eli said. "What's going on?"

"Hell if I know." Jonah put his truck into gear. "If you see her again, call me. Scratch that. If you see her, stop her and keep her with you while you call me."

His brother started to smile, then stopped when he saw how serious Jonah was. "Is she okay?"

"I don't know," Jonah answered honestly, not wanting to believe the list he'd found meant she would do something crazy. "But I need to find her."

He headed into town, stopping first at the community center but she wasn't there. He drove by the beauty and doughnut shops, and then the wings place. Going up and down each street, he kept an eye out for her truck, even stopped by the clinic to ask Callie if Vanessa had been in to see her.

Nothing.

He didn't see her truck outside of Crawford's General Store, but he went inside, anyway. Trying not to get caught up in too many conversations, he figured by the number of people asking him about Vanessa, no one had seen her in here today.

Back outside, he thought for a moment about getting a hold of the sheriff. Was that really necessary? He didn't have anything to go on except her crazy behavior and a bucket list—

"You look a bit lost, young man."

Jonah spun around. "What did you say?"

"I said you looked lost."

The old woman closed the distance between them, peering up at him with sharp, eagle-like eyes. "No, you're not lost. Not anymore. But someone else is."

"I'm sorry, have we met?"

She placed a wrinkled hand on his arm. "I'm Winona Cobbs."

The psychic. Vanessa had told him about this old woman who'd come to town to give lectures and hand out free advice. She'd approached Vanessa about the mural and shared stories about the history of Montana, which Vanessa had used in her research.

He had no idea what real talents this old woman possessed, if any, but he had to ask. "I'm trying to find Vanessa Brent. The artist you spoke with about the mural she's painting out at the resort. Have you seen her?"

The woman hugged her shawl closer to her chest. "No."

Jonah waited. She didn't say anything more, but her gaze never left his.

"I'm worried about her." He tried again. "Can you help me find her?"

Her eyes narrowed for a moment, then closed. She pulled in a deep breath, slowly let it out and repeated the action two more times. "I see a white owl," she finally said.

His shoulders slumped. This wasn't going to work. Grabbing his keys, he headed for his truck. "Okay, thanks."

"And a waterfall."

That got his attention. He turned back. "A waterfall?"

"A white owl and a waterfall."

If the psychic was right, Jonah knew exactly where Vanessa was.

But could he trust her? "Are you sure?" he asked.

"As sure as I am of you. The question is, are you?"

Jonah had no choice. He thanked the woman, who waved off his words as she continued on her way. Back in his truck, he headed out of town straight to Fall Mountain and the waterfall that gave Rust Creek Falls its name.

It had been years since he'd been out this way. So much had changed. He drove past a picnic area and direction signs to a lower falls viewing area he didn't remember being here the last time.

No sign of Vanessa's truck at either spot.

Continuing farther up the mountain, he reached the turn off to the trail that would lead him to Owl Rock, so named because the large white boulder with twin peaks at the top which resembled the woodland creature. It protruded out over the falls as if keeping watch over them.

Checking his phone as he made his way up the trail, Jonah wasn't surprised to find service spotty at best. It didn't really matter, since Vanessa hadn't answered his previous attempts, but what if something happened and he needed to call for help?

Refusing to allow that thought to form, he was glad it was a clear and sunny afternoon. As he kept walking, the noise of the falling water led him to a clearing.

Then he saw her, standing by the rock and way too close to the waterfall for his comfort.

A glimmer of fear sprang to life inside him. What should he do? If he yelled to her, she could get startled, slip on the slippery rock and plummet to her death. If he did nothing, and she was up here for some crazy reason...

He did the only thing he could. He headed toward her as softly as he could and said her name.

Hearing Jonah's voice didn't surprise her.

She turned around, not bothering to hide her tears. What was the point? More would follow. "What are doing here, Jonah?"

"Do you really need me to answer that?" He came a few steps closer, his hands held wide at his sides. "You had to know I'd look for you."

Yes, she did know that. And while she appreciated his cautious approach, she wasn't about to do anything stupid.

On the contrary. What she had to do was probably the simplest, and yet the hardest thing that had ever been asked of her.

"You can relax, you know," she said, walking toward him. "I'm okay."

A raised eyebrow translated his skepticism, but he did drop his hands. "Yeah. Don't get mad when I say I don't believe you."

Her lips twitched, as if they wanted to smile, but then Vanessa looked down again at the square, glittery red box she held cradled to her chest.

"Red was her favorite color," she said instead as the tears returned. "Not crimson or burgundy or maroon. Nope, it had to be a candy-apple, fire-engine, the-brighter-the-better red."

"Here."

She blinked, bringing into focus the square cloth Jonah held in his hand. Looking up, she found him right in front of her now and a spurt of laughter somehow made it through the tightness of her throat. "Is that an actual hankie?"

He shrugged. "My mother raised me right."

Vanessa took his offering and pressing the soft material to her face, breathed in Jonah's familiar scent. Turning away, she wiped the wetness from her eyes, so thankful he was there.

That surprised her, although it shouldn't have. She loved him. It seemed right that he should be there.

Why was she just realizing this now?

Maybe she could get through this after all. "Today is Adele's twenty-sixth birthday…would've been. She was my best friend."

It was so hard to talk about her in the past tense. That someone so alive and vibrant should no longer be there.

"Tell me about her," Jonah murmured, the wary tension in his face easing.

"Adele Marguerite Dubront." She pulled in a deep breath, and then released it. The shudder that accompanied it was a sign she was okay to talk now. "A big name, but she so lived up to it. From the moment we met as little girls, she was someone I admired. Wanted to emulate. My best friend, my partner in crime. My sister."

Jonah stayed silent, but he moved closer, one hand warm and solid at her lower back.

"She was fearless, always the first one to try new things, say hello to people and then she'd listen intently to whatever they had to say."

"Sounds a lot like you."

This time her laugh had a harsh edge to it. "Oh, no. Maybe the person I've tried to be in the last few months, but before that…no, I was very much the stereotypical artist. Wrapped up in my own little world. Content with just my paints and canvases for company. But she wouldn't let me stay there. No, she would dare me and entice me and drag me along on another of her crazy schemes.

"All of which made finding out about her childhood battle with cancer so hard to believe. Until it returned with a vengeance last year. She'd beaten it once before. We were so sure she could do it again. And she tried. Gave it her best, but then we had to accept—*I* had to accept that she was going to be taken from me far too soon."

"Those are her ashes."

Vanessa closed her eyes, and nodded, not surprised Jonah had figured out what was in the box she held so tightly. "Her mother left me a voice mail a few days ago. When I called her back she explained about a special request Adele had left in her will. Something she'd asked her mother to keep from me until after…"

Opening her eyes, she focused on the beautiful waterfall directly in front of her. "Well, until I'd had the chance to move on with my life. Until I started working on our list."

"Your bucket list."

She spun around, stumbled over her feet, but Jonah was there to catch her. His arms strong and secure. "How do you know about that?"

"I went to the cabin to find you and I found it—you left it on the couch. I'm sorry, but I couldn't help reading it." His gaze held hers. "Especially once I saw my name. I didn't understand what it was at first and when I read the name of the cancer center—"

"You thought it might've been me who was—"

"You've been acting so strange lately, I was afraid…" He brushed back some of her curls, tucking them behind one ear. "I'm so sorry for your loss. I know what carrying that kind of weight can do to a person. But you've helped me lift my burden. Why won't you let me do the same for you?"

Could she? She wasn't sure.

"I know this is going to sound crazy, but I feel guilty." As hard as it was to do, Vanessa stepped out of his embrace and walked past him, farther into the clearing. "Meeting you…loving you—and yes, I do love you despite my best efforts to keep my distance—my feelings are so strong, Jonah. You make me happy. But why am I entitled to that when Adele never got that chance?"

"Because she would want it for you, Vanessa. You know she would, from what you've told me about her. You deserve to be happy, to be loved." Jonah followed, stepped in front of her and framed her face in his hands. "I love you, Vanessa. I have from the very first time I saw you. There's no excuse as to why it's taken me until now to tell you that. I love you."

Her soul soared at his words even as the fear that had invaded her heart remained.

"But you said… I tried so hard to keep things light and easy between us because I don't think I can handle another goodbye. There've been too many of them in my life."

"I'm not saying goodbye, Vanessa. Count on it."

"And then today you talked about buying property in Rust Creek Falls, which sounds a lot like you're planning to stick around." Vanessa talked over the top of his protest. "But that's scary, too. What if something happens to you this time?"

"Sweetheart, there are no guarantees in life. But there are promises, and I promise I am going to love you for as long as you'll have me." Jonah tightened his hold, his fingers pressing into her hair. "No, I'm going to love you for the rest of *my* life, no matter what comes our way. We'll make Rust Creek Falls our home and keep my place in Denver. Hell, I'm going to take you to Hawaii so you can see a live volcano."

Number twenty on her list.

Tears swarmed again, but this time they were ones of surprise and joy. "You'll do that for me? Help me finish my list?"

"If there is anywhere you want to go—anything on your list you still want to do—count me in."

She shook her head. "All I want, all I need is you. I think you're right. That's what my friend would want for me. For us. I love you, Jonah."

She grabbed at his jacket with her free hand, lifted herself up on her toes and kissed him, pouring all her love and passion into this moment. His hands slid to her shoulder and then circled around to her back, pulling her close until—

"Oh, I..." Vanessa stepped back and held out the box. "I still need to honor Adele's final wish. She wanted me to find the most beautiful, most perfect place..."

Jonah covered her hands with his. "Let me help."

They stood at the edge of the rock and held the box at an angle over the falls, allowing the down breeze to lift the ashes and carry them away.

Vanessa closed her eyes, offered a silent goodbye, thanking Adele for their years of friendship and for insisting she take their list to heart. If she'd never made that promise to take a chance Vanessa never would've found the love and happiness that filled her at this moment.

"You ready to head home now?"

Vanessa nodded, loving how wonderful those six simple words sounded.

She placed her hand in Jonah's and as they walked

back down the trail, she noticed a smudge of something dark on his cheek.

Dirt, perhaps?

No, she knew exactly what it was—her friend's stamp of approval. Instead of brushing it away, she peeked back over her shoulder and sent a quick wink to the heavens.

Vanessa studied the costume that hung on the back of the bathroom door.

She was supposed to be Pocahontas for Halloween. An idea she'd come up with to go along with Jonah's cowboy costume (men had it so easy!) when he'd reminded her just this morning they needed to be dressed up for the Halloween party at Callie and Nate's tonight.

Considering how quickly she'd pulled this outfit together, thanks to finding faux-suede fabric and a blue beaded necklace during a quick shopping trip to Kalispell, the costume had come together nicely except for her wayward curls.

She'd planned to straighten her hair now that her makeup was done, including the tribal tattoo wrapped around her right biceps, but putting the dress together had taken up most of the afternoon and Jonah was set to pick her up at any moment.

Thankfully her progress on the mural was moving at a quick pace. She still had quite a few portraits and landmark buildings to paint, but she was sure she'd finish well ahead of the December deadline. Seeing the mural unveiled at the resort's grand opening over the holidays would be very exciting.

A knock came at the door. She tightened the belt on her silk bathrobe and hurried to answer.

Jonah had decided he'd get dressed at his folks' tonight, despite the fact he was slowly moving his stuff to the cabin, something about getting his hands on a special addition for his costume.

She guessed it would be one of his father's rodeo belt buckles that Charles had showed off with such pride after a family dinner last night.

A dinner that turned into a celebration when Jonah shared his plans to make Rust Creek Falls his home again. There were still a lot of details to be ironed out, but everyone was so excited, none more than her.

Being happy and in love was wonderful!

Ready for a night of fun with their friends, Vanessa opened the door. "Hey, you're early! I still need to get dressed—"

Her breath disappeared. Her words were gone, too.

Jonah stood on the deck, looking amazing in dark slacks and a fitted jacket made from a beautiful red brocade material with a high collar and richly decorated epaulets at the shoulders. A collared shirt, complete with a cravat-style tie at the neck, a leather belt and a sweeping cape that just about touched the ground completed the look.

No, the sword he carried at his waist was what truly made him look like a member of a royal family.

"What's this?" she asked, unable to hold back her delight when he bowed deeply from the waist. "Where's my cowboy?"

"Gone for the evening, milady." Jonah straightened, then grinned. "I hope you will allow Prince Charming to escort you to the festivities this evening instead. I do believe meeting him was on your list."

Vanessa gasped, one hand pressed to her lips.

Number twenty-two: kiss Prince Charming!

She couldn't believe Jonah remembered her list and

had hunted down a fitting costume for tonight. "Well, actually, the goal is to *kiss* Prince Charming."

Jonah's grin widened. "Oh, I think we can arrange that."

Vanessa stepped back and waved him inside. "Where did you get that outfit?"

"My sisters are involved with a theatre in Kalispell that put on a version of Snow White last year," Jonah said, closing the door behind him. "When I asked if I could borrow it for tonight, they were very happy to help. As long as I agreed to pose for pictures."

"Well, you look wonderful. You're probably plastered all over the internet by now," Vanessa said, then laughed as she started back for the bedroom. "Give me a few minutes to get dressed and we'll be on our way."

"Hey, wait a minute." He took her hand, stopping her. "I've got something else for you."

"Really? What might that—" She turned back and once again found herself speechless when he eased the sword to one side before he slowly knelt before her, one knee on the hardwood floor. "Jonah!"

"I know this is sudden. We've only been a part of each other's lives for a short time, and it's only been two days since I said I love you. But with everything I am and everything in me, I know being with you forever is what I want."

He pulled a small velvet box from a hidden pocket and opened it to reveal a solitaire diamond ring that sparkled brilliantly in the light.

"You don't have to answer me now. Take as much time as you need," he continued. "I won't even say the words yet if you're not ready, but I want you to know—"

"I'm ready."

Her reply came out of her with such certainty Vanessa knew, to the depth of her heart, it was true. She'd been so lucky to find this special man. She didn't want to waste one more moment.

Not when time, and life, was so precious.

"You can ask me." She smiled at the look of pure love that filled Jonah's handsome face. "I mean, since you're already down there."

"Vanessa Brent, will you do me the honor of becoming my wife?"

"Yes!"

* * * * *

MILLS & BOON®

Why shop at millsandboon.co.uk?

Each year, thousands of romance readers find their perfect read at millsandboon.co.uk. That's because we're passionate about bringing you the very best romantic fiction. Here are some of the advantages of shopping at www.millsandboon.co.uk:

* **Get new books first**—you'll be able to buy your favourite books one month before they hit the shops

* **Get exclusive discounts**—you'll also be able to buy our specially created monthly collections, with up to 50% off the RRP

* **Find your favourite authors**—latest news, interviews and new releases for all your favourite authors and series on our website, plus ideas for what to try next

* **Join in**—once you've bought your favourite books, don't forget to register with us to rate, review and join in the discussions

Visit **www.millsandboon.co.uk**
for all this and more today!